CROSSING HOPE

KIMBERLY KINCAID

CROSSING HOPE

❀ Created with Vellum

DEDICATION

This book is dedicated to my father,

who is one of the very finest men I know

ACKNOWLEDGMENTS

Oh, y'all. This. Book.

I'm not going to even lie. CROSSING HOPE was a tough book to write. It's always difficult to end a series, especially one you really adore. And I was pretty much in love with everything about Cross Creek, right from the time I said to my agent, "So, I want to write about farmers..." and she didn't think I was crazy for not filling in that blank with something more mainstream (thank you, Nalini Akolekar!) But not only do we get to finally (FINALLY) see tough-as-gutter-spikes Marley get her HEA—and with the town bad boy, no less!—but I had to deliver a wrap-up to the Cross family saga, on top of it. To say it was emotional to get that job done is a massive understatement, and would have been utterly impossible without the following people.

Nicole Bailey, my editor, who has been with me from damn near word one, twenty-six books ago. Thank you for keeping me in line, and also for keeping track of my inability to get a timeline right. Jaycee DeLorenzo, my cover designer, who is magical in all the ways. Wander Aguiar, Andrey Bahia, and Andrew Biernat, I am so very fortunate to have worked with you on the cover image, which (as you know) I love like a love song, baby! Rachel Hamilton, thank you for being my right hand, and sometimes my left hand, too. Without you, I am lost, girl!

Erin Nicholas, Erin McCarthy (who whipped my BUTT in word sprints, but are pretty much the entire reason the last 65 pages of this book exist), Jennifer Bernard, and Mari Carr, thank you for making me laugh when I wanted to cry. Cat Parisi, thank you for...well, being you! Linda, Elena, Natalie, Leah, Rich, Marly (coincidental, but funny, right?!), Deb, Emerald, and all of the unbelievably wonderful people at Stafford House of Yoga, thank you (really, seriously, thank you) for tending to my Zen as I wrote this book. You carried me more than you know, and I am so grateful.

Avery Flynn and Robin Covington, I would never consider a minute of this journey without you. Thank you is not enough (yes, I know I can show my love by way of wine, Oreos, and gummy bears!)

My girls, who make me laugh every single day and also put up with taking goofy pictures of me at the farmers' market for my Insta. My daughters actually inspired me to write this series the way that I did, because each of them has a distinct "birth order" personality. Marley kind of messed with the birth order of things in Cross Creek, but I love that my girls put their mark on this series.

And what can I say about Mr. K? I write true love because I know true love. I am blessed beyond measure to know it with you.

1

Marley Rallston was bored, irritated, and sad, in that order. Bored, because she was standing in a mile-long line at The Corner Market with an armload of flour, butter, and brown sugar instead of in the kitchen, figuring out how to make oatmeal cookies that didn't spread out over a baking sheet like liquid-hot lava. Irritated, because the person in front of her in said line was Amber Cassidy, who Marley didn't so much know as know *of*, and who also happened to be Millhaven's town gossip—which meant that by nightfall, everyone with ears would know Marley had made a rare appearance in town. And sad, because...well, that had pretty much been her default for the past year since the mother she'd thought had been her only living relative—and who'd certainly been the closest person to her—had lost a horrible and heartbreaking battle against cancer.

But not before she'd dropped the emotional grenade that not only was Marley's father alive and kicking and running his family farm with his three sons out in the middle of God's country, but she wanted Marley to swear she'd go find him after she died. Oh, how Marley had been tempted to say no. She'd spent twenty-four years thinking her father was dead, the poor, unfortunate victim of a freak accident. She'd even felt sad about him from time to time, the man who'd never had the chance to know his daughter. But the joke had been on her, hadn't it? Tobias Cross had known all about her, even before she'd been born. Not that he'd ever done a damned thing about it, other than write a monthly check and steer clear of her as if she'd been the nastiest strain of some deadly virus. And now Marley was flat-broke and stuck living under the man's roof.

On second thought, she'd take irritated for the win.

"Oh, my land," Amber drawled, depositing Marley back to the reality of the line in the crowded market, which hadn't moved so much as a millimeter, kill her very much. "Marley Rallston, is that *you*, honey?"

Amber blinked her too-long-to-be-real lashes at Marley in surprise that was also markedly false, and Marley showed her teeth in a gesture she hoped passed as a smile.

"Yep, it's me." Of course, she just had to be wearing a semi-ancient tank top and ragged pair of cut-offs that both bore the signs of the three exhausting hours she'd spent sweating in the kitchen. Damn it, she should've known better than to think she'd get away with replenishing the ingredients she'd wrecked without being caught looking like a car crash.

Amber, on the other hand, looked like she'd just shimmied off the pages of a fashion magazine, her summer-blond hair and full face of makeup flawlessly in place despite the raging heat outside. June in Millhaven? *So* not the same as June in Chicago.

"Well, it sure is *nice* to see you out and about," Amber said with a grin that was more wolfish than welcoming. "I'm not sure if you remember me. We met a couple of months ago when you and Cate were havin' breakfast at Clementine's Diner. I'm Amber. Amber Cassidy. I'm a stylist at The Hair Lair, right up the street."

She stuck out a hand tipped in perfectly polished, perfectly fuchsia fingernails, and ah, hell. Marley might rather be anywhere other than standing here in her Sunday un-best, talking to the woman, but she couldn't justify being blatantly rude. "I remember," Marley said, awkwardly juggling the items in her grasp in order to meet Amber's handshake.

As soon as she had everything balanced and her fingers extended, though, Amber surprised her by tugging her forward. "Oh, this feels too city. I'm a hugger! C'mere, darlin'."

"Oh—" Before Marley could figure out a passably polite way to feint, Amber had wrapped her broomstick-thin arms around her shoulders, leaving Marley no choice but to endure the shockingly powerful hug and finish with a stunned, "Kaaaaay."

Marley's heart thudded in her chest. The response, along with her suddenly shallow breathing, her clammy palms, and the cold spear of panic in her belly, wasn't normal, she knew.

But she liked people at arm's length. Literally. Figuratively. And everything in between.

Which was just one of the ten thousand reasons she was the odd woman out on Cross Creek Farm.

"So," Amber said, shifting back—although only a half-step—and wagging a tenth of her manicure at Marley. "I've got to tell you, you're a tricky one."

"I am?" Marley's brows lifted, enough confusion filling

her mind to edge out the unease she'd felt at Amber's unexpected breach of her personal space.

But Amber just nodded and gave up a you-don't-have-to-play-coy-with-me smile. "You *are*. You've made it hard to get to know you, spendin' nearly all your time up there at Cross Creek rather than comin' on into town on the regular."

Specifically, Marley had spent nearly all of the last nine months either in her room at the main house, at her crappy retail job a few towns over, or in her oldest brother Owen's kitchen, taking informal baking lessons from his live-in girlfriend, Cate. It wasn't a hair she wanted to split, and especially not with Millhaven's biggest blabbermouth, so she simply said, "I guess I'm not really an out-and-about kind of girl."

Amber smacked her forehead lightly and laughed. "Silly me. Of *course*, you're probably makin' up for lost time with your daddy. I can't even imagine what it must be like to have found him after all these *years*!"

"Mmm." The sound was all Marley could manage. Her defenses plucked at the back of her neck, digging deep as they broadcast the let's-go-let's-go-LET'SGOLET'SGO-LET'SGO message in her brain, the words reverberating as if they'd been shouted into a canyon.

Amber yammered on, oblivious. "And your momma, Lord rest her soul, losin' her best friend and then turnin' to Miss Rosemary's widower for comfort"—she paused to clear her throat over the euphemism—"then leavin' Millhaven so suddenly like that before you were born. Honestly, the whole thing is just enough to take my breath away."

Pain snatched Marley's remaining scrap of balance, slicing into her from every direction, and oh, God, why wasn't this line *moving*? Time for Plan B, before the ache taking over her rib cage betrayed her by making itself obvious.

"Darn it," Marley said, faking as much *whoopsie* as her admittedly limited acting skills would allow. "I totally forgot vanilla extract. Can't make these cookies without it, so..."

She jerked her head toward the back of the market before pivoting on the thick heels of her black motorcycle boots and moving the rest of herself hastily in that direction. For a split second, she felt a stab of guilt for the untruth. The reality was, Marley had barely been able to scratch together the cash for the ingredients already in her arms. Every last dime she could squeeze out of her meager paychecks went toward paying the avalanche of medical bills that had started rolling in just weeks after her mother had been diagnosed with stage 4 pancreatic cancer a year and a half ago. The pragmatic part of Marley's brain told her it was a blessing that her mother had only suffered for six months.

The rest of her wanted time that didn't exist to go along with the money she didn't have to get out of this town where she didn't belong.

Okay, she thought, sliding in as deep a breath as her lungs would allow. So, she didn't normally lie, because she never really gave so much as a single fuck what anyone thought of the truths she had to tell. But the fib to Amber was a means to an end. At least now she could hide among the shelves of canned goods and bushel baskets full of local produce and weekly specials and wait for the line to thin out. Then she could buy the ingredients she'd really come for and head back to Owen's while he worked on the farm and Cate balanced the books at the main house. Marley would have the kitchen to herself. Maybe she'd be able to find a tiny chunk of peace.

After all, baking always calmed Cate. It was the woman's refuge, her sanctuary, her happy place. Marley didn't get quite as into it as all that, but she liked being in the kitchen well enough—certainly better than her job of selling stupidly trendy clothes in the mall—and she was passably decent at it. Or at least, that's what Cate said, although not in those precise words. She'd gone with "natural affinity", which Marley definitely thought was pushing the border of bullshit territory. Today's oatmeal cookies would agree, the tricky little bastards, and Marley was tempted to point to them and say, "see?" But she was also determined to find *something* to pass the time and keep her sane while she earned enough money to pay off her debt and get gone.

Considering her debt-to-paycheck ratio, she was going to have a lot of time to kill.

She turned the corner at the top of the soup and pasta aisle, relief filling her chest at the sight of the empty space in front of her. The row, which stretched out under her boots in laminate hardwood rather than regular old, ho-hum white linoleum, was flanked cozily on either side by shelves marked with handwritten signs. The Corner Market wasn't like any grocery store Marley had ever seen before. The front of the place had a strong farm stand feel to it. Rough-hewn, wood-slatted bins held fresh ears of corn and fat, jewel-colored watermelons on either end of the rows of bushel baskets, which were filled with everything from apples to zucchini. Much of the produce was local, including selections from Cross Creek Farm, along with others from their rival, Whittaker Hollow. Even the items that had clearly been imported from other parts of the country, like bananas and citrus fruits that needed full-time hot climates to grow, were carefully placed in shallow wooden trays that showed off each selection, rather than haphazardly tossed on display shelves without thought.

The back half of the market, where Marley thankfully now stood in as much peace as she was going to find (in Millhaven, anyway), wasn't much different, dotted with small, strategically placed stands holding fresh produce to complement the dry goods and other items on the shelves. Bananas and berries stood in baskets in the cereal aisle. Tomatoes, some with the emerald-green vines still attached, sat gently piled on tall, free-standing displays in the aisle offering their canned brethren, along with all the pasta. Marley had never seen pasta sauce come from anywhere other than a jar before she'd ended up stuck in Millhaven. In fact, there were scores of local customs she'd either never seen or wasn't privy to as the only person in town who hadn't been born and bred there.

Shaking off the squeeze that the thought had sent deep into her belly, Marley moved farther down the aisle, shoulders tight to her spine. It didn't matter that she didn't know the small-town protocol or the ass-backward quirks that the people who lived here swore by—even if the sauce Owen made from scratch was one of the most mouth-wateringly delicious things she'd ever tasted, including every dish she'd ever ordered from her mother's favorite Italian restaurant in Chicago. Marley had only come to Millhaven because her mother had begged her to right before she'd died. She'd just had the shit luck of getting hit with the over-90-days-late final notice from Chicago Memorial Hospital two days after she'd pulled her wheezing, rusted-out Toyota up the gravel drive at Cross Creek Farm.

Two days after *that*, she'd had no choice but to drain her bank account to pay as much of the debt as possible. Her meager savings hadn't taken more than a chip out of the total, so she'd done the only thing she could to save herself from bankruptcy. She'd set up a payment plan and gotten a job to ensure she could keep to it.

And as soon as she made that final payment in ten months and fourteen days (if she got overtime at the stupid boutique, please, please, please), she was getting the hell out of Dodge. Away from the father who'd had another family and hadn't wanted her. Away from the small town where she stuck out like a dark storm cloud on a gorgeous, bright blue horizon. Yep, in ten months and fourteen days, she'd be headed to her favorite place, AKA Anywhere Other Than Millhaven, Virginia.

Not that she was counting, of course.

A sharp gasp of surprise yanked Marley back to the here and right-now of the pasta aisle she'd wandered down. Shooting off a few rapid-fire blinks, she registered the sight in front of her. A girl—who looked to be eleven or so, but between her shockingly skinny frame and the long, stringy hair hiding half of her face, it was tough to tell—crouched behind one of the free-standing displays in the aisle. Her light brown eyes widened in fear, then sheer panic, as she looked at Marley, who had clearly caught her unaware. The girl threw out her hands to snatch up the half-opened, fully threadbare backpack at her feet. Only, the zipper was too far undone and the bag too crammed full to make the swift trip to her shoulder, and the top gaped open, sending a trio of cans clattering to the floor in loud succession.

"Oh!" The girl gulped and ducked down to retrieve the cans, which only made three more tumble out onto the laminate. Marley knelt on auto-pilot, putting the flour, butter, and brown sugar she'd been holding out of the way and reaching for the can of tuna that had bumped up against her boot.

"Here, let me..." Marley trailed off at the same instant her brain played connect the dots with what was in front of her eyes. There was no shopping basket or cart anywhere in sight. The girl, who had been hiding behind the display, was now poised to run, her eyes darting around Marley toward the daylight at the front of the store.

Oh, *hell*. "Are you stealing these groceries?" she asked, taking extra care to keep her voice soft and low. The girl was painfully thin, her arms like the branches of the saplings Owen and Marley's middle brother, Hunter, had planted in the apple orchard a few months ago. Her shorts bore the kind of holes that weren't a fashion statement, and her T-shirt was easily two sizes too small, a fact that was emphasized by the way she nervously tugged on its hem as she took a deep breath to answer.

"I..."

Something in Marley's stare must've told the girl that any lie she could conjure would be worthless, because she dropped her quavering chin. "We don't have anything to eat," she whispered. "It's just me and my mom, and she's trying, but she just lost her job because of cutbacks, and"—the girl broke off with renewed panic—"You can't tell. *Please*. If I get in trouble for this, the Department of Family Services will take me from her, and I'm her only family. She's my *mom*. I'll put everything back right now, I swear, but I can't—"

"What's going on over here?" A guy who looked to be a little bit older than Marley had rounded the far end of the aisle, brows furrowed. His polo shirt bore The Corner Market's logo, and the fact that the thing had a collar meant that he was—shit—likely the manager.

"Nothing," Marley said, trying to step in front of the backpack. "Everything's totally fine."

But the manager—Travis, according to his nametag—wasn't having it. "I heard something fall." His eyes narrowed on the backpack Marley had no prayer of keeping from his view. "Wait a second. This bag is full of groceries." His gaze winged to the girl, then to Marley, then back to the girl, where it hardened. "These aren't paid for. Sierra, are you... you're *stealing*."

Travis's eyes were lasered firmly on the girl. And why wouldn't they be? She was the one clutching that backpack like a life preserver in middle of a vast, deep ocean.

But Marley understood the exact brand of panic in the girl's stare. Okay, no, she might not have ever been hungry like that, nor had she ever stolen so much as a stick of gum from her mother's purse in her entire twenty-five years. She *did* know what it was like to protect her mother, though, and to do whatever she had to in order to survive. God, it was why she was here in this Godforsaken town in the middle of the Shenandoah Valley in the first place. Her mother had begged her to come find Tobias after she'd died, and even though Marley had wanted—not a little—to say no, she couldn't.

Just like she couldn't let this kid get hauled off to jail and taken away from *her* mother, just for being hungry and trying to survive.

"It's mine."

"I'm sorry?" Travis took a step back in surprise, but Marley countered it by moving forward and nailing him with a stare.

"The backpack is mine," she said evenly. "I put it down, and Sierra was just handing it to me. That's when everything spilled out."

"So, *you* were stealing these groceries?" Travis asked, his expression taking the express route from doubt to dead-seriousness in about two seconds flat.

Self-preservation was a strong instinct, and Marley's was currently prickling a hot path of warning up her spine. Still, she overrode it in a breath.

"Yep. I sure was."

"I have to call the police," Travis warned, his hands finding his hips with authority. "We prosecute all shoplifters. You're going to be arrested for this."

At that, Sierra let out a sound, caught somewhere between a huff of shock and a squawk of protest, and Marley's gut bottomed out. She looked at the girl, making sure their eyes had locked good and hard before shaking her head almost imperceptibly. She already didn't belong in this town, and she was certainly already the hottest topic for the rumor mill. Yeah, getting arrested would sting, but she'd been through worse.

Letting this girl, who was hungry and frightened, get snapped out of her house just because she was trying to survive?

Not going to happen.

Marley firmed both her shoulders and her resolve, turning toward Travis with certainty. "You do whatever you've got to do," she said.

And with that, he led her to the office in the back of the market.

2

Greyson Whittaker could count on one hand the things in life about which he gave a rat's ass. His family's six hundred-acre cattle, feed, and produce farm tucked right in at the foothills of the Shenandoah Mountains headlined the list.

No, check that. Whittaker Hollow *was* the list. Everything else was pretty much take it or leave it as far as he was concerned.

Along with every*one* else. Including—and especially—his old man, who just so happened to own the place.

But since they'd lost a section of fencing at the far end of their apple orchard courtesy of the nasty thunderstorms that had blown through the area two days ago, and Jeremiah Whittaker cared far less about the farm bearing his name than Greyson did, Greyson was hauling himself to the co-op down on Town Street for the materials he'd need to repair the damage. His old man might not invest his time in anything other than being a mean old son of a bitch, a job at which he'd excelled for most of Greyson's life and had practically earned a fucking Master's degree in over the past nine years, but that land meant everything to Greyson.

The way the sun spread over the hay fields on a perfect spring afternoon. The glow from that first breath of daylight hitting the dew-laced grass and lighting it up better than the Fourth of July and Christmas combined. The sweet, heady smell of freshly picked peaches, the unexplainable magic by which they tasted best with the warmth of the summer sun still clinging to their soft, velvety skin. Yeah, he thought, letting a smile slip over his mouth to replace the scowl he wore as a default. His father could hate the place as much as he wanted. He could hate Greyson, too; Christ knew they'd started covering *that* ground in wild and vivid detail nearly a decade ago and never looked back. But Greyson didn't care about the rift. He didn't care about all the barbs that had been thrown hard and stuck under his skin for so long, and he definitely didn't care about the ones he'd learned to throw back, at his old man and pretty much everyone else. He could love Whittaker Hollow enough for the both of them, and he'd work it by himself with the cattle managers and farmhands if he had to.

Speaking of ground they were already covering.

Snuffing out his smile, Greyson allowed his features to harden. It didn't matter that he didn't care much for the people who had raised him; for his bitter old man, his disinterested mother, who had mentally checked out of her obligations to both family and farm the minute Greyson had turned eighteen, or his three older sisters who had never shown any interest in Whittaker Hollow and moved off the land as soon as they'd had the chance. He didn't need any of them in order to do what he loved, nor what he wanted. He didn't need any of them, period. Hard stop.

And he liked that just fine, thanks. Relying on folks,

needing them and trusting them and giving a shit, or, worse yet, letting *them* give a shit about him? That was just a recipe for fucking disaster, right there. Smarter to just go for the stiff-arm right from the get and keep people where they were gonna end up anyway.

After all, everyone in Millhaven had pegged him as his father's son decades ago. Might as well live up to that family legacy, since he sure as shit wasn't going to prove it wrong. But it was better to push first than have to push back.

And if there was one thing Greyson had learned the hard way, it was how to push. Fiercely and relentlessly and right in the tender spots where it hurt the most.

Like father, like son.

"Oh, quit whining," he muttered under his breath, tightening his grip on the steering wheel of the over-the-hill Chevy Silverado he'd never, ever part with. His life might not be full of family dinners or fishing trips or time around the campfire, but he had Whittaker Hollow. As long as he could work the land, he'd have all he needed.

Thoroughly ignoring the sign that read *No Parking: Loading Zone*, Greyson guided his dinged and dusty truck into the stretch of space directly beside the no-frills brown clapboard building that housed Millhaven's farming co-op. Technically, he knew he wasn't so much bending the rules as forcing them into a full-on kink by leaving his truck here since he hadn't come for fertilizer or feed and he wasn't making a delivery. But he'd never been as big on the rules as he was on pushing his luck, and anyway, he was only going to be inside for five minutes—ten, tops, if Billy Masterson got to jawing from behind the counter. In a town that was roughly the size of a Saltine cracker and about as fancy, illegally parking in the loading zone for a quick run into the co-op wasn't likely to rock anyone's foundation. Plus, Greyson's give-a-damn had been busted for far too long for him to care if it did.

He adjusted his baseball hat against the ruthless midday sun and set his work boots on the pavement, aiming himself at the co-op's front entrance. The combination of heat and humidity did its best to knock his breath from his lungs, but Greyson knew better than to sling in a deep draw of the stuff and let it punch his ticket. Inhaling on a lazy five-count, he shouldered his way past the co-op's glass and metal doors and ambled over to the counter, where Billy Masterson stood talking to Eli Cross.

So much for that easy fucking breath. "Billy. Eli," Greyson gritted out, as if the latter word had tasted like dirty ashes. If there had ever been love lost between the Crosses and the Whittakers, it had been far before Greyson could remember. Or maybe the dawn of time, to hear his father tell it.

"Greyson," Eli acknowledged, while Billy—who could give Amber Cassidy a run for her paycheck in the gossip department if the spirit freaking moved him—didn't even bother trying to mask the fact that he was soaking in every goddamn syllable. Funny, Eli didn't put a whole lot of piss and wind behind the greeting like he'd done ever since they'd first tried to beat the crap out of each other nearly twenty years ago in middle school.

Not that the guy's newfound chill was going to stop Greyson from going on the offensive. "Thought you got too good for us simple folk and blew out of town last fall, Cross," he said pointedly.

Of course, Greyson—just like every other person in Millhaven with a working heartbeat—knew that Eli *had* left town after deciding to make a one-eighty career change from farmer to travel journalist. Like a bad penny, the guy still turned up every now and again. Usually, it was to help out at Cross Creek Farm, but in this case, his freshly minted wife was roundly pregnant. Since Scarlett was the photographer half of their nauseatingly cute journalism team, Greyson figured he was stuck with his old nemesis in town until the kid popped out.

"I did," Eli replied with a shrug. "But I'm doin' some local writing and freelancing for a bit, along with helping my family out now that it's the growing season. I've got some space in my schedule," he added slowly, "if y'all want me to take a look at your website to spruce up the copy."

A breath of surprise moved through Greyson's chest at the authenticity in Eli's tone, but it only lasted for a half-second before he surrendered it to his frown. Eli might have mellowed out some since settling down with Scarlett, but he, along with his two brothers and their old man, had always thought he was so much better than everyone else. And now, as if what the Crosses needed was a story as big and happy as a Norman Rockwell painting, there was a long-lost sister in the mix. Not that anyone had seen much of her since she'd come to town late last year.

"I don't need any help. I'll pass," Greyson bit off.

"Suit yourself." Eli powered the words with another shrug before turning toward Billy to place an order that seemed to go on for a month. Cross Creek must be pretty flush to need that much fertilizer and feed, a fact that meant Greyson would have to bust his ass triple-time in order to keep up, let alone surpass their production. Of course, the Crosses had had the good fucking luck to expand their revenue by building an on-site store front which had opened last month. Word of mouth (AKA Billy and Amber) had it that business at Cross Creek was booming better than ever this season.

Sure. There were three of them full-time, plus Eli, plus Cate McAllister running their books, Scarlett transforming their website into a magazine spread, and Hunter's wife, Emerson, organizing their marketing. Goddamned Crosses. If there were three of him running Whittaker Hollow full-time, and all that extra help besides? He'd have their luck, too.

But there *had* been three men in his family to run the farm once. Not that it had turned out the way any of them had thought it would.

Banishing his crappy headspace once and for all, Greyson crossed his arms over his sweat-damp T-shirt and waited out Eli's order. After the guy had (*finally*) finished and parted with an "if you change your mind about the website, just holler", to which Greyson had simply scowled, Greyson was able to get the fencing supplies he'd come for.

"You wanna pull around to the loading zone so we can get this stuff in your truck?" Billy asked, jerking his chin toward the side of the building.

"Already ahead of you, dude."

At least there was one stroke of luck on his side. Greyson palmed his keys and headed back into the brutal sunshine, rounding the corner to where he'd left the Silverado.

And found Sheriff Lane Atlee leaning against the driver's side door.

Shit. *Shit*. So much for luck, or anything even remotely resembling the stuff, being on his side. "Help you, Lane?"

The guy's white-blond brows winged high enough to breach the tops of his Ray-Bans, heading up toward the dark brown brim of his Millhaven Police Department uniform hat. "I'm pretty sure you mean Sheriff Atlee," he said coolly. "And as a matter of fact, yes, I believe you can. Would you like to tell me what it is that you're doing parked in this here loading zone, Greyson?"

"Loading?" Greyson asked. But since he'd been unable to keep his tone from veering into smartass territory as he'd replied, a muscle in Lane's jaw ticked with impatience.

"For the last eleven—no"—Lane looked at his watch—"twelve minutes now?"

Greyson's gut dropped. "You've been standing here waiting for twelve minutes?"

"I have," Lane confirmed. "And in case you haven't noticed, it's pretty hot this afternoon."

"It's June," Greyson said, prompting Lane to push off the Silverado's quarter panel and step forward abruptly.

"I don't think you want to go your usual route with me today."

Greyson opened his mouth to argue, but then thought better of his instincts to push. He might be ballsy to a fault, but Lane was not only built like an armored tank, he was also technically in the right.

Time to cut bait and get back to the farm. Lord knew nothing would get done there until he did, and winning a pissing match with Lane wasn't worth the time lost.

"Okay," Greyson muttered. "Can you just write me the ticket so we can both get on with it? I've got fences that need mending." Not to mention a hundred thousand other chores that needed done before quitting time.

Lane shocked the crap out of him by shaking his head, then went for a double by saying, "'Fraid not."

"Excuse me?"

Somewhere, in the very back hallways of his brain, it occurred to Greyson that he was arguing *not* getting a ticket. But Lane's expression was just a bit too gleeful for that little jewel to mean anything good for Greyson. Especially since not only was Lane the sheriff, but he'd been Owen Cross's best friend since long about the third grade...which was coincidentally about when the whole Cross/Whittaker rivalry had taken root in Greyson's memory.

"I'm not writing you a ticket," Lane said, capturing Greyson's attention and holding it in his grip.

Although Greyson's next question wasn't one he wanted the answer to, still, he had to ask. "Why not?"

"Because," Lane said, just in time for Billy to arrive on the loading dock with a bundle of fencing wire on his shoulder. "Writing you a ticket doesn't seem to deter you from parking illegally."

"Oh, man. You parked here again?" Billy asked, and Jesus, the guy wasn't helping.

"Only for a minute," Greyson snapped. "Look, Lane—"

"Sheriff *Atlee*. And you can save your breath. This is the sixth parking ticket you've racked up this year, Whittaker."

A fact Greyson knew as well as Lane, because the collection of unpaid tickets had taken up residence in his glove box, not eight feet from where he currently stood. "Fine. Write it up and I'll go down to the courthouse and pay them all, right now." It would take time he didn't have, not to mention money he shouldn't lay out on anything that wasn't related to the farm. But since it would also get him off the damned hook, he'd deal with both of those little setbacks later.

Still, Lane wasn't budging. "Sorry," he said, although his smile made the word tough for Greyson to swallow. "See, Section 124 of the traffic code states that once a citizen obtains six non-moving violations, that earns said citizen a trip to jail."

"You're going to *arrest* me?" Greyson choked. "For fucking *parking* tickets?"

"Watch your mouth," Lane flipped back, standing at full attention. "And to answer your question, yes. I am absolutely going to arrest you for fucking parking tickets."

Billy dropped the fencing wire to the loading dock with a thud. "You're hauling him to jail?"

"Yep." Lane took the pair of shiny, silver handcuffs from his utility belt as proof, and oh, for Chrissake.

"You don't need to cuff me. I'm not going to fight you." This whole thing was bullshit (okay, fine. Mostly bullshit. There *were* enough tickets in his glove box to wallpaper the Silverado's back windshield), and he sure did like to push. But he knew better than to start a brawl with Lane right here on the loading dock. No matter how badly a dark little part of him wanted to.

Lane tilted his head against the unrelenting sunlight for a minute before replacing the cuffs on his utility belt and turning toward his cruiser, which was parked a handful of feet away. "Let's go, then."

A thought vaulted into Greyson's mind, sending the first real strike of panic through him over the incident. "What's going to happen to my truck?"

Lane paused, his expression betraying both his confusion and his surprise. "Well, I can't leave it here in the loading zone. Cody Garrity'll have to come tow it to the impound."

The answer made sense, seeing as Cody was Millhaven's only mechanic, and as such, owned the only tow truck within a solid twenty-five mile radius.

Still... "You need to make sure he's careful when he hitches it up," Greyson insisted. "No manhandling it. And no scratches to the paint, you hear?"

"The thing is already scratched to high heaven," Lane

pointed out, but Greyson's irritation flared, and he stabbed his boots into the pavement to stand tall.

"I mean it, *Sheriff*. No damage to the truck. At. All."

Whether it was Greyson's tone or the unyielding look he'd just worked up to match it, he didn't know. But something got the message across, loud and goddamned clear. "Okay," Lane said, shifting a gaze at Billy. "I'll radio for Cody to come pick it up as soon as we get in the cruiser. Can you make sure he's careful?"

"Yeah," Billy said to Lane, then nodded at Greyson. "I'll make sure."

Lane jerked his chin once in thanks. "Good. Guess that means it's just me and you and a ride downtown, Whittaker."

"Great," Greyson said through his teeth.

This day officially couldn't get any worse.

3

As soon as Greyson saw Amber Cassidy and her BFF, Mollie Mae Van Buren, lean their bottle-blond heads out the front door of The Hair Lair just in time for Lane to drive his police cruiser by the place, he knew his day had officially gotten worse. He paused for a second to curse Billy's inclination to gossip like a middle schooler, although his frustration burned bright, then burned out. Millhaven was a small town, with circles more tightly knit than the socks and scarves old Mrs. Ellersby sold every year at the annual Watermelon Festival. It wasn't as if the news wouldn't have made the rounds at both Clementine's Diner and The Bar by nightfall, even if Billy *had* kept his trap buttoned up—or, more likely, his fingers off his text screen.

And it wasn't as if anyone would really be shocked that Jeremiah Whittaker's son had finally found his way to the back of a police cruiser.

Lane pulled the car to a stop in front of the small, squat police station, popping the rear door open for Greyson to exit. "Come on," he prompted, gesturing toward the main entrance. Despite the reputation that preceded Greyson like a game day banner, he had never actually been over the threshold of the police station, so he let Lane guide him past the glass door and down the narrow hallway leading farther into the building.

"You're really going to arrest me over a bunch of unpaid parking tickets?" Greyson pushed one last time, even though he knew the odds of getting out of this now were likely lodged between slim and none. But the fields at Whittaker Hollow weren't going to tend themselves, and his father sure as hell wasn't going to do anything more than the bare minimum to make things happen. The question might be a Hail Mary dressed in lottery-ticket wrapping paper, but Greyson had gotten by on less before.

Lane snorted. "We've already covered this ground. If you want to argue, you can take it up with Judge Abernathy."

"Great." Judge Pearl Abernathy had achieved relic status before Greyson had even been born, and she was battier than a belfry, on top of it. So much for gaining any ground there. The best he could hope for at this point was that Lane would at least be fastidious about his job and book Greyson quickly so he could figure out bail and get back to Whittaker Hollow by supper.

Stuffing his hands into the pockets of his jeans, Greyson walked down the hallway just a half-step ahead of Lane. They passed a small office with Lane's name stenciled on the glass door, along with a utilitarian desk in an even smaller open area beside it that was currently unoccupied. The nameplate on the far corner marked the space as Woody Collingsworth's, and sure, Greyson couldn't have been nabbed by the soft-spoken nineteen-year-old deputy. At least that, he might've had a prayer of verbally muscling his way out of.

"Here we go. Home sweet home, for now." Lane pulled a key ring from his utility belt, coming to a halt outside the single, eight-by-eight holding cell at the end of the hallway. The thing was furnished—a generous word—with a long, thinly padded bench that was likely meant to double as a cot, a toilet that was shockingly clean but also highly un-private, and not much else. Greyson supposed he'd think the whole setup was antiquated if he hadn't been born and raised in Millhaven, where the worst crimes to go down consisted of bar fights that ended in handshakes when one party beat the other, fair and square, and the occasional idiot teens playing mailbox baseball or shooting out street lights with BB guns. At least there was air conditioning, and maybe he'd get in a wink of shuteye while he waited for Lane to write up his paperwork. But the sheriff had no sooner trundled the steel bars along their track than a pair of footsteps sounded off from behind them, causing both Lane and Greyson to turn in surprise.

Woody, Greyson recognized quickly enough, with his one-size-too-large uniform and his Adam's apple bobbing nervously above his crookedly knotted tie. The woman beside him?

Yeeeeeah. *Definitely* a far better subject, and oddly, not one he readily recognized. Greyson let his gaze move over her slowly, from the ground up. Her black motorcycle boots gave her just a hint of toughness without being overkill, especially with the way her long, shapely legs tapered into them at mid-calf. Toned thighs gave way to frayed cutoff shorts and a white tank top that fully held Greyson's attention, snug enough to showcase the woman's curves, yet not so tight as to leave nothing to the imagination. Dark, ruffled hair hid part of her face, but the half Greyson could see made his blood thrum faster in his veins. Full, peach-colored mouth set in a scowl he was tempted to wipe right off of her. Strong chin, high and defiant.

The woman shifted her head, her hair tumbling from her forehead, and *God damn* it. Those eyes, flashing indignation with just a hint of wide surprise, were bright, beautiful Cross blue.

Which meant she wasn't just off limits, but entirely out of the fucking question.

MARLEY'S BOOTS clapped to a halt on the linoleum at the same time her heartbeat cranked way, way up in her chest. She blamed the former on the way the deputy—who had nervously picked her up from The Corner Market—had stopped short beside her, as well as the sight of her oldest brother Owen's best friend standing a few feet away, his face locked in disbelief. The latter was entirely the fault of the man planted next to Lane, though. Between his tanned skin, the tall, muscular frame that nearly gave Lane's a run for its money, and the inky black tattoo curling from beneath the sleeve of his T-shirt all the way to his left elbow, Marley really couldn't help the visceral reaction.

Even if the guy was leveling her with a dark and stormy gaze that said he didn't like what he was looking at in return.

"What the hell is going on here?" Lane's voice crash-landed in Marley's thoughts just in time to chase the flush from her face. What did she care what this scowling stranger thought of her, anyway? She had bigger problems at the moment, thanks.

Case in point. "I, uh," Deputy Collingsworth stammered, turning roughly the color of summer strawberries as he cleared his throat. "I made an arrest."

"I can see that," Lane replied tightly. "What I meant was, would you care to *elaborate* on exactly why it is that you've arrested my best friend's little sister?"

Marley's gut fluttered, but she refused to let the sensation get anywhere near her face. She'd known exactly what she was doing when she'd claimed those groceries as her own. Even if the steel bars and jail cell were a whole lot more real now that they were standing starkly in front of her.

Deputy Collingsworth straightened. "She was shoplifting at The Corner Market. Travis Paulson caught her red-handed, and she admitted it, to him and to me. What else was I supposed to do?"

Shock streaked over Lane's face, but it didn't last. "Radio me, for starters," he hissed, and the guy next to him released an audible, oh-please scoff that sent Marley's brows hooking up. She opened her mouth to tell Lane and the deputy and God and anyone else within earshot that she didn't want any special treatment. If Lane had been at the market, he might've seen what Travis and the deputy had missed, and she could not—*would* not—let Sierra be taken from her mother. Jail or no.

But Lane was already shaking his head, the thought forgotten. "You know what, never mind. We've got a more immediate issue to deal with here."

"Okay," the deputy said, enough of a question hanging in his voice that Lane huffed out a breath.

"I've also made an arrest, as you can see." He jerked his chin at Tall, Dark, and Scowling. "And we can't put two people of the opposite sex in the same jail cell."

The guy's face changed then, sending another curl of

heat through Marley's blood. "By all means. Ladies first," he said, gesturing grandly at the single cell. His smirk was its own entity, taking over his unnervingly rugged and (ugh) undeniably good-looking face as if it had a life of its own. He could fill Wrigley Field with his arrogant attitude and ultra-cocky bravado. Even then, he was brimming with so much of both that he'd probably have to use a crowbar to cram it all in. Too bad for him and his sexy little smile, Marley was packing boatloads of backbone, herself.

And she was in just the mood to let it fly like a fifty-foot flag.

"Oh, no. Really. Age before beauty," she maintained, planting her hands on the hips of her cutoffs and smiling so sweetly at the wide-open door to the cell, she damn near needed a root canal. "After you."

The guy's black brows shot toward the tousled waves falling over his forehead. "It wouldn't be gentlemanly of me to step on your cute little toes. Please. I insist."

Oh, my God, was this guy even for real?

Marley parted her lips with every intention of informing his arrogant ass exactly where she was going to plant those *cute* little toes of hers—along with the rest of her boot-encased foot—when Lane stepped between the two of them with a frown.

"While I'm half-tempted to let her have at you"—he fastened the guy with a sub-arctic stare—"that's enough. Marley"—he turned toward her, arms crossed over the front of his uniform shirt—"get in the cell. Please."

"What?" she gasped, her shock turning to indignation, lickety-split. "Why *me*?"

Before Lane could answer, Mr. Full of Himself kicked his smirk into fifth gear. "Guess being a Cross doesn't get you out of everything in this town after all, huh, darlin'?"

"I'm not a Cross," Marley snapped, her heart crashing against her ribs, and the guy's chin went up in shock, with Lane's and the deputy's quickly following suit. *Shit.* Time to get him—and everyone else—out of her emotional dance space, once and for all.

"My last name is Rallston," she said with cool indifference as she strutted into the jail cell and pivoted on her heels to be sure she still had him, eye to eye and glare to glare. "And I don't play dirty to get out of being arrested. Unlike some people."

He looked like he was going to pop off with a haughty (and true, damn it) comment about how she was the one who'd been tossed into the business side of the jail cell while he still stood frustratingly on the freedom side.

But this time, it was Lane's turn to smirk. "I wouldn't get too excited about your situation, Whittaker." Lane slipped the handcuffs from his utility belt, his light blond brows all the way up. "Turn."

"You're serious," the guy said slowly, his grin faded as fast as Marley's bloomed over her face.

"As a heart attack. As a man and a woman, I can't put the two of you in the same cell. But I can't let one of you walk, either, and I don't have anywhere else for either of you to safely wait to be booked." At this, he shot his deputy a withering stare. "So, you get the outside, while Marley here gets the inside. Now, are we gonna do this the hard way, or..."

"*Fine*," he bit out, turning to the side to allow Lane to handcuff his left wrist to the bars of the now-closed cell door. Lane made a promise to book them both as quickly as possible, then muttered a low, "in my office, Deputy Collingsworth?" before turning to stride down the hallway with the deputy in tow.

Marley's glee at the guy's comeuppance receded just

enough for her to replay the exchange between him and Lane with more care, and wait...

"*You're* Greyson Whittaker?" she realized out loud, and God, didn't that just figure?

"In the flesh," he replied. At least his smirk made a lot more sense now. Her brothers certainly talked enough smack about him. Even Hunter, who was notoriously even-keeled, made no bones about his dislike for the guy.

"For the record," Greyson threw over his shoulder, his dark eyes glinting in the over-bright fluorescent lighting as he sent a gaze right into her. "All the stories you've heard are true."

Unable to help herself, Marley knotted her arms over her chest and replied, "I see. So you did lose five grand to my brother Eli in that bet last fall, huh?"

Ah, that got him. "I paid him every penny," Greyson ground out, although the snap of his shoulders and the muscle that had visibly tightened beneath the healthy dose of stubble on his jawline said he hadn't been happy about the result or the reminder.

"Hmm." Marley made the sound to cover her shock. She hadn't known he'd made good on the bet, although the events leading up to it had happened before she'd arrived in Millhaven. Anyway, it didn't much matter. She wasn't exactly sticking around to record things. The less she knew, the easier it would be to forget she'd even come here.

They settled into silence, with Marley perching on the bench—which was surprisingly comfortable, all things considered—and Greyson shooting her a salty glance, likely at the fact that she had a place other than the floor to park her butt. But he'd earned what he'd gotten, trying to brazen his way out of trouble, and she didn't feel the least bit sorry for him. Not even when she wondered if those handcuffs felt as cold and hard as they looked, or if his arm would fall asleep if they had to wait here for a while before Lane and Deputy Collingsworth came back to get them.

Of course, Greyson wasn't one to be outdone by simple logistics. Turning with care, he shifted his body around so the side of the handcuffs that Lane had attached to the bars slid down low enough for him to sit on the linoleum with his back to her. Time crawled by like a glacier carving a valley through a mountainside, the silence pressing against Marley's eardrums and making her fidget. She'd never been arrested before, and even though she didn't regret an ounce of what she'd done to land herself in her current predicament, she was pretty much out of her element. She didn't know how long this would take—an hour? Two? Ten?—or how much bail for this sort of thing would cost. Would she have to tap into the payment she'd planned to make to the hospital for the month? She hadn't technically stolen anything, so retribution would be easy, but what if the manager from the market decided to prosecute anyway, like he'd threatened? If she didn't have bail money, she sure as hell didn't have money for a lawyer. For pity's sake, she couldn't even spring for vanilla extract.

There was no way this wasn't going to set her back financially, which meant there was no way she'd be able to keep to the payment schedule she'd meticulously crafted to get her out of Millhaven ASAP. The thought made Marley's stomach drop, the unease that accompanied it quickly driving her bat-shit crazy.

Something else. Anything else. Right now.

"So," she said, her voice sounding terribly loud in her own ears even though she'd painted her tone with as much boredom as she could drum up. "What'd you do to land yourself in here, anyway?"

"What do you care?" Greyson asked back, matching her boredom and raising her some attitude.

God, he was such an *ass*. But, sadly, he was the only ass around, and Marley was likely to go off the deep end if she had to sit there, lost in thoughts of the family Greyson had just pigeonholed her into *or* what might happen to her and her finances now that she'd been arrested for shoplifting.

She stretched out on the bench, propping herself up on one elbow so she could still see him even though his back was still fully to her. "I'm bored. Plus, you already know what I did. It only seems fair."

"You're a Cross. What do you know of fair?" Greyson snorted. But the last thing Marley was in the mood for, now or ever, was to be lumped in with the family rivalry that seemed to be alive and thriving, stronger than ever. She wasn't a Cross, and she never would be.

"Don't act like you know me, because I guarantee you, you don't. And I already told you. My last name is Rallston. I'm *not* a Cross."

For one blazing-hot second, Marley's stare zeroed in on Greyson's back. He wasn't wearing his T-shirt so much as the cotton had just surrendered to his work-hardened muscles, holding fast to the cords and hard curves just enough to dare her imagination into action. His sleeve had slipped farther over his bicep, revealing more of that mouth-watering tattoo, the dark design swirling over hard, smooth skin.

Marley didn't want to find him attractive. He was cocky. No, *obnoxious*. He was arrogant and made stupid assumptions.

And, okay, fine. He was also really. Freaking. Sexy. Coal-black lashes. Full, firm mouth. Wide hands, callused and rough, yet strong. Strong enough to hold anything...

She realized, just a beat too late, that he'd turned to look at her, his chin resting against his shoulder so just his eyes showed over the top of his T-shirt. His smirk translated flawlessly though, crinkling the edges of those darker-than-coffee eyes with edgy danger rather than anything suggesting humor.

"Not a Cross, huh?"

Marley willed her voice not to shake. "No."

Greyson's smirk grew darker, his stare along with it. "Whatever you say, darlin'."

The word sent an unexpected and very intense shot of heat down Marley's spine, and it pooled even more hotly between her hips when it landed. Which was stupid, honestly. She'd heard the word bunches of times before; for God's sake, that gossip, Amber Cassidy, had aimed it at her only a couple of hours ago in The Corner Market. But something about the way Greyson had said it, the way he'd leaned on the *r* and rolled over that *l* with ease, yet still made the whole thing slide off his tongue with just a hint of sexy suggestion, kept that warmth firmly in place in her body.

In that brief, impulsive moment, Marley wanted nothing more than to slide off his tongue. Which was dangerous for so many reasons.

Not the least of which was that it was the first thing she'd *wanted* at all since arriving in this Godforsaken town, other than to get the hell out.

"Don't call me 'darlin'," she snapped, putting enough emphasis on the word to make it sound like the meanest sort of insult rather than something that had made her want to take off her panties and fling them at him. "You know what, forget it. I don't care what you think or why you're here. In fact, I can't wait to be booked so I can get the hell out of here and never have to lay eyes on you again."

Greyson stiffened, although whether it was in surprise or something else, Marley couldn't tell. "The feeling's mutual, I can promise you that. *Darlin'*."

"Perfect," Marley gritted out. "Then at least there's one thing we can agree on."

Then she turned to her side, giving him her back, closed her eyes, and pretended to fall fast asleep.

4

T*wenty-seven bottles of beer on the wall, twenty-seven bottles of beer. Take one down, pass it around...*

Yep. It was official. Greyson had lost his goddamned mind.

Okay, he thought, shifting his weight from one side of his numb ass to the other. So he was bored to the point of insanity, and his ass matched the arm that was handcuffed neatly to the bars by his left ear. But he was nothing if not stubborn, and *definitely* nothing if not tough. He'd endured far worse than the soft, feminine breaths sounding off from the other side of the jail cell, not to mention the hellfire and brimstone attitude that had preceded them. Marley Rallston might have a lot more mettle than he'd assumed she would, but he had a hundred more important things to spend his brain power on than the headstrong brunette.

Except.

Greyson had to admit that after months of her being little more than a rumor of near-mythical proportions, it was a curious thing she'd set so much as a baby toe outside of the perfect haven of Cross Creek Farm, and a *damned* curious thing that she'd ended up in the pokey on her first real foray into town. And to shoplift groceries from The Corner Market, of all the weird-ass things, when he'd bet everything he owned that her pantry was brimming and her family's farm flush with the literal fruits of their labor? Then to go all guns-blazing when Greyson had called her a Cross —which she *was*, no matter how puffed up she got over it, because damn, those Crosses all had that same holier-than-thou attitude. But why would she come to town after all this time if she hated her family enough to renounce them? The longer he sat here rolling over the particulars, the more he had to admit that nothing about Marley's actions or reactions made any damned sense.

It also doesn't matter, dumbass. The reminder sliced cleanly, bringing him back to the police station floor with a snap. He didn't give a shit about anything that wasn't fenced in by the borders of Whittaker Hollow, least of all a woman who was as brash as she was bullheaded. Plus, no matter how hard Marley argued to the contrary, both her Bahama-blue eyes and her bloodline really did label her a Cross.

Which meant she was mouthy, presumptuous, and far more trouble than she was worth. No matter how fucking hot he'd felt in the pit of his belly when he'd looked over his shoulder and caught her staring at him with a glint of something far too familiar in her stare.

She'd looked hungry. And not in a whoops, I skipped breakfast, yes, I want fries with that sort of way.

Greyson rolled his eyes and gave himself a mental thump to the skull. Probably, he just needed to get laid. It was a feat easier said than done in a town the size of a pinprick, and one where Greyson had lived since birth. Not that he'd ever had trouble attracting willing participants—he might be chock-full of rough edges and hard straightaways, but he hadn't been born ugly. At least, not if his track record was any indication. But small-town living had its drawbacks, the biggest of which (as far as his libido was concerned, anyway) was that he'd exhausted his options for local dating by the time he'd finished high school. Now, at the ripe old age of twenty-nine, he might as well drain the dating pool, fill it with a bunch of dirt and concrete, and build a fucking park. Greyson usually hauled himself to the bars in Camden Valley, or even farther out to Lockridge, when he got a wild enough hair about being unlaid. He hadn't made the trip in a while, with it being the growing season and all. If the ruckus that both his brain and his balls were currently making about Marley goddamned Rallston was any indication, he was far overdue.

She pulled in another slow, steady breath from behind him. Christ, even her inhale/exhale made him want to turn around to watch her chest move, and wasn't that all the encouragement he needed to scratch the get-laid itch, ASAP?

Heavy boot-steps thumped a brisk, measured rhythm over the linoleum from the far end of the hallway, sending Greyson's heart into a matching beat and his legs awkwardly under him as he found his feet and stood.

"It's about damned time," he muttered. He knew that shooting his mouth off like a two-dollar pistol was an iffy idea at best—clearly, he had zero leverage, here. But shitty odds had never stopped him before. Shitty ideas? Even less likely to keep him in check. The collection of parking tickets in his glove box was case in freaking point.

Lane frowned, but surprisingly didn't push back. "Okay, you two," he said, dividing his glance between Greyson and Marley, who had pushed up from the bench in a swift, soundless move, looking suspiciously bright-eyed and alert for someone who had allegedly been snoozing her day away. "Both of your arrest reports have been entered into the system, so the next step is booking."

His gaze settled on Marley, then, as if maybe she'd come up with some perfectly reasonable explanation for her actions and he'd be able to spring her, no harm, no foul.

No chance. She slid her hands into the pockets of her cutoffs and kept her gaze fastened firmly ahead, leaving Lane no choice but to continue and Greyson no choice but to be more curious than he wanted to over why she hadn't tried for the out.

"In the interest of efficiency, I'm going to process you one right after the other. You'll be fingerprinted, and have your mug shots taken. Then, once that's done, you'll both be escorted next door for your bond hearings with the judge."

Again, Lane paused, only this time, it was to look at Greyson. "You do get a phone call, too. If you want to try to get in touch with your old man to make arrangements for bail—"

"No." Every part of Greyson turned to steel except for his pulse. *God damn it.*

He dragged in a breath, slipping a no-shits-given-here expression over his face even though it took effort. He might've seen his father's true colors years ago, and liked them then as little as he did today, but that didn't mean he had to let anybody see his. Least of all Lane Atlee and Marley Cross. Rallston. Whatever.

"I'll be needing Cody Garrity's number," Greyson drawled, packing his tone with maximum levels of boredom and arrogance. "I want to be sure I can get my truck tonight, before he closes up shop."

"Suit yourself," Lane said after a beat of obvious surprise. "Let's get moving, then."

He turned, reaching for the side of the handcuffs he'd looped around the bars of the jail cell, when Marley finally broke her stubborn vow of silence.

"What about me?"

The question moved past her lips simply, her voice carrying just the slightest edge of huskiness from having not been used for a while. Her shoulders were still set in that unyielding line that radiated both tension and toughness, and Lane's brows tucked in obvious confusion.

"The rules prohibit us from processing more than one person at a time. As soon as I'm done with Greyson, you two can switch places, then you'll both go see Judge Abernathy. It won't be long."

"That's not what I meant." Marley's pretty, peach-colored mouth pursed in a frown. "Don't I get a phone call, too?"

"Oh. Uh. Well, yes, but I..." Lane paused for a nice, long look-see at the floor, clearing his throat. "I already called Owen. He and Hunter and Eli will meet you at the courthouse."

A noise of frustration flew out of her chest. "You made my phone call *for* me?" Marley asked, incredulous, and Greyson had to admit, the move had taken stones the size of country watermelons on Lane's part. Not that he was nearly as shocked as Marley seemed to be that the guy had given her brothers the heads up. Everyone in the Cross's inner circle always looked out for their own, like the sort of rah-rah, made-for-TV movie that made his sisters sigh with overblown gushiness and him want to do a reverse swan dive with the contents of his stomach.

"You're entitled to call whomever you'd like," Lane said, ever a stickler for the rules. "You get a crack at the phone, same as Greyson. But come on, Marley." He exhaled in a slow leak. "You're my best friend's little sister, and you're sitting in my jail cell. You didn't really think I *wouldn't* call him, did you?"

Marley's scowl dug in, good and hard. "I don't need my brothers to bail me out."

"Look, I know y'all are still working through some things, but they care, okay? Plus, you might not be crazy about your family bailing you out, but someone needs to do it," Lane pointed out quietly.

There was no denying that the big oaf was right, at least about bail. Not that it hadn't made Greyson want to spit fire when he'd applied the little nugget of reality to his own situation, because, yeah, it so freaking had. He figured he'd cross that bridge when he got to it. What he *hadn't* figured was that Marley would go the same route, once again forgoing the easy out of letting her brothers or her father come to her rescue. Tobias Cross was a righteous old SOB, but he'd always had a reputation for being a do-gooder. Greyson had zero goddamned doubt that, even with the jam she'd landed herself in, the old man would never hang Marley out to dry.

Weird that she didn't seem to want to give him the chance to prove it.

For once and for all, think about shit that matters! Lord knows your farm isn't going to tend itself.

Greyson made a sound that didn't consider being anything other than impolite. "I don't mean to break up this truly touching moment, here, but can we get on with it so I can stop being handcuffed to this jail cell and start getting on with my life, please?"

"Put a lid on it, Whittaker," Lane said, although—*yessss*—he continued his trip closer to unlock the cuffs, freeing Greyson's wrist with an economy of movement. "It's not as if you've got a hot date, or anything."

The words skittered dangerously close to the ugly truth, and Greyson made an attempt at a smile that didn't take.

"I don't think Judge Abernathy would appreciate your lack of consideration," he volleyed.

Lane grumbled under his breath, but at least he seemed to have the epiphany that they were wasting time. "Whatever. Let's go."

They went through the whole mug shot/fingerprinting/phone call process without exchanging more than the necessary Q and A, which was fine by Greyson. Lane waked him back to the cell, unlocking the thing and sliding the door open with a clang.

"Okay, Marley. Your turn," Lane said, gesturing to the wide-open space behind him.

Marley hesitated. The hitch lasted only long enough to send Greyson's brows up, though, before she swung her boots to the floor and pushed herself to standing, then breezed coolly out of the cell. She smelled like oatmeal cookies, warm and soft and sweet, which was the complete opposite of how she was.

And didn't that just trip his fucking trigger?

You know what, screw this. He didn't care that it was smack dab in the middle of both the week and the growing season. He was going into Camden Valley *tonight* to fix his sex drought, good and proper.

After Lane finished processing Marley, and Greyson spent his time thinking about tall blondes who looked nothing like her, Woody came back to the cell to spring Greyson for the trip to the courthouse. Calling it a trip was, to be honest, a stretch, since the whole thing involved more of a quick stroll than anything else. Woody led the way, with Marley and Greyson in the middle and Lane at their backs. Marley walked the way she did everything else, full of chin-up attitude that was far hotter than it had a right to be. Greyson forced himself to focus on the steps it took to get him over the sun-bleached sidewalk connecting the police station to the front of the courthouse property, then the bricked stairs to the building itself, and finally, through the massive doors of the front entrance.

The courthouse was one of the oldest buildings in Millhaven, second only to the church on the opposite side of Town Street's main square. Like the church, and most other buildings in Millhaven, come to think on it, it had also been beautifully maintained, with nearly all of the architecture having been either left intact or updated as needed to keep with the original, Southern small-town style. Tan on black marble floors checkerboarded out beneath Greyson's feet as he moved through the metal detectors—the only obvious update the courthouse had seen in decades—then fell back into step beside Marley as they walked past large windows, sturdy benches, and darkly paneled wood doors adorned with brass plates noting room numbers and office names. When they arrived outside the main courtroom, Greyson's heart began to beat faster against his will, but he stuffed the feeling down in favor of an extra helping of his usual noncommittal scowl.

"What now?" he asked. "Do you want to handcuff me to the judge's bench?"

"Do you really want to tempt me, when you know she wouldn't question it if I did?" Lane asked back, and, shit. He had a point. Most folks in town called Judge Abernathy "eccentric", which, Greyson supposed, was the polite word for it. He'd always gone with "a couple eggs shy of a dozen", himself. Either way, whatever he was in for with her couldn't be good.

Lane must've taken Greyson's lack of immediate

response as a concession, because he continued quietly. "You're the only two on the docket. When the judge comes out, Orville will call your cases, and I'll escort you to the defendant's table when it's your turn. Then the judge will read the charges and ask you how you plead, and Vernon'll ask for a certain amount for bail."

"Sorry, who?" Marley blinked. Lane must've realized in the same moment Greyson did that she was out of her element, and he shook his head in apology.

"Orville and Vernon Stackhouse. They're identical twins. One's the bailiff, and the other is Millhaven's prosecutor."

"The prosecutor," she repeated, and although her demeanor remained bulletproof and her stare didn't waver, she paled just slightly enough to give herself away.

Lane nodded. "Yes. Since you both declined an attorney"—his gaze flicked over Marley, but she returned it with that blue stare that still wasn't budging, so he continued—"you'll answer all of her questions yourself, then she'll set bail and give you both trial dates. Any questions?"

"Nope," Greyson said, trying to ignore the queasy feeling that the thought of a trial date had sent to the depths of his belly. Marley, who had been oddly quiet ever since Lane had taken her for processing, simply shook her head.

"Good." Lane nodded. "Then let's go."

He moved forward, leading them down the aisle bisecting the large, rectangular courtroom. The population of Millhaven being what it was (or, more to the point, what it *wasn't*), the high-ceilinged room itself was mostly empty, the bench seats of the gallery occupied only by Owen, Hunter, and Eli Cross—all of whom wore matching, terribly worried expressions—and Greyson's sister, Kelsey, who looked more ticked off than troubled.

Gut dropping, Greyson added *throttle Billy Masterson and*

his big goddamned mouth to his list of things to do when he got out of this mess. He followed Lane to the front of the courtroom, where he had the spectacular luck of having to sit next to Marley on one side and Lane on the other. The big guy arranged just enough space between them to ensure that incidental contact was out of the question. Marley kept her distance, too, but somehow, Greyson managed to feel the tension in her left shoulder with his right anyway, the warmth of her bare leg next to his seeming to melt through his jeans and slide right under his skin.

"All rise," came Orville's monotone, not a nanosecond too soon for both Greyson's dick and his sanity. "This court is now in session. The honorable Judge Pearl Abernathy presiding."

For all the power she held in the eyes of the law, Judge Abernathy couldn't have looked the part any less. She couldn't weigh more than a hundred pounds even, and that was probably in her robes *and* soaked to the skin. Her gray hair was pulled back into a tidy bun that made her already-prominent cheekbones stand out like the curves on a full, ripe apple, and her reading glasses—this pair with bright purple frames, although that could change on a dime depending on which of the two dozen pairs in her arsenal was closest to her grasp at any given moment—magnified her already-large eyes to nearly doll-like status.

"Well!" Judge Abernathy sat, propping her elbows on the large oak bench from which she presided and dropping her chin into her palms with an excited grin. Christ, Greyson was screwed. "I have to tell y'all, this is more hullabaloo than I've had in my courtroom since Matty Beaumont got that burr under his saddle and drove his tractor through the side of Silas Gardner's barn. S'pose Silas should've known better than to load up on Harley Martin's moonshine and tell half the town that Matty's old basset hound is prettier than his wife. Anyhoo!" She clucked her tongue as she shifted back to riffle through a few sheets of paper that had been placed on the bench in front of her. "Shoplifting. Unpaid parking tickets. My, my. Y'all *have* been misbehaving, haven't you?"

The mischief in Judge Abernathy's tone, and everything it implied as she linked Marley and Greyson together with her stare made Greyson's face go hot.

"Not *together*," he said, his mouth pressing into a hard line as he punctuated his lightning-quick claim with, "Ma'am."

Marley stiffened and went saucer-eyed beside him on the bench as she shook her head, and at least there was one thing they agreed on. A noise of protest sounded off from behind them, a grumble of disdain that Greyson would bet his left nut belonged to Eli Cross and had been launched at the mere suggestion of impropriety regarding his sister, who —news flash—wasn't exactly a delicate flower, but hey. Whatever helped the jackass sleep at night.

"Order in the court," Orville interrupted, giving Greyson some high-octane stink-eye from his spot next to the judge's bench. "Don't address the judge until your case has been called and you're standing before her, son."

Greyson knew—God, he *knew*—that pushing was a bad idea. Borderline stupid, really. But the word 'son' burrowed deep, trapping his breath in his throat and daring him over the line.

Before he could say anything, though, Judge Abernathy waved a hand through the air. "Ah, right. All these formalities. I suppose we should get this party started properly. Orville, why don't you call Mr. Whittaker's case, here, so he and I can get down to business?"

Marley snorted, mostly under her breath. "What ever happened to ladies first?"

"*Order*," Orville snapped, and Greyson's patience went along for the ride. He had a farm to get back to, land that needed tending and work that needed done. Not to mention the shit he'd have to endure from his old man once he caught wind of what had happened today. All Marley had to do was go back up to that big ol' farmhouse, high on the hill at Cross Creek, and do...whatever it was she'd been doing there for the last nine months, while her old man probably coddled her into next fucking week.

He pushed without a second thought. "Ladies first only applies when there are ladies *present*. As it stands, I don't see any."

Greyson instantly recognized the words as meaner than most. The bitter taste they had left in his mouth told him so, and the sharp pang in his stomach seconded the motion.

One corner of Marley's mouth lifted, and wait...

"You know," she murmured, and yep, sure as the sun came up in the morning and the roosters crowed along with it, she was smiling. "That is, by far, the most intelligent thing you have said all day. I'm not a lady. In fact, I'm not even close. And don't you forget it."

For a beat, then one more, they sat there, their stares locking them together as if they were gravity itself, some law of nature far bigger than either of them could fight. Greyson's heart thundered in his rib cage, pressing his pulse in a wild rush against his eardrums, and even though he'd normally rather be up to his hips in pure manure than back down, he averted his eyes first.

She still looked hungry.

Orville crossed his arms over his chest and looked at Judge Abernathy, who apparently had to give the actual order for him to act before he could do it. Greyson had torn his stare away from Marley's just in time for him to catch the look on the judge's face, and an icy ball of dread the size of a cantaloupe formed in his gut.

Because now Judge Abernathy's huge, Anime-cartoon eyes were lit with curiosity, and he knew better than to think he was getting out of this mess any time soon.

5

Marley couldn't breathe. Technically, she knew there was nothing wrong with her lungs, nor any of the other anatomy required for the job. But when Greyson had fixed her with that stare, so dark and deep that she'd still be falling into it if he hadn't had the sense to turn away, something had short-circuited in her system. It was as if, in that brief slice of a moment, he'd somehow managed not only to look at her, but to *see* her.

No wonder he'd turned away.

Marley forced herself to inhale, then stamped the thought into dust. She had so many other things to worry about right now. Bail. A trial date. The fact that her brothers had all looked at her with far more concern than anger as she'd walked into the courtroom.

The way the judge was staring at her with enough curiosity to sink a cruise ship in about three minutes, start to finish.

"My, my," Judge Abernathy trilled, an impish smile shaping her mouth. "That was quite the exchange. I reckon I should've expected it, seeing as how one of you is a Whittaker and the other a Cross. Dogs and cats have more affection for each other than y'all."

"My last name is Rallston. I'm not a Cross," Marley said, the words sailing out of her by default, and the bailiff guy... Otis? No, Orville, let out an exasperated huff.

But Judge Abernathy simply tilted her head. "Nevertheless, here you are, acting like one. At least when it comes to present company." Her humungous eyes traveled to Greyson, and she tapped a finger on the bench in front of her. "As a matter of fact, that gives me an interesting idea. Come on up here, you two. Before Orville here goes into apoplexy, and so I can holler at you both properly."

She lifted her hands, the long, black sleeves of her robe flapping around her birdlike arms as she motioned for them to come forward and stand at the large oak table on the left side of the courtroom, but all Marley could do was gape at the woman.

Thankfully, Greyson seemed to be just as stunned as she was. "I'm sorry?" he asked. But Judge Abernathy simply raised a brow over the rims of her crazy glasses.

"Oh, come now, Mr. Whittaker. You might be a lot of things, but I hardly think hearing impaired is one of them."

The prosecutor, who was a mirror image of the bailiff but for the suit and tie instead of the uniform that matched Lane's, finally chose that moment to throw in his two cents from the right side of the courtroom. "I think, Judge, that perhaps what Mr. Whittaker is saying is that this is a bit, ah, unorthodox, as we're here for two separate bail hearings for unrelated incidents."

Funny, none of that seemed to register with the old bird. "Psssh! Of course it's unorthodox. It's my courtroom. Don't worry." Judge Abernathy sighed heavily, dividing her glance between Orville and Vernon, who both wore matching expressions of here-we-go-again. "I might not be stodgy enough to do things in a customary manner, but it'll all be on the up and up. I do know the law, after all."

She tapped her temple and winked, and oh God, she was *serious*.

"This is crazy," Marley whispered. She'd known Millhaven was backwards, but this took the crown. Not that she had any recourse, what with the whole having-been-arrested thing and all, and neither the prosecutor nor Lane argued with the judge's request, so she pushed to her feet and followed Greyson to the defendant's table.

"There!" Judge Abernathy smiled brightly. "That's so much better. Now, before we get to brass tacks"—the look she sent in Vernon's direction read *yes, bail*—"there is one thing we need to address. Mr. Whittaker, if you don't see a lady in front of you, you need to get yourself to Doc Sanders for an eye exam, sooner rather than later."

Greyson got as close to remorseful as he probably ever would, dropping his stubbled chin toward the marble floor. "My apologies. I didn't mean you, ma'am."

"Lord mercy, but you've got the sense of a goat," Judge Abernathy said with a shake of her head. "I don't mean me, either. I know exactly who you are, Greyson Whittaker. Your reputation precedes you, and there is that old saying about the apple and the tree."

Greyson went rigid beside her, and if Marley didn't know any better, she'd have thought the words had hurt him. But since she was pretty sure he was all bravado and dark, dirty stares and not much else, she let a smile escape at his comeuppance.

The gesture lasted for less than a heartbeat. "Oh, don't be too quick with that smile, Miss Rallston. You've got a tree of your own, now, don't you? It does make you two quite the interesting pair."

A flush of warmth stole over Marley's face, creeping all the way up into her hairline and over her ears. "Respectfully, uh, ma'am?" Unsure of how else to avoid the bailiff's death glare, she raised her hand, waiting until Judge Abernathy nodded before continuing. "But we're *so* not a pair."

"Ah, but you both have a penchant for getting into a pickle, now, don't you? Let's see, here." Scooping up the sheaf of papers in front of her, the judge slid her reading glasses lower on the bridge of her nose, her lips moving silently as she read. "Well. Given your reputation, Mr. Whittaker, I can't say I'm surprised about these parking tickets. But we'll get to that in a tick. As for you, Miss Rallston"—she peered at Marley—"I'll admit to at least being curious."

Marley's pulse knocked at her throat. She'd known this part, where the judge set bail and decided how to punish her, would suck. But it was still better than Sierra and her mom being pulled apart just because they couldn't make ends meet, even if it cost her. Bracing herself, Marley waited for the judge to say something, to give up a dollar amount that would likely tempt her to cry (not that she'd ever *dream* of actually doing it in front of all these people—or, you know, anyone. Ever), or, God, worse yet, make her stay in jail for a little while first.

She didn't. Instead, the silence stretched through the courtroom until every single eye in the place had bored into Marley from some angle or another, and finally Judge Abernathy leaned forward.

"That was your cue to tell me what happened at The Corner Market today, sugar bee."

"Oh." A rush of embarrassment moved through Marley's chest, partly from the duh factor and partly at having been called 'sugar bee' as a grown woman, *by* a grown woman. The less she said, the better, though, so she nodded at the papers between Judge Abernathy's fingers. "Well, it's just like it says in the arrest report, I guess."

"Sheriff Atlee is excellent at his job," the judge agreed. "He's written a very thorough account. But all things being equal, I'd like to hear this yarn straight from the horse's mouth."

The prosecutor cleared his throat. "Begging your pardon again, Judge, but...well, isn't all of this better suited for an actual trial, rather than a bond hearing?"

The thought of having to come back for an actual trial gave Marley a serious case of the shakes, and she struggled for an inhale that barely made the trip past her lips. God, couldn't they just get it all over-with right now?

Judge Abernathy smiled serenely at the man, and although it was soft enough for her to be the only one, she caught the "oh, shit" Greyson had let escape on a barely there whisper.

"Mr. Stackhouse, let me ask you a question. Have I ever walked into your house and told you how to run the place? How to balance your bank statement, or what to have for Sunday supper?" Judge Abernathy asked.

Vernon's mouth fell open, his spine going stick-straight against the back of his chair. "Why, no, Your Honor. Of course not."

"Well, then, I'd thank you kindly for not interrupting and telling me how to run mine." She turned back to Marley and asked, "Miss Rallston, are you certain you don't want an attorney while I ask you a few questions? Because you're not obligated to say a word, and if you've changed your mind, we can absolutely accommodate you."

The woman's expression had turned genuine, so much

so that Marley believed her, despite all the eccentricities she'd trotted out like a show pony since she'd taken the bench. But it was a question Marley could answer with ease. An attorney would only cost more time and money, and having one wouldn't change one ounce of her answers or her situation, anyway. Better to just answer the judge's questions and get on with it.

"Yes, ma'am. I'm sure."

"Alrighty, then." Judge Abernathy looked at Vernon, who nodded in deference, then she leaned forward to refocus her gaze on Marley. "Now, where were we? Ah! You were telling me how you thought today was a good day for allegedly developing sticky fingers."

Marley froze. She hated lying—she'd never seen the point—and this woman might be nuts on toast, but she *was* a judge.

Marley chose her words with caution. "Yes, ma'am." Not a lie. That was the topic of conversation.

The judge's brows dipped. "You didn't have anything better to do than put"—she paused, tilting her chin over the arrest report on the bench—"five cans of tuna fish, four cans of tomato soup, two packages of instant noodles, and a Snickers bar into your backpack and hightail it out of The Corner Market without paying for said groceries?"

"It...seemed like a good idea at the time," Marley said, and okay, yeah. She'd slanted the truth there with the heavy implication that she'd been the one to put the groceries in the backpack. But bending the truth with the store manager *had* seemed like a good idea at the time, and she still didn't regret taking the blame. Since Sierra *couldn't* take the blame without being taken from her mother, it would have to do.

"I see," Judge Abernathy said. "And is there anything you'd like to add to this account of what happened today?"

"No, ma'am." Marley's rib cage tightened beneath her tank top, and she resisted the urge to fidget, even though it took a metric ton of effort.

Surprisingly, the judge didn't push. "Interesting," was all she said before shifting her gaze to the spot where Lane stood in the gallery. "Sheriff Atlee, am I correct in assuming all of the groceries in question have been safely returned to their shelves at The Corner Market, undamaged?"

Marley turned to look at him over her shoulder, just in time to catch his nod. "Yes, Your Honor."

"Oh, goodie. I do love it when retribution takes care of itself. Not that it means you're off the hook, sugar bee. Nor you, Mr. Whittaker."

Again, Greyson tensed beside her, and again, Marley's curiosity tripped despite the fact that she knew she shouldn't care less about anything other than getting out of this predicament as unscathed as possible. "I'm not really sure what her shoplifting has to do with my parking tickets," he said. "I didn't *steal* anything."

"And I didn't break the law *six* times in a row," Marley shot back with a glare.

"Ah, and there it is," Judge Abernathy replied with a smile that could only be labeled beatific, and seriously, was anything about this process going to be normal? Hadn't this woman ever seen *Law & Order*, for God's sake?

Greyson looked at the judge, his dark brows lifted in obvious confusion. "I'm sorry, ma'am. There what is?"

"What landed you both here in the first place," Judge Abernathy replied, not skipping so much as a heartbeat. "You wanted to know what your cases have to do with one another? Well, I'll tell you, Mr. Whittaker. You and Miss Rallston, here, may have allegedly committed separate offenses, but you both need an attitude adjustment, lickety-split. Lucky for you, we're going to take care of that right now."

Vernon cleared his throat, and Judge Abernathy rolled her eyes. "Alright, alright. Go on, Orville, and read the charges against Mr. Whittaker and Miss Rallston—separately—so we can get to the good part."

"Finally," Greyson muttered, entering a guilty plea a minute later as the bailiff read the charges against him. Although Marley's stomach clenched when it was her turn, she managed to get the word "guilty" past her lips, and she pressed the soles of her boots into the floor a little harder, standing tall to take whatever bail the judge finally sent her way.

"Okay, you two. Here it is. I am prepared to release you both on your own recognizance, provided that you meet a few stipulations, and that the prosecution agrees to the terms."

Greyson's "what?" crashed into Vernon's "Your Honor", but neither one of them held a candle to Marley's thankfully internal "holy fucking shit". The judge was going to let them off with no bail at *all*? Not that Marley was complaining—God, she was half-tempted to rush the bench and kiss the woman on the mouth—but how was this even possible?

The prosecutor won out, recovering his wits first. "Your Honor, while I hold the deepest respect for the court, I must revisit my previous claim that these proceedings are all rather, ah. Unusual."

"And that is what makes them such fun, don't you think?" Judge Abernathy asked with a laugh. "Come now, Vernon. I'm not suggesting we skip trials altogether. But if we can focus on the steak and not the peas, why shouldn't we bypass all the blah, blah, blah of drawing this out and enjoy a lovely dinner together right now, hmm?"

"All the evidence seems to be in order and both pleas have been entered," he replied slowly, likely beginning to realize that both cases would be slam dunks in his win column. "I suppose it wouldn't hurt to have the trials now, as long as both defendants agree."

"Atta boy. How about you two? Would you like to proceed?"

"It'll save time, right? We can just cut through all the cr—ah, stuff that takes up time, get our punishments right now, and we won't have to come back?" Greyson asked. His trademark cockiness had strangely fallen away, but his stare still remained as dark as it was intense, and wow, he wanted to get out of here as badly as Marley did.

"Yes, indeed," said the judge. "I will remind you that the choice is yours. If you'd like a court-appointed attorney—that's a freebie, now—and a trial date in the future, I can make that pony prance, too. But if you want to get on with it right now—"

"Yes."

Marley's answer vaulted out and collided with Greyson's in a simultaneous burst, and the back of her neck prickled with heat. She had no doubt he wanted to be tethered to both her and this courtroom for as little time as possible. He'd probably be thrilled to never clap eyes on her again. And weren't they just BFFs in that regard?

"Excellent!" Judge Abernathy clapped her hands like a kid at a carnival, her robes swirling around her arms. They went through a few minutes of legalities that included case numbers and trial dates set for the right-here, right-now and evidence being entered for each, and then the judge pushed her glasses over the bridge of her nose, all business.

"Alrighty, now. First thing's first. Does either defendant

—that's y'all," she paused to say to both her and Greyson, "have anything to add to the evidence presented herein?"

Somewhere in the far reaches of Marley's brain, it occurred to her that she was still being lumped in with Greyson. But the judge seemed to be A) interested in efficiency, which was a big yay for Marley, and B) off her freaking rocker, so Marley opted for a simple "no, ma'am," in the interest of getting the hell out of the courtroom with her punishment in-hand as fast as the space-time continuum would allow. Greyson echoed the sentiment, and Judge Abernathy nodded.

"So noted. Miss Rallston, you've entered a guilty plea to the crime of attempted shoplifting, and this court finds you as such based on the evidence at hand. Mr. Whittaker, your parking tickets speak for themselves, and since you're not contesting them, this court also finds you guilty of violating Section 124 of the Town of Millhaven's traffic code. Now... what to do with you both?"

Greyson snapped to awareness beside her, his body strung with enough tension that she could practically feel it on her skin. "Us *both*?"

"You've committed separate crimes, to be sure, but it's the opinion of this court that y'all will benefit from the same penance. First, the nitty gritty." Judge Abernathy swung her gaze to Marley, and ugh, here it came. "Miss Rallston, to finish your retribution for the attempted shoplifting, the court will require an apology from you to The Corner Market. Mr. Whittaker, you'll have to make good on those tickets by week's end. All six, paid in full."

Marley allowed herself the tiniest exhale. Okay, that didn't sound so bad. Maybe the judge had just been making them sweat a little, like some sort of scared-straight life lesson or something. Maybe—just maybe—she'd get out of this without a high-dollar price tag attached to her permanent record.

"Yes, ma'am," Marley said, and even Greyson had the good sense to nod in agreement.

"I'll take care of it on my way out, Judge," he said.

"Thank you kindly, but I'm not done with you troublemakers just yet."

Before Marley could fully register the words as the sucker punch they were, Judge Abernathy followed through with the haymaker. "I'm also sentencing you each to two hundred hours of community service."

"Two *hundred*?" Marley blurted. Holy shit, that might as well be a lifetime!

Not that it seemed to bother the judge one whit. "Yes, I think that'll serve nicely."

"Begging your pardon, Judge," Greyson said. "But it's the growing season. I've got a farm to run."

Marley noticed that he spoke the words not with argument or attitude, but with something that looked dangerously close to actual panic. The sentiment disappeared even more quickly than it had arrived, though, almost as if it had been purposely extinguished, and he straightened, clenching his fists at his sides.

"I've got a job, too," Marley volunteered, a fresh wave of dread crashing over her at the thought of trying to balance her work hours—which already required a built-in hour and a half for travel to and from Lockridge—with that much community service.

"Mmm," Judge Abernathy murmured. "We'll get things arranged around your work schedules. Justice needs serving, but not at the expense of your livelihoods. That's not how the law works, now. Louis Kerrigan needs help over at the animal shelter on the east side of town. I'm sure he can figure out a way to get the two of you in there for some good, hard teamwork."

Marley's jaw unhinged. No way. No *way*. She couldn't possibly mean... "Wait. Greyson and I have to do the community service *together*?"

Several voices rippled through the gallery behind her—she could easily parse Eli's as more disgruntled than the others, although none of them sounded thrilled.

Greyson least of all. "You want me to spend free time I don't have at an animal shelter. With *her*?"

The disdain in his words hit Marley with an unexpected sting, and she crossed her arms over her chest to cover it up. "Believe me, I'm as underwhelmed as you are."

"Well, it wouldn't be a punishment if y'all were thrilled with it," Judge Abernathy pointed out over a smile. "But with you two tussling like cats and dogs, it only seems appropriate for you to learn to take care of them properly. To answer your question, Miss Rallston, yes. You and Mr. Whittaker will be required to serve your two hundred community service hours together, as your work schedules allow, under Louis's supervision. Ninety days should be enough time for y'all to get things done. You can report to the shelter first thing Saturday morning to get started. I'll tell Louis to expect you. Oh! And, of course, you'll both be on probation for the duration of your community service. No more toes out of line for either of you. Any questions?"

Marley opened her mouth to fire off no less than a dozen of them, all with vehement protests attached. How on earth was she supposed to work enough to keep up with her payments to the hospital *and* slog her way through two hundred hours of community service, especially since those hours would probably feel more like millennia working next to Mr. Tall, Dark, and Douchebag? Her boss at the boutique was hardly what Marley would call accommodating (and more like what she'd call a preferential bitch). Adjusting her work schedule to allow for this fresh hell was going to be damn near impossible, and without that job—or, more specifically, the paycheck it garnered—she'd never get out of Millhaven.

Except she couldn't exactly say that, nor could she fess up in front of the crazy judge and her decent-to-a-fault brothers and Greyson goddamned Whittaker that she hadn't stolen those groceries at all, but rather, that she'd lied about doing so in order to keep a scared, hungry pre-teen girl from being taken from her mother. Marley might be older, and her circumstances different, but that end result was the same.

She knew what it felt like to be taken from her mother, and she knew how deeply it hurt. So she did the only thing she could.

"No, ma'am. No questions."

"Wonderful," Judge Abernathy said after Greyson's silence extended long enough to count as a concession, too. "Then this court is adjourned."

6

Marley rolled over, drifting in the no-man's-land of being mostly asleep, partly foggy, and wholly relaxed. She was warm, her body loose and her mind fluid, her thoughts sliding from one to the other with ease. Her mother sat beside her, leaning over the bed and smoothing her hair away from her face, and even though Marley knew she was too old for the gesture, she leaned into it anyway. But then the hands grew different, the face in front of hers fading too fast for her to even cry out. The hands were on her arms now, and there were more of them, grabbing her wrists and shoulders, pulling her in different directions, away from her mother. A new face, young and scared and framed by long, stringy hair, appeared in the background, light brown eyes wide and pleading for help, and Marley's heart surged up to lodge in her throat, blocking her scream.

The harder she struggled, the more hands appeared. On her shoulders. Digging in to her forearms. Invisible fingers latched on to her, the contact close, too close, like clammy breath in her ear. They pulled her away, holding her down, and oh, God, she couldn't breathe, couldn't see that spot in her nice, warm bed where she'd felt so happy, where she knew she belonged. Panic rolled through her chest, and she searched wildly—where was it? Hadn't she just been right there with her mother? And where was Sierra now? God, she had to get back. She had to find the place where she'd been. She had to help them both.

Marley struggled harder, to no avail. Her fear grew slick in the depths of her belly, her panic pouring over her like ice water. But then the dozens of hands became one set of arms, the hold on her strong and unyielding, yet somehow, she wasn't frightened.

Gotcha, darlin'...

Marley woke with a ragged gasp. Levering up with a jerk, she shot off a series of rapid-fire blinks, registering the wash of golden sunlight streaming through the sheer curtains, the birds chirping happily outside the window. The reality of losing her mother, of being stuck in a town where she didn't belong, of everything that had happened yesterday, crashed back into her like a wrecking ball, filling her with sadness so deep that, for a second, it was actually painful.

"Shit." She dropped her chin to her chest. Squeezing her eyes shut, she forced her pulse to slow and her breaths back toward a normal pattern. In. Out. In again, this time, a sip deeper. A step further from the loss. The sadness.

"There," she finally whispered with a nod. Nightmares were part of Marley's regular repertoire, and she was used to coaching her way out of them when she woke. She'd be fine in a minute. She just needed to forget the panic, to clear her mind of the fear that clawed into her pretty much every time she closed her eyes. It had only been a dream, and almost certainly a product of yesterday's mental stress.

How the hell else would Greyson Whittaker and his

stupid, sexy drawl have ended up in her head, and *comforting* her, no less?

Flinging the quilt off her legs, Marley planted her bare feet over the floorboards and padded to the bathroom. She scrubbed her teeth, then her face, with more enthusiasm than either probably required, gathering the fortitude she'd need to get through her day. Her brothers had all made separate attempts to talk to her about her arrest after she'd been dismissed from the courtroom yesterday afternoon, ranging from stern and serious (Owen) to laid-back yet concerned (Hunter) to joking and jovial (ah, Eli), but she'd met them all with enough one-word answers to shut down any chance of deeper conversation before retreating to her room. Marley got that they were doing their family-obligation thing, each of them trying to fix the problem in his own way because they felt like they should, but, truly, the less she dwelled on what had happened, the easier it would be to forge ahead with her agenda.

Complete this community service as fast as possible. Change her work schedule as little as possible. And think about what Greyson Whittaker's ridiculously muscular arms would feel like around her aching, needy body as *never* as possible.

Marley was so busy snuffing out the thought—and the pulse of heat it had sent to a spot between her legs that had seen far too little action in the last year and a half—that she didn't do her customary look-and-listen before descending the stairs to the main house and making her way into the kitchen in search of a cup of coffee or six.

Which was how she managed to walk smack into Hunter just as soon as she crossed the threshold.

"Crap!" Marley's hands flew up just a beat after her

brother's, and he caught her biceps with his palms, steadying her with ease.

"Whoa," he said, replacing his surprise with a smile as soon as she was solid on her feet. "You okay, there, kiddo?"

She'd long since stopped trying to get her brothers to drop the various, little-sisterly terms of endearment they had on a regular rotation, even though her belly still sank with each one. It made them feel better, she supposed, to try to make her part of the family, and they were decent guys. Good, even. Not that she'd ever be part of the family. After twenty-four years of not wanting her, Tobias wasn't likely to change his colors now. Just as she wouldn't belong here, even on the other-worldly chance that he did.

"Yeah, sorry. Guess I just need to caffeinate." Marley ducked her chin in equal parts apology and chagrin, the latter tripling in her gut as she realized that—while Tobias was not-so-suspiciously absent—all three of her brothers, plus Hunter's wife, Emerson, all stood in the kitchen.

Shit. Marley made her way to the coffeepot on the far side of the kitchen, feeling every set of eyes on her as she went. But, true to form, Hunter just gave up a nonchalant shrug.

"No worries. I think we've all been there," he said, moving back to the spot where Emerson stood at the far end of the butcher block island in the center of the kitchen. The room had always reminded Marley of one of those kitchens in a home and garden magazine, all light and airy, with everything in its rightful spot even though none of it looked staged or overly organized, as if every object had a place to belong and simply gravitated there to nestle in seamlessly. The white ceramic bowl holding nectarines and plums on the time-scuffed butcher block. The oversized mugs and matching plates behind the glass-paned cabinet over the coffeepot. The big, inviting oak table that they'd recently placed a leaf in and long, cushioned benches on either side of rather than chairs, so Emerson and Scarlett and Cate would always have room. Everyone always paired up so perfectly, each one of her brothers and their significant others finding their proper space and fitting in like puzzle pieces.

Well, everyone except her, that was.

"So." Emerson cleared her throat softly, pulling her auburn curls over one shoulder before sending a careful look in Marley's direction. "How are you doing this morning?" *Translation: are you ready to talk about what happened yesterday yet?*

Marley's stomach tightened and dropped behind her dark green sleep shirt. Truly, there wasn't enough coffee for this. Not even if she spiked what she'd just poured with a gallon of Kahlua.

"Spectacular. You?"

Despite her defensiveness, Marley meant this question. Emerson had multiple sclerosis, a disease Marley had known nothing about when she'd landed on her ass in Millhaven last year. While Emerson had far more good days than bad thanks to a solid wellness plan and a support system that might as well be made of titanium for how carefully Hunter and the rest of the Crosses looked out for her, Marley knew the road wasn't an easy one, and her sister-in-law had never been anything other than genuinely kind to her. Marley might not want to dive headlong into bestieship with the family she hadn't even known she'd had at this time last year, or, hey, even stick around town for any longer than was absolutely necessary. But she couldn't justify going full-frontal bitch on Emerson, even if she'd rather be boiled in oil than talk about having been arrested yesterday.

"I'm okay," Emerson said. The silence that hung in the air afterwards had all the subtlety of a brick sailing through the French doors, and okay. Time to maneuver her way out of this.

Marley pressed her back to the counter, cradling her mug to her chest. "Shouldn't you guys be, I don't know. Working, or something?"

"We *are* working," Owen volleyed, and Marley had to bite back an involuntary smile at the edge of stiffness in her oldest brother's voice. God, he was probably Type A in his sleep. "We were just getting the weekly marketing plans all set before Hunter and I head over to the north fields to check the irrigation system and bale hay with Dad."

The word "Dad", so easily slung around, like "chair" or "weather" or "car", stuck into Marley like a bee sting, unexpected and sharp, and she grunted into her coffee in reply. Although she'd set eyes on Tobias twice after returning home yesterday, and she was certain he'd gotten the full story from her brothers about how she'd been arrested for shoplifting, he had been the only person who hadn't made some sort of effort to get her to open up about the heap of trouble she'd gotten herself into.

Not that his silence had shocked her, really. He'd spent her whole life not making an effort. Why start now?

Marley mashed down the ache in her chest and yanked on her armor, good and tight. "You guys just aren't usually all hogging my breakfast spot," she muttered, bringing herself back to the reality of the abnormally crowded kitchen.

"It's nice to see you, too, sprout." Eli gave up a grin that was caught somewhere between confident and charming, and she softened despite her conviction not to.

"I'm only four years younger than you, you know," she pointed out, and Eli's grin became a laugh.

"Yeah, but I'm practicing. I've only got two and a half months to go before Jordan arrives." He paused, and Marley noticed just a beat too late that his blue stare had lost a bit of its crinkle around the edges. "Speaking of which, we missed you last night."

Ah, right. The family pep rally at Eli and Scarlett's new place to paint the baby's room. "Yeah, sorry." Marley took a large sip from her mug, the coffee burning a path to her belly. "I had a thing."

Since she was pretty sure Eli wouldn't count her sitting in her room with a pint of Ben and Jerry's, flipping through old photo albums and having an extended conversation with a mother who could neither answer nor even hear her an actual thing, she kept the particulars to herself. But despite her brothers' efforts, she could barely make it through the weekly Cross family dinner that went down every Saturday night without feeling like a total outsider, let alone survive something as family-oriented as painting the baby's room. Plus, there was little point in getting *that* close with everyone when she was only going to turn around and leave as soon as she could, anyway.

And hey, speaking of which... "So, yeah. I should go get ready for work."

Marley pushed off the counter, her sights set on the exit leading back to the hallway and the front of the main house. The squeak of the back door that allowed entry to the kitchen through a small mudroom to her right stopped her in her tracks, though, and the sight of Lucy, the black and white mutt who was always within a four-foot radius of Tobias's boots at any given time of the day or night, sent her heart tripping against her ribs and her coffee sloshing up the sides of the mug still in her hand.

"Mornin', Emerson," came Tobias's voice from the doorway of the mudroom, followed by a tip of that caramel-colored hat he was nearly never without. "Boys," he added, nodding across the kitchen at Eli, Hunter, and Owen. His gaze screeched to a halt when it got to Marley, widening for just a split second before darting away.

"Good morning, Marley. Can't say I expected to see you down here," Tobias said quietly. His tone was impossible to read—God, it always was—but she read between the lines well enough.

"Sorry to disappoint you."

Owen made a sound of irritation, which was his default reaction to this bob and weave she and Tobias had been doing ever since she'd come here to fulfill her mother's dying wish of meeting the man face-to-face. But Tobias shook his head, almost imperceptibly, as he ignored the barb, and hell if that wasn't *his* default to the whole fucked up situation, too.

Second verse, same as the first. Hell, at this point, they might as well have a script.

"Well," the old man finally said a beat later, running a palm over the front of the plain gray T-shirt he'd tucked into his jeans. "I s'pose we should get to work on that hay before it gets too hot out."

"That sounds like a good plan," Hunter agreed, likely in an effort to smooth over the sinkhole full of awkward Marley had inserted into the otherwise lovely conversation.

Emerson nodded, following his lead. "I need to get into town, myself. Mrs. Ellersby has a nine thirty appointment for physical therapy, and as sweet as the old woman is, I don't want to put Doc Sanders out by making her wait."

"Ah. You be sure to tell the doc hello from all of us," Tobias said with a smile.

"Sure thing." Kissing Hunter's cheek, Emerson murmured goodbyes to everyone, and Eli grabbed his laptop from the kitchen table.

"I'm going to head home to check on Scarlett and work for a bit, too. I'll walk you out."

Everyone began to scatter, Marley included, but Owen pinned her back into place with a stormy blue-gray stare. "I'll meet you in the north field in a minute," he said to Tobias and Hunter, although—oh, goody—he didn't budge his gaze from hers. "I've got something to take care of here first."

Tobias's pause surprised her, although Hunter's didn't. "Okay," Hunter said slowly, moving toward the mudroom only after Tobias had turned to pave the way. Lucy's tags sounded off in a muted jingle, the back door clapping shut a few heartbeats later, and Marley didn't wait to go on the defensive.

"I know what you're going to say," she told Owen, and yep, that serious-as-sin-on-Sunday crease tugging his dark brows into a V made her guess official.

Owen crossed his arms over his chest and frowned. "Then why do I have to keep saying it?"

"You don't," she pointed out, but her brother wasn't having it.

"Apparently, I do, because it's not getting through. You've been here for nine months, Marley. When are you going to give him a chance to get to know you?"

Never. I am never giving him a chance.

The answer surged up from behind her sternum, burning on her tongue and begging to be said. It wasn't just that she was angry and didn't want to, although both were so, so accurate. But even more than the fact that she didn't want to give Tobias a chance was the raw, real truth that she simply *couldn't* give Tobias a chance.

Just like she couldn't keep having this conversation. God, she needed to get out of here, out of this kitchen and out of this house and out of fucking Millhaven, as fast as humanly possible.

"My being here is temporary," Marley said. She hadn't shared the how or why of her being stranded in town with her brothers. If they knew about her debt to the hospital, they'd only try to help her pay it, and trading one debt for another wasn't on her list of "oh, goody, please, sign me up". Plus, it wasn't their burden to right. Lorraine had been her mother, not theirs.

Owen dropped his voice, low and quiet. "It doesn't have to be temporary. Look, I know"—he broke off—"I know losing your mom was hard for you. But you don't have to leave. You don't have to lose us, too."

Annnnd this conversation was officially over. "I'm not *losing* anything. I'm just not staying. And I'm damn sure not giving Tobias a chance. It's far too late for amends."

With that, Marley turned toward the stairs, knotting her arms over the front of her sleep shirt to cover up her wildly beating heart and locking down her resolve to pay her debt so she could hurry up and get gone.

7

Greyson shifted back on his boots and watched the post-dawn sunlight filter over the corn field he stood in front of. Leaning against the barn at his back, he let his eyes linger on the slender green stalks, memorizing the way they whispered and swayed in the breeze. Calm spread through him, the sort that could only come from this, and he pulled it in like a deep, vital breath. There was a chill in the air that wouldn't last, but for now, it made the canvas jacket he'd thrown on over his T-shirt comfortable and the warmth of the travel mug of coffee between his palms a welcome sensation. He hadn't had time to go into Camden Valley for any *other* welcome sensations like he'd planned to a few days ago—hell, he'd barely had time to shower before collapsing into bed for the past two nights. Not that busting his ass to stay on top of things had made him more tired in the long run. Greyson didn't exactly hate the work, and by that, he meant that he was honestly made for it. But with this community service looming like summer storm clouds on the horizon, he'd had to get forward so he wouldn't get behind.

Because getting behind wasn't an option. He loved this land far too much to treat it with complacency.

Sometimes, the apple did fall far from the tree after all.

The sound of approaching footsteps captured Greyson's attention, and oh, the fucking irony. "You set for today?" he asked as soon as his old man was close enough to be in earshot, although he didn't take his eyes from the softly sunlit corn field in front of them, as if the visual could anchor him in the shit-storm that was about to go down.

His father grunted dismissively. "You didn't give me much choice, now did you?"

Greyson exhaled, wishing he'd thrown something stronger than coffee into his travel mug. Whiskey. Moonshine. Turpentine. At this point, he wasn't goddamn picky. "The community service is just temporary, Pop."

"Two hundred hours hardly seems temporary," his father said, his frown hanging heavy in his voice. "Kelsey said the Cross girl's got a mouth on her, too," he continued with a snort. "You got yourself into a hell of a jam, didn't you, boy?"

Greyson's molars came together with a clack, the calm he'd cultivated doing a complete mic drop/peace out. "I didn't get myself into a jam with *her*. And thanks for the news flash."

The verbal jab was just enough to get his father off his back without making the old man want to counter, and hell if Greyson wasn't a master at finding that sweet spot after all this time.

"Anyway," he continued. "I'm going to finish up in the orchards and check in with the cattle managers to make sure they've got what they need for next week before I head out. The farmhands left for the market in Camden Valley a little while ago. They'll bring the box truck and whatever doesn't sell back at two."

He'd been irritated not to be able to spend at least part of the day at the farmers' market like he usually did on Saturdays during the season. Their farmhands knew the schedule, sure, and they were capable enough. But Greyson liked to be as hands-on as possible when it came to putting Whittaker Hollow's produce into people's hands. Chalk up reason number four hundred and sixty-two why this community service was going to be an epic pain in his ass.

"Guess you've got it all figured out, then, huh?" his father asked, and it was all Greyson had not to point out that one of them fucking had to.

"Yep," he said instead. He didn't have time for this. There was work to be done. "I'm headed down to the orchards. I'll see you Monday."

His father made a noise that Greyson supposed was meant to be an acknowledgment, only it lacked the conviction it needed to be anything other than a non-verbal "whatever". But since it wasn't a fight Greyson had the time or energy to pick well enough to win, he went about the rest of what needed to be done, making sure Whittaker Hollow was set for the long, hot day ahead before grabbing the keys to his truck from the hook in the off-set garage where he usually hung them.

He didn't usually set foot in the ungracefully aging two-story farmhouse where his parents both lived and where he'd spent the bulk of his life. He had moved out of the place three days shy of his twentieth birthday, and while he'd step over the threshold if the occasion absolutely called for it, he always hated every second he had to spend there. In fact, he didn't even live on the property, having never bought a small parcel of the land from his old man the way he'd intended to when he'd graduated high school and he, his father, and his uncle had planned to run Whittaker Hollow together, the three of them.

God knew it wasn't for lack of wanting to live on the land that bore his family's name. But that dream was more ghost now than anything else, and Greyson couldn't chase it.

Not unless he wanted to let it break him.

Thrusting the thought and the bitterness that accompanied it aside, Greyson drove to the far edge of town, where Louis Kerrigan ran the local animal shelter. The place stood on a road more rural than most, which, for Millhaven, was saying something. Aside from a few tin-can trailers and very old, just as decrepit single-story houses dotted on either side of the barely paved asphalt, there was nothing that qualified as actual civilization this far from Town Street. Just wide, sprawling fields of tall grass and weeds parading as wildflowers, tall, thickly trunked oak trees lush and loaded with foliage, and the endless sky stretched out like a fat blue canvas overhead.

Although, like everything else in Millhaven, Greyson had known exactly where the animal shelter was located since about middle school, he'd never had cause to go inside the place, proper. In fact, he'd never even made it past the turnoff for the dirt-clumped gravel driveway. But when he rectified that and took the long, winding drive to its end, he caught sight of a Toyota that looked like it was being held together with a handful of rusty bolts, a pair of rubber bands, and sheer, dumb luck. Marley stood in front of the thing, her eyes hidden by a pair of aviator sunglasses and her hands tucked into a pair of olive green cargo shorts that showed off her legs just enough to make Greyson want to bang his head against the Silverado's steering wheel.

He put the truck in *park* and slid out, arching a brow at

her from beneath his baseball hat. “You waiting for an engraved invitation?”

“No.” She scowled, a gesture that shouldn’t turn Greyson on, yet it *so* did. “I just got here. And...well, to be honest, I didn’t think I was in the right place, and I didn’t want to just go barging in.”

Do not fuck with her. Do not fuck with her. Seriously. Do not... “Is there someplace else around here you could’ve mixed the place up with?”

Okay, so he was fucking with her. But it really couldn’t be helped. They were smack in the center of nowhere, for Chrissake.

Marley’s frown deepened as she swiveled a gaze over their remote surroundings. “Very funny. But it’s not my fault that nothing around here shows up on my GPS,” she muttered.

“You get cell service out here?” Greyson asked, a pop of shock moving through his chest. She was working some serious voodoo magic if her cell phone was anything other than a high-tech paperweight right now.

“God, no,” she said, waving her phone at him with a scoff. “Why do you think I thought I was lost? This thing is useless in this town.”

As overbold as she was, she also wasn’t wrong. “Yeah.” He shrugged. “Unless you’re on Town Street or near someplace with a hotspot, you’re pretty much out of luck with that.”

“Tell me something I don’t know,” Marley said with a smile too sweet to be anything other than thoroughly sarcastic, and, hey, if that was the game she wanted to play, he was all fucking in.

“There are these things called maps,” Greyson drawled with a smile to rival hers. “Made out of paper, pretty colors.

As it turns out, they're kind of useful when your phone isn't."

Marley flushed, and *bingo*. "Can we just get this over-with, please?"

"It would be my pleasure."

Greyson hung back for a second to let her move in front of him, because damn it, even though they'd gone toe to toe over the whole ladies-first thing, it really didn't feel right to barge in front of her. Marley's black sneakers crunched over the gravel of the parking area—which was big enough to hold his truck and her clunker and not much else—and over the weed-laced walkway leading to the shelter. In hindsight, he couldn't really blame Marley for wondering if she was in the wrong place. The small, squat building was dilapidated at best, the brown clapboard siding in dire need of a good stripping and painting and the pair of windows facing the drive looking as if they hadn't seen a cleaning in at least a decade. The sign nailed to the front door read *Millhaven Animal Shelter* in crooked, hand-painted letters, and okay, yeah, Judge Abernathy might need a check-up from the neck up, but she sure hadn't been wrong about Louis Kerrigan needing help out here. Christ, if the inside of this place was as bad as the outside, two hundred hours might not even put a dent in things.

Marley paused at the threshold, but only for a second. Setting her shoulders and straightening her spine beneath her black muscle shirt, she pushed her way through the front door, stepping into the cramped, musty lobby and walking to the counter that lined the back of the space.

"Hi," she said carefully to Louis, who hadn't looked up from the disorganized mountain of paperwork on the desk in front of him even though he'd have to be dead-drunk or legally blind not to have noticed her come in. "We're, um, here for the community service thing."

Louis finally fixed Marley, then Greyson, with a beady stare, his desk chair protesting with a loud groan as he shifted back for the full effect. "Uh-huh," he grunted. "Judge sent me the paperwork."

The pause that followed weighed approximately seven hundred pounds, and Greyson felt himself slip another notch closer to hell. "Okay," Marley tried again. "So, did you want us to get started, or…?"

"Rules first," Louis said, and it didn't escape Greyson's notice that the man's stare had migrated in his direction, as if he expected Greyson to break every last one of them, right out of the gate. "There's plenty of work to be done 'round here, so I expect y'all to be on time, every time. No cuttin' corners. No yappin' on your cell phones while you work. None of them ear bud things, neither. If I call for you, you need to hear me. I only give directions once, so make sure you're listenin' the first time. And a job's only done when I say it's done good enough. Any questions?"

Greyson bit back the temptation to laugh at the irony. "Nope. That was pretty clear."

"Good." Louis narrowed his eyes at them with suspicion. "And no shenanigans between y'all, either. I realize that ain't likely, what with you bein' a Cross and you bein' a Whittaker, but still. I got rules."

An image of Marley, her head tipped back and her pretty face flushed with pleasure, flared through Greyson's mind, strong enough to wedge his protest in his throat.

Marley, however? Way quicker on the draw. "That's *so* not going to be a problem. And for the record, I'm actually not a Cross. My last name is Rallston. Two l's."

"Is Tobias Cross your daddy?" Louis asked as he pegged

her with a frown, and damn, Greyson had never seen anyone's shoulders go so rigid in his life.

"Biologically." Marley slid the answer through her teeth. "Yes."

"Then you're a Cross. At least, 'round here, you are." Leaning back in his desk chair, Louis hooked a beefy thumb over an equally beefy shoulder. "Yard needs cleanin' up. Y'all can start there. Once that's done, the fence needs mending so I can let these dogs out without worryin' about them runnin' off. Supplies are in the shed. That should keep you two busy for the day."

Yeah, yeah. The work, Greyson could handle. But they needed to focus on the more important stuff. Namely... "Before we get started in the yard, can we talk about the schedule?"

Louis gave him a blank stare. "What about it?"

"Uh, everything?" Greyson asked, his pulse kicking faster in frustration. "I mean, I've got a job, so—"

"I got a job, too, son," Louis snapped. "Judge says y'all are mine for two hundred hours, so that's what you'll do. Not a minute less." He jabbed his finger into the papers in front of him on the desk, and Greyson's frustration redoubled its efforts.

"I'm not trying to get out of the work," he said, doing a piss-poor job of not letting his indignation seep into his tone.

Louis laughed without an ounce of humor. "Sure you ain't. Because a Whittaker would never try to bully his way out of a bad situation."

Greyson's fingers turned to fists at his sides, involuntary and tight. "I just want to know about the schedule. Like I said, I'm good for the work."

"Hmm." Louis's grunt conveyed his doubt like a special

delivery. "Then you might want to prove it by getting started." He sent a pointed glare toward the door. "That yard's not getting any cleaner while you stand here jawin'."

It was a challenge if Greyson had ever seen one, and he stepped forward, fully prepared to push first and push hard.

But then Marley surprised the crap out of him by lifting a hand and looking at Louis. "As much as it pains me to say this, Greyson's right. We *do* need to set some sort of schedule so we can get this community service done in the ninety days the judge allotted. Plus, I have a job, too, and he and I kind of have to know when to be here, since one of your rules was that we arrive on time," she pointed out.

Louis processed her logic for the same moment Greyson parsed through all the what-the-hell winging through his brain. "Fine," the man said slowly. "Evenings and weekends'll be all right, I s'pose."

Marley winced, but the gesture was so quick and her stance so tough afterward that Greyson couldn't even be one hundred-percent sure his eyes hadn't been playing tricks on him.

"When, exactly?" he asked, not wanting to lose the chance to get things one step closer to over-with.

"Tuesday, Wednesday, and Thursday evenings, four to eight. Then a full eight hours every weekend. Sundays will do."

After some quick mental math, Greyson realized that would put them just ahead of the ninety days Judge Abernathy had allowed.

"Done," he said. So what if it meant he wouldn't see a single day off all summer? The sooner they were done with this mess, the faster he'd be back on his farm full-time, the happier he'd be.

Marley seemed to have reached the same conclusion

with regard to the timetable, because she nodded. "Okay by me if that's as fast as we can do it."

"Good," Louis replied. "I ain't usually here after five or on Sundays, but you can be rest assured I'll be givin' y'all enough work to make sure you do every minute of the time you owe. Speakin' of which, that yard is waiting. Gate's unlatched."

"Great." In truth, Greyson meant the word far less sarcastically than he let on. At least now there was an agenda, a set of tasks to keep his body moving and his mind off the fact that he wasn't at Whittaker Hollow. Hard work, he knew how to do, and what's more, he didn't really hate it.

He followed Marley back through the front door and around to the side of the shelter. A six-foot privacy fence extended outward from the edge of the building, and they reached the gate easily enough.

"Okay," Marley said, putting one hand on the rusted handle. "It's just a little yard work, right? How bad can it really be?"

If the stench that hit them as soon as she swung the gate on its hinges didn't answer her question, then the sight that accompanied it sure did.

"Holy shit," she gasped, her eyes going wide over the hand she'd clapped over her nose and mouth.

"Literally," Greyson muttered as he shook his head.

Agenda or not, this was going to be one hell of a long day.

8

Marley was officially in the small-town equivalent of the fourth circle of hell. As if the lust-hate relationship her libido was currently having with her common sense every time she so much as looked at Greyson wasn't enough, she was spending her Saturday picking up dog bombs and not getting paid.

Having to tell her boss at the boutique that she was going to need three nights a week plus every Sunday off for the foreseeable future? That was just the cherry on top of her crap sundae right now.

Make that a dog crap sundae. *Ugh.*

Swiping a forearm over her sweaty brow, Marley scanned the yard as she took a second to catch her breath. She and Greyson had made a decent amount of headway in the past couple of hours, although now that the sun was almost directly overhead and beating down on them like a heavyweight boxer at a prize fight, she already felt herself flagging.

Not Greyson, though. Nope. He was working just as briskly as he had been the second they'd gotten started. In fact, he'd been the one to come up with a strategy for getting the job done, marching his way (carefully) over to the shed the first minute they'd been out here to turn up a couple of pairs of rubber boots along with two pairs of worn but serviceable work gloves. The semi-rusted shovels that had been hanging on the shed wall worked better than Marley had expected for scooping up the mess in the yard, and the plastic liner Greyson had put inside of the trash bin made it so neither of them had to actually touch anything that qualified as a biohazard. She still hadn't gotten used to the heat or the smell, or the fact that the yard looked like it hadn't been properly tended in months, and not one or two. But at least they were making progress, and by the end of the day, she'd be eight hours closer to freedom.

Never mind the hundred and ninety-two to go.

"Don't think about it," Marley muttered to herself. Returning her attention to the job in front of her, she peered into the section of overgrown grass by her boots, and wait... why was the grass...moving?

"Ahhh!" Her shriek was pure instinct, the words that followed it pure invective. Dropping her shovel with an abrupt thunk, she slapped her back against the nearest surface, which just so happened to be a gigantic oak tree. The bark scraped against her skin through her muscle shirt, but the adrenaline pumping full steam ahead in her veins turned the sensation into barely a sting as the grass-that-wasn't-grass continued to move.

"Problem?" Greyson asked from a few feet away, his tone as slow and easy as syrup on Sunday-morning pancakes.

She looked at him as if he'd lost his goddamned mind. Which surely he had, because... "That's a *snake*," she said pointedly, even though the creature—gah!—was now slithering over the bald patch of the yard between them, coiling and recoiling as if trying to decide which one of them to devour first.

Greyson cocked his head for a lazy inspection. "It's a black racer. They're harmless." He lifted a muscular shoulder halfway before letting it fall back into place. "Well, unless you're a mouse or a frog, I guess."

"Are you crazy? How can that"—she jabbed a finger at the snake—"be harmless?"

"Because its venom won't kill you?" he asked, and *seriously*?

"Oh my God. Do they still bite?"

He considered the question for what felt like a century. "Pretty much everything bites if you piss it off enough."

Marley's heart tripped faster, fear sliding up her spine in icy fingers. "Greyson—"

"Okay, okay." Slowly lowering his shovel, he stepped closer to the snake. "I can't get any work done with you making such a ruckus, anyway."

He crouched down lower to the ground, walking slowly until he was only one stride away from the snake. Marley's belly squeezed, and she was half mesmerized, half terrified to look. Her awe won out, if only by a fraction, and she watched breathlessly as Greyson extended one arm in controlled increments. Dark eyes watching. Muscles primed. Waiting. Moving closer...closer...and then—

"Gotcha!"

Greyson had lashed his hand out and closed his fingers around the back of the snake's head before Marley's brain had even registered a single movement. A gasp barged past her lips as soon as the realization sank in, and she stared, unblinking, in total disbelief.

"No way that's harmless. That thing is *huge*," she blurted.

It was hard to tell with all the wriggling, but God, the snake had to be three feet long, at least.

"It's actually a baby," Greyson said, inspecting the animal with the sort of laid-back attention Marley usually put into things like tying her shoes. "They get much bigger when they're fully grown. But you can tell it's a racer and not a black snake because its belly is silver. See?"

He held the snake up, and even though his grip was firm yet somehow still gentle around the back of its head, Marley flattened her back against the oak tree even harder. "I can't *un*-see," she murmured, mostly to herself.

"You want to pet him before I put him over the fence?"

It took her a beat, then two, to realize that he wasn't joking or giving her shit by way of trying to scare her on purpose.

She frowned anyway. He really was crazy if he thought she was going anywhere near that thing. "I'll pass."

"And here I thought you were fearless," Greyson said with a smirk, and on second thought, there was the shit-slinging after all.

Marley planted her hands over her hips, although she didn't budge from the safety of her spot a few feet away from him *and* the snake. "I'm also not stupid."

"And I'm not a liar," he countered, a muscle beneath his stubble flexing just enough to betray the tension there. "I told you they're harmless, and I meant it. I'm not going to let you get hurt."

"You're not?" Marley heard the coarse implication of her words only after she'd spoken them, and she clamped her lips together, too late.

For a second, Greyson said nothing—even the snake in his grasp seemed to have stilled somewhat. But then he shrugged. "It'd take longer to clean up the damned yard that way, now wouldn't it?"

Turning away from her, he walked over to the stretch of fencing that was missing a section of intermittent boards, leaving a gap big enough for him to duck through to free the snake back into the wilderness—or, at least, somewhere farther from the yard. He reappeared a minute later, his expression mostly hidden beneath the brim of his faded blue baseball hat, and Marley bit her lip.

"So, you don't get along with Louis very well, huh?" she asked by way of a peace offering, the scrape on her back burning slightly as she reached down to pick up the shovel she'd dropped.

Surprise slid over Greyson's face, there and then gone. "No one gets along with Louis. He's pretty much a garden variety jackass," he said after a minute, tacking on, "Pardon my language."

Marley waved off the apology with a tart laugh. "Fairly certain I just said far worse when I saw that snake. And anyway, you're not wrong. He is sort of a jackass."

They fell back into a rhythm of scoop-dump, the pace steady but the silence less uncomfortable than before. Still, Marley's curiosity had been bubbling for hours, and it wasn't as if she had anything better to do.

"Why do you care what he thinks of you?" she asked, her heart skipping faster at the way Greyson's shoulders snapped around his spine.

"I don't." The handle of his shovel met the edge of the trash bin with a harder-than-necessary bang, and even though the rational part of her brain knew it was probably not a swift move, she didn't hesitate to push.

"Uh, news flash. Yeah, you do."

Greyson's black brows lifted as his shoulders went loose beneath his T-shirt. "No, I don't."

Yeah. Still not buying it. Also, still not staying quiet. "Seriously? As soon as he made that comment about you not doing the work, you were ready to jump all over him."

Greyson surprised her by not arguing, then surprised her again by saying, "Guess I'm just not real crazy about folks making assumptions, is all."

"I get that," she said, and Greyson stopped, mid-move, to turn and stare at her.

"You do?"

The laugh that drifted up from her chest felt far better than it should have, but Marley gave in to it, anyway. "You look shocked."

"Not exactly." He resumed shoveling, his movements looking effortless even though Marley knew full well that they weren't. "It's just...I thought that was more of a small town thing, where your reputation precedes you and people make assumptions based on that."

She thought about it for a second before answering. "I guess it kind of is. I mean, everyone around here *literally* knows everyone else. Which I totally find weird," she qualified with an arch of one brow. "But just because I don't live here doesn't mean I don't get it."

"You do live here," Greyson pointed out. There was a fair amount of "duh" in his tone, which she probably should've expected, but it rankled all the same. God, she never should've opened her fat mouth in the first place.

"That's temporary. I'm leaving as soon as I can."

"Yeah?" he asked, trading the sarcasm in his tone for curiosity, and shit. Shit! She wanted to talk about this about as much as she wanted to get a bikini wax on sunburned skin. "Where are you headed?"

Marley dug her shovel into the ground too hard, bringing up a healthy chunk of grass along with everything she'd intended to scoop up. "Not here."

"Okay."

Greyson drew the word out on that sexy drawl that was fast becoming her kryptonite, and ugh, she'd been an idiot to start the conversation in the first place. She needed to focus on getting this yard cleaned up so she could go back to the main house at Cross Creek and figure out a way to convince her boss to give her the weekday hours everyone always coveted.

What's more, she needed to *not* focus on the fact that, for a split second, she'd been deeply, hotly, wildly tempted to tell Greyson all the things she hadn't told anyone else.

"Look," she said, crossing her arms over her chest to lock in her emotions and lock down her resolve. "This yard is gigantic, and we've barely covered a third of it. We should probably skip the small talk and just get the work over-with so we can get out of here."

The surprise that burst over his face made Marley's cheeks burn, but not as much as the hard frown that chased it. "Fine by me. You're the one who got chatty in the first place."

"You don't have to worry," she said, re-gripping her shovel and turning away from him. "It won't happen again."

IT TOOK all of four hours for Marley's words to become a lie. She and Greyson had slogged silently through clearing the entire yard not just of refuse, but also of weeds, fallen branches, and assorted debris that had managed to migrate into the space. They'd exchanged as few words as possible along the way, including the handful that had them standing in front of the section of the privacy fence whose boards had either been knocked askew or were missing outright.

"Shouldn't be too hard to fix," Greyson said after a quick perusal, and Marley heaved an inner sigh of relief, both at the fact that the task would be easy and that he seemed to intuitively know how to get it done.

"Okay. Just tell me what you need me to do."

He squinted at her through the blazing afternoon sunlight. "You don't know how to mend a fence?"

Marley rolled her eyes before averting them, fixing her stare on the panel of wood listing at a near-drunken angle in front of her. "*Why* would I know how to do that, exactly?"

"It's kind of common knowledge around here, is all." Greyson shrugged, as if fence mending was akin to brushing one's teeth or knowing that the sun would rise in the east, and score yet another thing that put Marley on the outside looking in.

"This town is completely backwards," she mumbled. But, of course, Greyson heard her, and—of *course*—he just couldn't let a sleeping dog lie.

"It's perspective," he corrected. "Mending fences is one of those things that comes in handy 'round here, so yeah. Most folks know how to do it." He paused for a second, as if he wanted to keep pushing, but then he shook his head. "Anyway, we're going to need a few tools from the shed, along with some replacement boards. I'll be right back."

He pivoted on the heels of the weathered work boots he'd put back on when they'd finished clearing the yard and sauntered away from her. Even his gait was cocky, slow and sure and as easy as one plus one equals two, and Marley forced her eyes away from him even though some of her other parts wanted nothing more than to drink him in until she was good and satiated.

Sweet baby Jesus, he had a nice ass. Firm. Powerful. Just round enough to grab onto and—

Whipping her gaze in a complete one-eighty from where Greyson (and his ass) had gone, Marley searched for something—and at this point, anything would do the trick—to distract her so she could regain her fucking grip on reality. She looked through a gap in the fence, focusing on the stretch of land on the other side. A handful of trees dotted the space, thin and long like a shoreline, with a small, scraggly yard and a smaller, scragglier trailer beyond. A young girl stood in the grass, and even though her back was to Marley as she reached into the battered laundry basket at her feet to pull out a T-shirt and clip it to the twine strung over her head, Marley would've recognized that blond hair and too-slim stature anywhere.

It was Sierra.

Edging back so that she was mostly hidden by the part of the fence that was still standing, Marley peered past the boards, her heartbeat pressing against her eardrums like a baby bird's wings, flap-flap-flap-flap-flap. Sierra repeated the laundry-hanging process with a pair of shorts, a sundress that was threadbare enough to be nearly translucent, and a few other articles of clothing. Even from this distance and through the tank top the girl was wearing, Marley could practically see the bones in Sierra's spine as she bent, then stood, bent, then stood, again and again until the job was done and she headed back toward the trailer, and oh God, she had to do *something*.

"You didn't see that snake again, did you?"

Greyson's voice sent Marley's pulse bottle-rocketing to the moon. "What?" she asked, jerking around to look at him.

"Your face," he said slowly, his expression impossible to gauge from beneath the brim of his baseball hat and all that bravado he wore as well as a fingerprint. "You look like someone just walked over your grave."

Jesus. In a trillion years, she would never get used to all the totally bizarre sayings people had in this Godforsaken town. "I'm fine. Also, not dead yet."

Before he could tell her it was just a saying, blah blah blah, she dialed her voice to its most nonchalant setting and asked, "So, who's that girl?"

"What?" He dropped the fence boards he'd propped over one broad shoulder and the toolbox he must've turned up from the shed into the grass between them, but oh no. Marley wanted his full attention.

"The little girl," she said, stepping into Greyson's line of sight until he had no choice but to stop what he was doing and look at her. "The family, who lives there in that trailer on the other side of the fence. Who are they?"

The question had to have caught him off guard, because he answered her both quickly and without snark. "The Becketts. They've lived there for a handful of years. One of the few families in Millhaven not to have been born and bred here, actually."

"Really?" Okay, can't say she'd seen that coming.

"Yeah, really. Every once in a while, this charming little town of ours gets a transplant." Greyson gave her a pointed smirk, then tipped his chin to look past the gap in the fence. "As for the Becketts, it's just the little girl, Sierra, and her mother, Jade. I think she works in Camden Valley, but I'm not sure. They mostly keep to themselves."

"I thought everyone in this town knew everyone else," Marley said, exasperated. How else was she supposed to figure out how to help Sierra and her mom?

Greyson reached down and snatched up a board from the stack beside him in the grass. "And I thought you wanted to get this work done as fast as possible."

"I do," she said, proving it by flattening her palms over the board he'd jutted his chin at in a wordless *take this*, holding it in place while he bent to grab a hammer. "I'm just asking a question."

"Why?"

Marley noticed then that Greyson had moved in behind her, presumably to take over her spot at the fence now that he'd grabbed the hammer he needed to nail the board into place. But instead of reaching out to hold the plank steady so she could duck away from him, he simply stood there—close, close, God, so warm and tempting and *close*—waiting for her to answer.

She turned her chin over her shoulder, her lips parting just enough to usher out her exhale. The defenses that had sewn themselves into her fabric over the past nine months warned her—loudly and with zero remorse—to use the scant space Greyson had left between their bodies to side-step him, board and pride be damned. He was *right* there, their breath comingling and the heat of his body pressing into her back through the thin cotton of her shirt. Marley could smell the scent of something crisp—his soap, maybe—layered beneath a less definitive smell that was more masculine, more personal, especially as she pulled it inside of her on an inhale and held it. Her instinct told her to shutter herself, to grow spikes and find space. But then, for one bright, unexplainable second, Marley wanted to turn not away, but toward Greyson, so she could let the truth spill out of her like a waterfall.

The moment was gone as unceremoniously as it had arrived, leaving her with the sharp sting of having been slapped in the face. Was she nuts? She couldn't tell Greyson the truth about Sierra. She couldn't tell him the truth about *anything*.

She needed him at arm's length. Right. Now.

"No reason," Marley said, sliding neatly aside to hand the board off to him and reclaim the distance between them. "Forget I asked."

He blinked once, a slow lower and lift of those dark, see-all eyes. "You got it," he said, turning away from her.

But somehow, she knew he wouldn't.

9

After nearly a week of farm/shelter/farm/bed, Greyson had shot right past dog-tired and thudded to a stop just this side of utter fucking exhaustion. Things at Whittaker Hollow were exactly as he'd expected them to be, which was to say he'd been busy with work and short-tempered with his old man. Things at the shelter had met expectations, too; namely that he and Marley had spent two evenings this week completing menial chores while trading as little interaction as possible. Which should've been fine by him, really. After all, Greyson had wanted nothing more than to get in, get done, and get out, in that order.

Except all the silence was driving him ape shit, and the curiosity about Marley that he couldn't keep from doubling every time he turned around? *That* was driving him crazy in a whooooole different way. Now more than ever.

"Damn it," he muttered, his shoulders slumping against the over-worn driver's seat of his Silverado. Okay, so maybe he'd pushed a little too hard by stepping in so close when she'd gotten all nosy about the Becketts. But it had been a weird ask, and anyway, he *always* pushed too hard. Marley hadn't been expecting it, though. Greyson had been able to tell by the way she'd looked at him, those blue eyes flaring hotly, her mouth parted in surprise so sweet, he'd wanted nothing more than to taste it, long and slow on his tongue.

She'd moved away, of course, pushing back in response to his push first just as everyone did, and had continued to keep him at arm's length for the rest of this week. Louis had kept them running all over hell's half-acre, clearing out storage closets and organizing poorly kept inventory—dog food and grooming tools and crate after crate of things Greyson would bet his left arm Louis hadn't even known he'd had. He and Marley had yet to actually care for any of the animals they'd seen in the pens in the back of the shelter, but that'd have to change at some point here, soon. The place was only so big, and despite the reputation that everyone in town had painted him with decades ago, Greyson had enough work ethic to get done whatever chores Louis tossed at him, and right quick.

Why do you care what he thinks of you?

Greyson shook off both the memory and the fresh pinch the question sent between his ribs. He had bigger shit to think on than Louis Kerrigan's opinion of him, and damn little energy to spare on anything that wasn't related to Whittaker Hollow. They were about to be up to their elbows in grain, corn, and at least half of their smaller crops of locally grown produce. All the soil analysis and calibration he'd done to the fertilization methods they used on their peach trees had paid off in spades last year, and he was looking to not only repeat that success, but outdo it this season. It'd take all the energy he had, and probably some he didn't.

But that didn't matter. Louis Kerrigan's opinion of him

didn't matter. The fact that his father would likely be more hindrance than help in getting the work done didn't matter, either.

None of it mattered except the land.

Pulling up to the shelter, Greyson parked next to Marley's rusty, dusty Toyota—how the thing even ran was honestly beyond him—and hustled up the walkway, then through the front door. Marley stood in the waiting area, flushed and a little breathless, wearing—*whoa*—a red and black dress with a series of thin, intricate straps draped across her shoulders and a pair of spike-heeled sandals that gave him all sorts of really good bad ideas.

"Aren't you a little over-dressed?" The question didn't come out with nearly as much cockiness as Greyson had intended to pin to it, not that any straight guy over the age of eighteen could fucking blame him under the circumstances. That dress was a goddamned menace. But Marley scowled well enough in reply.

"I had to leave work early to get here in time as it was. I didn't even have time to change my shoes, let alone the rest of it."

The curiosity Greyson had just sworn off came rushing back to life. Traitorous little shit. "Where do you work?"

"Sage and Maggie's," she said, as if the words were slightly rotten, like milk that was a day past its prime. "It's a vintage boutique with a modern twist for today's upscale fashionistas."

He would not laugh. He would not laugh. He would not —"Sorry," Greyson said, his laugh escaping on a big, fat middle finger to decorum. "I don't have any idea what that means."

To his surprise, one corner of Marley's mouth kicked up instead of curling into a sneer. "It's basically a shop that sells overpriced, overly trendy women's clothes. In Lockridge Mall."

Christ, there was so much to unpack there. Finally, he decided to go with, "I guess that explains the dress."

"Nothing explains this dress. The shoes, even less."

"You two done yappin'?"

Louis crossed his arms and frowned from the spot where he'd appeared in the doorway leading to the back of the shelter, and Greyson wondered if the guy was churlish even in his sleep.

"Absolutely," Marley said, turning toward Louis. After a quick trip to the tiny bathroom to trade her dress and heels for a tank top and a pair of jeans that did nothing to stop the flow of bad ideas in Greyson's head, she reappeared at the front desk. "Okay. What's on tap for tonight?"

"Come on," Louis grunted. He led the way through the door, bypassing the storage closet and the small square of the office in favor of the larger, open space where the animals were. The area was shockingly tidy considering how cluttered and dingy the rest of the place was...or, at least, had been before Greyson and Marley had gotten their hands on it. The animals—seven, no, make that eight, dogs of varying degrees of mutt-dom, and four cats, all looking equally bored—seemed healthy and well-fed, and most of the dogs perked up with varying degrees of eagerness at the sound of Louis's footsteps and voice as he neared.

"The pens all need cleaning out. I'd'a done it today but I had to go into Camden Valley to pick up an emergency rescue and help them out a little. Their shelter's at capacity."

"So, you want us to actually take *care* of them?" Marley asked, the shock on her face plain as she eyed the cages built into the wall, the dogs in one section and the cats in another.

"Well, you ain't here for a tea party, are ya?" Louis took a few steps to the stainless steel table in the center of the room. "The cats all need feedin' once you're done cleaning out the pens. Instructions are right here, and the food's in the cabinet over there. Don't be givin' 'em anything that's not on the sheet," he warned, his stare flattening on Greyson as if surely *he'd* be the one to break the damned rules even though Marley had committed a crime to land herself in here, just the same as him.

"I can read," Greyson said between his teeth, although he purposely didn't pick up the sheet of paper from the table.

Marley sighed softly. "Okay, so clean the pens and feed the cats. What else?"

After a second, Louis loosened his stare from Greyson's and turned back toward the pens. "These six need to be walked," he said, gesturing to the cages on the left-hand side of the room. "At least twenty minutes apiece. No less. They ain't had a chance to run all day, and they need to get around. But this one here"—he pointed to a cage with a medium-sized dog with one front paw heavily bandaged —"can stay in while she heals. I already took her out to do her business, so she'll be alright."

Greyson scanned the pens, his attention snagging on the one in the corner, with something small and shadowy huddled up so tight, he could only see its tail and one wide, watchful eye. "What about this one?"

"She don't come out."

"Why not?" Greyson pressed, not heeding the warning in Louis's voice for even a nanosecond. "Is she sick or something?"

"No. She ain't sick or hurt. Just don't mess with her, you

hear? You leave her be and take the other six out, you understand?"

"I'm not going to *mess* with anything," Greyson snapped. For crying in a bucket, he might have sharper corners than most, but he wasn't a dog-harming delinquent.

Not that the look on Louis's face said that he was thinking anything but, of course. "Good. Once you do all that, there are boxes in the back hallway that need to be unpacked, and everything in them inventoried and stored. That ought to keep y'all busy 'til eight."

"Got it," Marley said with a nod. "Clean the pens, walk the dogs, inventory the stuff in the boxes. Stay busy 'til quitting time."

After a long second and one last dose of side-eye in Greyson's direction—which Greyson returned in kind—Louis grumbled and headed for the back door. The bang that followed announced his departure, and Greyson turned toward the pens, already formulating a plan to get the work done.

"Okay. It'll probably be easiest if we use two of the empty pens here to put the cats in while we rotate through cleaning their cages. Then you can walk the dogs two at a time while I stay here to clean out their pens. That'll kill two birds with one stone."

Cleaning the dogs' pens was the crappier job of the two, but Greyson didn't mind the work. It'd get them closer to out of here, at any rate, and Christ, he was tired enough to fall over.

But Marley grabbed his attention with a quick shake of her head. "You can walk the dogs if you want." She looked at the cages, an odd expression on her face that Greyson couldn't quite place, there and then gone. "In fact, go for it. I'll clean the pens."

It was on the tip of his tongue to ask her why on God's green earth she'd forfeit the easier, not to mention more fun, task. But he was tired as hell, and she'd made it clear she didn't want to socialize, so he shrugged despite his curiosity. "Suit yourself."

Stepping toward the closest vacant pen, he sprang the latch to open the door, repeating the process with an adjacent cage occupied by a gray and white cat with large green eyes and a nasty but well-healed scar on one ear.

"C'mere, you." Greyson moved deliberately, pausing for a heartbeat to let the cat check him out by way of a series of tentative sniffs before scooping it up. He wasn't normally a cat guy, but this one was pretty cute, and it snuggled in right quick against the crook of his arm, its purr sounding off like a tractor engine at the height of the harvest. Greyson spared a second to scratch behind its ears, giving the injured one a wider berth just to be on the safe side. The tension that had set up camp in his muscles loosened slightly, and he let a small smile escape.

"Okay, buddy. Into the pen you go," he said, giving the cat one last pet, then lifting it easily into its temporary quarters. He caught Marley watching out of the corner of her baby blues, and damn it, he was seriously going to have to do something about his curiosity if he wanted to make it through this community service without a hard-on of epic proportions. Her shoulders rigid, she reached into the cage in front of her and closed her hands around the orange tabby inside. The cat squirmed, its body turning and twisting like a fur-covered Slinky as Marley slid it from the cage and held it at arm's length, awkwardly cupping a palm beneath the cat's legs and hind quarters to help usher it into the new cage.

"Wow," Greyson said, unable to help it. "No offense, but you kind of suck at this part."

"Thanks. That's the sweetest thing anyone's said to me all day," she replied. But her tone held only half of its usual caustic wit, and ah, hell.

Greyson tried again. "I just meant you don't seem comfortable around the animals, is all. Didn't you ever have a dog or a cat as a pet, growing up?"

"No." Marley paused. Bit her lip. Examined him carefully for a minute before asking, "Did you?"

"No." A memory slammed into him, of a pretty black lab, never far from his uncle's work boots, but he tucked it aside in favor of the job in front of him. "I've been around animals my whole life, though. Cows and chickens and a handful of feral cats who live in our hay barn."

"Sounds charming," she said, and here, Greyson didn't hesitate.

"Actually, it is. Living on a farm is way better than any city."

A scoff crossed Marley's lips, but funny, she quickly traded it for a look of curiosity as she reached for the cleaning supplies Louis had left out on the table. "Have you ever been to a city?"

"We're not all uncultured out here in the sticks, you know," he told her, although he didn't get shitty about it. If she wanted to think cities were better than small towns, then so be it. He didn't have time to fix her crazy. "I go into Lockridge on the regular, and I've been to Richmond a coupl'a times. Washington, DC once. But as far as I'm concerned, there's no better place than here."

"That's what my brothers say." She lifted a shoulder before letting it drop. "Even Eli, and he doesn't live here all the time anymore. But it's perspective, like you said. I guess mine's just different."

Greyson wanted to push. He wanted to ask where she was from, and what was so great about wherever it was that she clearly wanted to go back, and why she'd even come to Millhaven in the first place, and about a thousand other questions ranging from nonchalant to downright damned nosy. But he stopped himself just shy of launch.

Every time he'd pushed her, she'd pushed back and clammed up. If he wanted answers, he was going to have to get them another way.

"Animals can sense when a person isn't comfortable around them," he said. "Kind of like most people can sense it, too. But they rely on instinct, so when they sense that you're not comfortable, they get uncomfortable back."

Reaching up, he unlatched the cage where he'd deposited the gray and white cat a few minutes ago. The animal came to him just as easily as it had the first time, nestling back in at the bend in his elbow as if the spot had been custom-made for it.

Marley? Not so much. "What are you doing?" she asked, taking a step back on the linoleum and eyeing the cat with a not-small amount of wariness.

"I'm giving you perspective." Greyson closed the space between them in a few strides. Shifting to balance the cat with one arm, he extended the other toward Marley. As soon as he made contact, just a businesslike brush of his fingers on the outside of her wrist, she tensed, a bowstring pulling taut.

"Hey, whoa." The metronome of his heartbeat tripped into a faster rhythm as he released her and stepped back to widen the circle of space between them. She hadn't yanked back, hadn't verbally protested or side-stepped or done anything else, even though he was one hundred-percent certain she'd seen him walking toward her, arm outstretched. The contact had been slight, lasting barely a second, but clearly, he'd made her uneasy.

"I apologize. I didn't mean any offense."

Marley blinked. "I know," she said, sounding every inch as if she meant it. A thought occurred to him, too late, and shit.

"If you're afraid of cats like you're afraid of snakes, you could have told me," he offered.

More blinking, and Lord, her eyes were as blue as the ocean in a travel brochure. "What? I'm not...I mean, okay." She took a deep breath, seeming to re-set herself. "I *am* afraid of snakes. That's just human. But I'm not afraid of cats or dogs."

Greyson waited, even though he had to practically bite a hole in his bottom lip to get the job done. Finally, Marley continued with, "It's just that I'm not a touchy-feely kind of person, is all."

"Really? You don't say. I never would have guessed."

The semi-playful, more than semi-smartass jibe was out before Greyson could grab it back. But then Marley laughed, making something deep and undefined move in his gut, daring him to say all the things that would make her laugh again.

"Okay, Cat Whisperer," she said. "What's your first piece of advice, then?"

"You can start by petting her," he offered, although he purposely let Marley make the first move toward him, along with all the moves after that.

To his surprise, she did, walking forward until she faced both him and the loudly purring cat still reclined lazily in the crook of his arm.

"So just pet her," Marley said, looking at the cat as if she were covered in spikes and scales. "Like this?"

Greyson watched her run a stiff hand over the cat's head a couple of times and tried not to wince. "That's…a start."

A tinge of color pinked Marley's cheeks, made more obvious by the glare of the fluorescent lights overhead. "You're supposed to be helping."

"Okay, you're right." Gesturing down at her hand, he looked at her in an unspoken request for permission to take it, which she granted with a small nod. "The first thing you want to do is let her get to know you. Cats do that with their noses. Then you can get down to petting her."

He took Marley's fingers and held them up for the cat's approval. "There, see?" he continued when the cat rubbed her nose against the thumb side of Marley's palm a few seconds later. "Not so bad."

"I guess not," Marley agreed, her stance loosening slightly and her touch growing more fluid as she curved her fingers over the cat's head, then repeated the process, again and again. The cat—who really needed a name, Greyson decided—rumbled out a rusty purr as she went lax against his chest and arm, preening under Marley's attention.

"Hey, she likes you. You want to take her?" he asked, shifting to make the transfer, but just like that, Marley's hand snapped back to her side.

"No. I'm good. She looks, um, really comfortable with you. But thanks for the tip."

Before he could protest, and oh, part of him really fucking wanted to, she'd moved back to the empty cage she'd started to clean, picking up the task with renewed focus. Greyson inhaled, ready to call her out on the exhale. But then he had a thought that stopped the words short in his throat.

Marley was pushing first so he'd push back, and then she could push away. It was a move he'd used thousands of times, and one he knew by heart. Shit, he'd practically scribbled his signature on it in permanent ink a decade ago.

He'd just never seen anyone *else* use it.

"You're welcome," he finally managed, putting the cat back in her cage and turning back to his job. As usual, Louis had given them plenty to do, and, as usual, they fell into a steady rhythm to get the tasks knocked off, one by one. Finally, after the last bag of kitty litter had been inventoried and stacked on a shelf in the newly reorganized storage closet, they switched off all the lights and headed out of the building, locking the door behind them. Greyson's muscles practically threw confetti over the fact that they'd get a little bit of rest soon, and he flipped his keys against his palm as he headed for his truck.

It took him a couple of beats to realize Marley had reduced her pace to snail status. "Aren't you heading out?" he asked, pointing to her car.

Her eyes went wide, just a quick flare of roundness before returning to normal. "Oh, um, yeah. Of course. I just need to make a quick call first."

The manners that had been buried way down beneath his bravado reared up, making him hitch. True, they were out in the middle of nowhere. It wasn't as if anyone would happen along to mess with her. But her car was halfway to the junk pile. What if the thing didn't start?

And what if aliens start dropping out of the sky? his overtaxed muscles countered. Marley was a big girl, capable and smart. On the off chance that she had car trouble, she'd call one of her brothers to come get her. She had her pick of the three of them, for God's sake. He needed to worry himself over what was important; namely, getting his ass into bed so he could grab some decent shuteye before having to get up at o'dark-thirty tomorrow.

"Okay," Greyson said, his manners giving up one last jab as he tugged open the door to his truck. "Goodnight, then."

"Goodnight."

Marley made a show of taking her cell phone from the back pocket of her jeans and thumbing a path over the screen. The light flashed over her face in the shadows that were just beginning to form now that the sun had slid past the tree line to the west, showcasing her serious concentration. Greyson started the Silverado, giving her one last look in his rearview mirror as he trundled down the gravel drive. There was something odd about her expression that he couldn't place, something just the slightest bit forced. He knew he shouldn't care—in fact, he shouldn't even be giving Marley or her car or her expression a second thought.

Except for the fact that she didn't even *have* cell service out here, Greyson realized with an upward snap of his chin. No one did.

Holy shit. The expression she'd been wearing had been a poker face, and a terrible one, at that. She'd lied about staying behind to make a phone call.

So what was she doing instead?

He'd put the truck in *park* at the mouth of the driveway before he even knew he would stop. The path was curved enough that Marley wouldn't see him if he made the trip back to the shelter on foot, which he did with about three minutes and a fair amount of ease. Greyson's heart thumped faster when he got close enough to put eyes on the parking area. Marley wasn't where she'd been minutes ago, nor was she in her car, or standing on the rickety, old porch of the shelter.

She was headed toward the fence line with two bags of... wait, were those groceries?

Greyson ducked behind a thick oak tree as Marley swiveled a nervous gaze over the yard, peeking out from behind the massive tree just in time to catch sight of her making her way past the fence and into the adjacent yard. From where he stood, he could just make out the Becketts' overgrown yard, the dingy clothesline spanning two crooked wooden posts, and the dilapidated set of steps leading to the back of the trailer. A small laundry basket sat on the top step, just out of the way of the door, and Marley made a beeline for the thing, tucking both bags of groceries securely inside before turning back toward the fence line.

And as Greyson slipped back to his truck, then past the driveway and into the deepening shadows, he wondered if Marley Rallston was ever going to stop doing things that made him want to know more about her.

10

Marley sat back against the red vinyl of the corner booth in Clementine's Diner and stared a hole in her menu even though she already knew what she'd order the second she'd walked in. It wasn't that she was in bad company; on the contrary, Owen's live-in girlfriend and probably soon-to-be-fiancée, if her other brothers' track record of getting hitched this year was any indication, was one of Marley's favorite people in Millhaven. And not just because Cate had waited until after the breakfast rush to ask her if she wanted to grab something to eat, when the most popular—okay, only, unless you counted The Bar, which Marley didn't—place to eat in town was bound to be less crowded. At this point in the day, in the no-man's-land between breakfast and lunch, most people were already out and about, doing their Saturday thing. Sleeping in was a foreign concept in farming towns, some fancy, far-fetched thing like sushi or craft beer, both of which had been available in abundance on pretty much every street corner in Chicago.

Marley rubbed a hand over her sternum and looked up

just in time to see Clementine sidle over to the booth, her smile warm and wide. "Good morning, ladies! Cate, it's so good to see you."

Cate stood to give the older woman a hug, and Marley quickly dropped her gaze back to her menu until Cate sat back down across from her, which was silly, she knew. The women were close. Cate used to work here, waiting tables, until she'd taken a full-time position at Cross Creek Farm, balancing the books and making all manner of baked goods for the on-site store and their tent at the farmers' market. Of course Clementine would hug her. Hugging was *normal*, for Pete's sake.

"It's good to see you, too, Clem," Cate said. "How are things here?"

Clementine's smile remained happily in place, her long, sleek braids sliding down her back as she tilted her head. "Oh, you know. Breakfast, lunch, supper. But we wouldn't have it any other way." She gestured behind the counter toward the kitchen, where her husband manned the grill and just about everything else. "What can I get for the two of you today?"

"I'd love a cup of coffee, and a ham and cheese omelet," Cate said, even though she'd never even looked at a menu. "Hash browns—"

"Instead of toast, I know." Clementine's eyes remained kind as she shifted her gaze to Marley. "How about you, honey?"

"I'd like a slice of peach pie and the biggest cup of coffee you've got," she said with as much efficiency as she could muster. Small talk had never been her jam, even before she'd gotten stranded here. Now that she was in a town that felt as backward as a field-sobriety alphabet? Even less.

"Pie for breakfast," Clementine said after a beat of

surprise. "You might just be a girl after my own heart. Coffee'll be right up."

Cate, who was about as no-nonsense as a tax audit, didn't waste a single second after Clementine had walked out of earshot to pounce. "So, when are we going to talk about the fact that you got arrested for stealing a bunch of groceries that you and I both know you didn't need?"

Marley's heart moved into her throat, and God, so much for giving a girl a little warning. "How about never?" she managed.

Of course, Cate wasn't so easily dissuaded. "Come on, Marley. You haven't said so much as a word about it to Owen or Hunter or Eli. You need to talk about it at some point."

"There's nothing much to say." Marley forced herself not to fiddle with the napkin-wrapped silverware or the paper placemat in front of her. Her brothers might let her skate if she got prickly enough, but Cate was a whole different story, and the last thing Marley wanted to do was lie to the woman. Especially since she was terrible at it. And double-especially when Cate skewered her with an I-don't-buy-it look like she was doing now.

"So, you just decided to swipe a bunch of canned goods for grins?"

"That's what the court record says," Marley answered through tight lips. "Anyway, I apologized and I'm doing my penance. Believe me, I won't get arrested again." All truths, thank God. Why couldn't she be bad at something useless, like whistling show tunes or reciting tongue twisters without flubbing the words?

"Hmm." Cate waited for Clementine to place two over-sized cups of coffee on the Formica and depart with the promise that their food would be up soon before continuing. "And how's that penance of yours going?"

Marley thought of the insane commutes and shortened hours she'd suffered through this week, both of which would translate to a smaller paycheck, and she channeled all of her energy into not frowning. "Fine."

"Greyson Whittaker can be..."

Cate let the sentence drift, but Marley was all too happy to supply the rest. "A cocky, Casanova pain in my ass?"

"I was going to say a little rough around the edges," Cate replied, dark brows up and smile far too knowing. "But *Casanova*? You think he's good-looking."

"No." Marley's protest came too fast, and damn it, she should've slept in and scrounged breakfast at the house. Time to do some damage control and move on. "I think he's arrogant and bull-headed. But I have to do community service with him, like the judge said, so..."

Marley capped the words with a shrug. There was no reason for Cate—or anyone, really—to know that not only did Marley think Greyson was indeed good-looking (biggest. Euphemism. Ever. Between his shoulders and his smirk, he should seriously be classified as some sort of stupidly sexy stealth weapon) but that he'd frequented her dreams for a week straight.

And every time, he'd been right there. Ready to catch her even though she hadn't known she was falling. *Gotcha...*

"I see," Cate said, stirring some cream and sugar into her coffee, then taking a thoughtful sip. "And it's working out okay with your job?"

"I guess." It was another stretch of the truth. Her boss at the boutique, Noémie (who Marley strongly suspected was really a Naomi and just trying too hard to be posh), had already given her a flawlessly lined side-eye at her request for three evenings a week plus Sundays off.

Cate paused, but only for a second before saying, "The

reason that I ask is that Owen and I were talking about the storefront, and how much of a natural you are at helping me with the baked goods. You know the products inside and out, and we could really use someone smart to manage that end of things. We were thinking that maybe you might—"

"No." Marley knotted her hands together to keep them from shaking. But she couldn't waver. Not on this.

"You didn't even hear me out," Cate said quietly. The frown that had tugged at the corners of her mouth with the delivery told Marley she was less than thrilled with her response. But nope. No way. No matter how much Cate frowned, she wasn't going to budge.

"I don't need to. I'm not interested in working at the storefront. I'm not part of the family." Before Cate could call her on the technicality of her genetics, Marley stuck on, "Not like the rest of you are."

"The only person who feels that way is you," Cate said, her voice soft enough to remove any accusation from the words, yet strong enough for Marley to know she believed them as the truth.

Which made one of them, anyway. Marley's fingers tightened so hard they throbbed in time with her clattering pulse. "Tobias chose not to make me his family a long time ago."

A sigh crossed Cate's lips. "You're going to have to talk to him eventually, you know."

"No, I'm really not."

"Your mother asked you to come find your family for a reason, Marley. She wouldn't want you to feel so alone, and she wouldn't have told you about Tobias unless it was time to mend that bridge."

Sadness welled up in Marley's chest, flattening her lungs and turning her breath into sand. It was farther than any of her brothers had ever gone with her, and damn it, *damn it*, she should've known better than to let herself be caught off guard by Cate's brevity.

"Don't," Marley bit out, and Cate reached across the Formica to touch Marley's hand.

"I'm not trying to upset you," she started, but between the words and the touch, Marley had redlined.

"Then stop talking about my mother." She pulled away, her voice steady even though the rest of her wasn't. "You didn't know her. You don't know what she wanted, or what she was like."

After a long pause measured by heartbeats and heavy silence, Cate nodded. "You're right. I didn't know her, and I guess I shouldn't presume to know why she asked you to come to Cross Creek after she passed. But whether or not you like it—"

"I don't," Marley snapped, aiming the words at her so she'd get mad. Arguing was so much easier, and anyway, it hurt less.

God, Marley was tired of hurting.

Cate's stare flashed with the color and intensity of a double shot of whiskey, but she finished her sentence with shocking kindness in her tone. "Whether or not you like it, or want to talk about it or even admit it, she *did* ask you to come here, and your father did take you in. That's a truth that isn't going to change."

Marley remembered, with strange and sudden clarity, the literal moments after her mother had died. The nurses had turned off the sound for the monitors, her mother having signed the DNR form weeks prior, despite Marley's protests. There had been no ominous beep signaling the end, just a few hard-scrabble breaths, and then the realization that it was over. Her mother, the closest person to her, the only person she'd ever loved and confided in and really showed herself to, was gone, yet Marley was still painfully here. A truth that wasn't going to change.

A truth that meant she couldn't let Tobias into her life under any circumstances.

"Maybe so," Marley said, trading the memory for an inhale that cemented her determination to do whatever it took to get out of debt and out of Millhaven as fast as possible. "But my being here is temporary. I never intended to stay. Anyway"—she looked at the door, past ready to make an escape—"I think I'm going to pass on the pie, after all. I have to get back to the house." Not home. Never home. "I've got to work this afternoon, and I really should get ready."

"Marley—"

"Thanks for the offer," Marley said, taking out enough cash to cover her coffee and the pie for which she'd abruptly lost her appetite. "I'll see you later."

Turning on the heel of one sneaker, she cut a fast path out of the diner, past the gleaming glass door with its cheery bells, down the neatly cobbled walkway lining Town Street. She'd parked a few blocks away—that's what she got for thinking it was so nice out today, she'd enjoy the walk—and she headed briskly past the barber shop, then the hardware store. Thankfully, The Hair Lair was across the street, although now that Marley thought about it, she wouldn't put it past Amber Cassidy to bolt through traffic to get a good scoop. She tugged her keys from her wristlet and reached for the handle on the Toyota's driver's side door when a flash of something familiar caught her eye from a few feet away.

Make that *someone* familiar. Tobias was standing in front of Doc Sanders's office as if he'd just come out of the place. Too stunned to move, Marley battled with her racing pulse, staring even though she knew she shouldn't. Tobias squinted through the mid-morning sunlight, his eyes shuttered beneath that caramel-colored hat he always wore. They widened as soon as they landed on her, recognition lighting his features. He smiled, just enough to make his eyes crinkle at the edges, and his arm lifted. But then he stopped halfway through the movement, panic streaking over his face as if he'd suddenly realized where he was and what he'd been about to do, and dropped his arm stiffly to his side before averting his gaze. The sting of the rejection forced Marley's body into gear, fingers to door handle, key to ignition, seatbelt over chest. She needed to get gone, sooner rather than later.

Some truths would never, ever change.

11

"It's only eight fifty. You're early."

Marley looked up from the piece of paper in her grasp, and seriously, was it too much to ask that Greyson would have bedhead or bad breath or a coffee stain on his just-snug-enough-to-showcase-every-damned-muscle T-shirt, just once?

If his broken-in jeans and freshly showered smell and sleepy, Sunday-morning stare were anything to go by, the answer to that question was a big, fat hell yes.

"We agreed on nine, so you're early, too," she said, trying to look bored as she propped an elbow on the stainless steel worktable in the center of the back room at the shelter. "Anyway, I just got here."

Okay, so it was a relative version of the truth. She'd been here for a full ten minutes. But she wanted to get this community service over-with, and the faster they got through everything Louis had planned, the closer she'd be to history. Plus, she'd wanted to work up to being around the animals today. Not that she didn't like them, or think they were actually pretty cute, even. It was just a hell of a lot easier to stick to the whole arm's length thing when she didn't have to cuddle anything.

You wanted to do a hell of a lot more than cuddle Greyson in your dreams last night.

The thought hit her like a line drive, swift and unexpected, snapping her chin upward and her spine straight. But come on—it had been a *dream* that Greyson just happened to have been in, not an on-purpose fantasy. Sure, having his arms around her in her mind had felt intoxicating, and okay, maybe those dream-hands had done a few other things and she'd woken up with her train halfway to the orgasm station. Still. She couldn't control her dreams, for God's sake.

Apparently, she also couldn't control her face, because Greyson had narrowed his eyes, his dark lashes sweeping over her with a look of growing concern. "You okay? You look—"

"Mmm hmm!" Marley interrupted. "Yep. I'm great. Just perfect." Also, babbling. What the hell was *wrong* with her? "So, Louis left us a pretty long list of things to do today," she managed to spit out, and Greyson's concern turned to irritation. *Whew*.

"Of course he did," he muttered. Moving closer, he asked, "What are we looking at?"

"It's more of the same, basically. Cleaning the pens, walking the dogs, tending the yard." Marley didn't add that Louis had written *and don't mess with that one dog!* in big, bold letters at the bottom of the page. Greyson was pissy enough about the old guy. "It looks like he wants us to start building some sort of dog run outside, too. There are plans and a list of materials that are supposed to be out back."

Greyson took the plans from her, scanning them carefully. “Okay, this shouldn’t be too bad. It’s going to take us all week, at least, but the design is pretty straightforward.”

“I’m glad you think so,” Marley said. The plans might as well have been in Mandarin for how well she could decipher them. “At least one of us is good at this.”

“You managed all that inventory the other day way faster than I would’ve. Not to mention, you were pretty much the boss of that storage closet project,” Greyson said, and once she got over her surprise—which, admittedly, took a few seconds—she answered.

“Yeah, but that kind of stuff is easy.”

“Not for everyone.”

Marley followed him over to the cages along the far wall, falling into the routine of getting ready to clean out the pens. “I guess some things just make better sense to me than others.”

“Me, too.” Greyson gave up a nod, then a soft laugh. “Maybe batty old Judge Abernathy knew what she was doing when she threw the two of us here together, after all.”

“Let’s not get crazy,” Marley said, although she couldn’t help but laugh, too. “I’m pretty sure she’s still not all there.” She tapped her temple with a finger. “But maybe she did get lucky.”

“So, how come you stole a bunch of groceries from The Corner Market, anyway?”

Marley covered up her jumping pulse with a lift of her brows. “For someone with a granite-reinforced work ethic, you’re awfully chatty today.”

“It’s called multi-tasking,” he said, sliding the fat, gray and white cat with the scar on her ear out of her cage with care. “Anyway, if we’re going to spend all this time together, I’d rather not be bored.”

Damn it, she needed to deflect. Telling the truth about

what had happened at The Corner Market wasn't an option, especially with the curiosity brewing in those dark-chocolate eyes of his.

She pasted a sassy smile to her lips. "You're so charming. Really. I bet you've got girls lined up around the block, just dying to go out with you."

"I might," he countered, with just enough of a dare in his tone that Marley bit.

"In a town this size? Doubtful. Even for you."

Greyson's smirk appeared just as she heard the words she'd spoken, and she heard—too late—what they implied. *Even for you, who is so hot, the fire department should follow you around with hoses, ready to douse you* and *the panties of all the women in your path.* God, this couldn't get any worse.

"Are you flirting with me?" he asked, and Marley made a mental note never to think things couldn't get worse ever again, even if she lived to be a hundred.

"No!" She needed to either kill this conversation or get it back on the rails and off the topic of them flirting, ASAP. "How come you never paid your parking tickets?"

If Greyson was thrown by the shift in the topic, he didn't show it. "Truth? I don't really know. I should've. I guess I had bigger things on my mind. Plus, I'm kind of used to bucking authority, so..."

Marley reached for a sweet-faced black and white cat and bit back a snort of irony. "Yeah, I got that. But what could be bigger than paying the tickets that would keep you from being arrested?"

"To be fair, I didn't realize I'd get arrested over it," he pointed out. "But to answer, I guess I was focused on my farm."

"Being focused on work makes sense," she said. She'd

been all about the paycheck ever since her mother's medical bills had started piling up.

"I didn't say I was focused on work. I said I was focused on my farm."

Marley rewound the words. Played them back. Yep, still nothing. "There's a difference?"

"Uh, yeah there's a difference." Greyson shot her a quizzical look, which she returned in kind, so he continued. "I don't mind the work. I mean, that's part of the deal. But even though there are sometimes long days and hard labor, that's secondary. The farm is what matters. That's where I belong."

"That is the weirdest concept to me."

The words had flown out before she could check them, and—ah, hell—Greyson's brows were already more than halfway to the fall of dark hair tumbling over his forehead, arched in full-on curiosity. But she'd made no bones about not wanting to stick around town any longer than was necessary. It's not as if it'd be some giant news flash to say it again.

Marley shrugged. "I don't belong here, is all."

"So, where do you belong?" he asked. They worked for a minute, then another, while Marley gave the question legitimate thought.

"Not here," she finally said. In the beginning, she'd assumed she'd go back to Chicago once she'd checked coming to Millhaven to meet Tobias as her mother had asked her to off her To Do list. But the more she thought about it, the less sure she became that she'd ever be able to drive past the old house they'd rented, or all the places she and her mother had loved to go, or—a chill raced over her skin, leaving goose bumps in its path—the hospital where her mother had died. But that was the bonus of not belonging anywhere. She had options. As long as her options took her far away from here, she'd be just fine.

"Okay. Where'd you come from?"

Greyson's voice was surprisingly devoid of all his usual pushiness and arrogance, and the tension knotting Marley's shoulders slipped loose along with her answer.

"I'd have figured everyone in town would know that by now. You guys pretty much live in each other's pockets around here."

"Fair enough." He paused to take the gray and white cat out of her temporary cage and scratch her belly, then put her back in her freshly cleaned pen before adding, "There aren't really any secrets in Millhaven. Still, you can't believe *everything* you hear."

Now it was Marley's curiosity that sparked. "Like what?"

"Like what, what?" Greyson asked slowly. But oh, no. She'd heard that hint of scorn in his tone. Lord knew she could spot sarcasm from a thousand yards away, and whether he'd meant for her to hear it or not, Greyson had just been chock full of the stuff.

"You just said you can't believe everything you hear. So, what shouldn't I believe?"

"It's kind of just a saying. I didn't mean it literally. You don't even talk to anybody around here," he pointed out.

Her mouth fell open in surprise. "You're dodging the question."

"You dodged the question about where you're from," Greyson countered, and Marley had to admit, he kind of had her there.

"Fine. I'm from Chicago."

"Really?"

God, the shock on his face was so complete that Marley almost felt bad teasing him. *Almost.* "No, I made it up." Her laughter softened any snap the words might've held, making him laugh, too. "Yes, really," she continued. "I had a distant great-aunt who lived just outside the city, so my mom figured it was as good a place as any to live. She moved there a few months before I was born, and I lived there my whole life, so yeah. That's where I'm from." Marley exhaled, then clamped down on her lip when she heard how much she'd said. "Anyway. Your turn."

"Oh." Greyson blinked. He must have realized she wasn't going to let it drop, because he said, "I guess all I meant when I said you shouldn't believe everything you hear is that people tend to make assumptions in small towns."

"People do that everywhere," she said, and his laugh slid through her, unexpectedly deep.

"Yeah, but around here, you can't ever get away from it. You probably thought you knew me before we ever ended up in that jail cell, right?"

"I..."

Marley wanted to protest, she really did, to say, "How could I have known you when I'd never even met you?"

But the truth was, she couldn't. She might not know a lot of people around Millhaven (okay, so she knew like six, and Scarlett wasn't even technically a local), but her brothers talked. They sure had enough to say about Greyson. "Yeah, I guess I did."

He turned to look at her over one shoulder. "And what did you think?"

"Um." Jeez, way to put a girl on the spot. Not that she wasn't down with honesty, because she was. But calling Greyson a jerk when he was *being* a jerk was one thing. Right now, he was just being real.

"Let me see if I can help you out," he said. "Cocky. Arrogant. Smug." He ticked them off on his fingers, one by one. "Rough around the edges. Downright mean. Am I warm?"

"Well, yeah," she said, because they both knew he wasn't wrong. "But you have to admit, you back at least some of that up."

"You wonder why?"

Marley opened her mouth to answer with the obvious, then stopped short. Okay, yes. He *could* be cocky and rough around the edges. He'd been damn near close to a total jackass when she'd first met him, and her brothers had stories for days. There had even been that bet with Eli last year. But Greyson had also been kind with the animals, and despite the curiosity he'd clearly shown earlier over her past and where she was from, he hadn't prodded nosily to get the details. Plus, he never hesitated to roll up his sleeves to do the work Louis heaped on them, always diving into each task with not just determination to get it done, but to get it done well.

"I do now," she said. "Why would you act like that if you didn't mean it?"

He closed the cage in front of him, turning to face her fully. "Because this is Millhaven. People believe what they're going to, and I'm never gonna prove them wrong. Trust me, I've tried. But my family legacy was laid out for me a long time ago." His voice took on a mocking tone. "That Greyson Whittaker's an ornery bastard. After all, the apple don't fall far from the tree."

Marley's pulse whooshed in her ears as what he'd said clicked all the way into place, like a row of Dominoes falling *tat-tat-tat-tat-tat* in a line. "So, it's a self-fulfilling prophecy? You act the way you do because that's what everyone expects of you as your father's son."

"Sometimes," Greyson said, and Marley's brows went up.

She didn't even care that her curiosity, and all of the interest in him that went with it, was probably on full display. "Why only sometimes?"

"Because that cockiness isn't always for show." He took a step toward her, then another, before stopping to level her with a smile so hot and so dark, she felt it on her skin like a touch.

"Sometimes, darlin', I really *am* that damn good."

MARLEY'S MUSCLES felt like someone had replaced them with old rubber bands and even older rubber cement. But since she could have either worked herself into exhaustion or closed the space between her and Greyson to kiss him and not stop until they were good and naked and screaming each other's names, she'd gone for what had been behind door number one for the sake of both dignity and decorum. He'd followed suit, just as Marley had figured he would. Titanium work ethic aside, he'd been flirting with her not because he was interested, but to prove his point. Everyone thought he was Millhaven's baddest bad boy. His father's son. Hard-edged and difficult.

God, she still wanted to kiss him.

Shaking off the thought, along with all the heat pooling low and tight in her belly, Marley peeked past the Toyota and over the path leading away from the shelter. She'd used the old "I should probably use the ladies room before I head out" excuse to linger today, shooing Greyson off with the promise that yes, she'd be just fine to lock up, and no, he absolutely didn't need to stay to walk her to her car. He hadn't protested much—thank you, lucky stars—and she'd loitered for an extra five minutes, just to be sure he was good and gone before she'd come back outside. Her grocery delivery had gone without a hitch the other day, and if she played things just right, all the rest of them should, too.

Sierra and her mother shouldn't be hungry. Marley had needed to stop at a Quick Mart in Lockridge to stock up on canned goods—after all, a trip to The Corner Market didn't seem like the best idea, given her reputation, and she hadn't wanted to raise suspicion. She might not be able to do anything big for the Becketts. Lord knew she was spending money she didn't really have on the handful of items as it was. But maybe if they had enough to eat, Sierra and her mom could start to get back on their feet.

Marley pulled the plastic bag full of canned beef stew, cling peaches (which weren't nearly as good as the real deal, but they were selfishly Marley's favorite, so in they'd gone), powdered milk, and peanut butter from the spot where she'd tucked it on the Toyota's floor mats. She'd snagged a pair of tomatoes from the bowl on the island in the main house at Cross Creek, too. Yes, she'd technically stolen them, she supposed. But they'd been too pretty to pass up, and they were healthy on top of it. She'd just skip having her share this week to make up for the indiscretion.

Moving as casually as possible, she walked to the fence line, crossing over into the Becketts' yard as if she had every right and reason to be there. The grass was overgrown, practically to Marley's knees in spots, and she sent up a fervent prayer that she wouldn't run across any snakes. She sent a glance over her surroundings as she got closer to the wooden steps leading up to the back of the trailer, taking in the clothesline, which now held a timeworn set of sheets and a few T-shirts and pairs of shorts, and the rest of the patchy grass. Soft sounds of water running and a radio in the background sounded off from inside—good cover,

Marley realized with a small sigh of relief. She crept to the stairs, where the laundry basket sat, just as it had the other day, reaching out to slowly, slooooowly slide the thing close enough that she could make her delivery and retreat.

Her hand jerked to a stop, mid-motion. There was already a bag full of groceries in the basket.

And she hadn't left it there.

With her heart in her throat, Marley peered around the scraggly yard again. Everything was as quiet and still as it had been the other evening, when she'd left the first round of canned goods here. Yet somehow, this new bag had appeared, seemingly from out of thin air.

Not wanting to tempt fate—she did have a pretty shitty track record for getting busted in the wrong place at the wrong time—she tucked her bag next to the one already in the laundry basket and made her way back to the fence line. Her brain spun with confusion, trying to come up with some viable explanation as to who had put the groceries on Sierra's back step and why, when an all-too-familiar voice invaded her thoughts.

"Do you want to tell me why you've been leaving groceries on the Becketts' porch for the last two evenings we've done community service?"

Marley bit back the scream in her throat, but only just. "Jesus," she said, slapping a hand over her sternum, her heart pounding steadily beneath the thin material of her T-shirt as she spun toward the giant oak tree Greyson had propped himself against. "Didn't anyone ever tell you it's rude to sneak up on people?"

"You say that like I have a care for manners," he drawled. "And you aren't answering the question."

Shit. Shit, shit, shitshitshit! "I—"

It was on the tip of Marley's tongue to deny the whole

thing, to go brash and bitchy and push him away. Explaining the situation would mean she'd have to explain *everything*, and Sierra could get into serious trouble. But Greyson had clearly seen Marley leave groceries on that step both times, and as weird as it was, if anyone would understand that things weren't always what they seemed, it was him.

So she looked him straight in those see-all eyes and said, "I didn't steal the groceries from The Corner Market on the day I was arrested. Sierra did."

12

Holy hell. Greyson didn't know what he'd been expecting when he'd called Marley out for sneaking around and leaving groceries on the Becketts' back step, but *this* definitely wasn't it.

"Wait," he said, trying like mad to process what she had said. "Sierra stole the groceries and you took the fall? But she's a kid. Christ, you don't even know her. Why would you do that?"

"Because." Marley knotted her arms over her chest, looking far more beautiful than she should with her chin hiked and her blue eyes blazing like the bright-hot core of a candle flame. "It's a long story."

Greyson crossed his arms to mirror her stubbornness. Beautiful or not, he wanted answers. "I've got time."

Marley huffed out a breath, the gravel beneath her boots popping softly as she shifted her weight from one foot to the other. "It's true that I don't know Sierra. Not really, anyway. But you do, right?"

"Not as well as I know a lot of other folks in town," Greyson said slowly. He hadn't been kidding when he'd said

Sierra and her mother mostly kept to themselves. "But yeah. I guess I know her and her mom well enough."

"Right. So you've seen how skinny she is."

Greyson's stomach tightened. He'd never really given it a mountain of thought before, having only seen the girl here or there at The Corner Market or town events, like Millhaven's Fall Fling or the Fourth of July parade, but... "Yeah."

"When I stumbled on her at the market, I caught her stealing groceries," Marley said. "It was pretty obvious that she was hungry and not some punk shoplifting for the thrill of it. She was going to put everything back, but then the manager saw what was going on, and..."

She trailed off, but Greyson filled in the blanks easily enough. *Damn.* "You said the bag was yours so she wouldn't get in trouble."

Marley bit her lip and nodded, her dark hair shushing over her shoulders. "It was kind of a snap decision. I don't regret it," she added, emphatically enough that Greyson believed her. "I guess I just wasn't thinking I'd get arrested and tossed in jail. Which is dumb, I know. Shoplifting is illegal."

"It's not all *that* dumb," Greyson countered. Hell, he'd been the same way with his parking tickets. "You thought you'd get into trouble, then get yourself out, right?"

"Yeah."

Greyson thought about it for a minute, his mind snagging on the one part of the story that didn't quite add up. "How come you didn't let Sierra take the blame? I get that she'd have gotten into trouble," he tacked on quickly. "But she's a kid, so she probably would've gotten a slap on the wrist. Especially if you'd gone to bat for her and said she was going to put everything back. So why not tell the truth?"

"I couldn't." For the first time since she'd opened her

mouth, Marley hesitated. "Sierra might not have gotten in nearly as much trouble for shoplifting as I did, but if I hadn't taken the blame, the Department of Family Services would have been notified, and she'd have been taken from her mom."

The defiant look in Marley's eyes came back in full force, pulling at Greyson's curiosity for the thousandth time today. He didn't know the particulars of Marley's family life—not anything that could be backed up with actual facts, anyway. God knew there were plenty of rumors churning through the gossip mill about her mother, who had been Tobias Cross's wife's best friend and had clearly had an affair with him after Miss Rosemary had died of breast cancer twenty-six years ago. But Greyson knew better than to take rumors at face value, just like he knew that look on Marley's face meant she wasn't going to say another word on the subject.

Realizing it was all he was going to get out of her, he tabled the topic. For now. "So, you took the blame for something you didn't do in order to keep a kid out of trouble. Why tell me?"

"What?" Marley blinked, and while Greyson might be content to let the rest of it slide, on this, he wasn't going to budge.

"You feel strongly enough about this to lie to the sheriff and a judge, not to mention I'm assuming your brothers and old man don't know what really happened."

"I didn't exactly *lie*," she argued, but at the sharp look he delivered in reply, she said, "I just got really creative with the facts."

Greyson waved a hand through the air, squinting at her through the lowering sunlight of the yard. "Okay, fine. But you could've easily stonewalled me just now, the same way you've been doing with everyone else, and I know your brothers. I'm sure they've all asked. Why tell me the truth and not any of them?"

"Because I trust you."

The words were simple. Only four of them, five syllables in total, uttered with less than a full breath. They shouldn't have made his brain command his feet to close the space between him and Marley, and they damn sure shouldn't be making his heart squeeze behind his breastbone.

Yet here he was, right up in her personal space with his pulse pounding like a nine-pound hammer, and fuck, she was so pretty, it damn near hurt.

"You trust me."

His voice came out low and rough, but she didn't shy away. She had plenty of wide open space to take a step back. God knew she sure was fierce enough to let him know it if he'd gotten too close.

But instead, Marley lifted her chin to meet his stare with just as much heat as he felt pumping through his veins. "Yeah. I do."

"That's probably not smart," he said, and there. *There* it was, that flare of stubbornness in her eyes that made his cock rock-hard and his brain short out.

"How is it not smart?" she asked. "You're the one who said I shouldn't believe everything I heard. You flat-out told me you're not always as bad as you seem, that it's mostly reputation, not fact, and..."

She kept arguing, and Greyson's composure—which had already been questionable at best, thanks—frayed with every sassy word. He knew, in his blood and his bones and in all the other parts of him that he *really* shouldn't think about right now, that what he wanted was a monumentally bad idea.

Which is probably why he didn't think twice about doing it.

Pushing forward, Greyson slanted his mouth over Marley's to capture her words, mid-sentence. Somewhere, in some far-off passageway in his brain, he realized she'd probably be pissed about that later. She wasn't the type of woman to take being shushed, and—he realized with a stab of panic—she'd gone still under his mouth.

But then she flung her arms around his shoulders with the sort of urgency that made him go still right back, and the truth slammed into him, hard and fast.

She wasn't just hungry. She was *starving*.

Greyson swung her around, walking her backward until she bumped against the nearest flat surface, which just so happened to be his truck. Her mouth was surprisingly soft considering how many arguments she liked to form with it, and he slid his tongue over her bottom lip, coaxing his way inside.

As it turned out, Marley didn't need any encouragement. Opening in a seamless glide, she deepened the kiss, her tongue meeting his in bold strokes. He reached up to tunnel his fingers through her hair, wanting to hold her right where she was so he could taste every delicious, forbidden inch of her. She arched into his grip, coasting her hands from his shoulders to his chest to his waist, gripping his T-shirt and holding him just as tightly as he was holding her, and he exhaled by way of a low moan.

"You keep doing that, darlin'," Greyson said, against her lips because no way was he willing to actually part from her now that he'd had a taste, "and I may not be able to mind my manners."

Marley didn't hesitate to kiss him harder, taking his mouth like a dare. "I thought you didn't have a care for manners," she said, shuddering in his grasp when he trailed a path of hot, open-mouthed kisses from her jawline over her neck. "Oh, God. Don't stop doing that."

Greyson's mouth shaped a smirk on her skin. "There you go, getting bossy."

"I'm"—Marley paused for a sigh that made him want to lay waste to every stitch of Godforsaken clothing between them so he could sink into her, fast and hard and deep—"decisive."

"You're bossy," he said with a laugh as he kissed his way to her collarbone. "Just like a Cross."

Every part of Marley stilled save her pulse, which beat wildly against Greyson's lips. "I'm not a Cross," she said, pulling away from him so fast, he was momentarily dizzy.

"I know, I just..." He shook his head, his own heartbeat cranking faster in his chest. "I guess in the heat of the moment, I just forgot."

"Well, don't."

She looked angry on the surface, her eyes glinting and her kiss-swollen mouth compressed in a flat line, and even though Greyson could see the deeper, more vulnerable emotion lurking beneath her attitude, his own irritation threatened to rise.

"Look, I get it. Family can be a pain. I'm not real crazy about mine, either. But—"

"Believe me, you don't get it."

Greyson's shoulders stiffened. *He* didn't get it? Maybe he hadn't gone all emo, heart-on-the-floor confessional earlier, but he'd still told her things no one knew. He'd confided in her, and she'd said she *trusted* him, for fuck's sake. How had he been dumb enough to fall for that?

No one ever trusted a Whittaker.

Out of pure, unbridled instinct, he pushed. Hard. "Right.

Of course I don't. Anyway, if you're done distracting me, why don't we call it a night? I've got more important things to do."

Anyone else would've flinched, or at the very least, pushed back. Greyson knew this as well as he knew his own name—in fact, he counted on it.

But as soon as Marley shrugged and said, "Fine by me," then walked away, he realized his error.

She wasn't like anyone else.

Two days later, Greyson's frustration levels had reached an all-time high. His waking hours had been full of back-breaking labor, thanks to the double header of a heat wave and a malfunction of the irrigation system that kept their largest corn field from turning into a wasteland. His nights? Well, those had brimmed over with dark and dirty thoughts of a brash, smart-mouthed brunette who he shouldn't want and couldn't have.

I trust you.

"Got those water lines under control?"

His father's gravel-road voice sent him winging around, and Jesus, he needed to focus.

"Yeah," Greyson said, giving the field one last look so he wouldn't have to meet his old man's non-committal stare. "It was a pain where no pill can reach to fix the damn thing, but the system looks set." So as not to piss off fate, he added, "For now."

"Hmm."

The noise was all his father gave up, and okay, yeah, Greyson needed to be somewhere else on the farm, working the land and getting his hands good and dirty so he could get his head screwed on straight, once and for freaking all. "Anyway. I'm going to check the peach orchard. If I can get things just right for these last two weeks before peak season starts, I think we'll be looking at our best season yet for produce, especially pick-your-own."

"Not sure it's worth the bother," his old man said with a lift of his shoulder that stopped halfway before listing down beneath his T-shirt, as if it couldn't be bothered to make the entire trip into a true shrug. "Those damn things have grown themselves the past coupl'a years. Babyin' 'em seems like wasted effort."

Greyson's molars met with a clack. Those peaches had been the crown jewel of Whittaker Hollow's reputation for the past three years, easy, thanks to Greyson's ball-busting work. They grew them leaps and bounds better than Cross Creek, to the point that the Crosses had stopped trying to compete, focusing their efforts on their fancy-schmancy specialty produce instead. But nothing grew itself out here, and it was a fact his father damn well knew. One that Greyson was in just enough of a shitty, sleepless mood to point out.

"Actually, they haven't grown themselves. *I've* grown them, and I've done a damned good job of it."

The implication hung in the humid afternoon air, just as Greyson had intended it to, and his father bit.

"How come you love it so much?" he asked, his voice more contempt than curiosity. But Greyson was sick of all the back and forth, all the little jabs that never amounted to anything other than scrapes and bruises.

This time, he wanted blood.

"How come you don't? This is your farm. *Your* legacy. You wanted to run the place once"—he lifted one hand in a preemptive effort to stop the protest his father's expression said he'd been working up—"and don't tell me you didn't, because I remember. You and Uncle Steve and I had plans for this farm. Big ones."

For a second, the hardness his father had worn for nearly a decade faltered, making Greyson's throat knot. But he'd pushed first, and oh, how his old man was an expert in pushing right back.

"And just look how those plans turned out. Steve got what he wanted. Then the bastard up and died. Now, ain't nobody gettin' what they want. Life's just full of broken promises."

For a beat, then two, Greyson stood there, paralyzed on the dusty path next to the rows and rows of corn. His heart twisted—he missed his uncle, too, for Chrissake, missed the belly laughs the guy used to give out like Halloween candy, the way his dark eyes sparked with excitement, pure and real, when he talked about the best ways to work the land. Greyson opened his mouth to say so, but his old man beat him to the punch, knocking him down for the count, as always.

"Do whatever you want with the peaches," he said, turning his back on Greyson as he started back toward the house. "You're going to anyway, and I don't give a shit."

13

Marley stood on the threshold of the shelter in her three-inch heels and ridiculously trendy, faux-leather-trimmed tank dress, and flat-out balked about going inside. She was risking Louis's wrath, she knew, or at the very least, some top shelf side-eye for being late. It was five past four—this stupid commute was going to make her motion sick, not to mention bat-shit crazy—and Greyson's dented and dinged truck was already parked in its usual spot in the gravel side lot, the dust settled around it as if he'd arrived a good ten minutes ago. But despite the fact that she'd had to battle an unnerving amount of traffic and nearly break her neck to arrive even close to on time, here she stood, unable to do anything other than *not* go inside.

You keep doing that, darlin', and I may not be able to mind my manners...

"Oh, for heaven's sake," Marley muttered under her breath. Okay, yes. So she'd had a weak moment and told Greyson the truth about Sierra, then an even weaker moment when they'd kissed. It'd been just a heat-of-the-moment thing. Consensual, sure. Hot? Oh, hell yes. But not *that* big a deal. She'd been kissed by plenty of guys. Dozens, even.

Except.

She'd spent the last year of her life keeping everyone at arm's length, literally. It wasn't just that Marley shied away from touching other people, although she definitely did avoid it at all costs. But sometimes she felt dread, or even straight-up panic, at the simplest physical contact. Her former landlady folding her into an awkward, cardboard cutout hug when she'd left Chicago. Cate putting a hand over hers to guide her through a baking technique. One of her brothers offering up a simple shoulder squeeze. Marley hadn't wanted to touch anyone, or let anyone touch her, for so long, it had become her default.

But she'd wanted Greyson to touch her. No. That wasn't quite right, she thought, her cheeks heating as she shifted her weight on the sun-baked porch boards. She'd wanted him to learn her with his hands, to kiss her and undress her and explore every last part of her body in slow, intimate strokes. In that moment, Marley hadn't just wanted his touch.

She'd *craved* it. And worse was that, for as abrupt as their parting had been and as hard as she'd tried for the last two days, she couldn't make herself stop.

The whole thing was ridiculous, she thought, turning the damned knob and making her way inside the shelter. Greyson might be hot (so. So. *So* hot. God, it was almost unfair), but he was also a jerk. He'd talked such a good game about not wanting to be judged by his family, then turned around and called *her* a Cross, lumping her in with her biological family like nothing-doing? Nope. No way. She should've known better than to deviate from her original plan of do the work, get out of Dodge. Do not make friends, do not kiss the hot guy, do not pass "go", do not collect two hundred dollars.

Marley rushed through the dingy lobby, making her way to the back of the shelter. She'd change her clothes once she let Louis know she was here. He was already going to be pissed.

"You're late," he said, proving her right as she arrived in the back room where he stood, arms crossed and eyes narrowed, beside an impossible-to-read Greyson.

"I'm sorry," she said genuinely. Just because she didn't want to be here didn't mean she hadn't earned the obligation. "I got a little caught up at work. If you want, I can stay a few minutes late tonight to make up for the lost time."

"Oh." Louis gave up a slow blink. "Well, as long as you get the work done, I s'pose a few minutes'll be alright. Just this once, though."

She exhaled in relief. "You got it. What's on the agenda for tonight?"

Louis went over their tasks for the evening, and although she and Greyson would be busy, no doubt, nothing was unfamiliar or sounded too terribly taxing.

"Okay," Greyson said after Louis had finished his rundown of clean-walk-organize. "Anything else?"

"No." Louis resumed his eyes-narrowed, arms-crossed stance. "But—"

"I know, I know." Greyson rolled his eyes, his voice loaded with come-at-me attitude. "Don't mess with the dog in the corner cage."

Louis lifted a finger for an air-jab. "I mean it," he said, huffing one last time before turning to walk back to the front room.

"I know you do, you judgmental jackass," Greyson

muttered, just barely under his breath, and oooookay. No way could Marley leave that alone.

"Whoa. What's with you?" she asked.

Greyson's frown intensified. "Nothing," he snapped, then seemed to think better of it, running a hand over his stubbled jaw as if he could erase the tension there. "Truth be told, I had a shit day."

"Ah. I'm familiar." Marley gestured to her outfit. "Exhibit A. I'm pretty sure these shoes are from Satan's signature line."

He surprised her with a laugh, and judging by the look that followed on his face, she wasn't the only one. "Guess there must be something in the water. You want to walk the dogs tonight?"

She'd gotten a little more comfortable with the animals last week—occupational hazard, and all—but still...*get the work done, get out of Dodge*. "Nah, you can."

"I've got an idea," Greyson said, looking at her thoughtfully. "Since we could both use something good, why don't we both do it?"

Marley's brows shot up. "You want to go together?"

"Well, you'll have to ditch your shoes, which I know will disappoint you something terrible." The heat of his smirk chased Marley's shock away in less than a breath. "But, sure. Why not?"

"Because it's nice?"

Marley heard the words only after they'd crash-coursed past her apparently non-existent brain to mouth filter. "Sorry. That just kind of flew out. But..." Oh, she needed to just say it. "We kind of parted on bad terms on Sunday. I didn't expect you to want to do any jobs where you had to spend time with me."

Greyson paused, sinking a thumb through the belt loop

on his jeans and blowing out a breath. "Yeah. About Sunday. I...kind of acted like an ass."

"I wasn't exactly the nicest, either," Marley pointed out, once she'd gotten past her surprise at his candor. Yeah, he'd thrown her for a loop, but it took two to have an argument. She hadn't failed to rise to the occasion.

As if he'd read her mind, he nodded. "Truce?"

Unable to help it, she arched a brow. "You make it sound like we're at battle."

"Our families sort of are," he said wryly. But she was tired of the labels, of him being a Whittaker and her being tagged as the Cross that she wasn't.

So she said, "I guess it's a good thing we're not our families, then. Truce."

Marley went into the bathroom to change, nearly groaning out loud at the shoegasm of kicking off those infernal heels that Noémie had insisted were an absolute "must-have". She was so much more comfortable in her cutoffs and Converse. Not that she'd ever find a job to support *that* sort of dress code.

"Okay," Marley said, stowing her bag on a shelf by the door. "Which dogs do you want to take first?"

Greyson tilted his head at the cages along the back wall in assessment. "We could probably manage three at once, if you take Gypsy and I take Boomer and Snickers."

Her laughter flew out in a quick burst. "You named them?" she asked, and he looked at her as if *she* was the crazy one.

"All dogs need names. Plus, it's a hell of a lot easier than saying, 'that brown one' or 'the spotted one', don't you think?"

Marley had to admit, he did have a point. "Fair enough. But Snickers?"

"What can I say?" Greyson shrugged, gesturing to the cage holding a medium-sized dark brown and caramel-colored mutt. "I was hungry, and come on. She looks like a Snickers, doesn't she?"

Huh. He kind of had a point, and hell if the dog hadn't responded to her name, her ears perking up and her eyes going bright. "I wonder why Louis didn't name them himself," Marley mused. "According to the records, some of them have been here for a while."

She'd started organizing all the records the other day, and it was going to be a crazy-big task. Louis swore he knew where everything was, but that made exactly one of them. Whatever system he'd conjured in his head seemed to be unacquainted with both rhyme and reason. Also, any technology from this century. Every single record the man kept was by hand.

"Maybe he didn't name them because he's an unfeeling ass?" Greyson ventured, and oh for the love of God.

"You let him get to you." Marley pointed the clasp-end of the leash she'd taken from a hook on the wall at him, her heart tapping faster against her breastbone when he actually stopped short of the cage he'd been heading toward to look at her.

"Aside from the fact that he's a crusty old bastard, he doesn't do a very good job around here. It took us forever to get that yard right, and that storage closet was a disaster zone."

She couldn't deny that he had a point. At least, about the state of the shelter. "Yeah, but the animals are really well cared for. Their vet records are all up-to-date and meticulously kept. Even if I did have to dig around quite a bit to find all of them."

Greyson leveled her with a look as if to say *see?*, and

Marley let out an exhale. "What I mean is, I think all Louis needs is some help managing the place. He's doing the important stuff, but everything else...not so much. And you *do* let him get to you."

"He's mean."

"Only if you push. And for the record, I thought you were mean when I first met you."

Hah! That got him. But Marley saw the shock on Greyson's face turn to a smirk just a beat too late, and damn it, damn it, damn it, she needed to build some sort of immunity against that thing before it turned lethal.

"And what do you think of me now?" he asked, pinning her with a stare that made her want to surrender her panties like a white flag.

"I think"—*so many things. So many dirty, delicious, inappropriate things*. A prickle of heat rippled down her spine—"that we should get to walking these dogs."

To her surprise, Greyson let her get away with dodging the question. Turning toward the cages along the far wall, he bent to unlatch the one where a sweet, older, Basset hound-looking dog (Marley was betting she was Gypsy) had been housed. But then he bypassed the latch, stepping all the way to the corner cage that Louis had forbidden them from.

"Greyson," she warned—had they not *just* had the conversation about him pushing too hard?—but he looked at her over one broad shoulder, not budging.

"What? I'm just looking."

She scoffed her disagreement, because while he might be just looking right now in this exact moment, chances were extremely high he wouldn't stay that way. "Louis said not to mess with him. What if he's rabid or something?"

Greyson scoffed right back. "Then he wouldn't be here,

that's for damn sure. Anyway, I've seen rabid animals before, and they don't act like this."

Marley tilted her head in a nonverbal *that makes sense.* Still. "Louis wouldn't have told us not to mess with him if he didn't have a good reason, and he's never negligent when it comes to the animals."

"Louis might have a reason for telling us not to mess with him," Greyson agreed, leaning down to look in the cage more closely. "But I'm not sure it's a good one."

Huffing out a sigh, Marley moved forward to look over Greyson's shoulder, peering into the cage that was two-removed from the other animals in either direction. The dog inside was on the small side, with the too-big paws and ears of a puppy. But that was where the resemblance ended. Instead of eagerly seeking attention or food or even curiously sniffing around the way puppies tended to, this dog had wedged itself into the farthest corner of the pen from the latch and curled itself inward like a sleek, black question mark.

"Hey, buddy," Greyson said, and even though he'd taken caution not to advance any closer and to keep his voice low and even, the dog whimpered, shrinking back against the already tight corner of the pen.

Marley's heart lurched in her rib cage. "I mean it, Greyson. I don't think—"

"Wait."

The dog's whimpering had gone silent, its small head lifting just slightly so that one dark eye was visible from the mass of matted black fur.

And it was looking right at her.

"Keep talking," Greyson said, wincing as the dog shrank back at the sound of his voice.

"What?" she asked.

But Greyson was already taking a step back, waving a hand to encourage her into the space he'd just vacated in front of the cage. "I think he likes your voice. Or, at least, he's not as scared of it as he is everything else."

"That's crazy." Could dogs even have a preference for that sort of thing?

"Maybe," Greyson agreed, prompting a frown to tug at the edges of Marley's mouth. "But that doesn't mean it's not true."

"So, what? You want me to have a conversation with a dog?"

Greyson shook his head. "No. You can have the conversation with me. Just let the dog hear you."

"Are you listening to yourself?" she asked with a laugh of disbelief. They had a ton of work to do, and he wanted to go all Animal Planet with a dog that had been clearly labeled off-limits to them.

"Could you just humor me, here? See, he's looking at you." Greyson said, killing the argument she'd been working up by tacking on, "We can switch up our game plan and clean the cats' cages first so the dog can hear your voice while we work. These guys can wait another half an hour for their walks"—he gestured to the section of pens in front of him, where all of the dogs looked traitorously content —"and we'll have lost nothing. Come on. All you have to do is talk."

Marley eyed the cage where the black dog had once again become little more than a shadow in the corner. "You like to push, don't you?"

"Right. Because you don't."

Greyson had delivered the reply with enough easy teasing in his voice that she answered without brass. "Sometimes. But not *always*."

She hung enough *like some people I know* in her tone that after a beat or two, Greyson lifted his hands in concession.

"Fine. Yes. I like to push."

"Why?" she asked, turning toward the nearest pen, which just so happened to be where that friendly gray cat with the ragged ear had been snoozing. Switching up their schedule wouldn't hurt anything, and it would keep Greyson in check—at least, a little. All in all, humoring him was a win-win.

He gave up a triumphant grin before beginning to work. "Why not?"

"It kind of makes you an ass sometimes," Marley said, and he laughed.

"Fair enough. But that's the point."

"You like being an ass?" Surprise pushed her pulse just a little faster in her veins.

Greyson's response came slowly. "It's what people expect."

"That doesn't really answer the question."

He paused for a second, scratching the orange tabby behind its ears. "Like I told you the other day, my family has a reputation around Millhaven, and we come by a lot of it honestly. My father is...not an easy man. He's never been particularly open, but his brother, my uncle Steve, was killed nine years ago. After that, things got a lot worse."

"Oh." A wave of sadness laddered up Marley's spine. She knew all too well what loss felt like when it was expected. Something sudden like that? Must have been devastating. "I'm really sorry about your uncle."

"Thanks," Greyson said with a nod. "He was visiting Washington, DC—he was a huge history buff, and wanted to see all the monuments. The Lincoln Memorial, the Library of Congress, the Vietnam War Memorial. The works. He was mugged a few blocks away from the Capitol building the night before he was supposed to come back to Millhaven. The guy shot him for forty-six dollars and an old Timex. My uncle never even made it to the hospital. He died right there at the scene."

Greyson told the story quietly, each fact stacked upon the one that had come before it, and the sadness that had traveled over Marley's spine became a chill.

"That's awful."

"The crazy part is, he'd never even left home before that, and he didn't plan to again once he came home. It was supposed to be a once-in-a-lifetime trip for his birthday. The only one he'd ever wanted to take."

Marley's heart squeezed. She knew all the platitudes, was so well-versed in you-poor-thing sympathy lingo that she could probably write a hundred greeting cards in her sleep. But the only words that weren't completely useless were the ones that were the truth.

"That must've been really hard for you," she said, and he nodded.

"Yeah," he said, surprising her by following up with a laugh, sharp and quick. "I was twenty at the time, though. Young and stupid. My uncle and I were close, definitely, but my old man...I think he took it really hard."

"You *think*?" Marley's hand stilled on the latch of the cage she'd just cleaned out. "You were both here, in Millhaven, running your farm together, right? How could you not know?"

Greyson paused. "Like I said, he's not exactly an easy man. He's always been tight with words. Even tighter with emotions. Well, other than anger, anyway," he amended. "He got real good at that one after my uncle was killed, and he's been that way ever since. Angry. Ornery. Always ready to pick a fight. Nobody even questions it anymore. They just expect it, from him and from me."

Marley thought for a minute, tumbling his words and what they meant around in her head over and over, letting them slowly click together with their bigger meaning. "Okay, so people expect you to act all cocky and brash. But have you ever tried *not* pushing?"

"Other than right now, you mean?" he asked, brows arched, and the seriousness of the conversation lifted enough for her to smile.

"Yeah. Like with Louis, for example." Marley held up a hand to staunch the argument she knew he'd work up, and God, his open-mouthed, rigid-shouldered stance kept him true to form. "I get that he's cranky, and that he pisses you off by making assumptions about who you are and how you'll act. But have you ever considered proving him wrong with your actions, rather than just butting heads all the time?"

Greyson opened his mouth to answer. Closed it. Then, finally, went with, "I've tried to prove everyone wrong before, but...well, I may not be mean by nature, but I'm not exactly sporting wings and a halo, either. I meant what I said when I told you this cocky thing ain't always for show."

"Yeah, I got that," Marley said. His bravado certainly seemed to fit him like the pair of impeccably broken-in Levi's that she couldn't seem to erase from her mind's eye. "But what's the old adage about actions speaking louder than words? If you show people you're more than they assume, I bet a lot of them will start to get it eventually, just like I did."

"Ah. So you don't think I'm just that arrogant jackass your brothers warned you about now?" he asked, so quietly that she didn't think. Just answered.

"No, I don't. I think sometimes you *act* like an arrogant jackass," she said, because as harsh as it might sound, it was also the undeniable truth, and sugar-coating? So not her thing. "But I also think people would believe you if you eased up a little and showed them that even if you are cocky, you're also not mean like your father. You might be a Whittaker like him, and you might run your family farm with him, but you don't have to fulfill every part of that legacy. Not if you don't want to. You can just be you without all the pushing."

"Maybe." Greyson tilted his head at her, his dark stare telling her that while his hands still moved from cage to cat to cleaner, then back again, his mind was fully focused on what she'd said. "But pushing isn't *always* a bad thing, you know."

"Oh, really?" God, it was just like him to argue, even if he was doing it with a smile on his ruggedly handsome face.

"Yeah, really," he said. "Sometimes people need a good nudge."

Marley laughed. "Like who?"

She realized, too late, that Greyson had stopped cleaning the cage in front of him, choosing instead to step toward her until less than an arm's length remained.

"Like you. The whole point of this conversation was for that little guy to hear your voice"—he pointed to the corner cage—"and I just did all the yappin'. So what's it going to be, Marley? Put up, or shut up?"

14

One of these days, Greyson was going to learn not to tempt fate. His conversation with Marley had been cruising along like a Sunday drive, with just the right amount of sexy back-and-forth to temper the deeper subject matter. They'd even managed a painless mutual apology for the attitude they'd traded along with that kiss three days ago, for Chrissake. He'd shared a little (fine. A lot) more about his family than he'd expected to, but that'd been oddly okay. Everything that had popped past his lips had felt natural, as if he'd somehow known Marley wouldn't judge or—worse yet—give him a raft of overdone sympathy about his uncle's murder and the way his father had grown colder and more distant over time. The more Greyson had told her, the more he'd wanted to know about her in return, to find out if she'd meant what she'd said about trusting him. He hadn't been bullshitting her about that dog seeming to be calmed by her voice, either, and you know what? Screw that.

Greyson was glad he'd pushed a little. Maybe fate shouldn't tempt him.

Marley dropped her gaze, but stood her ground in front of him. "I don't know what you want me to talk about. I'm not exactly well-versed in anything other than what sort of shoes you should avoid if you like not hobbling around in pain."

"There's a good place to start," he said. It was as decent as any, he supposed. "How come you hate your job? Shoes aside, of course."

"A couple of reasons, really," Marley said slowly. "The commute is hell and my co-workers are shallow, stiletto-wearing mean-girls. But the biggest reason I hate it is because, honestly? It's mindless. My boss is in charge of all the good stuff, like arranging the window displays and doing the inventory and organizing the schedules. All I do is fold midriff-baring sweaters and ninety-dollar skinny jeans and unlock fitting rooms for spoiled teenagers looking to spend money like they have an endless supply of the stuff."

An image of Marley, wearing a sweater that showed off her bare, tapered waist and jeans made to illustrate the flare of her hips barged through Greyson's mind, and shit, he needed to focus. *Fast*, before his dick got the message and decided to pop up for a hi-how-are-ya.

"Okay"—he cleared his throat and scrubbed the cage in front of him for a breath cycle—"that does sound pretty boring. What would you rather be doing instead?"

"Leaving town."

Marley's answer was so swift and decisive that Greyson couldn't help but ask, "Then why don't you? Not that I don't think you're crazy for wanting to leave," he qualified. "As far as I'm concerned, Millhaven's fucking perfect. But you clearly don't like your job, and you've made it plain that you don't want to be part of your family." No one made that much of a fuss about their heritage if they wanted to own it. "So, why stick around?"

"Truth?" Her pause was measurable only by the tiny hitch of her fingers on the water bowl she'd just emptied, but oh, Greyson had seen it.

"No," he teased, partly to put her at ease and partly to see her blush, because that was the sort of bastard he was. "Lie to me."

She paired an eye-roll with her soft laugh, and oh, mission accomplished. "I'm sure my brothers think it's because I'm still grieving for my mom and that I need to find myself, or figure out my path, or some crazy, cosmic crap like that. Like I'm in limbo, or whatever."

"But you're not," he said, and she shook her head.

"No, I'm not. I'm just in debt."

Curveball, meet catcher's mitt. "You're in debt?" he repeated, unable to curb his surprise.

She gave up a rueful smile. "Up to my elbows, actually. My mom had health insurance, but not everything was covered, and she..."

Here, Marley paused again, but something in her eyes warned Greyson not to tease her this time. He heeded it even though he was tempted to push his luck, or at least say *something*—Christ, the sadness that had suddenly torn over her face was making his instincts howl to get her to unload some of it so her burden would ease.

But then she shrugged, and the sadness was gone as fast as it had appeared. "Anyway. Even with the insurance and everything she left me, there's still enough debt left behind to keep me stuck here in Millhaven while I pay it off. My job at the boutique isn't ideal." Marley made a face that suggested this was a gross understatement, and from the sound of things, Greyson would agree. "But it was the first thing I could find, and the pay isn't terrible. I mapped everything out—what I owe, how many hours I have to work per week to pay things off every month. And as soon as that debt is settled, I'm out of here."

Ah. Well, that explained her willingness to do a job she hated with the heat and intensity of ten-thousand white-hot suns. Greyson remained quiet for a minute and turned the rest of it over in his mind. He knew his next words weren't going to win him any favor, but really, when had he ever let that stop him before?

"Look, I'm not breaking out my pom poms to do the Cross family cheer over here. God knows there's no love lost between us. But your brothers and old man won't help you out? I know you're a Rallston," he emphasized, not only because it was true, but also so she wouldn't put a kill switch to the conversation by way of telling him to fuck straight off. "But you can't deny that y'all *are* family. Blood is blood, and we tend to stand for our own 'round here."

"They probably would offer to help me pay off the debt," she said. "If I told them I owed it."

Greyson's heart beat faster in surprise. "You haven't told them?"

"The debt isn't theirs. I mean, technically, yes, they're my family," Marley said, her displeasure on full display as she turned toward the last cage in the row. "And Tobias is my biological father. But he made it really clear that he didn't want anything to do with me from the start. The only reason I came to Millhaven to meet him in the first place was because my mother asked me to. Just because I had the shitty luck of getting stuck here when the bills came rolling in doesn't mean I want a handout from anyone, though. Least of all Tobias."

"It'd get you where you want to be," Greyson pointed out, and wasn't he just the devil's advocate right now?

Not that it would win him any arguments, judging by the look on Marley's face. "I don't need pity money from him, or a handout from my brothers. It's not why I came here. Anyway, she was *my* mother. This debt is my responsibility. If I have to stay in Millhaven while I pay it off, then that's what I'll do."

Once again, Greyson wanted to push, or at the very least to point out that her mother probably wouldn't have made her promise to come meet the old man if she didn't think he'd do right by her. Trouble was, not only did he understand what Marley was saying, but he *got* it. As tempting as it might be on the surface to take the money and run, he wouldn't want a handout, either. A debt was a debt, plain and simple. How she paid hers off was up to her.

So he said, "Well, all things considered, I don't think this is the worst place you could get stuck while you make good on your finances."

"You don't have a lot of other places to compare it to," she said after a beat of surprise widened her sky-blue stare.

Well, hell. Of course, she kind of had him there. "True. But I think if you gave Millhaven a chance, you might change your tune about it being so backwards. In fact, you might even start to like it here."

"Doubtful." The sound that crossed her lips punctuated the claim, but Greyson ignored her lack of conviction. Here, he knew he could push, because here, he knew he was right.

"You just need the right person to show you what's what, is all."

"Oh, and you think you're that person?" Marley asked. She'd probably meant to stay tough, or at the very least, non-committal. But a fragment of a smile had made its way to both her face and her tone, and Greyson matched it with his very best smirk.

"Yes, ma'am, I do. Look, I'm not trying to convince you to stay." There was, after all, the old adage about leading a horse to water, and while he wasn't really a platitudes kind of guy, that one made sense. "You've got greener pastures and other places to be. I get that, even if I think it's crazy. But you might as well try to enjoy Millhaven while you're here. I mean, what else are you doing with your free time? Watching Netflix and sitting around that big ol' house, avoiding your old man?"

"No." The flush crawling over her cheeks belied the claim—a fact she must have felt, because then she said, "Only sometimes."

Pausing, Marley knelt down to peer into the corner cage, where the black dog had been watching her about as closely as Greyson had. The dog was still far from friendly, curled in a cautious knot along the back wall of its pen. He wasn't whimpering or shaking anymore, though, and hadn't been since Marley had taken hold of the conversation.

"I guess it wouldn't hurt anything to prove you wrong," she finally said. Whether it was the fact that she'd agreed or the thrill of the challenge itself, Greyson couldn't be sure, but he laughed all the same.

"Remind me to have some salt and pepper handy."

"What? Why?"

The anticipation riding through his veins was dangerous, he knew. But he liked it too much to care.

"For when you eat those words, darlin'. I don't throw down challenges I intend to lose."

~

Marley sat in the cheery, sunlit kitchen of the main house at Cross Creek Farm and cursed viciously under her breath. Slumping against her ladder-back chair, she scooped the cell phone she could barely afford off the table in front of her and re-read the message on the screen for the thousandth time since it had arrived in her inbox a handful of hours ago.

Hey chérie. Sry I had to cut ur hours. Here's ur schedule for this week.

Marley didn't bother recalculating the number of hours she'd been assigned at the boutique. She already knew achingly well that they added up to far too few, just as she knew Noémie wouldn't budge on changing them. Marley had called her the second she'd seen the text, explaining through gritted teeth that she really, really needed double the hours for which she'd been slated, and wasn't there anything Noémie could do. Her boss (the witch) had sighed heavily as if Marley were a kindergartener asking for a cupcake and said, "Well, you *did* ask me for a very specific schedule, and we can't all get the hours we want. If you're not willing to be flexible, I can't guarantee what you'll get, and the hours you asked for are *primo*." She'd paused here to no doubt allow Marley a second to be wildly impressed with her worldliness. Italian and French. Ooo la fucking la. "Anyway, you know how retail is," Noémie had chirped. "*C'est la vie*!"

It had taken all of Marley's restraint not to tell the woman where she could stick her haughty airs and poorly pronounced adages. Okay, yes, she'd known she might take a small hit to her schedule because she needed to dance around her community service hours. But while she and Noémie weren't exactly BFFs, Marley had thought that maybe her boss would at least *try* to help her out as much as possible. The schedule Marley had received had reduced her to more of an afterthought than even a part-timer at this point, and God, couldn't she find one place—just *one* place—where she actually felt like she belonged?

Like the animal shelter, you mean?

The thought winged into her from out of nowhere, tightening her fingers on her phone case and halting her breath in her lungs. She hadn't hated her hours at the shelter this week, having found a solid groove of work/banter/rinse/repeat with Greyson both Wednesday and yesterday. They'd stuck to lighter topics of conversation over the past couple of days, like favorite types of music (country for him, rock for her), the best shows to binge watch (how he could think *The Walking Dead* was better than *Jessica Jones* was seriously beyond her), and how to properly order a cheeseburger (there, at least, they'd been in perfect agreement. Medium-rare, with the works, steak fries, not shoestring potatoes. There was hope for him yet). Greyson had even helped her stealth her way into Sierra's yard, bringing his own stash of groceries to add to hers every time, and she couldn't deny the truth.

He might argue with her and nudge her and make her generally crazy, and yeah, he might be cocky (*so* cocky), but Marley liked him.

And yeah again, sometimes, even if it was only for a split second at a time here and there, she didn't feel like such an outsider around him.

Whiiiiiiich was ridiculous, she thought, her head snapping up and her shoulders going along for the ride. It was mandatory community service, emphasis on mandatory. It wasn't supposed to be fun. She wasn't supposed to like it, no matter how warm Greyson made her feel between her thighs when he smirked, and she *definitely* wasn't supposed to feel as if she belonged there. With him. Kissing him. Letting him kiss her back in all the right places until she were hot and sweaty and desperate to come.

Oh, God, this was beyond ridiculous.

So why did she want it anyway?

"Whoa, are you okay?" Owen's voice hit her like a bucket of ice water—which, in this particular case, wasn't a bad thing.

Marley straightened, forcing a nothing-to-see-here look over her face as she glanced across the kitchen at her brother, who—blessedly—seemed completely oblivious to the naughty-factor of the thoughts she'd been having when he'd walked through the mudroom door. "Yep, I'm great. I was just about to make the filling for some extra blueberry pies. Cate mentioned you guys were way low on them at the storefront, and I have time to kill today."

"Oh, that's a great idea," Owen said, his smile brightening over the bottle of water he'd grabbed from the fridge. "Those blueberry pies *are* my favorite."

Marley managed to laugh. Not that she minded, because Cate was cool, but her brother was such a dork when it came to his girlfriend. "You say that about everything Cate makes."

"It's not my fault it's all amazing," he pointed out. "Or that you two make such a good team."

Marley's laugh became surprise in an instant. "I don't know about team. She's the one who comes up with all the flavor profiles and recipes, and then she teaches me how to make stuff. All the really hard stuff falls on her."

"Yeah, but she said you're really good at keeping things organized, and that you always do whatever it takes to get a recipe right."

Marley pushed up from the table and moved toward the

coffeepot with a shrug. "A) being organized is just a good idea. I mean, who doesn't want to know what they've got and where it is? Secondly, there isn't much point in not doing whatever it takes to get something right. Why even bother in the first place if you're only going to half-ass things, you know?"

"Hmm. Actually, I do," Owen said. "Speaking of which, have you given any more thought to working at the storefront? We could really use someone like you running the place."

Damn it! Marley must be really off her game not to have seen that one coming. Owen had never exactly been suave *or* subtle.

"No," she said automatically. The argument rang hollow in her ears, though, as if it was growing threadbare from overuse. "What do you mean, someone like me?"

Surprise flickered over Owen's face, but he didn't waste any time answering. "You don't take any crap, for starters, and you don't pull any punches. I had to learn that the hard way."

Ah, right. Their big Come To Jesus talk after he and Cate had had that big blowout argument last spring.

"That was your own fault for being thick-headed," Marley said, a smile twitching at the corners of her mouth. "Anyway, you figured things out fast enough." All she'd done was point out the truth, really. Cate and Owen were so obviously perfect for each other.

"Yeah, but I wouldn't have if you hadn't set me straight," Owen said, his argument growing steam. "You're also pretty smart."

Shock rippled behind Marley's breastbone. She knew she wasn't a dumbass or anything, but no one had ever gone out of their way to call her smart, especially when other adjectives like *stubborn* and *sarcastic* were so readily available. "You think so?"

He nodded. "It's in the genes."

"God, now you sound like Eli."

Owen laughed, lifting his water bottle at her in salute. "I can't help it if it's true." His expression slipped into the seriousness she was used to from him, making her heart work faster in her chest. "You really are smart, Marley, and I've watched you work with Cate when she fills orders for the storefront and the farmers' market. I wouldn't tell you I think you'd be good at this just to blow smoke. You know that's not my style."

Okay, so that was probably true. Owen had never been one to go the bullshit route. In fact, sometimes he was a little too honest. It was why, of all her brothers, she got along with him best. Not that she'd confided the big stuff in him—he was, after all, their father's son. He'd been raised by Tobias, the only living parent either of them had.

Stop, her brain whispered quietly, cutting the train of thought to the quick, her defenses rerouting her to a safer topic. "Alright, so I'm not brainless. That still doesn't mean I'd be any good at running a storefront."

"Why don't we do a test run at the farmers' market tomorrow?" Owen asked. When Marley didn't offer an immediate protest—stupid, stupid delayed reaction—he continued excitedly. "It's the Fourth of July, and with the parade in Camden Valley, the market is bound to be packed. We'll need all the hands we can get. Hunter and Eli and I can show you the ropes, and Cate and Scarlett and Emerson will be there, too. We'll even pay you for your time."

Behold, the magic words. "You'll pay me just for trying it out?"

"Of course. I mean, don't get me wrong. You're gonna

earn every penny if you say yes." Both his tone and his wry smile backed up the words in spades. "But the rest of us get paid for time put in. You should, too."

"How much, exactly?"

Owen rattled off an hourly wage that made her chest fill with butterflies. "Just for working at the farmers' market?" Marley asked. It was more than she made at the mall, and, bonus, no shoes that stunt doubled as instruments of torture.

Owen, however, shook his head. "No, for helping *manage* the farm stand. Like I said, it's a lot of work, and you'll need to start with stuff like inventory and helping to pack up the truck today. There's a learning curve to making a day at the market a success." His gray eyes shifted to meet hers, his gaze fastening tight. "But I really mean it when I say I think this is a great idea. So, what do you say?"

"How soon could you pay me?" Marley asked carefully, and after a beat of surprise, Owen replied.

"Payday's every other Friday, and this is our off week, so...Cate can cut you a check for whatever hours you work in seven days."

Marley leaned back against the counter and weighed all of the variables. No, she didn't want any part of the family business (one check for the *no* column), but this was temporary (one for *yes*), and she was desperate (more *yes*). Anyway, it wasn't as if she'd have to actually work with Tobias, or be anywhere near him for that matter. After his scare with heat exhaustion last year, her brothers made sure he took both Saturdays and Sundays off. The fact of the matter was that, unlike her hours at the boutique, her bills weren't going anywhere, and she had thirteen days before the hospital's billing department was going to make an electronic withdrawal that would overdraw her account if she didn't feed the damned thing.

If working at the farmers' market could get her closer to her goal of bills paid, get out of town, then how much could it hurt?

"Fine, I'll do it. But only after I make the filling for these pies like I promised I would. And Owen?"

Her brother had enough good graces to school his goofy grin before she could roll her eyes at him. "Yeah?"

"Don't get too excited. It's just this once."

15

There wasn't enough coffee in the entire town for this.

Marley threw back the last of what was in her travel mug anyway, because hello, she might be exhausted, but she wasn't crazy. While it had been a ton of work, the prep part of the farmers' market job had been pretty straightforward—just a lot of inventory and organizing and a bunch of manual labor thrown in for good measure. With some help from Eli, then Hunter, she'd managed to get it figured out and finished before the sun had gone down last night. The really tough part would be today, when there were tons of people nearby, smiling and staring and mentally pigeonholing her into a family where she couldn't belong.

Just breathe, Marley instructed herself, indulging in a deep pull of crisp, early morning air. Well, she supposed her brothers, along with every other farmer, baker, and local vendor setting up a tent in the pavilion right now, would say it wasn't early at all. Seven-thirty in the morning was practically midday to them. As far as Marley was concerned, venturing out from beneath the warm, sweet haven of her bed before ten was pure lunacy.

Unless she was getting paid, in which case... "Okay," she said, making her way to the back of Cross Creek's triple-wide canopy tent. Her brothers had divided the prep tasks into unload (Owen), actual setup (Hunter), and organize (Eli). Considering Cross Creek had one of the biggest and most well-traveled stalls at the market, none of the jobs were a cakewalk.

Including hers, which was to be sure they made good time and that everything went according to plan. "Everything seems to be on track," she told Owen, checking the list of tasks she'd snapped to the clipboard in her grasp. "Hunter got the last of the tables set up and in order, and Eli's filling all of them with the bins of produce." Marley gestured over her shoulder. "Cate is on top of her section with all the baked goods and jam, Scarlett's got the displays, and Emerson is making sure all the signs with the prices on them are in place. The cash box is stocked, the iPad is charged and ready to go with a credit card reader, and the cooler is full of cold water. Oh!"—she flipped to the sheet of paper under the schematic she'd made of the layout—"And I don't know if you guys normally do this or not, but I made a break schedule, so no one gets hangry...and by no one, I pretty much mean me."

"Wow," Owen said, bumping her shoulder gently with his own. "See? I told you. You're a natural."

The contact made her pulse skip, but she was able to smooth it back to normal with a breath and an expression she hoped passed as a smile. "No, I'm just good at being bossy. Speaking of which"—Marley sent her gaze over the controlled chaos of all the crates of produce, bright, fat tomatoes and sun-colored squash and baskets of leafy greens that had been measured into pretty, bouquet-like bundles—"are you guys married to having this one section set up this way?"

"What, with the watermelons?" Hunter asked, turning his attention from the task of setting them up in the very front of the space.

Marley nodded, and Eli paused to slide a forearm over his forehead before examining the display. "We've kind of always done it this way, since the watermelons are so popular this time of year. We usually crack one open so folks can see how pretty they are, and let them draw people into the tent to see the rest of what we've got."

"Oh." Marley's cheeks flushed. Of course, that was a good strategy. One her brothers had probably tested time and again. "That makes perfect sense."

"Why?" Owen asked, and ugh, she should've known he wouldn't drop it now that she'd opened her mouth. "What'd you have in mind?"

Knowing better than to tell him to forget it, she said, "It's just that today is the Fourth of July, so I thought you might want to push the apple pies Cate made, together with the watermelons and sweet corn. Like, what's more American than apple pie? That kind of theme? It would be like one-stop shopping for a cookout, with everything other than the burgers and hot dogs right here together."

The silence that followed breathed down Marley's neck, the shocked stares of her brothers pressing into her for a beat, then another and another, until, God, she couldn't stand it anymore.

"You know what, forget it. You guys totally know what works, and mixing the baked goods in with the produce will probably confuse people. We can just—"

"No, wait," Eli said, his gaze turning to the front of the

tent where they'd stacked the crates of watermelons and his brows tucked as if his thoughts were cruising at a mile a minute. "Actually, that's a great idea."

Marley shook her head. "You don't have to humor me."

"I'm not. A lot of high-end grocery stores are doing the same sort of thing, putting popular meal items into package deals to fit a theme. If we could hook people in with the special, then get them to maybe add on a few things like salad greens or tomatoes and butter lettuce for their burgers or maybe some veggies for grilling..."

"We'd upsell a lot of produce that way, and cross over with Cate's baked goods," Hunter said, excitement sparking in his sky-blue eyes.

The excitement, it seemed, was contagious, because even staid-and-serious Owen cracked a grin. "That's great visibility for the storefront, too. If folks like the pies"—he paused to give up a look that translated to *and who wouldn't?* —"then they'll come out to the farm for more."

"I can help make the display," Emerson offered from across the tent, immediately looking sheepish as Marley's jaw dropped. "Fine, so I was eavesdropping. But if you want to do a special price for a pie and a watermelon and, say, a dozen ears of corn, I can make a sign right now."

"Oh!" Scarlett piped in, making her way over from the back of the tent, and jeez, did anyone in this family not eavesdrop? "I can snap a few pictures of the display once Emerson gets it all set up, and—wait, wait!" She turned to rummage through a bag she'd tucked nearby, pulling out a red and white checkered tablecloth with a triumphant grin —"I brought this to use as a background for some new photos for the website. We can go with a whole picnic theme, and I can upload the shots on social media right when the gates open. Fourth of July special!"

Marley blinked, unsure how her sorta-maybe idea had just exploded into a brand-new promotion. But then Cate chimed in, too, and Marley couldn't help but give in to the excitement beginning to buzz through her veins.

"I've got a box of those single-serve plastic containers in my trunk. We can even divide a pie or two up and sell them by the slice. People can dig into a piece right now for some instant gratification, then grab a whole pie to take home for sharing."

"Ohhh, that is a good idea," Marley said. She rocked back on the thick heels of her motorcycle boots and waited for Owen to tell everyone to get moving, to delegate any other tasks that might need to be done in order to get things set.

But he didn't. Instead, he simply looked at her. Her confusion must've been obvious—Lord knew she had enough *whaaaa?* winging through her to fill an industrial-sized dump truck—because then he gently said, "You're the manager, remember?"

"Oh." *Oh.* A warmth spread through her, one that had damn little to do with the sun rising higher in the sky overhead. "Okay. As long as you guys think it's a good idea, then let's do it."

She paused for a minute to confer with her brothers about the best pricing strategy, then passed the information on to Emerson, who was already working with Scarlett to get the display set up.

"Here, wait," Eli said, nearly dropping a crate of pickling cucumbers to the concrete as he rushed to the front of the tent. "Let me pick that watermelon up. You're not supposed to be lifting anything heavy," he reminded Scarlett.

She threw her head back and laughed, long and loud. "Eli, please. I've been carrying a watermelon around for the last two months." She gestured to the rounded curve of her belly. "This kid is going to be a linebacker, I swear to God."

Still, she let Eli pick up the watermelon and place it on the display table. Not that Marley would bet he'd have given her any choice in the matter even if she'd argued. That whole stubborn thing really *did* run in their blood. Grinning, Marley turned toward the back of the tent to make sure all of the specialty produce from the greenhouse had made it out of the truck and onto the tables.

And nearly ran smack into Tobias.

"Oh!" The clipboard that had been between her fingers clattered to the pavement, her balance threatening a serious labor strike. Tobias reached out to stabilize her, and even though his grip on her upper arms was just enough to keep her from toppling over, the contact made Marley's throat squeeze. For a beat, they stood locked in the moment, her unable to move and him holding her steady, and oh God, oh God, oh God, she seriously couldn't breathe.

"Easy, there," Tobias said, dropping his hands but not his gaze. "Sorry 'bout that. I didn't mean to sneak up on ya."

"What are you doing here?"

Okay, so the words escaped with far less grace than they could've, to the point that Owen flinched, clearly able to hear the conversation from the spot where he stood a few paces away, by the display of heirloom tomatoes.

If Tobias noticed her abruptness—or, more to the point, cared—he didn't show it. "I was up early. Old habits, and all. Had breakfast at Clem's, and figured I'd make the trip to see how y'all were farin'."

Marley crossed her arms in reply, as if the move would help calm the absolute ruckus going on in her rib cage. Just as she was about to make an excuse and blaze a fast path to anywhere other than right here, Owen stepped closer, blocking her in.

"Everything's going without a hitch," he said. "As a matter of fact, Marley just came up with a really great idea to help promote some of the biggest sellers at the storefront."

The deliberateness of how he'd trailed off made it obvious that he wanted her to dish up the details. But this whole family-business thing wasn't what she'd signed on for. God, she should've known better than to agree to work at the market, money or no.

The farm belonged to Tobias, and to her brothers. This wasn't the place for her.

It *couldn't* be.

"The idea was no big deal. Anyway, I really should go finish this up." Marley bent to pick up the clipboard at her feet, firming her shoulders as an added and-I-mean-it as she stood.

Tobias paused, just for a second before nodding. "Of course. It's...real good to see you here, helpin' out."

"Owen's paying me, and it's just a one-time thing." She managed to push the words past her lips even though they felt like they'd been made of dust, fragile and ready to fly apart. Gripping the clipboard extra tight to accommodate her sweaty palms, she measured her footsteps to the back of the tent—*one, two, three, shaky inhale, four, five, six, weak exhale*—but, damn it, Owen followed closely behind.

"You really can't cut him a little slack?" he asked, canting his voice low enough to keep the conversation from reaching the spot where Tobias now stood, talking with Emerson and Cate by the newly forming display.

Marley ignored the sheen of sweat forming on her forehead and between her shoulder blades. "No."

Owen swore, harshly enough to draw Hunter's attention. Great. Just what she needed was for this to become a family affair.

"Jesus, Marley," Owen bit out, his gray eyes flashing beneath the brim of his baseball hat. "When are you going to stop punishing him for something that happened twenty-five years ago?"

"I'm not..." Marley's heart raced, her words slamming around in her head like a car crash, and oh God, she couldn't see, couldn't think, couldn't *breathe*. "You know what, this was a mistake. I don't belong here."

She turned to go, or maybe, more accurately, to run. But Hunter stepped in, dividing a look between her and Owen. "Okay, both of you. Just hang on a second. Please?"

His voice was so calm, so even and right there, grounded in front of her, that Marley managed to inhale, just enough.

"This isn't the time or place for this conversation. I'm not saying it isn't important, or that it doesn't need to happen," Hunter added, the flicker of intensity lurking in his stare telling her that he wasn't thrilled about her exchange with Tobias, either. "But we're less than a half an hour from those gates opening on one of the busiest days of the year, and we've got to focus on what's in front of us. Marley, you worked real hard to organize things today. Obviously, you're upset. But it'd be a shame if you didn't see the market through."

She closed her eyes, torn. No, she didn't want to get all gather-'round-the-campfire with anyone, especially Tobias, but she had worked hard, and the fact remained that she was desperate for money.

Still... "I think I just maybe need a second."

"Okay," Hunter said. "Why don't you take a walk? There's a nature trail over there that winds the perimeter of the park, and it's pretty secluded. There are benches, too, if you just want to sit."

Marley blinked and refocused, looking at Owen. She'd agreed to run things, and he was paying her, which technically made him her boss for the day. At this point, he might not want to let her stick around.

Finally, after a minute that lasted for at least an hour, he nodded. "We've only got the display and a few small, last-minute things left to do. We'll be okay if you need a break. But Marley?" he added, his voice serious enough to send a chill over her skin despite the warmth beginning to bloom in the air around them.

"One way or another, we *are* going to talk about this. Soon."

16

It was official. Greyson was so sleep deprived and work-worn, he was flat-out seeing things. That was the only explanation for the fact that he'd swear on his uncle Steve's grave that Marley Rallston was making a beeline through the Camden Valley pavilion. But no, after a series of head shakes and a whole lot of WTF, Greyson realized Marley was, in fact, right here in the flesh at the farmers' market and striding toward the entrance to the nature path less that forty feet to his left.

And from the hunch of her shoulders to the shock of sadness on her face, she looked rattled as hell.

Instinct drove his legs to action before the rest of him had a clue he'd move so much as a single muscle. "I'll be right back," he said to his farmhands Clint and José, both of whose brows traveled up, but both of whom also knew better than to put their thoughts to words. Grabbing the prettiest peach he could find from the crate in front of him, Greyson made his way toward the path. The trail itself had recently been paved into a neat ribbon of asphalt so joggers and cyclists and parents with strollers could navigate things with better ease, enjoying the shade from the trees that lined both sides of the path and provided a thick canopy of leaves overhead. Benches had been scattered along the trail at strategically chosen spots, some scenic, others secluded. It didn't take long to find Marley sitting on the bench farthest from the path, and whoa, the tension rolling off of her carried the same sort of charge as the August air, right before a thunderstorm.

Lucky for him, he knew just how to ride out nasty fucking weather. "You know," he said, softly because even though he knew she was too guarded not to have seen him coming, he didn't want to run the risk—however small—of scaring the crap out of her. "I didn't realize you were gonna make this challenge to enjoy small-town living so easy on me."

"Who says I'm doing anything of the sort?"

Her only movement was the slight lift of one dark, slender brow toward her tousled hairline, but Greyson had made do with less. "I do," he said, gesturing to the empty half of the bench in a wordless request.

She nodded and slid over a few inches, her cutoffs shushing over the wooden planks beneath her. "Okay, I'll bite. How am I making it easy for you to win the challenge?"

"You showed up in one of the best places around without me having to drag you, and you look like you could eat."

Without waiting for her to work up some smartass retort, he tossed the peach at her in a slow, deliberate pop fly, which she caught with both ease and surprise.

"What's this?" Marley asked, and he'd be willing to bet all of the day's profit that her smile was as unexpected to her as it was pretty to him.

"That there is the best damn peach you're ever gonna

taste. And it's just the first of about a billion reasons to love living around here."

"Bold words," she said, but she was still smiling.

And God help him, he wanted her to stay that way. "True words. Go on and try to prove me wrong."

"You're so—" Whatever wildly creative adjective she'd been fixing to pin him with stopped short on her lips as soon as she got the peach close enough to her face to smell it, and a dark bolt of satisfaction speared clean through Greyson's belly as she drew in a deep breath, argument forgotten. Her blue eyes wide, Marley sank her teeth into the fruit, and the sound that left her was something he was sure his mind would torture him with all damned day.

"Oh, my God," she murmured, taking another bite, then another.

Christ, she was gorgeous. "Told you," he said, hearing the gravel in his voice and not caring if she heard it, too.

Marley seemed pretty caught up in eating, though. She licked her thumb, and Christ, he was so not going to make it out of this without the bluest balls this side of the Mississippi. "Okay, fine," she said, taking one more bite and conceding with a shrug. "It's a really good peach."

"The best," Greyson corrected, and although she rolled her eyes, for once, she didn't argue.

"The best."

He gave her a minute to keep eating so she could enjoy her peach without interruption. Finally, when she got down to the pit, he asked, "So, do you want to tell me why you're here at the farmers' market? Not that I'm bitching, necessarily—like I said, you're making the challenge easy on me by showing up." He paused here to dish up a smirk. Old habits, and all; plus, he liked the flush it sent over Marley's cheeks. "But I'll admit, I am a little surprised to see you."

"I'm here to help my brothers," she said, and Greyson let go of a soft laugh.

"You sound as if you'd rather be fried in a skillet."

"That's a vivid image. Also, gross," Marley said. But she laughed, too, so he pushed his luck a little farther.

"You got the idea, didn't you? Anyway, it's not really like you to do anything you don't want to. So, you must've wanted to help."

She nodded, turning toward him just enough that he could feel the heat of her bare knee near his, even through his jeans. "At first, I agreed to help because Owen said he'd pay me. But then..."

Understanding crashed into him all at once. He knew that look. Hell, he'd lived and breathed it every day of his life. "You like it. Don't you."

"I think I'm good at it," she said, that honesty that he found so goddamned attractive spilling right out of her with ease that made him momentarily envious. "And yeah, it was kind of nice to do something more challenging and fun than folding clothes. It feels easy without *being* easy, you know?"

Good Lord, did he. "So, what's the problem, then?"

She sighed, pressing her lips together, but ultimately didn't fight the words. "I just have a hard time with the family part of it. Cross Creek belongs to Tobias, and I...don't."

"You really do have a thing for pushing your old man away, don't you?"

Marley's shoulders stole around her spine, hard and fast, but Greyson was faster. Reaching out, he put his fingers on her forearm, and the touch—benign as it was—stopped her short just as surely as if he'd put his foot in a door she'd been aiming to slam.

"Hey, I get it," he said, because fuck, he *really* did. And something told him that right now, in this moment, Marley needed to know it, too. "My old man and I are like matches and gasoline, remember? But here's the thing about that. Whittaker Hollow might be his farm, but that doesn't mean I can't love it there, or be good at running the place."

"It doesn't?" she asked.

One corner of Greyson's mouth edged up in a sardonic smile. "I sure as shit hope not, because I do it every day. Look, Cross Creek might belong to your father, and y'all might not get along."

She tensed under his fingers, and that was a story she clearly wasn't ready to tell. Still, he held firm. "But if you like workin' at the farm, if that feels right to you? Then you should do it. Even if it's temporary. Even if it feels right to him, too, and the farm belongs to him. Having that in common with him doesn't mean you've got to be his daughter. Not unless you want to be."

For a minute, they sat there, his fingers resting firmly on her forearm and the breeze rustling the thick curtain of leaves overhead, sending flashes of sunlight down in tiny golden bursts. Finally, she nodded, slipping from his grasp, although not unkindly.

"I should get back to work. Thanks. For the peach and...everything."

"No problem." Greyson waited until she'd planted her motorcycle boots onto the path before adding, "And Marley?

"Yeah?" She turned just as he dialed his smirk to ten, and oh yeah, he was never going to get tired of that blush.

"Meet me at the shelter tonight at eight thirty. Wear decent shoes, and bring a sweatshirt."

"Why?" she asked, brows tugged low in confusion.

"I promised to show you why Millhaven is so great, didn't I?"

Marley nodded. "You did."

"The peaches are just the beginning, darlin'. I'll have you eating those words of yours yet."

"AND A DOLLAR forty-seven is your change. Happy Fourth of July."

Marley handed first the money, then the pie/corn/watermelon package to the woman in front of her, her smile as real as the ache in her muscles. She'd been moving pretty much non-stop ever since arriving back at Cross Creek's bright red canopy tent three hours ago, her belly full of peaches and her heart oddly at ease. Yes, she'd been thrown by Tobias's unexpected presence this morning, and yes again, she had reasons for needing to keep him at arm's length—*good* ones, even if her brothers could never understand them. But Greyson had been right.

She could still work here—she could still be good at this—and not be her father's daughter. It was only temporary, anyway. A faster means to a necessary end.

Marley would make sure of that.

Finally grabbing a chance to exhale, she surveyed the break chart she'd drawn up at o-dark-thirty this morning. Scarlett had already headed back to Millhaven to edit some of the photos she'd taken and update Cross Creek's website, so that left six of them for the break schedule.

"Hey, Emerson," Marley said, and the redhead looked over from where she was sitting at a card table by the open back of the box truck, filling cardboard containers with the last of the blueberries they had in reserve. "Are you okay? It's pretty hot out here." In truth, it was probably only a few degrees shy of hell, and her sister-in-law's MS had flared something awful in last week's heat wave. "Do you want the first break?"

"Nah." Emerson shook her head and smiled. "It's nice and shady over here, and you gave me all the easy jobs today."

"I don't think any of the jobs here are easy," Marley said, her back muscles squeezing in a great, big *hell no, they're not* as Emerson laughed.

"Fair enough. But I promise, when I need a break, I'll let you know. In the meantime, Cate can go first. She's been busting her butt almost as hard as you have this morning."

"Okay." Passing cashier duty to Emerson, Marley went to go give Cate a break. They *had* been warp-speed busy so far, with the baked goods and produce flying out of the tent and into customers' waiting hands at a steady clip since the gates had opened. She had to admit, it felt a hell of a lot better to be busy here, selling vital, genuine products to folks who really seemed invested in what they were buying, than to try and sell overpriced clothes to a bunch of women who didn't need them and didn't seem to care.

"Hey, Cate. Break time," Marley said, biting back a laugh as Cate sagged in relief.

"Oh, thank *God*. Not that I don't love everyone's enthusiasm for apple pie and sugar cookies," she added quickly. "But I don't think we've ever been so busy." She paused. "You're sure you want to send me on a break?"

Marley nodded. "I'm sure. First of all, you've earned it, and if you tip over, Owen will be pissed. Secondly, I factored in peak hours when I made the break schedule. We should be about to hit a lull."

"Huh, that was really smart. Things *do* usually get a bit quieter just before lunch time," Cate agreed. "Okay, I'm off, then. I'm dying for some of Harley Martin's pulled pork barbecue, and I promised Daisy I'd stop by her tent to see how things are going. She's got this new mint and eucalyptus massage lotion, and—"

"Since you live with my brother, I'm going to stop you riiiiiiight there," Marley interjected. "But if you could check with Daisy on whether or not she makes homeopathic bleach for my ears, that would be awesome."

Cate laughed, then bit her lip in a sorry-not-sorry sort of way. "I'll be back in twenty minutes."

"Have fun," Marley called out as Cate moved through the steady crowd. She took a quick visual inventory of the pies and quick breads and cookies on display, making sure there were a few samples of blueberry pie front and center before kneeling down to grab another couple of items to replenish the supply on the table.

"Well, well," came an all too familiar, all too sexy voice from over her head. "It pains me a little to say it, what with y'all being our biggest competitor, but that blueberry pie looks right delicious."

Marley's pulse became its own thing, wild and enticing as it beat against her ears. "That's because it is," she said, standing to look Greyson right in those black-coffee eyes that made her belly flip. "Would you like to try some?"

"Why not?" He took the small plastic cup from her outstretched fingers. She waited impatiently for him to take a bite, pride making her smile a foregone conclusion.

"Not bad for a city girl, huh?" She backpedaled slightly, since it was only fair. "I mean, Cate made the crust, which is the hard part, of course, but—"

Greyson cut her off with a shake of his head. "It's really good."

"The best?" she teased, and he laughed.

"The only way it'd be better is if you'd made it with peaches."

Marley's mouth watered, her brain instantly spinning with new ideas. "You're biased."

"So are you." With just enough of a smile on his mouth to be suggestive of all the things he could do with it, he lifted his chin at her. The gesture was oddly intimate, like an inside joke only the two of them got, and damn it, Marley was running out of reasons not to like him.

A *lot*.

The soft sound of a throat being cleared dropped her back to reality, blushing all the way. Marley looked at the woman standing beside Greyson, taking in her kind face and no-nonsense blond-gray ponytail, but she was certain they hadn't met.

Greyson, however, seemed to know her well. "Hey, Doc. How are you today?"

"I'm well, Greyson. Thanks for asking. You?"

He slid a look at Marley out of the corner of his eye and grinned. "Can't complain."

"Well. That's good to hear," the woman said, her smile spilling into her tone. She looked at Marley expectantly. But rather than waiting for an introduction, she extended her hand. "And you must be Marley Rallston. I'm Ellen Sanders. It's nice to finally meet you."

Ah, Millhaven's town doctor. She was Emerson's boss, and each of Marley's brothers had mentioned the woman on occasion in casual conversation. Doc Sanders was, like everyone in Millhaven other than Marley, it seemed, a long-time local. Of course she'd probably heard all the whispers and rumors about Marley's return to town months ago.

"Yeah, I...don't get out too much," Marley said, semi-apologetically.

"I understand," Doc Sanders said, so genuinely that Marley believed her. "I was very sorry to hear of your mother's passing."

The unexpected mention throbbed through her like a bruise, but she resisted the urge to flinch. It was no secret that her mother had died. Plus, the doctor's kindness was plain to see. "Thank you."

"I didn't know her well, but I do remember her. She was a lovely woman." Doc Sanders paused for a gentle smile before saying, "At any rate, I just wanted to say hello. I had a big breakfast at Clementine's Diner, so I'm going to get my steps in before I head to the parade."

Marley's brain caught up to her mouth, which had been working—or, more to the point, *not* working—on a delay from all the emotion crowding through it. "Wow. Clementine's must've been busy this morning."

"I'm sorry?" Doc Sanders asked, looking self-conscious all of a sudden.

"It's just that Tob—" Marley stopped herself short. Where her father had eaten breakfast was none of her business. Whether or not he'd talked with the doctor while he'd been there? Even less. "You know what, forget I mentioned it. It was nice to meet you, Dr. Sanders."

"Oh, just Doc," the woman said, smiling at both Marley and Greyson as she turned toward the milling crowd. "Stay cool in this heat, you two."

Greyson lifted a brow at Marley, fixing her with a lopsided grin. "That might not be too likely, all things considered."

"You're awfully sure of yourself," she said, letting just a little bit of sass touch the words despite the way her pulse pressed harder in her veins at his closeness, the anticipation that they'd get even closer. Touch. Kiss.

More.

His grin turned to a laugh, as if he felt it, too. And *liked* it. "Yes, ma'am, I am. Now, where were we?"

"How about nowhere near my sister?"

The butterflies in Marley's stomach turned to stone, all of them dropping in unison. She wasn't about to make apologies for anything she did, thought, or said, and that included flirting with Greyson. Still, she knew how her brothers were, about her *and* about Greyson. This was going to tumble downhill if she didn't play it right. Especially with the brother in question.

"Eli." She pressed up to her tiptoes to make sure she was as close to eye level with him as she could get. "Greyson and I do community service together. I'm not sure keeping our distance from each other is realistic."

Eli remained unmoved, both literally and emotionally, standing beside her like a very pissed off mountain. "Working together is one thing," he said, not moving his eyes from Greyson, who was—shocker—standing just as firm and returning the favor of her brother's glare. "But...*that*"—he broke off to swing a finger between her and Greyson—"is another."

"So what if it is?" Greyson drawled. "Your sister's all grown up, Cross. You might not have noticed, but she's pretty capable of taking care of herself."

Shock cemented Marley into place. The hiccup gave Eli the advantage, though, and oh, he took it.

"Greyson," he said, the word slipping through his teeth. "This is over the line. Even for you."

Marley planted her hands over her hips. She was right freaking *here*, for God's sake! But before she could knock them both over the head for being chest-thumping Neanderthals and welcome their asses to the twenty-first century, Greyson broke his stare from Eli's and turned it to her.

"Why don't you ask your sister what she wants?"

So many answers. God, there were *so* many answers to that question. Finally, she went with, "I want you two to knock it off. That's what I want."

"Marley," Eli said by way of protest, and Greyson's fingers slid to fists at his sides. A look formed on his face, his stubbled jaw hardening like granite, the meanness of a retort that would no doubt spark a brawl clearly coming together in his mind.

But then he met her eyes, giving up a curt nod before stepping back. "Okay. I'll see you later," he said, turning to walk away.

"That guy is a serious dick," Eli muttered, and Marley recovered her wits enough to make an impolite noise.

"Were you honestly expecting a cup of cocoa and a warm hug, Eli? You were a jerk first. A *big* one."

"Eli was a jerk?" Hunter asked from a few feet away, and Eli crossed his arms, lowering his voice to keep their conversation from reaching the ears of anyone passing by.

"Greyson Whittaker was hitting on Marley. So, in a word? Hell yes."

Hunter let loose with a rare and shockingly harsh frown. "That's two words, dude. Both of them called for. Greyson *hit* on you?" he asked, lifting his brows at Marley.

Oh, for the love of… "Contrary to popular belief, I am an adult, and yes, I just so happen to be in possession of a vagina," she pointed out icily. "Is it that shocking that someone might show interest in me?"

Although both brothers had momentarily startled at the mention of Marley's anatomy, Hunter recovered first.

"It's not that. Look"—he blew out a breath while Eli

resumed mumbling a few more obscenities under his own—"I know this isn't what you're used to, but Millhaven's a small town, and you're our little sister. There are a couple of unspoken rules a person just doesn't break."

"And flirting with me is one of them?" Good grief! How was a girl with older brothers supposed to get laid around this place?

"It is for Greyson," Eli said. "I mean it, Marley. He's just bad news."

"He also happens to be right," Marley said, and *finally*, something that got both of their attention.

"Beg your pardon?" Eli asked, turning toward her on the pavement.

She stepped right in to meet him. "Contrary to what the two of you apparently think, I'm perfectly capable of handling myself. And that includes around a guy like Greyson Whittaker."

Even if that guy was turning out to be nothing that he seemed, and she was the only one who knew it.

17

There were fifty different reasons this was a bad idea. The part of Greyson that enjoyed self-preservation knew it—had listed them all with enthusiasm, in fact, in an effort to keep the rest of him out of his truck and off the path to the shelter. Despite her arguments to the contrary, Marley was a Cross. She may not have been born into her name like her brothers, but anyone even halfway paying attention could see how right she'd looked at that farm stand today, selling sweet corn and grinning like it was Christmas morning as she'd handed out samples of blueberry pie. Greyson might not know the root of their family rivalry, but that didn't mean it didn't exist, or that it wouldn't be an issue, both with Marley's brothers and his old man. Her brothers, he could handle, although it'd probably sting a bit when they tried to kick the crap out of him. His father, though? Already made Greyson's life difficult, and that was on their good days. Add to it that Marley was dead-set on leaving town as soon as she could, and that her chances of return hovered somewhere around nil, and yeah, come to think of it, he might even be lowballing it at fifty reasons why going to meet her tonight was a spectacularly bad plan.

But there was one stunningly good reason that it wasn't, and that gorgeous brunette, so fierce and full of chin-up, eyes-blazing attitude, yet selfless enough to sneak groceries to a family she didn't know, was going to be waiting for him, because he'd asked her to.

Marley trusted him. She needed something good to get past that sadness in her eyes.

And even though no one had ever accused him of being good in his life, Greyson was going to give it to her.

He pulled into the gravel driveway and parked, a thread of shock moving through his belly as he realized Marley had already arrived. She leaned against her car, her long, jeans-clad legs kicked out in front of her and crossed at the ankles as easy as Sunday morning, her smile a perfect mix of brass and wide-open beauty, and fuuuuuuck, this was the best bad idea he'd ever cooked up.

"You're early," she said, watching him as he walked around the front of his truck.

"You got here first," he pointed out, and she pressed her lips together, her expression as close to shyness as it would probably ever get.

"Well...yeah." Pushing off her car, Marley took a few steps forward, cutting the distance between them on the path in half. "So, how come we're here, exactly? I know you're supposed to be showing me how great Millhaven is and all, but I'm already pretty well acquainted with the shelter."

Greyson nodded, looking around the dusk-tinged front yard, where fireflies were just starting to make themselves known in the tall grass along the tree line. "I know. I told you to meet me here so you wouldn't get lost. There are no street signs where we're headed, plus"—he darted a glance at the Toyota—"I wasn't sure your car would make it."

"I'll have you know this car has survived a lot," Marley said, the teasing smile on her lips making it to both her eyes and her tone.

He took the challenge like a shot of whiskey, quick and sharp and so damn good. "Right. Including Y2K."

She laughed. "Your truck looks just as old."

"There are a couple of things you should know about country living," Greyson said, holding his arm out, then forcing himself to focus when the bare skin of Marley's forearm slid over his as she took it. "One is that you don't blaspheme a man's truck."

"Oh, I'm not speaking ill. I actually kind of like a ride with character."

"It was my uncle's."

The admission slipped out, but it didn't feel weird to tell her the little-known truth. In fact, Greyson missed talking about the guy.

"Steve, right?" she asked after he'd ushered her up into the passenger seat, then climbed behind the wheel to start the engine and pull out of the drive.

"Yeah. He and my old man were only a year apart in age. My uncle never got married or had kids of his own, so he and I were close. I always felt kind of lucky, like I had two dads."

Marley processed this for a minute, the wind from the cracked-open windows stirring her hair around her shoulders. "Was he close with your father, too?"

"In their own way," Greyson said slowly. He supposed they must have been—they ran the farm together, and that was no easy task—but... "My old man is tough to read, and he doesn't talk much. To be truthful, I always got the feeling there was something weird between him and my uncle, like an argument they never had out loud. But the three of us got on pretty good. At least, as far as the farm was concerned."

"You must miss him." This, Marley aimed at the passenger window, beyond which the leaves of the passing trees and the fields beyond them were all fading into the gray and purple shadows.

He gave her the truth, plain and simple, the only way he knew how. "I was twenty when he died. Not a day goes by that I don't think about him, though."

"You don't sound sad about it," Marley said, with far more awe than accusation.

"I'm not. Well, not anymore," he amended. Directly after the murder, he'd grieved and raged simultaneously, his only happiness coming from working the farm and the day the man who had killed his uncle had received a life sentence with no possibility for parole.

Greyson took a breath and continued. "It took me a long time to realize it, but feeling sad isn't what my uncle would've wanted. He had a great life, doing what he loved, and I got to be a part of that. Did he die too soon? Yeah." The man had been just shy of his fifty-third birthday, for Chrissake. "But he would've been hoppin' mad to know I was sad every time I thought about him. So now, even though sometimes it's tough, I make myself remember the good things."

"And that works?" Marley asked, her voice barely above a whisper as it rode the breeze inside the truck.

"Most of the time. But we're only human, you know? Sometimes, we're gonna be sad no matter what they would've wanted."

They rode for another few minutes in comfortable quiet until they reached the turnoff Greyson knew like a signature. Most folks had no idea it was anything other than a short, bumpy dirt road leading to a dead end. But he knew better than anyone how deceiving looks could be, and he navigated the path until it stopped, his headlights illuminating the tall grass in front of them for only a second before he cut them off along with the engine.

"Still trust me?" he asked. His heart beat faster in his chest when Marley turned to look at him through the shadows that had deepened to near nighttime, then faster still when she nodded.

"I do."

"Then let's go."

They got out of the truck, and her eyes must've adjusted to the lack of light, because she realized the scope of their surroundings. "We're in the middle of a field. There's nowhere *to* go."

Greyson lifted a hand. "How about up?"

"You're serious," Marley said, her face tilted to take in the water tower about fifty yards in front of them.

"I am serious," he agreed. A thought occurred to him, one he probably should've had before now. "You're not afraid of heights, are you?"

"No. It's the falling to my death part I'm not crazy about."

"I wouldn't let that happen." His heart slammed suddenly with a fierceness he hadn't expected, and he tugged in a deep breath to counter it. "Anyway, I've been up there a thousand times. It's not as bad as it looks, and when we get to the top, you'll see why it's worth it." Greyson checked the time on his cell phone, and yeah, perfect.

"If you say so," Marley said, although she didn't hesitate to follow him across the field. Their boots shushed through the grass, the outlines of the water tower and the trees lining the road beyond it coming into sharper focus as his eyes grew used to the dark more fully. Greyson was aware of Marley right behind him, the way she stepped carefully but with purpose, the smell of her skin, like some dark, exotic flower you'd see in a travel brochure. His cock twitched at the thought (well, probably at her nearness *and* the thought. God, how could she be so fucking close without touching him?) but he didn't stop until they got to the ladder built in to the support beam on the north side of the water tower.

Greyson turned to look at her, and yep. Still goddamn gorgeous. "Okay." He cleared his throat. "This isn't rocket science, but it's not something you want to fool around with, either. Hold on to the rails on either side, here"—he broke off to grab the steel bars running the length of the beam on either side—"concentrate on your footing, and take the step that's in front of you."

She didn't seem the type to back down from a challenge, but having her freeze partway up wouldn't do either of them any favors, so he added, "I'll be right behind you the whole way, and we can go down any time you want if you change your mind. No big deal. Cool?"

"Mmm hmm." Marley tied her hoodie around her waist. She assessed the railings, then the ladder trailing upward, both with shrewd stares. With surprisingly steady moves, she began to climb, and Greyson followed, step by step, hand over hand. They reached the platform that formed a ring around the bottom of the tower's reservoir a few minutes later. A shocked breath came out of her, as if she'd just now realized they'd be up this high, and damn, it was one hell of a turn-on that instead of being scared, she only seemed proud that she'd made the climb.

"Wow." She placed her hands on the support railing lining the platform, a sound length of steel that came in at her lower chest, with another two spanning at even intervals below.

"Forty feet," he said by way of agreement.

Marley tipped her ear toward her shoulder, the gears and inner workings of her brain clearly clacking away. "But it's dark out. I mean, it *is* kind of a rush to be up this high, but there's not a whole lot to actually see. How is this supposed to show me the awesomeness of Millhaven?"

"No one's ever accused you of being very patient, have they?"

At her snort in reply—the one Greyson had fully anticipated—he gestured at the platform in a wordless *have a seat*. "Don't worry. I didn't bring you all the way up here for nothing. As a matter of fact, right now, you happen to be in the best seat in the house."

"Really?" Marley asked, her doubt ringing through like church bells. Still, she sat, her back against the reservoir and her legs kicked out in front of her. A breeze stirred, not strong enough to make the tower so much as budge, sturdy thing that it was. Still, the cooler air made her shiver, and Greyson reached out to help her into her hoodie, wrapping the unzipped edges around her snugly as he looked up.

"Really."

Maybe it was providence, or possibly just dumb fucking luck. Whichever was to blame, for once, timing was on Greyson's side. A glittering flash of pink and purple light burst in the sky overhead, a loud pop and sizzle quickly following, and Marley's lips parted on a soft gasp.

"Oh! *Fireworks*."

He chuckled. "It's the Fourth of July, remember? They set them off from over there." Greyson pointed to a tiny cluster of lights in the near distance. "Everyone usually watches them from the park at the end of Town Street, but honestly? I think this is better."

Another starburst bloomed in the sky, the gold and white sparkles dim compared to the light in Marley's eyes. "It's not better. It's..." She waited until the darkness folded back around them to whisper, "Perfect."

Something moved in his chest, primal and deep. "I really want to kiss you right now."

"Okay," she said, leaning in close enough for her hip to press firmly against his, and he clung to his very last shred of logic.

"You know that if I do, things are going to get complicated, right?"

Another firework lit the sky, chasing the shadows. "Only if we let them."

Greyson's breath slipped out unsteadily, pushed hard by his slamming heart. "You know that if I do, I won't want to stop."

Marley's mouth curled into a smile he wanted on every last inch of his skin. "Okay."

"Marley—"

Her fingers flew up, pressing over his lips and stopping his words cold. "Greyson, stop talking," she said.

Then she replaced her fingers with her mouth, and for once in his life, he did exactly as he'd been told.

18

Marley knew she'd been flirting with trouble the second she'd seen Greyson pull up beside her at the shelter, and she'd damn sure known it when he'd told her their destination was forty feet in the air at the top of a water tower. But where most people would've run screaming, or at the very least forked over an unyielding "hell no" when faced with the prospect of doing something dangerous *with* someone dangerous, Marley hadn't thought twice.

She'd wanted to feel awake. Alive. Real in a way that she hadn't for far too long. And way up here, forty feet in the night sky with Greyson's lips on hers and the promise of so much more to come?

She didn't just feel alive. She felt *right*.

Reaching out to haul her in close, Greyson took the kiss from zero to oh-God-hot in less than a second. Marley wrapped her arms around him right back, seating herself deftly in his lap as he pressed his back flush with the reservoir. They were far from the edge of the platform, which was protected by the triple-tiered railing, anyway, so she arched against him, returning the kiss.

"Christ. You are so pretty. Do you know that?" he murmured into her mouth.

She hooked her fingers in his hair, surrendering to one more slide of his tongue over hers before her laugh won out. "You don't have to sweet-talk me. I already told you I want this."

Greyson pulled back, quickly enough to leave her dazed. "You think I'm just sweet-talking you so you'll have sex with me? That I don't mean exactly what I'm saying?"

He swiped a thumb across her bottom lip. A trail of heat followed in the wake of his touch, pinning Marley into place, and her heart thundered in a hard press against her ribs. "No."

Well *that* came out way breathier than she'd intended. She cleared her throat. "I just get that this is a heat of the moment thing. That's all."

"Maybe," Greyson agreed. "But heat of the moment or not, I still do the things that matter right. Speaking of which"—he looked around, just in time for another firework to pop over their heads and light up the hard set of his jaw —"come on."

Marley's surprise made her ask, "Where are we going?" even as she complied by moving out of his lap and pushing herself to standing beside him.

He leaned forward to kiss her, just one hard, fast press of his mouth. "My apartment. As much as I've been dying to have you, I'm not doing it here."

"No?" She lifted one corner of her mouth, just enough to tease him. "I guess there are boundaries you won't push, after all."

Greyson's eyes glittered, black on black in the shadows,

and Marley's breath went still at the sheer intensity on his face. "I would break every goddamn rule in the universe to get inside of you right now. But I mean to fuck you good and proper, which means we'll be needing more comfort and privacy than we've got up here. So, are you coming, or not?"

Oh. *God.* "What are you waiting for?" Marley breathed, hearing the waver in her voice even though she'd meant the reply to be tough. Sassy. "Let's go."

Grinning, he led the way back to the ladder, pausing just briefly to remind her to hold on tight and take each step with care. He lowered himself from the platform first, with her directly behind, and even though the adrenaline she'd felt going up wasn't shy about making a repeat performance in her veins for the trip back down, they arrived on terra firma both safely and quickly enough.

A prickle moved over Marley's skin as Greyson opened the passenger door to his truck to usher her in, then another as he laid his hand next to hers on the center console and pulled out of the field. His fingers inched closer to hers with every bump in the road, hers edging toward his in reply, until his pinky finger slid over hers in the barest suggestion of a touch. Marley swallowed her gasp and echoed the movement back to him, just a whisper of connection, skin against skin. The calluses by the blunt edge of his fingertip gave way to shockingly softer skin above his knuckle, both creating friction with that soft, steady contact. Greyson dragged the side of his pinky slowly over hers, up, then back, then up again, and even though Marley could think of a thousand more overtly sexual things he could do to turn her on, by the time he pulled into the parking lot in front of Millhaven's only apartment complex, her panties were already so damp, she was certain her arousal would be as wildly obvious as the fireworks still bursting in the night sky.

Maybe it was, because Greyson let go of an exhale that bordered on a moan before getting out of the truck. She followed suit, even though his frown said he wasn't happy she hadn't let him go the Southern manners route of coming to collect her. But tonight wasn't about manners.

Tonight was about feeling alive. Hard and deep and as soon as goddamn possible.

As if he'd read her thoughts, he said, "This way," leading her to a door that looked like all the others in the tidy, well-lit row. For a brief moment, Marley wondered why he didn't live on his farm the way everyone else around here did, especially since he so clearly loved the place.

But then they were over the threshold, the door shut behind them, and Greyson had erased the space between their bodies in less time than it took her to whisper his name.

"That's better," he said, the words hot on her skin as he kissed a path down her neck. She tugged at the edges of her hoodie to give him better access—ah, God, if he licked that spot above her collarbone again, she was going to fucking scream, and not in the bad way.

Greyson did her one better, yanking the cotton from her arms and tossing it to the floor, exposing her thin tank top and the hard press of her nipples beneath. "That's better, too. In fact..."

He reached down to grab the hem of his T-shirt and pulled it over his head in one fluid motion. Marley wanted to reclaim the space between them that the move had created. But holy shit, he was *gorgeous*, his work-carved muscles tan and smooth in the low light drifting in past the partially cracked blinds, and she was powerless to do anything other than stare as she drank him in. His tattoo spilled from the top of his shoulder downward, the swirls of black ink hugging his skin all the way to the bend of his elbow, emphasizing the sinews and curves of his biceps and triceps in a way that made Marley want to trace them with her fingers, her tongue. The flat plane of his chest gave way to leanly ridged abs, a trail of dark hair leading downward from just below his navel, and—Marley's breath went tight—the outline of his cock pressed hard against the fly of those perfectly imperfect jeans. Greyson wasn't linebacker huge, and with all the raw intensity rolling from his body and his stare, he wasn't magazine-pretty.

But he *was* leveling her with a smirk that made her thighs tremble, and oh God, she'd never ached so hard to be touched in her life.

"Like what you see?" he asked, his drawl as decadent as sweet cream, and Marley was done messing around. Grasping the edges of her tank top, she lifted until she was bare from the waist up, then flung the thing to meet Greyson's shirt on the floor.

"Yep."

His stare widened for half a second before glinting in the shadows. "You're..."

"Not wearing a bra," Marley confirmed, sending up a brief prayer of thanks for whomever had invented the whole tank top/built-in bra thing.

"Really fucking hot," he corrected, grabbing her hand. They moved through the small living space and past the even smaller kitchen that Marley could just make out in the ambient light from beyond the blinds. Greyson led her through a doorway to what had to be—*yes*—his bedroom, where the fireworks sent glimpses of silvery light past the curtains and over the space. Stopping at the foot of the bed, he turned to face her, his hands resting on the denim at her hips. They didn't stay there, though. The heat between Marley's legs pulsed faster as he unbuttoned her jeans, then faster still as he lowered the zipper. His fingers brushed over her sex, and a noise rose from the back of her throat that she barely recognized as belonging to her.

"I want—"

"I know," Greyson said, pressing closer until his mouth hovered over hers. "I promised to fuck you, good and proper, and I'm a man of my word." He firmed his touch between her thighs as proof. "But we do things a little slower out here in the country. I'll get you where you want to be. But first, you're gonna enjoy the ride."

Unable to trust her voice, Marley just nodded. Greyson lowered her jeans, and she aided the process by kicking out of her boots, letting him undress her until all she was wearing was a pair of dark gray cotton hip-huggers.

"There." He straightened, his fingers trailing up the outside of her arm, her shoulder, her chin. Marley knew he was looking at her closely, taking her in just as she'd done to him a few minutes ago. Rather than feel self-conscious at the fact that not only was she damn near naked, but he was far more dressed than her, she felt bold. Every sweep of those brown-black eyes turned her on more than the one before it, as if she could feel Greyson's stare like a touch, gentle in some places, hungry and deliciously rough in others. His gaze found her breasts, and her nipples instantly tightened, her pulse knocking hard at her throat. Marley watched as his eyes lowered over her belly, dipping over the top of her panties and lingering right where she felt slippery and desperate and *God*, so ready to be touched.

The thought lit like a wildfire inside her mind, and she

slid a hand over her belly, her fingers resting at the top edge of her panties.

"Marley." Greyson's voice was low, all gravel. But the word wasn't a warning, she realized with a start as she saw the look on his face.

It was reverent.

He dropped to his knees, lifting his eyes back to hers. "Show me."

Surprise unfurled in her chest, chased quickly by wicked desire. She didn't hesitate, hooking her thumbs along the sides of her panties and pushing them lower over her hips. Greyson caught them halfway down her thighs and slid them free, looking up at her. Waiting.

So Marley did what he'd told her to. Sweeping her hand between her legs, she circled her index finger over her clit, releasing a moan at the sparks of pleasure moving through her.

Greyson loosened a swear in reply, splaying one hand over her hip to hold her steady. "You are the sexiest goddamn thing I've ever seen."

"Greyson," she murmured, loving how he watched. She widened her stance slightly on the floorboards, pushing her fingers tighter to her core. But as good as it felt, she needed more. "Please. I don't just want to come." Marley looked down to catch his stare. "I want *you*."

Not even one beat passed between when she'd finished speaking and he pressed his mouth to her sex. Her muscles clenched at the intimate contact, at the way his tongue so expertly joined her fingers on her aching clit, and her chin fell forward on her chest.

"*Ah*." Pleasure bolted through her, coming from everywhere. Surrounding her and filling her up. Greyson smiled, a gesture she both saw and felt as his stubble grazed the sensitive skin of her inner thighs.

"You taste even prettier than you look. Now take what you need, darlin'. I've got you."

And he did. After three strokes with her fingers and his tongue working in tandem, he'd memorized her body, giving and taking in flawless rhythm. Marley slid her hands low to deepen their connection, knotting her fingers in his hair. Rocking her hips against him, she rode his mouth, the need in her core pulsing harder with every thrust of his tongue. Desire coiled like a spring, deep in her belly, beckoning. Begging.

And then Greyson closed his lips over her clit, his tongue swirling hard, and she flew apart. Her release rolled through her like thunder, turning the moan in her throat into a broken cry. Marley didn't even try to hold back as her orgasm intensified for one bright second, pulling her muscles taut and her breath to stillness before leaving her in a blissed-out, boneless state. She was vaguely aware of Greyson standing, then wrapping his arms around her shoulders. His nearness felt so simple, yet so vital and purely good, that it reignited the heat inside of her, and she pulled him back toward his bed.

"Come here," she said, and although he chuckled, he stretched out beside her.

"Still bossy, I see."

Marley arched a brow, reaching into the slim space between their bodies to run her hand up his denim-clad thigh. "You're not surprised, are you?"

"Nope." He sucked in a breath when her fingers reached his cock. "In fact, I'd be disappointed if you weren't."

"Ah. Then you'll probably love this."

With a lightning-fast twist of her wrist, Marley had

undone his jeans and yanked them open with clear intent. Slipping her palm under the fabric but over his boxer briefs, she curled her hand around his length and pumped. Once. Twice. A third time—

Greyson cursed. "When you're right, you're right," he said, toeing out of his boots, then taking off his jeans. She made quick work of his boxer briefs as soon as the rest of his clothes were past tense, and oh, she didn't want to wait.

"Condom." She made a move to dig up her own jeans, which at this point were who knew where, although she'd find them *and* the condom she'd tucked into her back pocket in the name of not getting knocked up. But Greyson beat her to it, reaching into the slim drawer on the table beside his bed to produce a condom from its depths. A few economical moves had it exactly where it needed to be, and one more had him kneeling between her thighs.

But Marley had other plans. Hooking one leg around the corded muscles of his waist, she used the leverage to switch their positions on the rumpled bed sheets.

"I'm not the only one who should enjoy the ride," she said, straddling him just below his navel.

His laughter hit her deep, traveling from her chest to her core and tightening everything along the way. "By all means," Greyson said, raising his hips until the head of his cock was pressed against the entrance to her core. *Close, so close.*

"Ladies first."

Marley rocked back at the same time he pushed forward, the movements joining them evenly. Her inner muscles locked at the sudden pressure, making her momentarily breathless and unable to move. Greyson's fingers grasped harder at her hips, his low exhale filling the air between them, and he looked at her, eyes wide open and wild.

"So pretty. You're so goddamned beautiful." He lifted her, ever so slightly, watching her face. Her body. The hot, tight place where he was buried between her legs.

Marley began to move, adjusting to the fullness, then wanting more, fully turned on by watching him watch *her*.

"Greyson." Pressing her shins firmly against the mattress, she anchored her balance, angling herself upright in his lap as he thrust into her from beneath. The change allowed his cock to uncover a spot deep inside of her that made her gasp, and she rocked faster, desperate to chase the sensation.

"Right there," Greyson ground out, his stare as palpable as his touch as he gripped her hips, arching up to fill her faster, again and again. His fingers dug into her even harder, the pleasure/pain of his touch and the near ferocity in his eyes daring her closer the edge. "I've got you, darlin'. Show me how good you feel with my cock inside of you."

The words were like gasoline on the slow burn building inside of her, igniting and exploding all in an instant. Marley stilled, the intensity of her orgasm leaving her powerless to do anything other than *feel*, the pleasure and release combining to wash over her in wave after wave. Greyson remained true to his word, holding her firmly and slowing his movements, until finally, he simply held her steady, still seated in his lap. Gliding a hand from her hip to her cheek, he captured her gaze. It grounded Marley in the moment, bringing her back to her body and the fact that he was still rock hard inside of her, and she leaned forward to kiss him.

"Show me," she said softly. "Show me what *you* need."

The moment stretched out between them, making

Marley's heart flutter. Then Greyson began to move, and the flutter became an all-out gallop. Lowering his hand from her face, he grasped her hips, holding her flush against his lap as he thrust his hips up and down in powerful bursts. Each push grew more urgent, his grip tightening and his expression so intense, it knocked the breath from Marley's lungs. But he'd held on for her, and what's more, she reveled in the fierceness of his ministrations, wanting every dark and dirty second more than the last. She didn't let go, moaning openly when his breath became erratic, harder still when his moan joined with hers. Greyson lifted his hips in one final, punishing thrust, his body going bowstring tight beneath her as he arched into her core with one last shout of her name.

Marley sagged over him, her head finding his shoulder. Their breath sawed out in unison, chest rising and falling rapidly together at first, then slower, deeper. After a minute, they disentangled, and Greyson moved quietly through a door she presumed led to a bathroom. He was only gone briefly before returning to the bed, and even though she knew pretty much anyone else would feel the sort of awkwardness that went with the maiden voyage of a post-coital routine, she didn't.

Instead, she just did what she wanted, slipping her arms around Greyson and letting him pull her all the way under the covers beside him.

19

Greyson smelled wildflowers. To be fair, what he smelled was almost certainly Marley's shampoo, or maybe it was her body lotion, or, Christ, maybe her skin somehow magically smelled like the honeysuckle and jasmine growing untamed and lush around the corn fields on the south side of Whittaker Hollow's property. Either way, he was inhaling the scent of it because Marley was naked in his bed, curled up beside him, and even though he knew her closeness, the way he'd told her things and let her really see who he was, should make him want to push her away, it didn't.

He held her tighter, and holy crap, he was screwed.

Even more fucked up? He didn't care. So he was screwed. The sex had been just short of other-worldly, and he'd meant what he'd said. She was truly beautiful.

Also, a Cross, who just so happened to be saying *sayonara* to the town he loved as soon as her bank account was in the black.

God, he was screwed.

"You okay?" Greyson asked, finally breaking the silence between them.

Marley nodded into his shoulder, the slide of her skin warm and sweet. "Mmm hmm. You?"

"Yeah." Keeping her tight against him with one arm, he reached down with the other to pull the covers over her shoulders, wanting to keep her warm. She settled back in, her voice soft as it curved into his ear.

"You're nothing like what you seem, you know."

Ah, shit. "Right. Like Millhaven's best kept secret," he teased, pressing a kiss to the top of her head.

But she wasn't laughing. "It makes me wonder why you push all the time," she mused. "I mean, I know you said it's because people expect it, and I get that it's hard to prove folks wrong sometimes. But I really like the guy underneath all that bravado. I think other people might like him, too, if you stopped being so prickly and just gave them a chance to see who you are."

Greyson's gut tightened, then dropped. "Anyone ever tell you you're brutally honest?"

Now she laughed. "All the time. But I don't see the point in living my life any other way."

The words traveled directly to his sternum and settled in, good and hard. He thought of how Marley was, how she'd given herself over so fully in bed, taking all the pleasure she'd wanted without caring what it had looked or sounded like. She'd been unapologetically fierce since he'd met her in that jail cell, yet honest with him about the kindness that had landed her there, too. She wasn't afraid to be who she was, and even though Greyson outsized her *and* outmuscled her, the longer he sat there, the more he realized she was the stronger of them.

"Doesn't it scare you to put yourself out there like that?"

he asked, grateful for the shadows in his room that acted as cover. "To let everyone see just who you are, even though they're probably going to judge you?"

Her heartbeat quickened against his rib cage, and it was the only sign of her surprise. "Maybe a little. I mean, I don't go sharing every emotion I own. There are a few things I keep close to the vest. But for most things, it's not worth it to cover them up. I am who I am. No apologies."

"*You* keep things close to the vest." Okay, fine. So it was a deflection of sorts. But seriously, she wasn't the sort to go tight-lipped about...well, anything.

"Sure," Marley said. When Greyson's silence translated to the what-exactly-do-you-not-let-loose-with that was flying through his head, she whispered, "Sometimes I talk to my mom. Not anything huge or earth-shattering, but"—she paused for a shrug—"we always used to fill each other in at the end of the day, so I still talk to her. I've never told anyone I do it, though. I know it sounds kind of weird."

Whether it was the honesty of her words or the fact that she'd given them up to him and only him, Greyson couldn't be certain. But his own truth came shoveling out to meet hers without a second thought. "Please. That's not weird. I talk to my uncle all the time."

"You do?" She lifted her head from his shoulder, propping one elbow on the bed sheets beneath them in order to look at him fully.

And Greyson let her. "Yep. I mean, I don't do it when other people can hear me. Not because I worry that talking to him is crazy," he added. "But my conversations with him are private. No one else needs to hear 'em."

"You don't think it's even the tiniest bit crazy that we talk to people who aren't alive anymore?" Marley asked, but he shook his head.

"Nope. The way I see it, my uncle doesn't need to be here to hear what I've got to say. And I might just be guessing, but I reckon your mom's the same. There's nothing crazy about wanting to keep her in your life."

Marley smiled, slow and sassy and beautiful. "You're not too bad at this whole true colors thing, you know."

Heat flared back to life in his veins, and he hooked his hands under her arms to pull her close. She might be a Cross with one foot out the door for greener pastures, but right now, in this moment, Greyson didn't care.

Right now, in this moment, what they had was enough.

"I'm good at lots of things," he said, his cock twitching against his thigh as her breath caught and her stare glittered on his.

"You want to prove it, sweet talker?"

He flipped her to her back with a laugh. "Why, yes, ma'am. I sure as hell do."

A few hours later, Greyson floated in the no-man's-land between sleep and wakefulness, blissed out of his fucking mind. Scraps of memory filtered lazily past his mind's eye—Marley's chin-up lack of fear at climbing the water tower. The heat of her mouth as he'd kissed her. The shake and shiver of her body as he'd done so much more, then done it again for good measure.

The fact that she was tucked up tight next to him and they'd both fallen asleep, and shit, shit, *shit*!

"Hey," Greyson whispered, his gut panging at having to wake her even though he knew it was necessary. Christ, he'd been an idiot to get this careless.

Marley stirred and gave up a loose, sleep-laced sigh. "What time is it?"

He looked at the clock at his bedside, and ah, hell. "Just after two. I need to get you home."

"Oh," she said, her body going stiff and her voice suddenly loaded with awareness. "Okay. I'll just grab my clothes."

She sucked at hiding her true feelings, and now was no exception. Her disappointment slid right under his skin, and he captured her face to cradle it between his palms.

"Marley." Christ, he could look at her for a month. And wasn't that just some dangerous shit, all by itself. "It's not that I don't want you to stay."

She shook her head. "No, it's cool. We both totally knew what this was going into it, and I don't regret—"

Greyson leaned in to kiss her, hard and fast. It was the only surefire way he knew to grab her attention. "I don't want you to leave. Trust me, I'd like nothin' better than to greet Sunday morning with you, right here like this."

"Okay." Her brows lifted, turning the word into a question. "So, why don't you?"

"Because your..." He caught himself just in time. "Tobias would worry if you stayed out all night, and when I told you I do the things that matter right, I meant it. I know you're an adult," Greyson continued, because if he knew anything about the woman in his arms, it was that she was about to argue. "And that you say you're not a Cross. But you're livin' in his house, and I mean to do right by you. So, yeah. I've got to take you home."

After a pause that felt like an ice age, Marley nodded. "Alright," she said, and he was relieved to see that she meant it.

But as she slid out of his bed and into her clothes, the part of him that backed up his reputation as a selfish bastard already wanted her back.

~

Marley slipped out of her boots on the front porch of the main house and tiptoed her way over the threshold in the dark. The house was perfectly quiet, as if the structure itself was asleep along with everyone else on the property. It had taken her months to get used to how hushed things got around here at night, no city sounds, no sirens or echoes of basslines from the too-loud radios of cars passing by. The quiet *was* kind of nice, though. It gave her the peace to lose herself in thoughts about what she'd do once the debt to the hospital was paid off, or how she could go about getting her version of Cate's pound cake recipe just as dense and buttery as the original.

And now she could add dreaming about what it had felt like to have Greyson's hands on her, and how intently he'd watched her as she'd come undone again...and again...

A soft, yet distinct jingle dropped Marley right back to the reality of the living room. Her feet shushed to a halt, and she knelt down in confusion as Tobias's dog, Lucy, tap-tap-tapped her way across the hardwood floor.

Guess the old girl was a pretty good guard dog, after all. Still... "What are you doing here?" Marley whispered, scratching the dog behind the ears the way Greyson did with all the animals at the shelter. "You never leave Tobias's side."

"You know what they say about old dogs," came a gravelly voice that made Marley's heart fly all the way up her windpipe. "I don't reckon Lucy'll be learnin' new tricks anytime soon."

"Jeez, you startled me!" Marley yelped, clapping a hand over her chest and channeling all of her energy into not tumbling backward onto her ass. Sucking in a breath to counter her slamming pulse, she peered into the shadows, catching the faint outline of the wing chair in the corner where Tobias sat.

"Sorry," he said, the apology genuine and his voice thick with sleep. "I'll admit I dozed off and didn't hear you come in."

Surprise collided with the adrenaline coursing through her veins, making her blurt the first thing that popped into her head rather than making a defensive retreat. "It's the middle of the night. Why aren't you in bed?"

"Well." Tobias paused, but only briefly. "I reckon because you're not in bed."

It was on the tip of her tongue to remind him that she wasn't some high schooler with a curfew, and that he hadn't been there to worry over her whereabouts when she had been. But something stopped the protest short.

Tobias would worry if you stayed out all night...

When Marley had been younger and lived at home, her mother had always said she couldn't truly sleep until Marley had come in for the night. No matter how late she'd decided to stay out with friends. No matter how often she'd texted with an *I promise I'm fine*.

Tobias might not be her father in any sense other than the biological, but Greyson hadn't been wrong. She *was* living in his house. At the very least, she owed him courtesy for that.

"I'm sorry if I kept you up by staying out late. I was"—okay, yeah, she should probably bite her tongue on that one, too—"safe. I just lost track of time."

"Ah. Well, it's good to see you back. You must be tired. I won't keep you," he said, shifting up out of the chair with more effort than it would take most people. "G'night."

Tobias headed not toward the front of the house, but the back, and Marley's brows shot up along with her confusion.

"Aren't you going to bed?" She stood and pointed to the stairs—he seemed exhausted—but Tobias shook his head.

"I was going to make a cup of warm milk first. Helps get me back to sleep, good and sound." He paused. "I could make one for you, too, if you'd like."

Marley shouldn't, she knew. But the offer had seemed to come without the expectation of a share-fest, and anyway, Tobias didn't look entirely steady on his feet. She was already going to be a zombie when the sun came up. Five extra minutes to be sure he got safely to bed wouldn't really hurt.

"Warm milk, huh?" she asked, following him into the kitchen. "Isn't that a myth?"

He flipped the light switch for the single-bulb fixture over the sink, which cast a gold glow through the deep nighttime shadows that had long since blanketed the room. "Could be. But it's never failed me yet."

The circles beneath his eyes suggested he'd seen his fair share of insomnia lately, and the thought made her throat go tight. "Hmm. With a track record like that, how can I say no?"

Tobias smiled, taking two mugs from the cabinet over the coffee maker. Next, he claimed a small saucepan from a shelf beneath the island, then the milk from the fridge, and, lastly, a small dark brown bottle from the pantry.

"You add vanilla extract to it?" Marley asked, mystified.

"Secret ingredient, passed down by my granny Joan," he said. "Better than the honey most folks use. Sometimes I throw in a little bourbon, too—now, that idea was all mine—but I figure for tonight, this'll do."

She couldn't help it. She *wanted* to help it. But instead, she laughed. "Now there's a small-town remedy I can get behind."

Tobias chuckled, the weariness in his blue-gray eyes fading a fraction. He filled the saucepan partway with milk, sight-measuring a splash of vanilla extract in next before swirling them together with a wooden spoon and clicking the burner beneath the saucepan to life.

"You seemed to fit in right nice today at the market, if you don't mind me sayin' so."

Marley crossed her arms over her chest out of instinct. "I guess."

"Hunter said it was one of our best days of the season so far, second only to the Watermelon Festival last month," Tobias continued in that quiet, no-nonsense way of his. "That's quite somethin'. You should be proud."

"Me?" Her mouth fell open. "Why?"

"Why not?" he asked, so nonchalantly that Marley blinked in surprise. "Seems to me you put in more than your fair share today."

"Well, I did, but so did—"

Tobias waved the wooden spoon at her. "Ah, no 'buts'. You did your part of the work, plain and simple. No harm in bein' proud of that."

She opened her mouth to push back by default, but then she closed it with a start.

She'd just cautioned Greyson against pushing so hard, and he'd pointed out—smartly—that she could still be here at Cross Creek and not be her father's daughter. Today had proven it.

Marley might not be able to be part of Tobias's family, or hell, even come close. But her mother wouldn't have begged her to come to Millhaven for nothing, and Greyson had been right.

She didn't have to push so hard to keep the arm's length she needed. She could still do her part and not belong here, like her brothers and their significant others. She and Tobias could be civil—they could hold conversations like this one, even—and it wouldn't make him her father. Her family.

It couldn't.

"I know I've been...kind of difficult these last few months," she started, and after a beat of surprise, Tobias shook his head.

"Your momma passed. Loss like that can hit a person hard."

It occurred to her that he was speaking from experience. Miss Rosemary had been young, only in her thirties when she'd died of breast cancer and left him a widower with three young boys to raise. In the days before she'd died, Marley's mother had told her all about the woman who had been her best friend, although she hadn't spoken much of Tobias. *You'll learn who he is for yourself*, she'd said. At the time, and for a *long* time, Marley had thought she might've meant it as a warning. But sitting here, now, taking in his tired eyes and slumped shoulders, she realized it might have been hopeful.

She swallowed hard. "It can. But I guess I've just been angry that you never tried to find me. I know my mother said she didn't want you to when I was young, but after I turned eighteen, you could have reached out. Called or sent me an email, or *something*. And..."

"I didn't," he agreed. "You're right, Marley. As much as I wanted to honor your mother's wishes when you were a child, I should have done better by you once you were old enough." Taking the saucepan off the burner and quieting the stove, he turned toward her, his expression as serious as it was honest. "I told myself I didn't because it'd disrupt your life, comin' out of the woodwork like that, and that it wasn't fair to you for me to just turn up, like an old penny. But the truth is, I was scared. As hard as that is for this old man to admit."

"You were scared?" Marley echoed. Her heartbeat pushed faster in shock. She'd always assumed he'd been non-committal, so happy with the life he'd cultivated here with his farm and his sons, that he hadn't cared about her, the extra. The outcast. The forgotten child, swept under the proverbial rug.

He nodded, sheepish. "Reckon I was. Thought maybe you wouldn't want to know me. Us. Your momma and I, we weren't..."

"In love with each other. I know," Marley said. Her mother had been graceful with the details, and Marley would spare Tobias the awkwardness of rehashing them. He and her mother had been desperate to erase their grief after Miss Rosemary had died. The woman had begged them both to be happy, to look after one another and comfort each other. Neither of them had expected they'd end up how they had, together for one night, then faced with having a child.

"I told her I'd do right by you both, and I meant it. But leaving town was what she wanted," Tobias said. "I could have fought her harder, but I didn't. And for that, I have regrets."

Marley's heart beat faster, but her words came out steady and calm. "You shouldn't. I come by my stubborn streak honestly, although I'm sure you already know that. She wouldn't have given in. And we were happy." Her eyes burned with a sudden sneak-attack of grief, but still, she said, "I never wanted for anything."

"I'm glad. And I'm glad you're here, now. To be truthful, I thought"—Tobias paused, not as if searching for the words, but as if deciding whether to say them at all—"well, after this mornin', I thought maybe you'd decided you'd had enough of us here and that you'd gone."

"You thought I'd left town without saying goodbye?" Marley asked, stunned.

"You haven't made any bones about not stayin' for good, and you were none too happy when I saw you this morning at the market," Tobias said, dividing the cooling milk between both mugs and handing one over to her. "So, yes. It did cross my mind."

She thought of her brothers, of Cate and Scarlett and Emerson. Of the day she'd spent working with them. The night she'd spent with Greyson.

"I wouldn't do that," Marley said, backtracking as her defenses thumped out a warning against her breastbone. "Not without saying goodbye, I mean. I'm really not staying here in Millhaven. I just, ah. I have a lot of bills to pay from when my mom was sick, so I can't just up and leave yet."

Damn it, now he was looking at her with concern. "That's a lot to carry on your shoulders. If you need help with medical bills, I can—"

"No."

The word leapt out, loaded with sharp corners, and she shook her head in an effort to at least sand the edges down. "She was my mom. My family. The bills are my responsibility, and I refuse to be a burden to you."

"Marley," he started again, but nope. On this, she was absolutely *not* going to budge.

"Tobias, please. I've spent this whole time feeling like an obligation, someone you sent money to every month. If we're going to get to know each other a little before I leave, then I want it to be genuine. No more money." She cradled her mug in her palms, her fingers tightening. "And please don't say anything about it to Owen, Hunter, and Eli. We already sort of get along. I don't want to turn into a charity case."

A minute passed, turning into two, then three. Finally, Tobias said, "You really are your momma's girl. When Lorraine got her head set on somethin', there never was any talking her out of it. I'll keep mum about the debt if that's what you want. But if you change your mind—"

"I won't," Marley said, tacking on, "but thank you for the offer."

"You're welcome." He nodded toward the threshold leading back to the front of the house, his eyes still weary but his words warmer than the milk in her hands. "Now go get some rest, you hear? The sun'll be up before you know it, and tomorrow's a new day."

20

Greyson reached up to wipe the sweat from his brow, fairly certain that Satan's backyard didn't even get this hot in the summertime. Not that he'd trade it—all this sunshine was good for crops. For building dog runs, though?

Not so freaking much.

"Okay," Marley said, bringing the last premeasured board over from what had once been a hulking pile of them in the shed. "This should be it."

Greyson nodded, the sight of her tousled hair and those infernal cutoffs that he both hated and wanted to build a goddamn shrine to not helping to keep him from overheating. "Well, I hope so, because if it's not, then we screwed this thing up somewhere along the way."

She made a noise of doubt, rocking back on the heels of her boots to look at the dog run now taking over a good portion of the yard. "We just spent all day finishing it, and it looks great," she said. "No way is it wrong."

"It does look pretty good, huh?" Greyson asked, hammering the last board into place and making sure the door he'd just secured swung neatly into its resting spot, and that everything lined up just so to keep the animals safe.

"After all the work we just did? I think even Louis will be happy with it."

Greyson was tempted to dish up his smack talk du jour about how Louis probably wasn't even happy on Christmas morning, but he trapped his tongue between his teeth before the words could launch. The cranky old guy had mellowed out a little over the past week. Of course, Greyson hadn't been pushing so hard, either, so maybe there was a little truth to Marley's claim, after all.

Pushing first might be better than pushing back, but sometimes, he could get what he wanted by not pushing at all.

"We should test the run out," he said, sliding the thought aside. He and Marley had spent one hot night together. Sure, they'd followed it up with a great day, talking and laughing easily despite the whole manual-labor-in-the-dead-of-summer thing, and yeah, they'd preceded it with a week's worth of flirty conversations studded with just enough truth-telling to make him think in ways he never had before. But she wasn't sticking around.

Fuck, he wanted her to.

"Oh, we should!" Marley agreed. The excitement on her face brought him back to the moment for good, scattering the unease that had collected in his gut.

"Gypsy and Blue get along pretty good, and Blue could use some extra runnin' around," he said. They'd just gotten the puppy, whose exact age and breed was anyone's guess, a few days ago. Michelle Martin had found the thing running crazy alongside the road leading out of town and brought him in to the shelter. Somebody (correction: some raging dickbag) had abandoned him, probably because the dog was overactive as hell. If Greyson ever got his hands on the person who'd left the dog there to get hit by a car—or worse —he'd throttle the son of a bitch. He'd named the little guy Blue for his eyes, which were the color of cornflowers. The vet had said it was likely because there was some Siberian husky going on in the dog's lineage, and the size of his paws sure confirmed it. He might be a puppy (ish? Who knew) now, but he wasn't gonna stay small for long. So far, the only person the dog came close to heeding was Greyson, and even then, it was barely fifty-fifty. Poor, misunderstood mutt.

"Blue could *always* use some extra running around. Even in his sleep," Marley said, laughing. They made their way through the shelter's back door and headed for the main room where the dogs were all curled up, most of them snoozing in their pens. Marley had convinced Louis to invest in new beds for both the dogs and cats last week, pulling apart the budget and examining the numbers with a microscope to find the money for the added comfort. She paused to kneel down in front of the cage in the corner, crooning softly to the little black dog inside for a minute before moving to Gypsy's cage to take the old girl out with a gentle, well-practiced grab.

"You name that one yet?" Greyson asked, his eyes still on the corner cage. The dog—some kind of lab mix, maybe?—had shuffled to the front of his cage to stare after Marley intently, the same way he'd done on Thursday, when they'd last been at the shelter. He still shrank back a bit whenever Greyson, or anyone else, for that matter, gave it a go, so Marley had taken to talking to him in soothing tones, then talking to Greyson quietly right after, to try and make the dog more comfortable around both of them.

Marley clipped Gypsy's leash into place. "He kind of

looks like a Shadow, don't you think?" she asked, and God, it was perfect.

"I do. Shadow it is."

"Louis told me animal control found him at a puppy mill." The delicate line of her jaw tightened. "Said he'd been treated really badly. The rescue vet in Camden Valley fixed him up and neutered him, but they couldn't find him a home, so that's how he ended up here."

Greyson used the furious energy pumping through him at the thought of Shadow's treatment to grab a leash for Blue and move over to the dog's pen, where he was already making high-pitched cries of excitement and wagging not just his tail, but pretty much his entire brown and white body.

"Louis told you all that?" Greyson asked in belated surprise. The guy was hardly gabby *or* friendly.

"To be fair, I bugged him as sweetly as I could 'til he caved." Marley waited until Greyson had talked Blue down from a fever pitch—sweet Jesus, the dog was a ball of energy—and gotten him out of his pen without too much fanfare before continuing. "But I also told him Shadow seemed to be coming around a little. He said we could see about me and you taking him out and holding him a little this week. The poor dog has been through a lot."

Whoa, talk about a new development. Louis was stingy as hell with that dog.

"Okay, sure," Greyson said. He led the way back out into the yard, but they hadn't even gotten four steps over the grass before Blue went from sixty to a *hundred* and sixty, nearly pulling his arm out of its socket and tipping him forward with a brutally exuberant tug on her leash.

"Jeez, Blue! Easy! *Sit.*" Greyson locked down his muscles in an effort to hold the leash steady, and even though he'd firmed his voice pretty good over the command, Blue still went berserk. "Good Lord, dog. What's got you so—"

"Greyson." Marley hitched to a halt beside him, her eyes as wide as dinner dishes, and he lasered his stare across the yard to follow hers.

Right to the spot where Sierra Beckett stood just inside the gate on the far side of the fence.

"You didn't lock it," the girl said, pointing to the latch. "I don't mean to trespass. The sign says I shouldn't, I know, but I heard you talking when I was hanging the laundry, and... I'm sorry. I don't want to get in any trouble."

"No." Marley shook her head, adamant. "It's okay. You can come in, if you want."

Sierra hesitated, her gaze not on Marley, but on him, and Greyson lifted one hand in a small wave.

"This is my friend, Greyson," Marley said. "And I'm Marley. We haven't officially met. You're Sierra, right?"

She nodded, taking a few tentative steps into the yard, and God, the kid really was skinny, all arms and legs, like a scarecrow. "Yes. Is that your dog?" she asked, looking at Gypsy with the sort of hope that made Greyson's chest twist.

"No. I'm taking care of her, though. Greyson and I are doing community service here at the animal shelter." Reaching down, Marley gave Gypsy a pat on the head, while Blue strained at his leash in a bid for equal attention.

"Okay, Blue. I see you, buddy," Greyson murmured, kneeling down to pet the dog, but only after he'd followed his command to settle somewhat. "Do you want to come and pet them?" he asked Sierra. "I know Blue here seems a little crazy, but he just gets real happy around most people. You could start out with Gypsy, there, if you'd like."

Sierra squinted through the sunlight at Marley, who nodded. Sierra tiptoed over, bending down to place a gentle pat on the dog's head. But Gypsy was an attention hog, the sweet old girl, and she turned to enthusiastically lick Sierra's hand before flopping over onto her back in a blatant request for belly rubs.

"Hey, look at that. She likes you," Marley said, smiling.

Sierra let out a giggle and sat on the grass beside the dog. "She's really soft. And kind of silly."

Blue renewed his full-body wiggle, and Greyson led him over to the door of the newly minted run. "One dog at a time, now. You'll get your turn soon enough. For now, go on. Run it out."

Finally, a command he'd follow with ease. The dog scampered off, sniffing his way through the dog run and chasing the dappled shadows thrown down by the leaves of the oak tree overhead. When he returned to Marley and Sierra, the little girl's expression sobered.

"You've been leaving groceries on our back step, haven't you?" she asked, making his heart pump faster and Marley's chin come whipping up.

"Yes," Marley said, and wasn't it just like her to go for the full-frontal truth. "We have."

Sierra nodded, petting Gypsy. "My mom didn't want to take them at first. She said we shouldn't, because we didn't know who they were from, and that we shouldn't be taking handouts even if we did. But I told her it was okay. The things were all cans, like from the grocery store or the food pantry in Camden Valley. I said..." She paused to let Gypsy lick her hand again, and damn, Greyson's rib cage felt far too tight for the nameless emotion filling it up right now. "Maybe it was a guardian angel who had left the food. I knew it was you, though. I saw you walking one of the dogs a couple weeks ago, and then the food showed up that night, so I figured it out."

"It's not a handout in a bad way," Marley said, sitting down beside Sierra. "We just wanted to help."

Sierra nodded. "I know. I just wish I could help you back. You're so nice to me and my mom."

Marley tilted her head, her expression wistful. No, wait. Calculating. What was she...

"You know, there might be a way you could help us back," she said, and both he and Sierra looked at her with equal doses of *huh*?

"There is?" Sierra asked. "How?"

Marley pointed down at Gypsy. "Most of these dogs can't get enough belly rubs, and there are cats inside, too. We sure could use someone to play with them a little extra while Greyson and I clean out their pens. As long as your mom says it's okay," she added.

Shock pushed Greyson's brows higher on his sweat-damp forehead. Louis was probably going to pitch a hissy fit at the idea of letting Sierra come play with the animals. But it really *was* a great idea, not only because Marley was spot-on about the animals benefiting from the human interaction, but because it would give the girl a sense of belonging and community. Even Louis would be able to see that, and there was no denying the guy could use all the extra help he could get.

"Really?" Sierra's face lit up like a summer sunrise, and she swung her gaze from Greyson to Marley, then back again. "I could help you? And you'd both be here, together?"

"Yes, ma'am," Greyson said, dipping his chin at her and kneeling down low to look her in the eye before transferring his gaze to Marley's and letting it hold. "Marley and I will be here together."

She blushed something furious, but her nod was even. Sure. "We will. We'd love to have you come help."

Sierra jumped up and threw her arms around Marley. Marley tensed in surprise, freezing to her spot on the grass for a drawn-out heartbeat. But then she hugged the girl back, her face softening and her eyes drifting shut as Sierra thanked her and promised to take the very best care of the animals, and something Greyson couldn't quite identify moved through him. It ended with the hug, and everything slid pretty much back to normal, with Sierra giving Gypsy a few last belly rubs, then going back through the gate to finish her chores. Marley bent back down to praise the dog, looking perfectly at-home in her cutoffs and T-shirt under the blazing sun and the country backdrop, and Greyson's gut panged in realization.

She might not have intended it, and she might not be staying.

But she still fit in.

He watched Marley lead Gypsy over to the run they'd built and encourage her to check it out, waiting until the dog was securely inside before shifting back to look at her.

"That was a right nice thing to do, asking Sierra to come help us out."

She lifted a shoulder beneath her bright red T-shirt, but her smile nullified any nothing-to-see-here the gesture might've otherwise conveyed. "It was no big deal. She just wants to feel like she's doing her part. Plus, the animals will love the extra attention."

"Louis is gonna fuss," Greyson said, and Marley rolled her eyes, but didn't lose her smile.

"I'll talk to him on Tuesday."

"I'll do it."

Marley blinked, and okay, so maybe he'd work on his delivery a little. Greyson straightened, smoothing his palms over the front of his jeans. "What I mean is, I can do it. I'll explain that Sierra saw us walking the dogs and that she wants to help. And no"—he let a half-smile sneak through—"I won't push when he gets uppity. But I will convince him it's a good idea."

"Okay," Marley said. She didn't seem to think twice about it, and the quiet trust filled his chest.

"So, I've been thinking."

"That's dangerous," she replied with a laugh, but nope. Not even her sexy little grin was going to sway him. Not in this.

"About this whole showing you how great small town living thing is," Greyson continued, just as easy as you please.

"Mmmm." Marley adjusted the red bandana that had been keeping most of her hair at bay, one dark wisp making a jail break to frame her damp cheek. "Definitely dangerous."

He lifted a brow, but kept going. "You've seen the farmers' market, the fireworks, and I know you've been to Town Street. So I'm thinking now, all that's really left to see is the grand finale. The very best thing Millhaven has to offer."

"And what exactly is that?"

Greyson's heart beat faster, but this was right. *She* was right. "Whittaker Hollow."

The sound that crossed her lips was pure, sweet surprise. "You want me to come to your farm?"

"I do." He moved over the grass until they were face to face, close enough to touch. He knew this was risky, and not a little bit. She wasn't even big on her *own* family's farm, and no Cross had set foot on Whittaker property since Christ was a corporal.

And yet, he didn't care, nor did he hesitate. "I know you're used to a different lifestyle, and that you think we're all backwards out here in the sticks. To be truthful, we might be. But there's a lot of good to be had out here. You've just got to let yourself see it. So, what do you say?"

Marley smiled and pressed up to her toes, kissing him just once before answering, "I say yes, on one condition."

"And that is…?"

"You send me home with peaches when we're done. After all, if I'm going to make a decent pie, I'll need the very best ingredients."

21

Marley was getting far too used to sitting in the front seat of Greyson's truck. The fact floated through her mind with way less concern than it should've, but honestly, between the perfectly broken-in comfort of the well-cushioned leather to the gorgeous summer breeze flying in through the open windows, she didn't know a soul alive who'd blame her. She could practically *taste* the sunshine, she thought with a laugh. Don't even get her started on the way she'd never believe the landscape wasn't entirely Photoshopped if she wasn't sitting here, taking it all in with her own two eyes.

Millhaven might seem totally foreign to her sometimes, with its quirks and slowed-down pace and lack of a Starbucks within a thirty-mile radius, but Marley couldn't deny that the town and its surroundings were truly beautiful.

"What's so funny?" Greyson asked, and Marley realized belatedly that not only had her laugh been out loud, but it had come directly from her belly.

"Nothing's funny," she said, and ugh, no matter how she framed this, he was going to give her a river of shit. Might as well just pop out with it. "It's just that I was thinking about how pretty it is out here. That's all."

His smirk was instantaneous. *Annnnd here we go.* "Pretty, huh? As in, majestic, wide-open spaces, fresh air like you won't find anywhere else on the planet, rolling fields and blue skies, with stunning mountains off in the distance? That kind of pretty?"

"Yes." Marley's laugh stayed put, which only egged Greyson on, of course.

"Or did you mean the kind of pretty that includes underground caverns and Civil War history and a national park with over a hundred miles of nature trails? Because out here in the Shenandoah Valley, we have that, too."

"Okay, okay!" she cried, lifting her hands in surrender that wasn't hard to give, considering he was right. "I get it. Yes, it's *that* pretty out here."

"Yeah, I sorta like it, myself."

Greyson slowed the truck down, turning onto a narrow lane marked by a plain, neatly printed sign reading *Whittaker Hollow Farm, est. 1949* in glossy black letters. Marley's pulse whooshed faster, and she swiveled her gaze over the grassy fields on either side of the lane.

"So, tell me about your farm," she said, and although his chin lifted in surprise just the slightest bit, he didn't skip even half a beat with his answer.

"The land has been in my family for four generations, like a lot of folks around Millhaven who have larger farms. We actually settled here around the same time as your old man's family."

Marley had heard Eli say more than once that Cross Creek and Whittaker Hollow were the two oldest farms in Millhaven, usually followed by a few grade-A swear words applied to either Greyson or his father.

Brushing the thought aside, she asked, "How big is the place?"

"Six hundred acres, give or take." Greyson followed a branch of the lane that forked off to the right, with small groups of lazily grazing black cows behind the perimeter of wire fencing lining either side. "We have cattle up here on the front half of the property, and the crops in the back. Mostly feed corn, grain, and hay, although we do our fair share of produce and pick-your-own for things like strawberries, peaches, and apples."

"It's so peaceful," Marley said. Bracing her palms on the window frame of the passenger door, she leaned out, squinting against the early-evening sunlight so she could take in the fields of bright emerald corn stalks in the distance, the fundamental, earthy scent of the breeze swirling around her—God, all of it.

"I think so," Greyson said from over her shoulder, and even though she couldn't see his slow, sexy smile, she could hear it in every inch of his voice. He pointed out a few things along the path so she could gain her bearings, like where they were in relation to the main house, the hay fields, and Whittaker Hollow's apple orchard. The layout and smaller details were different than Cross Creek, of course. Not that Marley had spent enough time outside of the main house to know the lay of *all* the land there—Cross Creek had over a hundred acres on Whittaker Hollow, and the farm she was on right now was far from small. Cross Creek was pretty, too, she had to admit, offering the same sort of calming, pastoral quiet that made it easy to see why Tobias and each of her brothers loved the place in his own way.

The thought hung in her mind, and since her brain-to-mouth filter had enough rust on it to qualify as an underwater relic à la *The Titanic*, she said, "There's a lot of smack talk between our families, huh?"

Greyson's shoulders tightened against the driver's seat. "That's one way to put it."

"Okay, but do you know why, exactly?" Marley asked. "I mean, I get it. You're the two biggest games in town, you're naturally going to compete for business. It's just that the tension seems to run really deep. Was there some kind of huge blowout argument, or something in particular that sparked all this bad blood?"

"You know, that's a good question," Greyson said slowly. They got to a hand-painted sign promising *Pick Your Own, This Way!* and he maneuvered the truck over a pair of gravel-packed tire tracks leading off to the right, passing another sign that read *Best Peaches in King County* before shaking his head. "I can't think of ever hearing anything specific. And I know Amber Cassidy, so..."

Talk about a pairing Marley wasn't expecting. "You're friends with Amber?"

"Friends is such a strong word." Here, he gave up enough of a half-smile to take any true sting out of the claim. "But Billy Masterson, who works down at the co-op? He has a thing for her. Has since we were in high school. He and I get on pretty good, when he's not running his mouth to my sisters about me being arrested. So, yeah, I know her alright."

"Those two sound like a match made in heaven," Marley said wryly.

Which is exactly how Greyson replied. "Right? They're perfect for each other. Anyway, it's kind of hard not to know Amber, and we've hung out enough. If there was a story there, she'd have told it. Hell, it'd be legend by now."

He pulled to a stop in a small side lot that was marked

only by flatter patches of grass and the occasional stretch of bare earth, worn through from use. Marley tumbled around the possibilities for a minute, following him out of his truck and enduring his frown.

"Sorry," she said, looking back at the door she'd just slammed. Guess she wasn't used to the whole Southern manners thing just yet. "So, if it's not something specific, like an argument over land or some agreement gone sour, I wonder what's behind it."

"I don't know." Greyson took her hand. Her belly flipped a little at the touch, but he ambled along, as if he had not one care, and she felt too good to do anything other than lace her fingers through his and squeeze. "But the rivalry is definitely there, and it's always been strong. My grandfather wasn't exactly a kind man, either. My old man is a lot like him in that way. He might've gotten nastier about the rivalry after my uncle was killed, but...honestly, he got nastier about everything then."

Marley nodded. "Grief has a way of doing that to some people."

"To be fair, none of us are saints. Your family plays an even part," Greyson said, his tone not confrontational, but damn sure not kind, either. And wasn't that just like him? "Eli and I started brawlin' in the third grade and pretty much never stopped. I might push a lot, but he pushes, too. I know they're your brothers, but Owen, Hunter, and Eli have always been all too happy to talk shit about me and mine."

"My brothers do say you're a jackass."

It was brutally direct—not that Marley knew any other way, really. Funny, not only did Greyson not bat so much as a single, ridiculously long lash, but he didn't disagree. "That might be a fair assessment. I'm not a nice guy."

"I'm not sure I believe that entirely," she argued. "You're

great with the animals at the shelter, and with Sierra. And you're nice to me."

"Yeah, but getting along with you took a little doing." The corners of his mouth quirked up, his boots whispering over the grass as he led her toward the edge of a field full of trees growing in winding rows. "And, for the record, I call your brothers jackasses right back, you know."

"I call them jackasses, too, when they're acting like it."

"You don't get along with your family, do you?"

The question stuck into her, sharp and unexpected, making her pulse jump. "My brothers and I get along okay," she hedged. "Things with Tobias are..."

Okay, so they'd called a truce of sorts last night, and she'd gone to bed feeling happier than she had in recent memory. Still, she couldn't explain this. Not even to Greyson, even though a part of her was tempted.

But how on earth could she tell him that it wasn't that she didn't *want* to be Tobias's daughter, a true part of his family like her brothers, but rather that she *couldn't*?

"More complicated," she finished lamely. Greyson didn't call her out on it, though, and Marley found herself exhaling in relief. They made their way to the top of the field in quiet that wasn't awkward or ill-fitting. By the time Marley turned to take in her surroundings with more care, the ease she'd felt when they'd arrived had made itself at home again in her chest.

"Are you sure you're ready for this?" Greyson asked, letting go of her hand to gesture to the row of peach-studded trees in front of them. "Because it *is* the best experience in Millhaven."

Marley couldn't help it. She arched a brow. "Are you sure about that? Because last night—"

"The best experience you can have in public," he

amended. Stepping in, he wrapped one palm around her hip to pull her flush against him, hooking the index finger on his other hand beneath her chin to bring their mouths nearly just as close, and oh God, Marley didn't give a flying fig about rivalries or what her brothers said.

She wanted Greyson Whittaker. Badly.

He slanted a stare over her mouth, slow and hot. "Now, are we gonna pick some peaches, or do you want to get me riled up enough that I throw you over my shoulder and take you back to my place?"

"We can't do both?" Marley breathed, and Greyson laughed, kissing her all too quickly before letting her go.

"Of course we can do both. But peaches first."

Grudgingly (but not too, because wow, the orchard was seriously beautiful), Marley followed him down the grassy path between the first two rows of trees. Greyson gave her a basic primer on peach growing—how old the trees were, how his family had added to the orchard over time and how Whittaker Hollow had actually been the first farm in Millhaven to do Pick Your Own produce, although Cross Creek had followed suit later that same year with apples and pumpkins during the harvest.

He spoke with ease, his shoulders loose and his expression wide-open and reverent as he pointed out details and let his eyes sweep over the land. His rough edges still showed—strong, stubbled jawline, muscles flexing and releasing with the suggestion of power, and then there was that tattoo, the heavy black lines tribal and fierce. But Greyson looked so happy, so *right*, here on his farm, that the vitality of it warmed her.

This was where he belonged. And standing here beside him, even if only for this moment, Marley felt like she belonged, too.

GREYSON WORRIED that maybe he was dreaming. He didn't normally—okay, fine. Ever—go for the whole rah-rah, feel-good route. Sure, he'd been happy, and more often than not when he was here on his family's land. But this higher-level of goodness that felt not sappy, but light and giddy and sewn into his bones?

Yeah. Not his usual jam. And he knew he should be worried about it, but the problem was, he felt too good to give a shit about worrying.

"Okay," Greyson said, turning to look at Marley. Although the sun had arced toward the west side of the orchard, it was far from setting, the rays slanting down to tease out the coffee-in-cream-colored highlights in the hair peeking out from beneath Marley's bandana, and sweet Jesus in the manger, she was beautiful.

He cleared his throat. "Peach picking," he said, before the darker, baser side of him refocused on his earlier promise to throw her over his shoulder to drag her off to do wicked, wicked things. "It's not brain surgery, but there are a few things you should know."

"Okay." She stepped in beside him, close enough that her arm brushed his as the leaves on the lower branches of the peach tree in front of them brushed against them both. "School me, oh wise one."

"Hilarious. You should be a comedienne. Really." Of course, his reply lost a lot in delivery, since he paired it with a laugh. But then Marley was laughing, too, and Greyson found himself not caring that she'd successfully poked fun at him. "So, you're obviously going to look first, for a peach that's ripe and free of blemishes."

Marley nodded, tipping her head at the low-growing branches. "The ripe ones are more orange, right?"

"For this variety, yes." They grew both yellow and white peaches in bulk, and donut peaches and a few other heirloom varieties in limited quantity. Those were the ones he was still playing with, finessing soil compositions and methods for optimal yield and fertilizer ratios. "Next, you want to get your hand up under the fruit, nice and even."

"Like this?" Marley asked, cupping her palm under a peach at eye level.

"Mmm hmm. If you get too much resistance, it's not ready for pickin'. You shouldn't have to put your back into it."

"Okay. So just pull?" Her fingers curved tighter with the clear intent to put her words into action, but Greyson stilled her progress with a brush of his hand.

"Nope. Twist. It keeps the branches from being damaged, so they can produce fruit again in the next growing cycle." Reaching out, he turned his wrist in a move so well-practiced, he was sure he could do it in his sleep, even easier than breathing. The peach let go of the branch with a soft pop, dropping into his palm just as easy as you please, and ah, perfect.

"It's got some nice weight to it," he said, placing the peach between Marley's fingers. "Which is one way you can tell if it's ready to be picked. But the very best way you can tell if a peach is ripe is to smell it."

She didn't even pause before lifting the thing to her face and inhaling deeply. "Oh." The way her reply was more pleasured sigh than actual word made Greyson's body heat in ways that had nothing to do with the summer evening. "It smells delicious." She realized—likely because he was making it *really* goddamned obvious—just a beat later that he was staring at her. "What?"

Greyson didn't stop staring, but he did say, "Most people with no experience picking peaches probably would've thought that was weird advice at first."

"I think we've already established that I'm not really like most people." She pointed to the front of her muscle shirt and mouthed *from Chicago*. "Anyway, I trust you. You're the expert, so if you say smelling the peaches is the best way to tell that they're ripe..."

Marley trailed off with a shrug. She handed the peach back to him, and he fought the odd feeling growing in his gut long enough to find one of the baskets they always had nearby so folks coming to pick their own fruit had something to collect their bounty in.

"What about you?" Greyson asked, depositing the peach in the bottom of the basket, which held about a peck of fruit—a good amount to send her home with.

"What do you mean, what about me?"

He shouldered his way around a large branch, watching her examine the options in front of her for what to pick next. "I mean, I'm the expert at this"—he gestured to the row of trees now to their right—"so what are you the expert of? What do you want to do with your life?"

"I don't know," she said, the admission seeming to shock her. "I have a degree in business management from a small college outside of Chicago."

"Wow, really?" Greyson asked, hearing the gracelessness of his surprise only after it had crash-coursed out. "Sorry, that wasn't very kind." Especially since she was turning out to be one of the smartest people he'd ever met.

But Marley just waved off the indiscretion and continued to pick peaches. "No, you're not wrong to be shocked. I don't even think my brothers know, and honestly, I never did anything with it. I worked retail in Chicago for a little while, but you have to earn seniority the hard way in management. By the time I started getting traction, my mom had been diagnosed with cancer, and she needed full-time care. I always thought I'd run a store—I'm good at organization and planning and stuff—but then life got in the way."

A saying, long buried, whispered up from someplace deep in Greyson's mind. "Life is what happens when you're dreaming of what you're going to do with it." His uncle Steve had said that all the time, hadn't he?

"But not you," Marley said. "You're doing what you love, aren't you?"

"Yes and no. Yes, I love my job, and yes, I belong on my farm." Those had been Greyson's truths from the time he'd gone to Millhaven High School's junior prom. "But the circumstances of running it aren't ideal. My old man owns the place, so ultimately, there are decisions I can't make, no matter how much he depends on me for operations."

It wasn't a can of worms Greyson really wanted to bust open, though—fuck, the thought alone threatened to kill the great mood he and Marley had cultivated just by being here, picking peaches. "You seemed pretty at home, working at the farmers' market yesterday."

She nodded, letting him take the subject for a do-si-do. "Yeah. It's definitely better than the boutique. Owen wants me to work at the storefront full-time. Manage the place, do inventory and schedules and displays. That sort of thing."

Whoa. That sounded like a full-time gig. A permanent, stay-here-in-Millhaven, not-leaving-anytime-soon, full-time gig. "And what do you want?" he managed to ask.

"A couple of days ago, I would've said not that."

"But now..." Greyson stepped closer to her, his pulse accelerating as her pupils flared and her lips parted.

"I can't stay in Millhaven," Marley murmured.

He took the peach from her hand, placing it carefully in the basket, then the basket on the grass beside their boots. "You're here for now," he said, his cock encouraging him to slide his arms around her, bracing his palms over the back of her rib cage to pull their bodies flush.

"I am here for now," she agreed, tipping her chin up until their mouths were tantalizingly close. "But—"

"No." Greyson shook his head, cutting her off. "No buts. Life's too short for that. If this is the moment you've got now, then that's the one you've gotta live. The other ones will come soon enough."

For a heartbeat, he thought she'd argue. The bright blue flash of her eyes certainly suggested she was headed that way.

But then she pressed up to kiss him. "Okay."

Greyson kissed her back. Unable to keep himself in check, he slanted his tongue over the seam of her mouth, tasting and taking as soon as she granted him deeper access, kissing her as if he was starving and she was pure sustenance...

"Well, well. Ain't this cute," came a voice from behind them, and no, no. No, no, no...

Greyson lifted his chin just in time to see his father's sneer.

22

Greyson closed his eyes for a long beat before stepping back from Marley. His old man never walked these fields—for fuck's sake, he *hated* the farm.

But he didn't hate making Greyson's life a fresh hell, and damn it, nothing good was going to come from this.

Still, he had no choice but to at least try and give it a go. "Marley, this is my father. Jeremiah Whittaker," Greyson said. "Pop, this is—"

"Oh, I know who she is." His father lifted a graying brow and turned toward Marley, his frown deepening with each passing second. "Your daddy coulda spit you out for how much you look like him."

Marley stiffened. Shit, this was going to go south, fast. "I'm Marley Rallston," she said evenly. "Lorraine Rallston's daughter."

His father's laugh was all contempt, and it echoed over the orchard. "You're a Cross, sweetheart. Through and through. It's in your eyes."

The words were designed to taunt. Christ, Greyson knew

the routine so well, he could've scripted it. "That's enough," he said, his voice steady even though the rest of him? Not so fucking much.

"Oh, that's not nearly enough," his father snapped, but Marley shook her head.

"Actually, it is. I would say it was nice to meet you, Mr. Whittaker, but we both know that's less than honest. Greyson, I'm sorry to cut things short, but I think I should be getting back to Cross Creek."

He jerked his chin once in a tight nod. He didn't want her to go, but his father had pushed first, and pushed hard. Pushing back now would be an uphill battle Greyson wasn't aiming to fight in front of Marley, and he was already in for a pound of flesh over this. His father's expression made *that* wildly goddamned clear.

Weird that Greyson was okay with that. Scooping up the half-full basket of peaches, he turned to lead her back to his truck, but the meanly satisfied grin on his father's face stopped him cold.

"Hey, why don't you take these with you?" Greyson said, loosening the death grip he'd just put on the basket handle to hand the thing over to Marley. "I'll meet you at the truck in just a second."

"Greyson," she said, so softly that his father likely hadn't heard it. "This isn't worth it."

He shook his head. "I won't be long. I promise."

Thankfully, she took the basket and went. He waited until she was out of earshot to turn toward his old man, his hands on his hips.

"That was uncalled for. Even for you."

His father sent a nasty noise of disagreement through his teeth. "Just like you to do something stupid, like think with your pecker. Of all the girls you could be takin' behind the toolshed, you had to choose *that* one?"

Anger burned, low and hot in Greyson's belly. "Be careful what you say next, old man."

He should've known it was a warning his father wouldn't heed. "I ain't the one who needs to step lightly," he snapped. "You think that girl really has a care for you?"

"So what if I do?" Greyson snapped right back.

"You're a fool. That family thinks they're so much better than everyone else. All they really care about is themselves."

It was a line he'd heard a million times. Had it memorized for at least a decade. But, God, he'd never questioned it, just let it fit right in with the whole us-versus-the-world mentality that his father had planted in his brain, letting it grow vicious and wild.

"You don't know what you're talking about," Greyson said.

But his father, it seemed, had had enough. "I know that this is *my* farm."

Greyson opened his mouth, fully prepared to pop off with a healthy *what the fuck*? But there was something in his father's voice that defied definition—not soft, but subtle, almost insidious—and it prickled like a warning over his skin. "Whittaker Hollow has always been your farm," Greyson said carefully.

His father snorted, his shoulders strung tight with tension. "Plenty of folks in this area who'd help me run it."

The implication hit Greyson on a delay, knocking the breath clean out of his lungs. "You're...are you threatening to *fire* me?"

"I'm reminding you where you are," his father corrected. "And *who* you are. That girl's a Cross. You'll end up learnin' your lesson with her the hard way."

Greyson inhaled. Exhaled. Inhaled again, and said, "I don't need you to tell me where I am. I know every inch of this land, along with how to tend it. As for who I am, you're the one who might need the lesson, because you don't know me at all."

With that, he pivoted on his boot heels and walked away.

MARLEY PULLED the nine by thirteen baking dish out of the oven at the main house at Cross Creek, and okay, she'd admit it. The cobbler looked pretty decent, and it smelled even better. To be fair, she'd had plenty of time to tinker with the recipe, what with her thoughts spinning too hard to allow for anything resembling easy sleep. But between the conversation she'd had with Greyson and the near-argument she'd had with his father, Marley's brain had been dangerously close to maximum capacity all night long.

If this is the moment you've got now, then that's the one you've gotta live...

Placing the baking dish on the cooling rack beside the oven, Marley fiddled with the edge of the blue and white potholder between her fingers. Greyson had apologized fifty times on the way back to her car, and cursed ten times more than that. She wasn't angry with him, and to be honest, she wasn't even angry about what his father had said. There was no denying that the older man had been a jackass, or that his mean streak looked to be a country mile wide, as one of her brothers might say, but Marley hadn't expected less. There didn't seem to be much point in getting mad about him showing his true colors when they were exactly what she'd thought they'd be. Anyway, none of that changed how she felt about Greyson.

How flawlessly at home he'd looked on his family's farm. How her chest had fluttered, hard and sweet as he'd kissed her beneath the peach tree.

How she'd thought of him and only him when she'd slid her hand inside her panties last night and—

"Good gravy in the pan, what are you making? I can smell it all the way in the office."

Marley clutched the potholder, her heart rocketing against her sternum, and she spun to face Cate. "Oh! I, um"—*was not thinking of Greyson Whittaker naked, was not thinking of Greyson Whittaker naked, was not*—"was just messing around with a peach cobbler thing. It's probably not very good."

Not one to be deterred, Cate waggled her dark brows. "I could use a mid-morning snack. Why don't we find out?"

Marley knew better than to argue—Cate's ferocity easily topped out at grizzly bear status when she put her mind to it—so she simply shrugged, watching Cate dish up a lumberjack-sized serving of cobbler and blow on a bite before popping it into her mouth.

She straightened, mid-chew, and oh, shit, this couldn't be good. "Did you come up with this recipe on your own?"

"Yeah?" Marley ventured. Cate had taught her how to get the butter-to-brown-sugar ratio right, and how to add in some flour and spices. But Marley liked nutmeg more than most people, and she'd fiddled with a few other things, like ginger, to go with the peaches.

But rather than spit everything out and toss her plate into the sink, Cate let go of an audible exhale.

"Oh, thank God," she said, forking up another bite. "That means we can sell it. Where'd you get the peaches? I thought Owen and Hunter said they weren't even thinking of growing them here this season."

And the hits just kept on coming. "Ah, about...that. I know we usually bake with the produce that's grown here, but..."

Cate shook her head reassuringly. "It's okay if you grabbed them from The Corner Market," she said, leapfrogging to a conclusion Marley wasn't about to correct. "Not everything we sell at the storefront has to use ingredients that were grown here. For this, I'm sure your brothers would make an exception."

"For what?" Owen asked, the mudroom door banging shut behind him and Hunter, who was right on his heels, and Marley suddenly had a perfect understanding of how snowballs grew into act-of-God-sized avalanches.

"Marley made cobbler and it's to freaking die for. Taste." Cate held up a forkload of cobbler, and Owen obliged.

"Damn, that *is* good." He angled for another bite, but Cate cradled the dish to her chest, laughing.

"Get your own!"

After a quick hand-washing, Owen and Hunter both did. "Wow, Marley. This is really delicious," Hunter said.

"You guys don't have to humor me," she said. God knew she'd grown a thick skin ages ago.

But Owen just laughed. "Do you think we'd eat this much if we were just humoring you?"

Huh. He had a point. Their plates *were* half-clean already. "I can write down the recipe, if you want. That way Cate can play with it."

"I don't need to play with it," Cate said around a mouthful of cobbler. "I just want to eat it. And smart of you to think outside the box with the peaches. Cobbler is a summer go-to. I normally make it with cherries or blueberries, because that's what we've got here, but this is..." She trailed off to take another bite, making a noise of appreciation that Owen and Hunter both mimicked. "I can't wait to get trays of this in the storefront."

Marley's gut panged at the thought that had been threading through her brain since she'd gone to Whittaker Hollow with Greyson, and oh God, it really was now or never. "Right. So, about that job managing the storefront," she started, and all three forks lowered in unison.

"What about it?" Owen asked slowly.

She took a deep breath. Held it for a second. Then let it go. "Is the offer still on the table? For me to, you know, do that full-time?"

Owen's nod was immediate. Sure. "It is."

"I'd only be able to do it for the season," Marley emphasized, because it wasn't fair to be anything other than upfront. But even with the bump in pay and the money she'd save by not commuting, she'd still be stuck here for another six months while she paid off her debt to the hospital. "Oh, and I'd have to go around my community service schedule."

"Of course," Owen said, with Hunter adding, "That shouldn't be a problem."

"And I'd like a Saturday off here and there. I do have a life, you know."

"I'm sure we can swing that," Hunter said, pressing a smile between his lips.

Marley nodded, looking at Owen. "Same pay we agreed on for the farmers' market, right?"

"Seems fair."

"Okay," she said, her heart beating faster even though her brain warned the rest of her to keep it cool. "I'm in."

"Can I ask what changed your mind?" Cate asked. It wasn't exactly a question Marley could answer outright—not that she was in the habit of bending the truth, but come on. Old man Whittaker had freaked *out* at the idea of her and Greyson together. Telling her brothers about him right now, in this moment, would erase all the headway she'd just made.

"I got tired of my job in Lockridge, and anyway, the farmers' market was kind of fun. In a grueling, manual labor sort of way. So taking the job just sort of made better sense."

"Hmm," Owen said, a smile spreading over his face. "Well, I hope you like hard work to go with your good sense, kid. Because they don't call it the busy season for nothing. We need all the help we can get around here, and there's no time like the present to get started."

23

Marley was slightly sunburned, partly mind-boggled, and thoroughly worn out. No, rewind. Worn out wasn't exactly right. It was more like brutal soreness in muscles she didn't even know she'd had. She'd made more progress than she'd expected over the course of the week, though, as she'd transitioned to running the storefront full-time. Owen and Hunter had split the duties up until now, and while they certainly knew the products, along with exactly when everything would be in season and in what supply, a bunch of managerial things had slid through the cracks. Marley had certainly had her work cut out for her with a hacksaw, but she'd begun to figure it out, slow and sure. Noémie had taken her notice in stride, which was to say she'd been all too happy to quietly remove Marley's already-scant shifts from the schedule at the boutique, effective immediately. It had allowed Marley to really focus on learning the ropes at Cross Creek, and she had to admit, working alongside her brothers and Emerson, Scarlett, and Cate had been kind of fun. She'd even done some planning and idea-sharing with Tobias a time or two, all of it painless.

Tender, aching muscles aside, of course.

Lying back against her pillows, Marley melted over her mattress, and ohhhhhh yeah, that was the ticket. Her hair was damp from the shower she'd indulged in after dinner, having scrubbed every last inch of her skin twice, and the sheets were cool against her bare legs. Snuggling in, she turned off the light at her bedside and hugged her pillow to her chest, looking forward to a great, big Saturday morning snooze-fest tomorrow.

Her cell phone lit up her nightstand and her pulse all at once, her pulse taking a distinct lead when she saw Greyson's name on the screen.

Hey.

Marley grinned like the idiot she was. She'd seen Greyson at the shelter this week, of course, but that had been (mostly) work. Texting him from the quiet dark of her bedroom? Totally different, and yep. Totally decadent.

Hey, yourself.

What're you doing?

For a fleeting second, she considered making up something less lame than reality, but she quickly gave up that ghost. **I'm lying in bed, contemplating the merits of sleeping until I'm no longer sore.**

A beat of silence passed before the three dots started dancing over her screen again, followed by, **Shame you're staying in bed. I know a really good remedy for sore muscles.**

Marley's heart raced, her smile a wide and inevitable thing. **Do you, now?**

Yes, ma'am. Meet me at the shelter and I'll show you.

Give me twenty minutes, she typed, her smile turning into a laugh loaded with anticipation when he replied,

I'll be there in fifteen.

Throwing the quilt from her body, Marley ignored her squalling shoulders as she rummaged for a pair of semi-clean jeans. She jammed her legs into the denim, rooting around for a bra next. She owned exactly one piece of sexy lingerie, a teal lace triangle bra that made up for its lack of functionality with a whole lot of hello-there-spaghetti-straps form. Covering the thing up with a plain black T-shirt felt kind of like hiding a surprise, and she grinned as she thought of the look Greyson would surely give up when he lifted up one to discover the other. A swipe of clear lip gloss and a quick ruffle of her hair later, and Marley was as good to go as she'd ever be. She stuffed her cell phone in the back pocket of her jeans, grabbing her car keys from her dresser and a couple of condoms from the top drawer, quickly sliding them into her wristlet before tiptoeing out into the hallway.

Where she promptly stopped short. The door to Tobias's room was ajar, the light beyond shining softly. His muffled footsteps were heavy enough to suggest that he was still wearing his boots, and therefore still dressed, and Marley's heart squeezed, her legs auto-piloting to the doorframe.

She knocked, peeking over the threshold only after he'd given up a surprised, "Come in."

"Hey, I'm um...going to go out for a bit with a friend. I'm not sure how late I'll be, but I didn't want you to worry."

He studied her, his blue-gray eyes bracketed with heavy lines despite his smile. "Alright. Thank you for lettin' me know."

"Are you okay?" The question flew out before Marley could check it, her stomach knotting. He looked more fatigued than usual, as if a stiff breeze could knock him right over.

"Just tired," Tobias said, waving a hand. "The growing season seems to get longer every year. Right helpful to have you workin' the storefront, though."

"Oh. Well, you know. Owen's paying me." The default felt strange and too stringent, so she added, "But it is nice not to have to drive into Lockridge anymore, and working on the farm is pretty fun. Eli's even teaching me how to take care of Clarabelle."

The thousand-pound Jersey Brown cow her brother had taken on as a pet thought she was a lapdog. And since Marley now had loads of experience taking care of those, she figured adding a cow to the mix wouldn't hurt, especially since Eli was about to have his hands full with a baby.

Tobias chuckled, the weariness on his face easing slightly. "Well, then. Sounds like you've earned a night off. Have a fun time, now."

She paused. He'd looked pretty shaky when she'd first knocked on his door. Maybe she should stick around, just in case...

No. Not again. You can't do this again.

Marley nodded, ducking her head so Tobias wouldn't see the tears that had just betrayed her by springing into her eyes, unbidden.

"Okay, thanks," she said, and quickly closed the door.

GREYSON WAITED for Marley with far more anticipation than he should have. But between her picking up full-time hours at Cross Creek and him needing to tend to about six million things at Whittaker Hollow, not to mention the fact that she'd somehow managed to sugar-talk Louis into letting Sierra come help them with the animals at the shelter during every shift, he'd barely had a chance to get any time alone with her this week.

And God help him, he'd wanted it. Really. Fucking. Badly.

Greyson stared through the rolled-down driver's side window of his truck, watching the fireflies weave lazily through the tall grass at the edge of the shelter's property. With every passing hour that he spent with Marley, he was running out of reasons to resist the fact that he wanted more of them.

In fact, there was really only one reason. And his name was Jeremiah Whittaker.

Things with his old man had been status quo after their *non*versation about Marley on Sunday evening, which was to say they had only exchanged words when necessary this week, and none of them had been particularly polite. Greyson hadn't addressed the not-quite-veiled threat his father had issued about him being expendable, but Greyson knew that was likely because he wasn't. Yes, his father could technically replace him, but between the timing and the training, it would be at an expense so great, the whole thing would make cutting off your nose to spite your face look like a frigging paper cut. His father wouldn't dare.

Probably.

A pair of headlights cut through the dark, grabbing Greyson's attention and making his breath move faster in his lungs. Marley pulled up next to him, sliding out of her car and into his truck, not even skipping a beat as she leaned over the truck's console to kiss him.

"Look at you, with all that Southern hospitality," he

drawled a minute later, trying to redirect at least *some* of his blood flow away from his dick.

Yeah, not a chance. "You like that?" Marley drawled back. "I'm learning from a consummate pro."

Greyson nipped her bottom lip, not hard, but hard enough. "Just so we're clear. It's not my manners I'm aimin' to show you."

Marley laughed, throaty and deep. "Oh, good. I've never been one to stand on ceremony, anyway."

"Actually," he said, but only after another minute of kissing her, because he wasn't stupid. "I know I've already shown you a couple of places here in Millhaven, including the very best. But there is just one more I think you'll like."

"It's not going to involve me climbing any water towers, or otherwise putting myself in peril, is it? Because I wasn't kidding about being sore as hell."

"And I wasn't kidding about knowing a good remedy for that," Greyson said. "But no. No climbing, no peril. I promise."

"Okay." Marley reached for her seatbelt, no muss, no fuss, all trust, and heat that had damn little to do with their kiss or the thought of where he was taking her moved through his gut.

She had a heart like a hurricane, and if he wasn't careful, he was going to be tempted to steal it.

Greyson aimed his truck back at the main road, taking a few turns he knew as well as his reflection. They weren't headed far, and after only a handful of minutes, he turned off the main road, onto a path that couldn't be found on any map, but was practically legend in Millhaven.

"Are you sure this is a place?" Marley asked, her smile hanging so heavily in her voice that he didn't have to sneak a glance at her through the dashboard lights to be able to picture it perfectly.

"I'm sure."

"It looks like the middle of a field." She squinted through the windshield as if she was trying to see past the truck's headlights, swinging her gaze from side to side in growing confusion.

Greyson drove a little farther, then a little more, and eh, they were a little close to the main road, but with the trees off to the right, this would do just fine.

He stopped the truck, killing both the ignition and the headlights. "That's because it is. Specifically, it's the field in between Pete Hitchcock's poultry farm and Curtis Shoemaker's property."

"It's kind of smack in the middle of nothing, huh?" Marley asked, still peering around.

She wasn't gonna find much, but then again, that was kind of the point. "You just described more than half of Millhaven. But there's no better place to stargaze than the middle of nowhere. C'mon and I'll show you."

He got out of the truck, and either she wasn't kidding about those sore muscles of hers, or she was actually doing him a solid, because she let him move around to the passenger side to open her door and usher her out. Greyson paused, but only for a second to grab the featherbed and small duffel he'd packed up for just this occasion from the backseat. His boots whispered over the grass, his eyes adjusting to the lack of manufactured light enough to lead Marley to the tailgate and lower it.

"Okay," he said, jumping up into the bed to spread out the thickly-cushioned blanket. "This ought to serve right nice."

"It feels so...big out here. I know that probably sounds

dumb," Marley added with a self-deprecating shrug outlined by the moonlight. "I mean, space is space, right? And Chicago's the birthplace of the skyscraper. Willis Tower is a hundred and ten stories high, for God's sake."

Greyson didn't count himself a stupid man, but... "I can't even fathom that, to be honest."

Marley leaned one hip against the tailgate, gingerly pushing her way up to the edge to sit beside him, hip to hip, shoulder to shoulder. She smelled warm and sweet, and he wrapped an arm around her to pull her close, wanting more. Wanting everything.

"I'm not sure you'd want to when you have this," Marley murmured. "I mean, I like Chicago well enough. I grew up there. But out here, the bigness of things just feels different. Less overwhelming, I guess. More wide-open than just huge."

Greyson's gut twanged at the mention of Chicago and the probability that she'd go back. But he had this moment with her, right now. If she was going to live it, then so was he.

"That doesn't sound dumb at all, actually. And you're right. I don't want any of that, because I have this."

Tightening his hold around her shoulders, he tilted his chin up to look at the stars. The moon hung over the tree line of red oaks growing off to the left, half-mast and mostly full, brightening the dark canvas of the sky that held it. The stars were out in full force, shining in clusters and swirls. The light from both created silvery shadows, and now that Greyson's eyes had adjusted fully, he could see the uncut wonder on Marley's face as she looked up, too.

"So," he started, the part of him that had earned his bad reputation snapping its jaws at the fact that the word had caused her to pull back as she transferred her gaze from the sky to his face. The rest of him, though? Totally fucking hooked on her stare. "About those sore muscles of yours."

"Ah, right. You have a magic remedy."

If Greyson had been hooked on her stare, then he didn't even want to know how to define the sensation that had just rampaged through his chest at the smile she'd just given up. Honestly, how could one woman be so brash and yet so sweet underneath?

Unable to resist, he kissed her once, quick and hard, before grabbing the duffel he'd stowed by the truck's wheel well. "I do."

Marley's brows pulled down tight, springing upward a moment later as he unearthed a green and white bottle from the depths of the bag. "Is that…?"

"Mint and eucalyptus massage lotion," Greyson confirmed, laughing when her shock didn't budge. "What, you think your brothers' wives are the only people who know Daisy Halstead? I grabbed this from her the other day at the farmers' market. It works great after a long day's work. Or, in your case, a long week. You want to give it a go?"

He expected some smart-assed answer from her. Lord knew he was half-tempted to get fresh with her, albeit in a bit of a different way. But instead, Marley whispered, "You'd rub my muscles with aromatherapy massage lotion just because I said they were achy?"

"It's the best way to make them feel better." Reaching out, he slid a hand over her forearm to press firm circles in the spot just above her wrist until—bingo—a sigh drifted past her lips. His hand traveled up to cup her face, his thumb chasing the vibration of the sigh from her bottom lip. "Let me make you feel good, Marley. I promise, I've got you."

She nodded, shifting without hesitation to slide off her flip-flops and move to the center of the featherbed. Greyson shucked his boots, joining her a second later, massage lotion in-hand.

"Turn," he said, his blood heating when, rather than arguing over being bossed around, she followed his command. But then Marley lifted her T-shirt over her head to reveal a thin, lacy bra with delicate straps crisscrossing between her shoulder blades, and Greyson realized his error, too late.

He could flirt with her, and he could fuck her—hell, he could even get as crazy as to fall for her—but when it came to this woman, so fierce and headstrong on the surface, yet breathtaking and beautiful underneath, he didn't have any control at all.

"You okay?" she asked over her shoulder, her tone teasing just enough for him to know *she* knew the effect she'd had on him.

"I'm very okay. And you"—he pressed a hand to the back of her rib cage, biting back a moan at the silk of her skin under his rough, callused fingers—"are goddamned gorgeous."

"You like it?" Marley grinned at him, only half of her peach-colored mouth visible from Greyson's vantage point behind her, and he leaned in, closing the space between them, chest to back, until his lips were a scant inch from her ear.

"The lace is nice and all, but I like *you*, darlin'. Now lay back and let me show you what Southern hospitality really looks like."

Marley's grin became a soft gasp, but again, she did what he'd told her to. She stretched out on the featherbed, front-first, and Greyson took a second to warm some of the massage lotion between his hands. The stuff smelled pretty good, not too frilly or overpowering, and Daisy had promised it would work wonders on the aches and pains he collected like baseball cards around the farm. Swinging one leg over Marley's lower back, he took care to balance the bulk of his weight between his shins so he didn't hurt her, then angled forward to place his hands on her shoulders.

"Ahhh," she sighed, arching into Greyson's touch. His cock, being the greedy, impulsive thing it was, instantly perked to life, but he kept himself (mostly, because let's face it, he was still a guy, and Marley was definitely hotter than homemade sin) in check. Her muscles were knotted up pretty good, but lucky for her, he knew just how to loosen that tension. Starting with the tops of her shoulders, he pressed slow circles over her skin, using his thumbs to unravel the tautness there, bit by bit. She softened into the featherbed, her breaths deepening.

Every pass of his fingers relaxed her body further, each sigh in response making him harder and more desperate to do away with his jeans and her jeans and every other barrier that stood between them so he could sink into her, good and hard. Greyson bit his lip in an effort to resist—Marley deserved better than some rough, graceless fucking.

But then she shifted her hips up and back, just enough to create the space she needed to flip over beneath him.

"Greyson." Another lift and lower of her hips, and Jesus God, she was *trying* to end him. "Do you want to touch me?"

She had to be kidding. The way her nipples were pressed against that tissue-thin lace that was barely covering her breasts to begin with had his hands begging him to turn her bra into scraps.

He flexed his fingers before curling them in tight restraint. "Yes."

She looked up at him, her eyes glittering in the moonlight. "Here?"

Marley brushed the index and middle fingers on one hand over her collarbone, then dipped them low between her cleavage, and need spread out, hot and low between Greyson's hips.

"Yes," he grated, still holding back. This was supposed to be about the experience. About making her feel good and being right here for her, like he'd promised. He couldn't just brazen his way through it like he did with everything else, all deep, dark attitude and uncut intensity.

Marley, however? Not one to be deterred. "What about here?" Her fingers glided over the midline of her belly, not stopping until they reached the top of her jeans.

"Yes." Greyson scraped in a breath. He could do this. He could go slow. He fucking *would* go slow, even if it killed him.

"And...here?" She skimmed the seam of her jeans, and his already fraying control snapped by another thread.

"Yes." He caught her wrist, stilling her movement and bringing her stare up to meet his. "But I don't want to go fast."

"Bullshit."

The challenge was so unexpected, yet so brashly hot, that it turned Greyson on as much as it stunned him. "What?"

"You heard me," Marley said, levering herself up so they sat face-to-face, even amid the tangle of their legs. "I know you're holding back. You're wound so tight, you're practically humming. So if you want me, take me. I'm right here."

"I want to." Hell, it was the biggest understatement Greyson had ever uttered in his entire twenty-nine years. Her mouth was so close, her chest right on his, and Christ, he *wanted* her. "But if I touch you right now, it's not going to be slow or sweet. If I touch you right now"—his cock jerked, the impulsive part of him he'd been trying to keep under control pushing the words past his lips like a promise—"I'm going to rip those clothes off of you. I'm going to fuck you, hard and deep and fast, and I'm not going to stop until the only name you know is mine."

Marley cupped his face between her palms, and as crazy as it was, Greyson felt the touch everywhere.

"Don't you see?" she whispered. "I want you like that, Greyson. I don't want pretenses. I want *you*. Just as you are."

She kissed him then, just a light brush of her lips to seal the words into place, and he was no more good. Knotting his fingers in her hair, he pushed her back to the featherbed in a rush, bracing his free arm behind her just in time to absorb the brunt of the impact. Marley arched in encouragement, her tongue meeting his in greedy strokes as they deepened their kiss in equal measure.

His hands moved to the straps of her bra, grasping tight. "This *is* pretty," he said. "But it's seriously got to go."

"It does," she agreed. But the infernal thing was a complicated web of teeny little straps, each of them keeping him from what he wanted, and Greyson couldn't help it. He pulled. Pulled again, and then...

Rrrrrrip.

"Sorry," he murmured, actually feeling a stab of remorse, albeit a small one.

Marley laughed. "I can get another bra, cowboy. Now are you gonna take off the rest, like you promised, or what?"

His fingers were on the button of her jeans before she'd even finished the question. Greyson did away with his T-shirt and his own jeans next, stopping for just a second to admire Marley's delicate pink thong before yanking his boxer briefs off to join the laundry scattered over the bed of his truck. The only thing he wasn't rushing was making sure he got the condom right, but that only took a few seconds, and then he was nestled right where he wanted to be, between Marley's thighs.

"These are pretty, too," Greyson said, running his finger along the inside edge of her panties, his pulse moving faster as he registered their dampness. She murmured his name, followed it up with a honeyed "please", and the reckless part of him took over. Shoving her panties aside but not off, Greyson pushed two fingers into her heat, letting his thumb slide over her clit in a firm stroke.

"I don't care if you rip them, too." Marley punctuated the claim with a sexy, want-filled moan. "In fact, if you don't take them off and put your cock where your fingers are *right now*, I'm going to rip them off myself."

Oh. Fuck. Yes.

"Far be it for me to keep a lady waiting," he drawled, slipping her panties off and readjusting his body to fit his hips over hers. God *damn* it, she was wet—he nearly lost his breath just from brushing against her entrance with the head of his cock. But Marley hadn't exaggerated, apparently, about wanting him hard and deep and fast, too, and she reached between their bodies to guide him into the snug space between her legs.

"Jesus, you're—" So many words ricocheted through his head, yet his mouth couldn't form a single goddamned one as he thrust all the way inside of her. Her inner muscles gripped his cock, the tight resistance easing slightly after a breath, and Marley curled her fingers around his waist.

"Oh, God, so are you." Planting her feet on either side of his legs, she used the leverage to rock her hips higher. Greyson let her set the rhythm with her hands, too, a dirty thrill moving through his chest as she pulled him closer, seating his cock deeper inside her core. He answered every request with a harder thrust, moving faster and with more purpose every time.

"Greyson." Marley's grip changed, her nails turning in to his waist to produce a sweet sting.

"Tell me," he demanded, knowing it was brash and not giving a shit. "Tell me how you want it."

She moaned, her sex so hot and slick, Greyson nearly lost his focus. "Harder. Please, harder."

No known force in the universe would've kept him from obliging. Leaning forward to brace one hand by her shoulder and press their bodies flush from hips to chest, Greyson kept the steady pace of his movements while increasing their pressure. He was hazily aware of the bed of the truck biting at his knees through the featherbed, of the burn in his muscles as he thrust, again and again. But he didn't care. Marley gasped, her body quickening beneath him, her breaths shallow and her inner thighs splayed wide in a wordless plea. She began to shake, her body taut with the force of her climax, and Greyson rode her through every moan and sigh and cry before she finally went lax. He fought the urge growing at the base of his spine, the one daring him to keep thrusting and taking until his own orgasm had had its way with them both.

Marley looked up at him, eyes bright. "Don't stop," she said, soft yet oh so sure. "I meant it, Greyson. I want *you*. No holding back."

He didn't. Gripping her shoulder with one hand and her waist with the other, Greyson pumped into her, quickly reclaiming the rhythm they'd built. The change in angle allowed him to thrust deeper, his cock sliding forward and his body following until no space remained between them. Marley knotted her legs around his hips to keep them joined as they rocked together, and the move was like a flame touching kindling. Need combined with the dark, dirty want already coursing through him, his balls tingling and going tight with the signal of imminent release. Greyson didn't fight it—in fact, he let it have him, let *Marley* have him, coming deep inside of her with a call of her name.

And right there, under the stars and in the haze of release, Greyson realized that he wasn't in danger of stealing Marley's heart, after all.

He was in danger of her stealing his. And the worst part was? She'd already gone and done it.

24

Marley was content to stay exactly where she was, doing exactly what she was doing, pretty much indefinitely. A little weird when she considered that she was naked in what could technically be considered a public place, but she and Greyson really were out in the middle of nowhere, and anyway, his arms felt far too good around her to move, indecent exposure or no.

"You alright?" Greyson murmured into her hair. They'd adjusted a little post-sex, with him grabbing a thin blanket from the duffel and tucking it around them and her finding her way into the crook of his arm. The nighttime air was cool around them, something Marley hadn't really noticed in the heat of the moment with Greyson. But now that they'd settled in, she felt perfectly comfortable, the air balancing out the warmth of Greyson's body beside her and the stars glittering overhead as if the whole world was in front of them.

"I'm great," she said with a laugh. But Greyson didn't return the favor, the small smile he gave over instead totally not cutting it in the I'm-great-too department, and Marley pulled back to look at him more fully.

"What's the matter?"

"Nothing." He must have known she was about to call him on the untruth, because he shrugged and amended, "I'm not unhappy."

"I'm not unhappy, either," she said slowly, trying—and failing—to interpret his expression.

Greyson's dark eyes glinted in the shadows, the intensity he always wore like a second skin thrumming beneath his warm, bare skin. "That's the thing, though. We're both happy, right here. Just like this."

Marley pulled her brows together, now thoroughly confused. "I'm sorry. I don't understand."

"Look, I know better than to tell you what to do," he said, his voice quiet even in the hush of night around them. "That's not my place, and you take to being bossed around about as well as I do. But this, what we have together? It feels too right for me not to stand up for it. I know you never planned to stay in Millhaven, and that you have reasons why. But there are reasons to stay here, too, and I want to be one of them. I want you to stay."

For a second that might've lasted for ten, all Marley could hear was the *thump*-thump-*thump*-thump of her own heart threatening to beat its way out of her chest.

"I like being with you, too," she finally managed. God, it was so true, it nearly hurt to say. "I don't want to leave. I mean, not like I did before. I like working at the storefront, and spending time with you, like this, is..." She trailed off, trapping the word *everything* between her teeth before it could betray her by escaping. "But I can't stay here once my bills are paid, Greyson. You don't understand."

He shifted to his side to face her, pinning her with a stare. "Then help me understand it."

"I can't," Marley said. But her voice quaked, turning the claim uncertain, and Greyson lifted her chin with the tip of his index finger.

"Hey. When I said I had you, I didn't just mean it in bed. I meant it for this, too. Help me understand, Marley. Let me in."

Whether it was the way he hadn't let her keep him at arm's length despite all her defenses or the fierceness in his tone that told her he meant it, he really *had* her, she didn't know. But the dam burst inside of her, walls she'd taken so much care to build and reinforce and build some more crumbling down in a swift, unexpected burst.

"My mother got sick suddenly. One minute she was fine, living her life and going to work and having dinner with me on Sunday nights, and the next, she felt nauseous and lost her appetite, like she had some sort of stomach bug. Less than a week later, we were sitting in her doctor's office, hearing phrases like large, malignant mass, and aggressive chemotherapy, and highly invasive cancer."

The re-telling, even though it was all factual, scraped at Marley's throat. Greyson didn't interrupt, simply put a hand on her arm, and the simple contact anchored her, giving her the power to continue.

"Everything happened in a blink. The chemo, the radiation, the move to hospice care. Six months after that day in the doctor's office, she was gone," Marley whispered, the tears she always tried so hard to fight pricking at the backs of her eyes, and God, she was so tired of fighting. "My mother was the only parent I knew, the one person I cared about more deeply than anyone else, and I lost her, just like that, over something I couldn't control."

Greyson's hand moved from her arm to her face, and it was only then that Marley realized, yep, those tears had breached her eyelids to slide over her nose and cheek.

Still, she didn't stop talking. "I took care of things—funeral arrangements, boxing up her belongings, insurance paperwork—but grieving was hard. Dealing with those first few months of loss nearly wrecked me, so many times I can't even count them. God"—Marley let out a joyless laugh—"I *still* have days where I'm so sad, I up and start crying just because I miss her, and it's been a whole year since she died."

"That's understandable," Greyson finally said. "She was your mother, and you were close."

"Exactly. We were *close*. I don't even know how to do that anymore. When people get too close now, I panic, and when I panic, I put everyone at arm's length." Dread claimed Marley's chest, crowding between her ribs.

But, once again, Greyson was right there, unyielding. "Not everyone. You don't do that with me. Listen, I know you miss your mother. I do. I miss my uncle, too. But you can't let the past dictate the present. Or the future. Your mother sent you here for a reason. She didn't want you to be alone."

"I don't want to be alone, either," Marley said, the confession leaving a hole deep inside of her from where she'd kept it buried for so long. Holding her brothers, and even Tobias, at arm's length for this long had been exhausting, and fighting the closeness they'd tried so hard to create with her had hurt, not because she hadn't wanted it, but because she *had*.

Greyson thumbed away another tear from the bridge of her nose. "You don't have to be. You don't have to put everyone at arm's length, Marley. You can stay."

The possibility burned bright, beckoning. But then

Marley shook her head, her defenses slamming into place. She couldn't go through the pain of losing another parent. She *couldn't*.

"I can't stay. If I let Tobias care for me, I'll care back. A *lot*. So, I can't be his daughter, and I can't let him be my father. If I stay, and something happens to him...if he dies..."

"He's going to."

Greyson's words sent her pulse skyrocketing. "Excuse me?"

"Tobias is human, Marley. He's going to die one day, just like you and me and everyone else in the world," Greyson said quietly. "But the question isn't really 'what if he dies'."

"It's not?" Marley couldn't help the sarcasm mixing with the emotion in her voice. Of course it was the question. It was exactly why she'd kept Tobias—hell, everyone—at arm's length for so long.

But Greyson said, "No. The question is, what if he dies and you never knew him. What if he dies, and you never let him know *you*, even though you've got the chance to."

The words stunned Marley so completely that all she could do was listen as he continued.

"Do you want to know the first thing I thought about you, when we were stuck in that jail cell? I thought 'damn, that's a Cross'. Not because your hair is dark and your eyes are blue, although, yeah, there's a resemblance. But it was your spirit. The thing that makes you, *you*. And you can fight that as much as you want, and you can be scared of it, too, but neither of those is gonna change the truth. You belong here."

Marley's tears continued to fall, and Greyson continued to clear them away. "Look, I might not be your family's biggest cheerleader, but even I can see that Tobias cares about you. So do your brothers. They'd never bring you into the fold at Cross Creek if they didn't. You're truly good at managing the storefront. You're happy doing it. And...I care about you, too. I want you to stay."

She swallowed, and oh God, oh God. "I want that, too, but..."

"No buts." Greyson brushed a finger over her lips, and oh, he tasted like hope. "Life's too short for that, remember?"

"I'm scared," Marley admitted, letting him pull her closer. Letting him have her, just as he'd promised to.

And he did. "I know you are, darlin'. But I've got you. I swear it."

As he dropped his face to kiss her, gathering her tight and safe in the cradle of his arms, Marley believed him.

And for the first time in a long time, she felt like she was right where she belonged.

Right up until two blazingly bright headlights cut through the darkness, followed by the telltale glare of blue and white police lights.

If Greyson didn't know any better, he'd swear he was cursed. But as it stood, he was just curs*ing*. Smack in the middle of what was undeniably the most important conversation he'd had...fuck, pretty much ever, and he had to be interrupted by the cops?

"You have *got* to be kidding me," he muttered as Lane Atlee stepped out of his police cruiser and started walking toward the back end of the Silverado. Lane looked all business, although in fairness, Greyson could count the number of smiles he'd seen the guy crack on one hand with fingers to spare, and his frown multiplied with every bootstep through the grass.

"Jesus, Whittaker," the sheriff clipped out. "Can't you stay out of trouble for...oh, holy shit."

Greyson had been so caught up in the depth of the conversation that he and Marley had been having that he'd forgotten until right now exactly how naked he and Marley both were, and exactly how close Lane was with her brothers. *Fuck.*

"Hi, Lane," Marley said, squinting at the painfully bright floodlight. "Any chance you'd be willing to tone that thing down a bit? I kind of like my retinas unscorched."

"Marley?" Lane's face turned roughly the color of the cherries Greyson had been trying his hand at growing in their greenhouse, and damn, could this get any more awkward?

Lane stepped back to the cruiser, killing the floodlight but not the headlights, then walking back to a spot about ten feet from the tailgate of Greyson's truck. "Damn it, Marley. What are you doing out here? No, wait. Don't answer that."

"Probably best if I don't," she agreed, and Lane blew out a breath.

"I'm going to need you both to get dressed while I figure out how to handle this."

Greyson's pulse tapped out a steady stream of *wait, what?* "What do you mean, how to handle this?"

Lane lifted a brow all the way to the brim of his hat. "Y'all are trespassing—"

"Oh, come on," Greyson interrupted, knowing he was in no position to push, what with him not wearing any pants, and all, but still. "Everyone in Millhaven knows this land doesn't really belong to anybody, Lane."

"Sheriff *Atlee*," Lane bit out. "You're also breaking indecent exposure laws—"

This time, it was Marley who interrupted. "Actually, we're both covered up by this blanket," she said, gesturing down to the cotton that was thankfully plastered to her and Greyson's naked bits, but Lane so wasn't having it.

"You're not decent underneath it," he argued. It was on the tip of Greyson's tongue to point out that Lane was just as naked under his clothes as Greyson was under this blanket, but Marley shook her head ever so slightly, and he thought better of it while Lane went on.

"And you're both still on probation for the laws y'all already broke," he said, and shit, he did totally have them there. "So, yeah. I need to figure out how to handle this. Your keys in the ignition?"

"Of course," Greyson said. Where else would they be?

"Good. Leave 'em there and don't move while I call the judge."

"Lane." Marley's voice stopped the guy in his tracks, and he pivoted back to face them. "Look, I think it's pretty clear that Greyson and I aren't doing anything malicious, and we promise"—she nudged his shoulder, prompting him to nod—"to pick up and head out of here right now. But do you really need to call Judge Abernathy?"

Lane looked uncertain. "Technically, I don't suppose I do. No one called in a complaint or anything. I just happened to see Greyson's truck from the main road as I was driving by. But y'all are, ah, indecent, and..."

"That is absolutely true," Marley agreed. "And I know that's a law you'd never bend, yourself. Not even to, say, go skinny dipping with Daisy in Broward Pond."

Lane paled, snapping to complete attention, and *damn*, it took every ounce of Greyson's willpower not to laugh.

"Well," the sheriff said. "I guess if you happened to get decent in the next two minutes, that'd fix our little problem."

"I think Greyson and I can manage that."

Marley clasped the blanket to her chest, turning to gather her clothes, but oh, no, that's not how this was going to go down.

"Turn around," Greyson said, making both Lane and Marley pause.

"Pardon?" Lane asked.

But Greyson didn't even think of budging. "Turn around while Marley gets dressed."

"Of course." The guy looked offended at the suggestion he'd do anything but offer Marley the utmost respect. "As long as you turn around, too."

"I'm pretty sure the cat is like, fifteen hundred miles away from that bag," Marley murmured, but when Lane simply stood there, his arms crossed hard over the retaining wall of his chest, Greyson nodded.

"Fine by me, as long as she gets privacy."

Greyson turned, and after some quick rustling and the soft *prrrrp* of a zipper, Marley hopped down from the tailgate, leaving Greyson to right his clothes and gather up the featherbed.

"Before y'all go, I'll be needing a word with Greyson," Lane said, which—duh—Marley immediately protested.

"Lane, I'm an adult," she said, planting her hands over her hips.

Atlee didn't blink, and Greyson hadn't expected him to. "It's okay, Marley. I'll only be a minute," he said. Grumbling under her breath, Marley walked toward the Silverado's passenger side. As soon as she was in the cab and the door was shut, Lane fixed Greyson with a menacing stare.

"As the sheriff, I'm going to tell you that I don't want to catch you out here again. No matter who you're with or what you're doing."

"Fair enough," Greyson agreed. He didn't love being told what to do, but the guy was the freaking sheriff. He could live with it.

"Now, as the best friend of that woman's oldest brother?" Lane continued, his tone growing both frost and teeth. "I'll tell you this. You might not have to answer to the judge for getting indecent with Marley out here where anyone could've seen you, but with what Owen, Hunter, and Eli are going to have to say about it? You're gonna wish you were in jail."

Greyson was an inch away from Lane before his brain had a single fucking clue he would move. The guy could eat him alive without breaking a sweat, and right now he totally looked like that was the immediate plan. But Greyson didn't give a shit.

"Respectfully, those Cross boys can spit nails 'til the sun comes up, and if they want to try to kick the crap out of me, they can give that their best shot, too. But let me make one thing perfectly goddamned clear. As long as she'll have me, there ain't nothing in the world that'll keep me from their sister."

25

The main house at Cross Creek looked like a fifty-foot Christmas tree had had a love child with the Fourth of July. Every single light on the main floor was lit up nice and bright, and as Marley counted one, two—yep, all three of her brothers' trucks in the lot beside the house, she cursed Lane Atlee for the ninetieth time in the last thirty minutes. She'd known he'd call Owen, who would in turn call Hunter and Eli, of course. Greyson had told her Lane had all but promised to get on the phone before they'd even gotten out of the field. He'd also volunteered to come face the music with her, telling her he'd take whatever consequences came with it. Although Marley's belly had flipped at the offer, she'd declined. The conversation was already going to be a tinderbox. No sense in adding an open flame.

Pulling in a deep breath, Marley set her shoulders around her spine and opened the front door. Hunter sat on the living room sofa, his light brown hair sticking up as if he'd been tugging his hands through it. Eli and Owen were at opposite ends of the area rug covering the hardwood floor, as if they'd both been pacing on opposite loops. Marley's stomach bottomed out at the sight of Tobias in the chair by the dark and quiet fireplace, his brow creased in concern. The four men froze for just a beat at the sight of her, and then her brothers' voices all crashed together like a high-speed collision on I-90.

"Thank *God* you're back—"

"What on earth were you *thinking*—"

"I'm going to wring Greyson's goddamned *neck*—"

Annnnnd redline. "Stop right there!" Marley jammed her flip-flops into the floorboards and stood as tall as her frame would allow. She turned toward Hunter, since he'd spoken first. "I am back, as safe and sound as I've been all night. What I was thinking"—she turned toward Owen, who'd launched that little gem—"was that I wanted to spend time with Greyson after a long week of work. And no"—this got leveled at Eli, who looked as mad as she'd ever seen him. Not that it was going to change a single breath of what she had to say—"you're not going to wring Greyson's neck for wanting to spend time with me, too. Not unless you want to go through me to do it."

Eli shook his head. "He doesn't want to *spend time* with you, Marley."

His tone easily conveyed his disdain. But for God's sake, it wasn't as if she hadn't been in that field, too, just as willing as Greyson.

"First of all, you don't know what he wants, or what he's really like," Marley said. "And secondly, just because he wants to sleep with me doesn't automatically mean he's *only* interested in sleeping with me, and it damn sure doesn't make him a monster. We're consenting adults."

All three of her brothers made varying noises of protest, and even Tobias's jaw flexed tighter at the implication, making Marley bite her lip. Not because she'd fudged the truth, and *definitely* not because she was the type to hold back, especially over something like this. But she could also respect the fact that, while she wasn't going to hide the fact that she liked Greyson in a more-than-friends way, there were probably parts of that attraction best left unspoken.

"Look, Marley," Hunter said, ever the calm one. "No one's trying to jump down your throat or tell you what to do. It's just that we've known Greyson a lot longer than you have, and he's..."

"An arrogant bastard with no honor," Eli bit out, and Owen nodded in agreement.

"He's bad news, just like his father. Old man Whittaker has always been a nasty son of a bitch, and Greyson's no different."

Marley's heart pounded, her protest hot on her tongue. "Oh, yes, he is."

"Marley," Owen started, but she'd reached her limit. Lifting a hand, she looked at each of her brothers in turn.

"No. You three have said your piece, and now I'm going to say mine. You might have known Greyson longer than I have, but I know him far better than any of you do. I've spent the past month with him at that shelter," she added, mostly to quell the argument brewing on Eli's face. "And I'm the only person who bothered to look past the reputation to see the man behind it."

"Greyson comes by his reputation honestly," Eli said. "He's the one who threw down that bet last fall that his farm was better than ours."

"You didn't hesitate to accept," Marley shot back, and that hushed him up, at least for a minute. "Fine, so he pushed. But you pushed back, and both of you were standing up for the same thing—your farm. I don't think any of you can really fault Greyson for having pride in his work. He loves Whittaker Hollow as much as you love Cross Creek."

Since that had stunned them all into silence, Marley took a step forward and continued. "Look, I know Greyson might be rough around the edges, but do you honestly think I'd put up with any crap from him?"

"That is a good point," Hunter said after a beat, returning Owen and Eli's twin stares of *seriously, dude?* with a shrug. "What? She's not wrong, about the bet or the fact that she's not the sort to be taken advantage of."

"Still." Owen shook his head. "This is Greyson *Whittaker* we're talking about, here. We're supposed to just believe he's turned over some new leaf because he's taken a shine to our little sister? Sorry, I'm not buying it."

Anger rose like a storm tide in Marley's chest. "I'm right here, you know—"

"I'm not buying it, either," Eli cut in. "Greyson has always had an agenda, and—"

Hunter jumped into the fray. "Okay, yeah, he's always been a dick, but—"

"Right, because you three were angels," Marley protested. "Come on, you guys, this is just—"

"*Enough*."

Tobias's voice boomed through the living room, startling everyone to complete silence and making Marley wonder where on earth he'd been hiding all that power.

"All this jawin' is making my head hurt. Boys"—he stood, looking briefly unsteady before finding a stance that matched his tone—"I know you don't like Greyson none, and to be honest, he's earned that from you. Especially you," he said to Eli, whose frown was big enough to require its own zip code.

"You're damn right," Eli muttered, and Marley rolled her eyes. This whole thing was pointless. She opened her mouth to say so, but then Tobias shook his head.

"But Marley's right. She's an adult, and she's got plenty of common sense."

Wait. No way. Was Tobias *siding* with her?

If her brothers' expressions were anything to go by, she wasn't the only one with a metric ton of *whoa* running through her veins.

"You think Marley running around with Greyson Whittaker is a good idea?" Owen asked, his blue-gray eyes wide with shock.

"It doesn't really matter what I think," Tobias said. It was an artful way of dodging the question, Marley realized, but she wasn't about to split that hair, especially when he continued with, "But if y'all can trust her with the storefront, I don't see why you can't trust that her head's on right regarding how she wants to spend her free time, and who she wants to do it with."

"Pop, this is Greyson we're talking about," Owen said, although his disgruntled frown had softened into something surprisingly close to concern. "Old man Whittaker's son."

"No." Here, Marley stepped forward. "He's not like his father." She took a breath, and God, even though this should scare her, she'd never been so sure of anything in her life. "Greyson is a good man. I know you guys have had your differences, but there are two sides to every coin. I'm not telling you that you have to like my being with him. But I am telling you that you have to deal with it, because it's not going to change."

She measured the passing time by the rapid beat of her pulse in her ears, and finally, Hunter broke the silence.

"We're not trying to be jerks about this. We just want to look out for you."

"I know," she said, because beneath her irritation, she really did. "But I just want *you* to trust me."

After a stretch of silence that felt a mile and a half long, Owen finally said, "Okay." He didn't look entirely convinced, but he also didn't look as mad as he had when she'd walked through the door, so for now, Marley would have to take it. "I don't like it, and I think y'all spending time together is a terrible idea. But if that's how you feel about Greyson, then I guess I have to respect that."

"Thank you." She looked at Eli, whose clean-shaven jaw was clenched hard enough to crack walnuts, and of her brothers, she knew he'd be the last to come around. *If* he ever did.

"I can't promise you I'm *ever* going to like this," he said, proving her point. "You're my sister, and Greyson is..." He trailed off, closing his eyes and exhaling audibly. "He'd just better treat you like gold."

Marley nodded. "I get it." The adrenaline she had felt over the last hour started to flag, reminding her how tired she'd been when she'd crawled into bed in the first place. "Look, it's late, and you guys have the farmers' market tomorrow." She had some things she wanted to take care of at the storefront, too, even though she was technically supposed to have the day off. "Why don't we call it a night?"

Owen split his gaze between her and Tobias, concern flickering back to life in his eyes. "Yeah, that's a good idea. We could probably all use some shuteye."

Her brothers all said their goodnights, Eli grumbling one last warning of the nine kinds of bodily harm he'd dish up if Greyson gave him the slightest reason to under his breath before heading out the door. Weariness invaded

Marley's muscles, tempting her to slump, but instead, she turned toward Tobias.

"You stood up for me."

"I reckon I did," he said quietly.

"Why?" Marley's cheeks burned as she heard the lack of grace in the question. "I mean, I can't imagine you're thrilled about the whole me and Greyson thing, either. It must've been hard for you to give me the benefit of the doubt."

Tobias's laugh was little more than a small puff of breath. "I can't say you're wrong about me not bein' thrilled. Truth be told, I'm not. But who you spend time with isn't my choice to make. As for the benefit of the doubt, well, I meant what I said. You're a smart girl. Stubborn, like your momma. I believe you've earned a bit of faith from me."

"Oh." The words hit Marley unexpectedly hard, right in the solar plexus, and she swallowed once. Twice. "Thank you."

Tobias nodded, the lines bracketing his mouth deepening. "That said, if Greyson does wrong by you, your brothers aren't gonna hesitate to deliver a whuppin', and I'm not gonna stand in their way."

"Fair enough," she said. She might not ever understand the weird dynamics of small-town family life, but she knew better than to think she could change *all* of it. At least, not tonight. "But I meant what I said, too. Greyson might have a bad reputation, but he's a good man."

"You really have a care for him, don't you?" Tobias asked, his expression surprised in one breath, then chagrined in the next. "Ah, that's none of my business. I shouldn't have presumed to ask."

"No, it's okay." The words vaulted past Marley's admittedly feeble brain-to-mouth filter, but she didn't try to haul them back. "I don't mind."

This was far different than the conversations she'd always had with her mother, but God, she'd missed those so much. Talking to Tobias felt oddly comforting, and even though a tiny voice in the back of her head whispered that she should be wary and keep her distance, she ignored it.

"I do care about Greyson, and we're working on some great projects over at the shelter."

"Are you, now?"

The question was a lead-in, Marley knew, just as she knew that she could take it, or cut it short.

She smiled, her chest feeling light despite the fatigue in her body. This didn't have to be huge, and it didn't have to be forever, but right now, it felt too good to turn down.

"We sure are. Why don't you make me some warm milk and I'll tell you all about it?"

26

Greyson wasn't a balloons and confetti kind of guy. In fact, he wasn't even close. But as he looked around the now-tidy yard behind the animal shelter, with its gates wide open and folks milling around with cups of lemonade, reading pamphlets about giving a cat or dog a forever home and petting a few of their most people-friendly candidates, he had to admit it.

This open house wasn't so bad.

That wouldn't have anything to do with its coordinator, now would it?

Since Greyson couldn't answer that internal question with anything other than a resounding "hell yes", he rocked back on his heels to slide a look at said coordinator beneath the brim of his baseball hat. Marley stood about a dozen paces away, holding the orange tabby she'd named Marmalade so Moonpie Porter's son, Ethan, could pet it, laughing as the kid—who had to be maybe seven—went all wide-eyed and happy. Moonpie's wife, Jenny, was already looking at him with a can't-we-keep-her-please in her eyes, and that would make their third request of the day for adoption papers.

The idea for the open house had come on quickly, last Saturday night (aka, The Day After They'd Almost Gotten Arrested...Again) as he and Marley had split a pizza in his tiny kitchen. She'd taken the whole event from concept to reality in a week, start to finish. They'd had to spend every evening at the shelter in order to prep for it, putting in extra hours each time, but once she'd gotten the idea, she'd been relentless. Greyson and Louis both had had no choice but to go along with the well-thought-out, well-executed plan to get as many animals adopted as possible.

Marley lifted her chin, her eyes moving over the crowd. As soon as she caught him looking, her smile lit up, so bright and beautiful that Greyson actually felt it smack in the center of his chest, and damn, he would worry that he'd gone completely soft, except for one tiny thing.

He *knew* he had, and it felt so good, he didn't care one whit who knew it.

The sound of a voice clearing from beside him had Greyson's head turning on a swivel, his gut tightening at the sight of Louis's ultra-serious expression.

"Louis," he said, testing the water.

The other man nodded, one lift of his beefy chin. "Y'all did okay with all of this."

Annnnnnd talk about the last thing Greyson had been expecting. "I just did the heavy lifting," he said past his surprise. "Marley's the one to thank. This adopt-a-pet open house was her idea."

Louis scowled. "I'm tryin' to say thank you. I don't reckon I've ever had so many folks out here in a day, lookin' to adopt, and the truth is, these animals deserve good homes."

"Oh." Cue up another batch of surprise. "Well, you're welcome."

"You were a bit ornery when you started, but..." Louis broke off, looking at the dog run Greyson and Marley had busted their butts to build, where a handful of people were ooohing and ahhhing over a few of the dogs. "I might'a misjudged you a little bit."

Greyson knew he should want to go hoarse from crowing. Louis *had* misjudged him. But instead, Greyson said, "I didn't make it easy. All the same, I appreciate the apology."

Louis grunted, and although his expression wasn't quite as cross as usual, it was far from qualifying as happy. Still, he shook Greyson's extended hand. "Right. Now that that's done, I'm going to see to getting Boomer's paperwork processed. Curtis Shoemaker wanted to take the old dog home today. Normally, we do a home visit, but Curtis has worked the same farm since the dawn of the ages, so..."

"That he has," Greyson agreed. "Go on and work on applications for as long as you need. Marley and I have got this covered."

He watched Louis trudge off to the office. If only calling a truce were so easy with his old man. They still hadn't done much other than trade clipped conversations about day-to-day operations at the farm, along with a couple of glares and hard frowns. But even those were wearing thin for Greyson, as if putting all that effort into pushing back was more exhausting than it was worth. Better to save that energy for what mattered, like the farm itself, and Marley.

Before he could let the thought sink in with the sort of gravity it deserved, she appeared at his side.

"Hey! I think the Porters are going to adopt Marmalade. Isn't that great?"

"It is," Greyson agreed. "Louis just said Curtis Shoemaker's taking Boomer home, too."

Marley's grin doubled, her blue eyes putting the perfect summer sky to shame. "Oh, good. Boomer's such a sweetheart. Now we've just got to work on finding the perfect home for Snickers. He'll be lonely without his buddy. But I saw Billy down at the co-op earlier this week when I went in for canning supplies. He said he'd love to have a dog to keep him company on his fishing trips. I'll bet he and Snickers would get along great."

"You're really good at this, you know that?"

The words were out before he could stop them, and they made Marley laugh. "What, hooking people up with their perfect pets?"

"Fitting in," he corrected, putting his arm around her. "You see all these folks out here?" He gestured to the handful of people scattered over the yard, playing with the dogs and flipping through photo albums of the animals who were resting or snoozing inside. "They're part of this community. And so are you."

Her face flushed, prettier than any peach he'd ever picked. "I just want to help. And anyway, you worked just as hard as I did. Maybe harder."

"Doubt it." Chucking decorum out the window—not that he'd ever been its number-one fan to begin with—Greyson pulled her close for a PG-13 kiss. Marley kissed him back with a laugh, both of them jumping slightly at the sound of an oddly familiar voice laughing along with her.

"My, my," said Judge Abernathy, her smile as big as her cartoon eyes behind her glasses, which today were framed in bright green polka dots. "I must say, I never imagined cats and dogs to get on *this* well, but I'm certainly glad y'all's community service turned out to be a success."

"Yes, ma'am." Greyson grinned, tipping his hat at the judge. "I suppose we have you to thank for it."

"Only if you've learned the error of your ways. I don't expect I'll be seein' either of you in my courtroom again, now, will I?"

Marley shook her head. "No, ma'am. You sure won't."

Judge Abernathy gave up a knowing smile. "Mmm. Well, it's right nice to see how far this place has come, along with the folks who are working in it. Louis tells me you put in a lot of work to spiff this place up and get it running right, plus extra hours all week to make this open house happen."

She hung the statement between him and Marley like a question, so Greyson replied, "We did, but finding these animals homes in the community is a good cause. Plus, Marley and I, uh, clearly don't mind spending time together."

The twinkle in the judge's eye said she understood exactly how much he *didn't mind* spending time with Marley, and damn, maybe the old biddy was a whole lot less crazy than he'd thought. "Regardless, your dedication deserves recognition. After all, what is community service for if not to serve the community? You've both done it well enough that I believe we can consider your sentences complete."

"We don't have to do the rest of the hours?" Marley asked, her shock obvious, and yeah, make that two of them.

"No, sugar bee. I think you've both learned your lesson, and something tells me Louis is more on his feet than he's been in a long while, thanks to the two of you."

"Wow. Thank you, Judge," Greyson said.

"Don't thank me." Her smile became a cat-in-cream grin as she turned toward the lemonade tent with a wave. "Just do us all a favor and don't go turnin' up in my courtroom again, either." She took a few steps, not even bothering to drop her voice as she murmured, "A Cross and a Whittaker. Who'd have thunk it?"

Marley waited for the woman to be out of earshot, but only just, before she said, "Oh, my God. Talk about something I wasn't expecting."

"Me, either." The sudden concern on Marley's face tugged at him just enough to make him add, "We can always check in with Louis from time to time to make sure he's on the level."

She nodded. "That's a good idea. You know, just in case."

They moved through the yard, stopping to talk with a few folks here and there. Greyson went to get ol' Gypsy from her pen inside the shelter, not getting much farther than the threshold when a flash of blond braids and a gap-toothed grin caught his attention.

"Greyson!" Sierra hugged him tightly. Man, she'd really come out of her shell in the couple of weeks she'd been helping out around here. She looked happier, not to mention healthier, although that was likely due to the groceries and produce he and Marley had still been sneaking onto her back step a few times a week.

"Hey, Little Bit," he said, applying the nickname he'd given her on her second day of dog-walking duties. "How's it going?"

"Good. Come on!" She grabbed his hand, firmly enough that he couldn't do anything other than follow her through the yard, shrugging at Marley, who Sierra scooped up with her other hand a few steps later, leading them both toward the gate. Greyson's heart beat faster in the oh-crap kind of way as he realized the girl's destination; or, more importantly, who was standing there. Marley must have realized, too—the resemblance between Sierra and her mother was impossible to miss, and the woman looked none too thrilled

—but there was no getting out of this. Even if they wanted to.

Sierra came to a halt beside her mother, dropping both Greyson and Marley's hands. "Mom, these are the two I've been telling you about. Greyson and Marley, this is my mom."

"Jade Beckett," the blonde said quietly, offering her hand to them each in turn.

"Greyson Whittaker. It's nice to meet you, ma'am." Greyson tipped his hat with one hand, keeping his grip on Gypsy's leash firm with the other. "Thanks for letting Sierra come help us with the animals. She's a natural."

Jade nodded, running a hand over her threadbare sundress. "When I spoke with Louis, he assured me she wouldn't be under y'all's feet. Thank you for keeping her busy. My work schedule is...unpredictable."

"It was no problem at all."

Jade's smile grew tight, and she turned to look at Marley. "Sierra tells me you're the one who's been leaving groceries on our step."

Although surprise parted Marley's lips, she didn't hesitate, nor did she drop her gaze. "That's true. I am."

"I'm not looking for a handout," she said, but the words were far from argumentative. They were simple. Factual.

Which was exactly how Marley answered them. "I know."

"That said"—Jade's chin dropped, just a degree—"it's very kind of you. Things lately have been difficult."

Marley looked at Sierra, who had gone solemnly silent, her lips pressed together. "Sierra mentioned that you're looking for full-time work."

Jade blinked, and wait, where was Marley going with this? "I clean some houses here and there, for people in

Camden Valley," Jade said. "But it's just temporary. I'm trying as hard as I can to find something steady. Something better. I'd just...I'd like to stay closer, to be with Sierra when she gets home from school once the new term starts, and there aren't a lot of job opportunities here in Millhaven, is all."

"I might know of one."

Greyson's brows shot up as Jade's furrowed together. "I'm sorry. I don't understand," she said.

Marley smiled, and right then and there, Greyson knew not just what she was about to say, but that he was head over boots in love with her.

"I manage the storefront at Cross Creek Farm. It's a fairly new establishment—the storefront, not the farm"—she paused for a self-deprecating smile—"but we're growing like weeds out there. In fact, business is booming so much that I just got approval to hire an assistant manager."

A soft gasp crossed Jade's lips as she followed Marley's meaning. "You think I could do that job?"

"I think it's a lot of hard work, and you'd have to be committed to it," Marley said. "But I wouldn't mind training the right person, or holding off on placing an ad online until you and I had a chance to talk about it some more."

"Why would you do that?" Jade's cheeks turned red, and she shook her head quickly. "Not that I'm not grateful for the opportunity. I'd love to talk with you some more. But why are you so willing to help me and my daughter?"

"Because I'm part of this community," Marley said, nothing but honesty in her words. "And I know what it's like to need someone to show you back to the path so you can walk on your own."

Jade dropped her chin and whispered, "Thank you."

"My pleasure. Why don't you come by Cross Creek on Monday at about ten, and we'll talk some more."

Sierra hugged her mother and grinned, bending down low to pet Gypsy, who was still tethered to the leash in Greyson's hand.

He cleared his throat and sat back on his heels. "Maybe we should introduce your mother to Gypsy." The old dog was the little girl's favorite.

"She's cute," Jade said, laughing as Gypsy flopped onto her back and Sierra obliged her with some belly rubs.

"Mommy, can't we adopt Gypsy? Please? She needs a forever home, and you've always said how much you'd love to have a dog again, like you did when you were a little girl."

"Oh, honey." Jade tried on a look that Greyson would bet she knew all too well, one that said she wanted to say yes, but she knew she was going to have to disappoint her daughter. "Gypsy's very sweet, and I would love to adopt her," she said with honesty in her tone. "But dogs are expensive. It says right here on the flyer that there's an adoption fee, and—"

Greyson shook his head, canceling out the rest of her words. "Normally, that's true, but Sierra here is our star volunteer." He'd cover the adoption fee himself if Louis had a problem with waiving it. "It's still up to your mom, of course, and you should take your time to decide. Owning a dog is a big responsibility. But as for the fee, that's covered."

"Please, Mom? I already know how to walk her, and everything!" Sierra took the leash from Greyson's hand, leading Gypsy around in a circle in the grass as proof.

"She's already spayed and up to date on all of her shots, so you won't need to take her to the vet. We can get you all of her records," Marley murmured, softly enough to keep the information away from Sierra's ears in case Jade still wanted to pass.

The smile flickering over Jade's face was answer enough, though. "Why don't we go see Mr. Kerrigan in the office to at least take a look at the paperwork?"

Sierra grinned, hugging him, then Marley, before grabbing her mother's hand. Jade and Marley exchanged a pair of "see you on Monday"s, and the day had been so perfect, *she* was so perfect, that Greyson didn't think twice.

"Everyone around here is adopting pets. Even Blue found the perfect place to live." His farmhand, José, had adopted the rambunctious dog, who—as it turned out—was a great cattle herder. "Have you thought about maybe giving Shadow a forever home?"

Marley stopped. Blinked. Blinked some more. "He's a sweet dog," she finally said. "My favorite, if I'm being honest, and I know he's taken a liking to me."

"News flash. That dog adores you." He'd certainly lived up to his name around her over the last few weeks. Whenever he wasn't following Marley around the yard, he was curled up in her lap or sitting on her sneakers.

"Okay, yes," she agreed with a laugh. "I love him, too, but...well, I don't really have a home to give him."

"You could."

Greyson's heart pounded like thunder in his chest. They'd been interrupted the first time he'd said it, but this was worth repeating. A thousand times. Through a megaphone. Hell, he'd rent a fucking skywriter if that's what it took to get her to see it.

"You could have a home here, in Millhaven. I know you're scared to stay, and you've got scars from losing your mother. You've got good reasons to guard your heart. But you've also got me, and a father and brothers who want you to give them a chance. They want you to be part of their family. We're all here for you, and we're not gonna leave. So, what do you say?"

He took her hand and squeezed, hanging on tight. "Will you give this a shot? Will you stay?"

Marley smiled, slow and sweet, squeezing right back. "I trust you, Greyson. If you say it'll be okay, then I have to believe it'll be okay. Yes. I'll stay."

27

Marley knew there was a giant grab bag of emotions she could be feeling as she rummaged through her room for her car keys. Panic, because she'd had a long day at the storefront and was running late to meet Greyson. Excitement at the fact that they had the next twelve hours to spend together, uninterrupted and, in all likelihood, very naked. Happiness at the decision she'd made to stay in Millhaven, finally letting people past arm's length and into the heart that had been empty and hurting for an entire year.

Scared, whispered a voice from somewhere way down deep in her chest. Marley stopped her search, flexing her fingers over her dresser mid-reach and curling them into a tight ball to ground herself.

"No."

The voice retreated, filling her with relief. Yes, the prospect of losing someone close would always scare her. She was human, after all. But Greyson had promised things would be okay, and while Marley might not trust fate (thorny bitch), she did trust him.

Everything would be okay. It had to be.

"Ah, gotcha!" she crowed, her fingers closing over the keys that had been buried beneath the shirt she'd worn yesterday. Putting them in her wristlet, she hit the stairs running, her boots echoing over the hardwood floors. She realized, too late, that Tobias must have been napping on the living room couch, because he snapped to attention, his hair mussed and his expression disoriented, as soon as she reached the landing.

"Oh, crap. I'm so sorry," she said. He'd been sifting through farm catalogues when she'd gone upstairs to shower and change only thirty minutes ago. They put their orders in on the first Wednesday of every month, which was tomorrow. "I didn't realize you'd decided to take a nap, otherwise I wouldn't have been so loud."

He refocused after a few blinks, placing the Stetson he pretty much always wore back on his head. "No, no. I'm glad you woke me. I've got to finalize a few orders yet. I didn't intend to doze off."

"Wow. You must have really needed the rest." Marley's worry tapped to life, and she opened her mouth to ask him if he was okay. But then he smiled, his blue-gray eyes crinkling at the edges like usual.

"Reckon I must have. Sure did the trick, though."

Marley smiled back. God, she needed to stop overreacting so much. "Well, I'm glad you got a chance to sneak in a nap, then. I'm going to head to Greyson's, and I won't be back 'til tomorrow, since I'm off until Thursday. Can I get you anything before I head out?"

"Actually, I was hopin' for just a minute of your time." Tobias's gaze darted to the front door and back. "As long as you're not in too big a rush."

She might be running late, but for this, Greyson would

understand. Especially since Tobias looked so serious all of a sudden. "Not at all. What's up?"

"Well, it's about that money you owe the hospital."

"What about it?" Marley asked carefully, her heartbeat speeding up. She'd been able to make the payment with greater ease this month, but she still had eight more of them to go, none of them small.

A fact which Tobias must've guessed, because he said, "I'd still like to help you take care of the debt."

"No." She kept her expression soft to temper the steel of her determination.

Determination, it seemed, that she'd come by honestly on both sides. "You can call it a loan, if you like."

"One you won't let me pay back," Marley argued, and his non-reply was all the confirmation she needed. "Look, I appreciate the offer. I really do. But I meant what I said a few weeks ago. I don't want to feel like your obligation. I know *you* might not feel as if I am," she qualified. "But this is important to me. I want us to move forward with a clean slate. Even ground, you and me. Okay?"

For a second, Tobias said nothing, and she straightened her shoulders, prepared to go for a gentle-but-firm round two. Then he surprised her with, "Alright, then. Clean slate."

"Thank you."

"Now go on and get. And do your old man a favor and be careful."

"I will," Marley said, grinning. She opened the door to head out, but the presence of a figure, up-close and hand lifted to knock, stopped her short.

"Whoa!" She stepped back, brows shooting up, and what the... "Doc Sanders?"

"Oh! Marley." The doctor's eyes widened before darting over Marley's shoulder, as if she were searching for something. "I, ah. I was expecting...well, you startled me."

"What are you doing here?" Marley asked, thoroughly confused for just a second before biting her tongue. "Ugh, I apologize. I didn't mean it like that."

The doctor smiled, although the expression didn't quite stick. "That's okay. I was just passing by and I thought I'd drop these off for your father."

Tobias appeared behind Marley. "Hi, there, Doc."

"Tobias." The doctor dropped her chin slightly, not quite meeting Tobias's eyes. "I brought by those vitamins I was telling you about at your appointment last week." She held up a white paper bag, the pills inside rattling along with Marley's pulse.

"You had an appointment last week?" she asked.

Tobias's expression, which had been unreadable this whole time, didn't change. "Just a check-up. Doc Sanders here is the best around. She likes to keep us all in tip-top shape."

"Oh." Marley took a breath. She was being silly. The whole thing made perfect sense. Even though the doctor still had an odd look on her face, and the bag holding those vitamins was pretty huge. "Okay. As long as everything's good."

"Don't you worry about a thing. Everything is right as rain," Tobias said.

Marley repeated the saying all the way down the steps and to her car, but somehow, she couldn't quite convince herself that they were true.

GREYSON PULLED the baking dish of barbecue chicken out of

his oven, feeling like a goddamn rock star. True, the chicken hadn't been *that* hard to make, with the marinade having done nearly all of the work and the oven doing the rest, and the potatoes and green beans he'd grabbed to go with it had been five-ingredient wonders. But between the meal and the fact that Marley was due to arrive at any second—not to mention that he absolutely planned to have her instead of dessert, tonight and every night for the foreseeable future—life was pretty freaking stellar.

A knock sounded off on his front door, and speak of the devil. "Hey," Greyson said, opening the door and stepping forward to wrap an arm around Marley's waist. "I hope you're hungry, because..." He stopped short, his stomach squeezing with unease. "What's wrong?"

One dark brow rose as far as it could go. "Who says anything's wrong?"

Greyson pulled her over the threshold and into his apartment, closing the door behind her. "Well, let's see. Should I start right here, with the crease on your forehead?" He brushed a finger over the delicate furrow until it smoothed a little. "Or maybe the frown you've got going right here." Unable to help it, he slipped a kiss across her lips, soft and quick. "Or how about this tension, in these shoulders of yours?" His fingers traveled up, pressing into her knotted muscles. "You've never been one to hide what you're feeling, Marley. And right now, I can tell something's troubling you. Talk to me."

"It's probably nothing," she said, although between her tone and the look on her face, Greyson knew she didn't believe that.

Still, he wanted to erase the worry from her face as fast as possible, so he said, "That may be, but you'll probably feel better once you air it out."

"I think Tobias is sick."

"Okay." Greyson took a second to process her words. "Do you think he's got the flu or something?"

Marley shook her head, her words unleashing like a torrent. "No, not like that. I think there's something *wrong*. He's had two doctor's appointments in the last month, and he looks tired. He naps all the time even though he's cut back on his hours at Cross Creek, and just now, Doc Sanders came to the house to hand-deliver medicine, and—"

"Whoa, whoa, whoa, slow down," Greyson said. It was rare that *he* was the voice of reason—in fact, this might be one for the history books. But Marley was clearly upset. She needed reassurance, and fast. "I'm sure there's a logical explanation for all of this. Let's just start at the beginning."

"Okay." She took a breath, resting a hand over the front of her tank top. "Last month, after I had breakfast with Cate at Clementine's Diner, I saw Tobias coming out of Doc Sanders's office. But then today, he told me he'd just had another appointment this week."

Greyson thought about it for a second. "Maybe she just wanted to re-test something as a precaution. No big deal."

Marley looked unconvinced, but didn't argue. "He's tired, though. Like, *all* the time."

"Yeah, but you know how tough working on a farm can be," Greyson pointed out. "And you're running the storefront. Not that it's not hard work, but there's even more manual labor that goes into operations, and Tobias has been doing it every day for over thirty years." Christ, Greyson loved farming the same way he loved to breathe air, and even he was exhausted just thinking about it.

Marley bit her lip. "Okay, then how do you explain Doc Sanders showing up at the house just now?"

That one *was* a tiny bit strange. Still… "I don't know. How did she explain it?"

"She said she was on her way home and wanted to drop off some vitamins they'd talked about at his checkup."

"That doesn't sound so crazy," Greyson said. "I mean, this is Millhaven. House calls, especially for something routine like that, aren't entirely unheard of."

Concern dashed through Marley's eyes, making them glint in the light streaming in past the curtains. "Maybe not, but she looked strange. Uncomfortable. Not at all like the first time I met her."

A light bulb went off in Greyson's head. "Doc Sanders takes her job real serious. Maybe she just wanted to protect Tobias's privacy and wasn't comfortable talking about his appointment in front of you." He wouldn't put that past the doc. In fact, he'd be shocked if she *didn't* protect a patient's privacy with all that she had.

"Oh," Marley whispered, some of the tension easing from her face. "Well, I never thought of it that way."

"Look, if you're that worried about it, you should ask Tobias. But truly, I don't think this is anything to be worried about," Greyson said.

"You don't?"

"I don't." He inhaled, a feeling he'd known for far too long swirling in his chest. "You've got a great chance to know Tobias and to be a family. In fact, I'm a little jealous. I wish…" Greyson paused, but this was Marley. She trusted him. Cared about him, just as he was. "I wish I had that with my old man. I wish I'd had a chance to make the effort so he and I could start fresh."

"You still could," Marley said. "If I can mend things with Tobias, anyone can."

Rather than express his doubt and kill the lightening

mood, Greyson pulled her close and dropped his forehead to hers. "We're a hell of a pair, huh?"

Her laugh wasn't loud or strong, but God, it was the sweetest thing he'd ever heard as it chased his unease away. "We are."

He cupped her face, kissing her once, then twice. And as Marley deepened the kiss in soft, needful strokes and he picked her up to carry her to bed, dinner be damned, Greyson knew that as long as she was by his side and he was by hers, everything would turn out just fine.

28

"Hellllllooooooo?" Marley dropped her keys on the table in the foyer of the main house, closing the door behind her. Quiet was the only thing to greet her, signaling that her brothers and Tobias were all out in the fields. Cate's car hadn't been in the side lot, and Marley belatedly remembered that she was attending a daylong seminar on maximizing the efficiency of the bookkeeping software they'd started using earlier this year. Having the house to herself was odd, to be sure, but maybe she'd head on down to the greenhouse to see what kind of berries Owen had on-hand. She'd thrown blueberries into her peach cobbler recipe last week. Maybe she could grab some blackberries today. Those would go over great in a jam, too. If she worked really hard, she could probably get a few jars on the shelf by as early as next week.

Marley laughed, the sound floating through the empty house. Her mood was considerably lighter than it had been when she'd left seventeen hours ago. But between the reassurance of Greyson's words and the slow, sexy comfort he'd given her in bed, not once, but twice, she knew he was right.

He'd promised her everything would be fine. It was time for her to start believing him. It was time to be with him, be with her family, without being scared.

Once and for all.

Turning toward the stairs with her sights set on the shower, she kicked her feet into motion. But a piece of paper stuck between the pages of Tobias's farm catalogue on the front table caught her eye, a familiar logo freezing her to her spot.

"What the hell?" Marley picked up the catalogue, shaking the single page free. It was a printout of an account summary, with Chicago Memorial Hospital's crest stamped in the upper right-hand corner. Her name was listed as the account holder, all the information matching the account that she'd been chipping away at for the past year. Except the little box that listed the balance read *paid in full*, and wait, wait. This couldn't be right.

How could the debt be paid?

Hands shaking, Marley dialed the number on the printout, accessing her account with her PIN code. After an automated voice confirmed that—holy shit—she did in fact have a zero balance, she hit "0", at least ten different emotions of equal intensity balling in her gut as she waited for the phone to ring once...twice...

"Accounting department, Darlene speaking."

Marley tried to calm her voice, but she was pretty sure it was a no-go. "Hi, Darlene, my name is Marley Rallston. I'm looking at my account, and it seems the balance was paid off recently. But I didn't make the payment."

"Oh, no," Darlene said, her tone going brighter by a notch as Marley confirmed her account number and answered the security questions. "I took this call yesterday. I remember it perfectly. It was a lovely gentleman. He said he was a friend of the family. Had kind of a Southern accent? But he was very clear that he wanted the account paid in full."

"Can he do that? You know, without my permission?"

Darlene's laugh grew nervous. "Well, when someone calls to pay off an account, we don't usually argue. The payment cleared without a problem, so..."

Marley cursed internally. "Okay. Can you reverse it?"

"I'm afraid not," Darlene said. "All payments are final, and the account has been closed."

She was tempted to argue anyway. But since she knew it would almost certainly get her nowhere, and Darlene wasn't really the object of her frustration anyway, she thanked the woman and hung up. Why would Tobias go so far out of his way to do something he *knew* she didn't want him to? Marley had made it painfully clear, not once, but twice, that she'd wanted to pay the debt herself, and now, she wasn't struggling to do so. These were all things Tobias knew, because she'd made sure to tell him, so he *wouldn't* do something like this.

She spun to grab one of the walkie-talkies from the office, determined to get the answer straight from the source, when a memory plowed into her, knocking her breath loose. The day her mother had gotten her diagnosis from the oncologist, she'd gone directly to an attorney's office. Marley had thought the whole thing was insane—there were treatments, chemo and radiation and all sorts of options to fight. But the woman's advice hadn't been to set aside any money to pursue those, nor had it been not to worry.

Get your affairs in order, she'd said.

Oh, God. Had Tobias paid off her debt—debt she'd all but begged him not to touch—because he really *was* sick, and was getting his affairs in order? Was he righting the wrongs of their past and making up for not coming to find her seven years ago?

Was he cleaning their slate, like she'd said she wanted, to *end* things rather than to start over?

Swallowing her panic, Marley turned back toward the stairs. She had to get far, far away from here, right now. God, how had she been so stupid? She'd known he was sick. She'd *known* it! But Greyson had convinced her otherwise, pushing her to stay in Millhaven and promising her everything would be okay.

Okay. Marley barked out a bitter laugh. What did he know of okay? Maybe he'd had good intentions when he'd made those promises, but he'd never watched someone he loved desperately waste away, month by month, minute by minute. He'd never had to feed someone ice chips, only to watch that person throw them back up, along with blood and bile and all sorts of other, awful things. He'd never had to watch that person's hair fall out from all the toxic chemicals being pumped through their failing body, never had to pick out that person's fucking *coffin*.

Greyson had thrown the word—the idea of it—around so easily. *Okay*. He'd never watched anyone he loved die. Instead, he'd convinced her to put her heart on the line and stay. He promised her everything would be fine, that her family would never leave her, that Tobias wasn't sick, and like a goddamned fool, she'd believed him.

She couldn't do this. She couldn't stay and watch her only living parent die. The grief had nearly broken her once.

She had to get out of Millhaven before it broke her for good.

~

As soon as Greyson got within range of the Wi-Fi at his parents' house, his phone blew up like a supernova. Reaching into his back pocket, he grumbled out a healthy "what the hell?" at the seven—no, eight—missed calls. None of them were from numbers he recognized, but all were local. No messages. He'd only been harvesting corn for a couple of hours, for Chrissake. Who the hell was—

His phone rang in his hand, and he took the call, ready to dish up a ration of shit over the spam casserole. "Whittaker," he ground out, and the person on the other end let out a huff of...relief?

"Jesus, it's about time!"

"Hunter?" Okay, so this had just gone from irritating to weird in less than two seconds. "Why the hell..."

"Is Marley with you?" The guy sounded distraught, and every hair on the back of Greyson's neck stood on end.

"What?"

Hunter made a noise of frustration. "Is Marley with you? I need to know."

"No, I haven't seen her since this morning," Greyson said, switching to offense in the same breath. "Why? What's wrong?"

"You haven't heard from her at all?" Hunter asked. "No texts, no voicemails? Nothing?"

Greyson worked for his inhale, dread pooling in a heavy layer beneath his frustration. After pulling his phone away from his ear to double-check, he said, "No. I'm only going to ask you one more time. What the hell is going on?"

"We're not..." Hunter broke off, and a muffled female voice, not Marley's—Cate McAllister's, maybe?—sounded off in the background. "We're not entirely sure, but it looks as if...well, it looks like she's gone."

"Gone," Greyson repeated, as if the word was in some

ancient foreign language that hadn't been spoken aloud in centuries.

"Her room is completely cleaned out. Bed made, drawers empty. Her car is gone from the side lot, and she took herself off the schedule at the storefront. Left a resignation letter, effective immediately."

For one, single heartbeat, Greyson stood there, suspended in time, in a world that was normal. Good. Right.

And then the gravity of what Hunter had said, of what the words *meant*, smashed into him like a wrecking ball, leaving nothing but shattered debris behind.

Marley couldn't be gone.

"I'll be right there." Greyson looked down, shocked to find his legs already in motion.

Hunter sputtered. "I don't think..."

"I don't give a rat's ass what you think," he snapped. None of this made any sense. Marley had been sleeping, safe and sound in his bed, just this morning. She'd promised to stay. She'd said she *trusted* him. She'd never leave, and especially not without a goodbye.

There had to be a good explanation for this. He just needed to find it, and the best place to start was the source.

Greyson made it to Cross Creek Farm in record time, thanking his lucky stars that Lane hadn't set up any speed traps along the route. He didn't have to bother knocking on the front door at the main house. As soon as his boots hit the bottom step of the porch, Owen swung the thing open and greeted him with a nod.

"I guess we should've known better than to think we could keep you from comin'," Owen said, ushering him inside. And whoa, it was a family affair up in here. All four Cross men were in the living room, each looking as freaked out as Greyson felt. Emerson, Cate, and a very pregnant

Scarlett all sat on the couch, murmuring quietly to one another and scrolling through their cell phones.

"I'm going to assume y'all have tried to call her," Greyson ventured. Eli shot him a look hard enough to cut diamonds, and he held up his hands. "Okay, okay. Just checking. Right to voicemail?"

"Yeah," Hunter said, and Greyson's defenses churned past his confusion.

"Me, too." He'd tried three times on his way here. *Hey, this is Marley. Sorry I missed your call...*had greeted him on the first ring.

"Clementine hasn't seen her today," Cate said, lowering her cell phone with a frown.

"Neither has Lane or Daisy," Emerson added, and Scarlett turned the bad news into a trifecta.

"She hasn't been to The Corner Market or anywhere on Town Street, either."

Greyson's temples pounded. How the hell could Marley be gone? "The last time I saw her was at five o'clock this morning, when I left my place. She was asleep."

Eli looked at him, eyes narrowing. "Was she acting weird last night? You didn't piss her off, did you?"

"I'm going to pretend you didn't ask me that," Greyson said through his teeth.

Thankfully, Owen stepped between them on the area rug. "And I'm going to take that as a no."

"That's a no," Greyson confirmed after a deep breath. "She wasn't upset when I saw her. Wait..." Oh, no. No, no, *fuck* no.

When people get too close now, I panic, and when I panic, I put everyone at arm's length.

He swung to look at Tobias, who had been oddly silent. The man looked positively ashen, his brow creased in concern and his mouth pressed into a flat line. "She was worried you're not well," Greyson said, realization sinking into him like razor wire.

"What?" At least three voices loosened the question, but God, it made sense.

"She saw you with Doc Sanders yesterday. Said you've looked tired." Greyson had to admit, she sure as shit hadn't been wrong about that. "She told me she's scared of losing another parent, but I never thought..."

All of a sudden, everything came into crystal-clear focus. This wasn't a mistake, and there wasn't a good explanation for it. Despite everything she'd said last night, despite her promises to stay, Marley had left Millhaven without so much as a goodbye. She was *gone*. Greyson had opened up to her, shown her exactly who he was, and let her convince him to show other people, too. He'd risked his father's scorn, his stupid heart—God, *everything*—by falling for her, and she'd said she trusted him. It had never occurred to him that he shouldn't trust her back.

And didn't that just make him the world's biggest idiot?

"She thinks Pop is sick, and that's why she left?" Hunter asked, and Cate exhaled softly.

"It makes perfect sense."

"Okay," Eli said, his voice barely making it past all the anger welling up in Greyson's chest. "She can't have gotten that far, and there aren't a whole lot of routes out of town. I bet if we split up, we'll find her."

"You want to go *after* her?" Greyson asked, shock crowding his chest.

"Uh, yeah," Owen said. Damn, the guy had already pulled up a map of the Shenandoah Valley on his phone. "That's our sister, and we're going to bring her home, where she belongs. If we hurry up, we should be able to make good time and catch her before it gets too late. Greyson, you can ride with me, Hunter can ride with Eli and Pop, and—"

"I'm not going."

Every head in the room turned toward him. Hunter, who had always had the coolest head among his brothers, stepped closer, dropping his voice while the rest of the family moved together to examine the map.

"Are you really going to be a dick about this?" Hunter asked. "Right now, when Marley needs you?"

Greyson's laugh held zero joy. "Needs me? For Chrissake, she *had* me," he hissed. "I told her I wouldn't leave her, and like a dumbass, I meant it. Too bad she didn't return the favor. She didn't even stick around long enough to ask questions. Instead, she took off without so much as a goodbye."

"She's scared of the answers. She needs us. She needs *you*," Hunter said, but nope. No way. Greyson couldn't go there. Not when he'd been trampled this hard.

He should've stuck with what he'd known, what had worked for him for his entire life.

Pushing first was always better than pushing back.

"No, she doesn't. Marley made her choice, and Millhaven isn't it. Do you really want to chase her down when you know she ain't comin' back? That girl does what she wants. And if what she wants right now is to leave all of this behind, then fine by me."

A muscle flexed in Hunter's jaw, signaling his irritation. "Don't let your pride get in the way, Whittaker. I get that you're pissed, but I also think you care about *that girl*."

"No," Greyson said, his hurt and his anger and his defenses coming together to shove him toward the door. "I *did* care about her, but she left. And if you think she's coming back, you're a bigger fool than I am."

29

Marley's eyes burned something fierce, although whether it was from the seven hours of driving into the blazing sun, then the headlights that had just begun to rise on the opposite side of the highway, or the fact that she'd cried every single tear her body could manufacture, she couldn't be sure. Either way, the plastic-encased diner menu in front of her slipped in and out of focus, and after her ninth attempt at reading the options, she was pretty much ready to give up.

"Hi, hon," said the platinum blond waitress, who was—thank Jesus, Mary, and all the stars in the sky—armed with a carafe and an empty mug. "Coffee?"

Marley would've kissed the woman on the mouth if she'd been able to muster the energy. "Please."

The waitress filled the oversized mug, then asked, "What can I getcha to eat?"

Since Marley hadn't been able to scan the menu despite her best efforts, she went with a safe diner bet. "I'll have a piece of pie. Whatever today's special is would be great."

"You got it."

The waitress sauntered off, leaving Marley to her thoughts, oh yay. She'd fought two urges to turn around and go back to Millhaven, once when she'd crossed the Virginia/West Virginia border, then again when she'd crossed into Ohio a few minutes ago. The drive had been slower going than she'd hoped—in fact, she was still nearly a hundred miles from where she'd planned to stop for the night. Her defenses felt stiff, atrophied from non-use and covered in dust. But Marley would have to toughen back up, fast. She needed to put Millhaven behind her, to resist the temptation to turn around and head back east, to leave her heart unguarded and make herself vulnerable to a pain she'd never survive.

Never mind that right now hurt pretty fucking badly.

"Here ya go," chirped the waitress, placing a dish of pie in front of her. Marley's stomach pitched when she realized it was loaded with peaches, and oh God, she missed Greyson. The farm. Her family.

She wanted to go back.

"No," Marley whispered. Pushing the plate away, she firmed her resolve, yanking her armor back into place. No matter how right and good Greyson's arms had felt around her, how happy she'd been at Cross Creek and how much she'd felt like she belonged there, she couldn't go back.

She'd had a family once before. Been someone's daughter. Loved that person with all of her might, and that person had died.

She couldn't lose everything again. Even if that meant not having anything.

Marley shook her head, reaching for the wristlet she'd placed on the vinyl bench seat beside her and turning to ask the waitress if she could get a to-go cup for the coffee. But the sight of the four men who had just barged into the diner sent her heart to her windpipe.

"Marley! Thank God," Owen said, the first one to catch sight of her, as he'd been leading the pack. Hunter and Eli let out similar exclamations, and—Marley realized with a start—even Tobias was there, looking wholly relieved. Owen got to her first, tugging her into a bear hug, and holy shit, what was happening?

"Jesus, kid. You had us worried," Owen said as he released her a full ten seconds later, and finally, Marley gathered her wits enough to speak.

"What are you guys doing here?" God, she didn't even know exactly where *here* was, let alone why on earth they'd follow her all this way. "How did you even find me?"

"It took some doing, I'll tell you that," Eli said, nudging her back toward the booth she'd just vacated. She was so shocked that she went, letting him sandwich her in as Owen, Hunter, and Tobias sat down across from them. "We've been to so many diners and truck stops, it's almost stupid. But there were only two real routes we thought you'd take. Cate and Emerson are on the other one. Scarlett stayed home in case you turned up there. Oh!" He swung a gaze at Hunter, who already had his cell phone in-hand.

"Got it. I just texted everybody to let them know we've got her and that everything is okay."

Marley's brows winged toward the ceiling. "Um, are you crazy? Everything is *not* okay."

"We found you," Owen said, nodding at the waitress as she lifted her carafe of coffee in question from behind the counter. Eli dropped his gaze to the piece of pie Marley hadn't touched, his eyes lighting.

"Oooh, pie. Granted, it's peach. Not my favorite." He pulled a face to back up the claim. "But I'm starving."

Yep, it was official. Marley was in the goddamned Twilight Zone. "You guys chased me across three states to sit here and eat pie?"

"No," Hunter said, waiting for the waitress to fill the four mugs she'd brought with her before telling Marley, "We chased you across three states to bring you home."

"Cross Creek isn't my home," she whispered. The words sounded hollow in her ears, though, and Owen didn't hesitate to call her on them.

"Yes, it is, Marley. I know you're scared of having a family again, but...well, Pop, do you want to take this one?"

Tobias nodded, and sweet Lord in heaven, would she ever be able to read this man's expression? "Your brothers and I had plenty of time to talk during the drive," he said quietly. "But there are some things you need to know. First off, I'm not dyin'. Well, not anytime soon, I don't reckon."

Relief ricocheted through Marley's rib cage, followed by a full dose of confusion. "You're not? But you've been so tired lately. And then there were all those appointments—"

"I *am* anemic," Tobias said. "I didn't say anything to any of you because I didn't want you to worry. That's what those pills were for. They're iron supplements. And it's true, I haven't been myself lately. But the reason for that isn't that I'm sick."

Her heart squeezed as finally, his expression grew emotional. "It's that I'm retiring."

Marley's shoulders bumped against the back of the booth. "W-what?"

"Truth is, it was a hard decision to make, and I fought it pretty good. That led to some sleepless nights. I love Cross Creek. Always have. But after all these years, and that scare I had last summer, well, I *am* tired. Owen and Hunter have things well under control, and Eli'll be here for a bit after the baby is born. With you runnin' the storefront, plus Cate and Scarlett and Emerson workin' as hard as they do, too, well, I knew the time was finally right. Cross Creek is family owned and operated, just as it's meant to be. So, yes. I'm retiring."

Marley's thoughts whirled like a carnival ride, and she grabbed the first one dancing by. "Okay, but *all* those trips to see Doc Sanders were for anemia? Isn't that diagnosed with just a simple blood test?"

For the first time, Tobias dropped his eyes, and whoa, even her brothers were exchanging weird looks.

"Not...exactly," Tobias said. "Yes, I did have an appointment that first day you saw me outside of her office, but Doc Sanders"—he paused to clear his throat—"Ellen and I have been spending a bit of time together."

Oh. My. God. "You're *dating* Doc Sanders?"

"I s'pose I am. I realize I should have said something before now, but to be honest, I wasn't sure how to tell y'all."

Owen leaned in, likely in an effort to allow Tobias to recover from the blush that had bloomed beneath his salt-and-pepper stubble. "I think it's great, Pop. Doc Sanders is a real nice lady, and you shouldn't be lonely."

Hunter and Eli nodded in agreement, and Marley's brain caught on the one last thing that had aimed her feet at the door seven hours ago. "You paid off my debt. Why would you do that if you weren't settling your affairs?"

"I know you said you wanted a clean slate," Tobias said. "And I do apologize for not heedin' your wishes. But you're my daughter, Marley, and in this family, we look out for our own."

"But Lorraine was *my* mother," she said, and Eli shook his head, pinning her with a Caribbean-blue stare.

"She might have been your family, but you're ours. You

could've told us about the debt. Of course we'd have helped you pay it."

Marley's heart raced, her throat tightening as tears sprang to her eyes. "It's not the same. Me, and you guys. I'm not...family like you are. Cross Creek isn't my home."

"Is that what you think?" Hunter's laugh was soft. "That we don't care for you the same as we care for each other?"

"No," she said automatically. "Maybe. I don't know. I *am* different than you three."

"You weren't raised in Millhaven like we were, no," Owen said. "But if there's one thing I know above all others, it's that home isn't a place. It's a feeling. It's knowing you can be as ugly as you need to be, and you'll still be loved. It's knowing that you're cared for, every minute of every day, no matter what. It's knowing that you're safe. That you belong to someone, and they belong to you right back. Home is where your family is, and we are your family. Your home is right here."

Marley began to cry in earnest, then, because in that instant, she knew Owen was right. "I'm so sorry. I shouldn't have left the way I did. I just got so scared after everything that happened with my mother." She looked at Tobias, everything so clear in hindsight. "I *really* thought you were sick. I panicked, and...God, I'm so, so sorry. I don't want to leave. I want to go back to Millhaven. That's where I belong, as long as you'll have me."

"Of course we will," Tobias said softly. "Let's get you home."

But as her brothers and Tobias crowded in to hug her, dry her tears, and take her back to the farm, Marley's heart still ached.

She wouldn't be exactly where she belonged without

Greyson. Greyson, who had believed in her. Cared for her. Greyson, who she'd left without saying goodbye.

Greyson, who probably hated her right now as much as she loved him, which meant she was going to have to do everything in her power, no matter how crazy, to get him back.

30

Greyson's muscles fought between burn and burnout, but still, he kept moving. He'd left Cross Creek yesterday evening and gone straight home, diving headfirst into a bottle of Jim Beam, no glass. He'd run the spectrum of emotions, dwelling mostly in the gray area between pissed off and defiant, because, hey, better the devil you know. He'd had a weak moment somewhere around ten thirty, when he'd been drunk enough to tumble into bed but sober enough to realize that his pillows and bed sheets smelled like wildflowers—all of them, because Marley was a consummate cover hog. He'd snatched every stich off the bed with a curse, wadding them up and throwing them all on the floor before finally crashing face-first on his couch. The few fitful hours of sleep he'd managed, coupled with the ice-cold shower and piping hot pot of coffee he'd mainlined before heading out the door two hours ago had been enough to sober him the rest of the way up, but, funny, they hadn't touched the gaping hole in his chest, or the anger and sadness that had filled it.

Marley was gone. She'd left him without a goodbye, and

she wasn't coming back. He really needed to get his head together, focus on his farm, and get the fuck over it.

"Somethin' must be under your skin pretty good," came a voice from the barn doorway, and son of a bitch, this was the last thing Greyson needed right now.

So, of course, it was exactly what he got. "The work needs done," he said, breaking stride with the lift-and-toss of the hay bales in the bed of his truck only to shrug.

His father raised one graying brow. "You're bailin' hay, which is a job we pay farmhands for, when the roosters have only been up for an hour? Seems less'n smart to me. Unless you want to walk around dog-tired all day."

"Maybe I do," Greyson said, sweat dripping from his forehead into his eyes, making them sting.

His father, who normally would've lost interest by now since Greyson was, in fact, working on the farm, lingered. "This wouldn't have anything to do with that Cross girl haulin' out of town yesterday, would it?"

Greyson's gut tilted, and he dropped the bale of hay that had been in his grasp to the barn floor with a heavy thump.

"What?" A smile twisted at his old man's lips. "Her sisters-in-law called half the damn county lookin' for her. You didn't think word wouldn't get around, did ya?"

"I didn't really pay it much mind," he said, although, fuck, he should've. Millhaven's grapevine had probably caught fire once word got out that Marley had taken off.

His father raised one hand in a dismissive wave. "Ah. I told you that girl was trouble. Them Crosses always did think they were so much better than the rest of us."

Something deep inside of Greyson snapped, sending his words up like a rising tide. "Why are you so goddamned angry all the time?"

"Because life's full of broken promises." The words,

which always emerged in bitterness, were oddly quiet. Quiet enough that, instead of pushing back or mouthing off like he'd always done in the past, Greyson simply listened.

"Nothing was supposed to turn out this way," his father finally said, because for the first time ever, Greyson had given him the chance instead of trying to get in a tangle with the man. "The farm. The work. The legacy. None of it."

Greyson's jaw unhinged. "What do you mean, it wasn't supposed to turn out this way?"

"You really don't know, do you?"

"Apparently not," Greyson said, unable to keep his attitude fully in check.

But his father surprised him further by letting go of a soft laugh. "I always thought Steve had told you, or at least mentioned it, since he was going to be your boss and all. Figures he'd have left that to me, too. I did get everything else."

Greyson's what-the-fuck-ometer spontaneously combusted. "Seriously, Pop. What the hell are you talking about?"

"Your uncle, that's what. You remember what he always used to say, about there bein' two types of folks around here?"

"Yeah," he said slowly, calling up the phrase in his mind. "The people who love Millhaven, and the people who leave it."

Greyson's old man nodded. "He always was a lover, ever since we were kids. Our daddy raised us on this farm just like his daddy raised him. Steve never wanted to do anything else. Always felt right as he could be, workin' the land. Reminds me of you, actually."

"But not you," Greyson said, and holy shit, it all made perfect sense.

"No. I worked on this farm for over twenty years, and never did love it. After my daddy died and left us the place eleven years ago, Steve and I agreed. I'd stay long enough to make sure everything was in order and running right, then I'd sell my half to him and leave Millhaven with your momma. You and your sisters were grown, they were all married. Steve promised to make you his right-hand and leave the farm to you when he passed. The only thing he wanted was to see Washington, DC one time before he took over."

Something loud and insistent sounded off close by, and Greyson was stunned to discover it was his heartbeat in his ears. "But then he was killed before you could sell him your half."

"He was." Bitter sadness carried his father's words. "I lost a brother I wanted, and gained a farm I didn't, all in one day. Life's what happens when you're busy makin' plans."

Funny, Greyson had always attributed the phrase to his uncle, but right here, in this moment, he realized it was his father who had always uttered it. "Why didn't you sell the place anyway?" he asked. The thought made him nauseous, and not a little, but still...if his old man hated Whittaker Hollow that much, surely he'd at least considered the option.

"It didn't feel right," his father said with a shrug. "It's been in our family for a long time. Sellin' it to Steve would'a kept it that way. Sellin' it to a stranger, well, who knows what would've become of it, or if they'd have given you a job. At least if I kept it, I knew you'd get to run the place, even if I had to stay while you did. Kinda figured it was just my lot to live and die here. I just didn't realize it would make me so angry to do it."

"Why didn't you ever tell me any of this?" Greyson asked.

"I thought you knew about Steve. Plus, talkin' about it wouldn't have changed anything."

Greyson could count at least fifty different ways it might've changed things, but saying as much probably wouldn't help. Not right this minute, anyway. "So, where does this hatred for the Crosses come from, then?"

"Some of it is pure rivalry," his old man said, gesturing to the open barn door behind him. "You of all people know what it's like to want to be the best around here."

Yeah, he kinda had Greyson's number, there. "And the other part?"

His old man paused. "Old man Cross got to live his dream. He was close with his sons, they're livin' theirs, too. Truth be told, a lot of it is just bitterness grown over time. Hell, even you got to live the life you wanted. I ain't too proud to say I feel like all I got were broken promises."

"It doesn't have to be that way, you know."

The look on his father's face was a testament to his doubt, but rather than push, Greyson just went for honesty. "Look, I'm not saying we can make changes overnight, and even though it would make us both happier than pigs in a mudpile, I can't buy you out of Whittaker Hollow." At least, not unless the bank gave him a monster of a loan, and even then, putting the farm up as collateral gave him hives the size of silver dollars. "But maybe if we sit down and really look at operations, we can figure out somethin' that'll work better than fighting like cats and dogs."

"It ain't like you to be so level," his father said, and Greyson's stomach knotted. At least Marley's influence might come to *some* good. Even if she'd never be around to see it.

"You, either. But I'm tired of picking fights instead of having conversations. This is who I am, Pop. I can't promise I'll always be a dream to work with. I've got rough edges, same as you. But I love this farm, and I swear I'll do the best I can to help you run it."

One corner of his father's mouth lifted, barely, but it was enough. "You know we're probably still gonna tussle over how to get things done. Ain't none of this gonna be easy, and it ain't gonna come quick, neither. There'll be a lot of hard work in front of us."

Greyson mirrored his father's expression, and you know, maybe the apple didn't fall too far from the tree after all. "That's okay," he said, extending his hand to his father for the first time in a decade. "I'm kinda counting on it."

After all, he was going to need all the hard work he could get to fill the Marley-sized hole in his heart.

TEN HOURS LATER, Greyson had to admit defeat. He'd stockpiled just enough energy to make it from his truck to his apartment to his shower to bed, although he'd probably be snoring before his head even landed firmly on his pillow.

The pillow that was currently on his floor, and would probably smell like wildflowers no matter how many times he freaking washed it.

"Knock it off," he muttered, pulling the Silverado out of Whittaker Hollow's driveway and onto the main road. His cell phone had remained quiet all day. No calls from Marley, and nothing from her brothers, either. Not that he'd expected anything—he'd told them she wouldn't come back. Once she made up her mind, there was no changing it.

And hadn't Greyson learned *that* the hard way.

Leaning a little harder on the gas pedal, he made his way toward his apartment building. His exhaustion was growing teeth, the dull thud behind his eyes pulsing along to the soundtrack of his heartbeat. He focused on the road in front of him, covering the ground as fast as he could, and ah, yeah, only a few minutes to go. Maybe less if he could hustle just a little faster...

Lane's police cruiser appeared from out of nowhere, blue and white lights flashing full-bore, and seriously? *Seriously*? If Greyson didn't know any better, he'd have said the guy had set himself up strategically, just waiting for his ass to come barreling by.

He pulled over, swearing every inch of the way so it would be out of his system once Lane arrived at his window, which happened about ten seconds later. "What seems to be the problem, Sheriff?"

"Greyson." Lane's expression was practically impenetrable, his eyes shielded behind the brim of his uniform hat and his mirrored Ray-Bans. "Can you step out of the vehicle, please?"

He had to be kidding. "I was only going like ten miles over the speed limit," Greyson protested, gritting his teeth. "Listen, I get that you've got a job to do, but I've had a really long day, and I'm not—"

"In the mood, I know," Lane said, and wait, what was that look that had flickered over his face? "This'll go quicker if you don't argue."

"What will?" Greyson asked.

"I need to take you down to the precinct."

Irritation flashed, deep and hot in Greyson's chest. Okay, fine. So maybe it had been twelve miles over the speed limit. Fifteen at the absolute worst. But still... "You're arresting me? *Again*?"

Lane stepped back, his jaw like granite, and gestured to his cruiser. "I don't like this any more than you do, Greyson. Step out of the vehicle. *Please.*"

Greyson nearly argued. He nearly told Lane to fuck straight off, that he could haul him in front of the judge just so Greyson could prove that Lane had a grudge. But Judge Abernathy had said not to ever show up in her courtroom again, and even though Greyson was pissed, he also knew fighting Lane fell under the heading of Epically Dumb Things.

"What about my truck?" he asked, and Lane nodded once in assurance.

"I'll take care of it like last time." He led the way to his cruiser, going through the whole mind-your-head routine as he deposited Greyson in the back. The trip to the police station was quick, the walk through the front doors uneventful, and finally, Greyson broke the silence.

"Are you seriously going to throw me in jail for going a few miles over the speed limit?"

"No," Lane said, although he kept walking down the hallway.

Greyson resisted the urge to pull up in shock. "No?"

Lane gave him a look akin to a nonverbal "was I unclear?", and Greyson had to ask. "Okay, then why did you drag me here, exactly?"

"That is an excellent question." Lane stopped in front of the jail cell and looked pointedly past the open door. "And there's your answer."

Marley stood in the center of the eight-by-eight space, wearing the same white tank top and cutoffs and motorcycle boots she'd had on the day Greyson had first met her, right on this very spot, and holy shit. Holy *shit*.

She was back in Millhaven.

"In you go," Lane said, and finally, Greyson's mouth caught up with his rushing thoughts and his slamming pulse.

"What if I don't want to talk to her?" he asked, his anger not one to take a knee. Marley didn't look shocked that he'd asked, although her bright blue eyes went wide with pleading that threatened to wreck him.

"Thought you might go that route," Lane said, touching his handcuffs. "You were going fifteen miles over the posted speed limit, which, according to section 146 of the traffic code, is a moving violation punishable by—"

"Okay, okay," Greyson said. "I get it." He took the few steps necessary to get himself well over the threshold, because Lane was anything if not thorough, and yep, the door clanged into place a second later.

"You owe me, Rallston," the sheriff said, and Marley nodded.

"That skinny dipping thing? Consider it in the vault." She drew a line over her lips with one finger, finishing the movement with a twist of an imaginary key. Lane grumbled as he walked away, leaving Greyson alone with Marley and every last one of his churning emotions.

"Can't say I was expecting to see you back in town," he said, crossing his arms over his chest.

"Yeah." She looked him right in the eye even though he was giving off every junkyard-dog vibe he could rustle up, and God, he had to hand it to her. Marley was tough. "I was hoping we could talk about that."

"You had Lane *arrest* me just so I'd talk to you?"

"Technically, he didn't arrest you. You're not in any trouble, and Owen was right behind him to get your truck. It's probably in the parking lot right now. If you still want to leave in five minutes, I'm not going to stand in your way. But I'd really like it if you'd listen to what I have to say in those five minutes."

Greyson opened his mouth to say no. He *should* say no. But what came out was, "Fine. I'm listening."

Relief splashed across Marley's face, so genuine that it chipped at his resolve even further. "I did a really stupid thing in leaving yesterday," she said. "I had good reasons. Or, at least, what I thought were good reasons. I'm sorry I had Lane bring you here so I could tell them to you, but I knew the only way I could get you to listen was to do something extreme."

"We're in jail," Greyson pointed out, and Marley smiled.

"Would you have answered if I'd called?"

Well, shit. "No."

"And would you have opened your door if I'd shown up at your apartment?"

She had him there, too. "Probably not."

"Considering the circumstances, jail seemed like my best option." She took a step forward, and it was then that Greyson noticed the shadows smudged under her eyes, as if she'd lost as much sleep as he had last night. "I owe you an apology. It's not enough, I know, but I owe it to you all the same. God, I owe you so much more than that."

"You don't owe me anything," Greyson said, the words way more truthful than ticked off.

"But I do," she said. "All this time, you've shown me that I belong here in Millhaven, and I was too scared and stubborn to see it. I thought Tobias was sick even though he's not, and I panicked. I ran away, when what I should've done was trust. I'm so, so sorry, Greyson. You weren't wrong. Eventually, bad things are going to happen, because that's life.

But I can't be afraid to live it, and to let people in for as long as I can as I do. I can't be afraid to love."

"Oh." His arms loosened to his sides, hope glimmering somewhere deep in his chest, covering his anger. "Well, I'm glad Tobias isn't sick." He'd gathered as much yesterday, when none of the Crosses had said so, but still.

"I am, too, but that's not why we're here," Marley said. She took another step forward, only an arm's length away now, and Greyson's heart pumped faster, his breath going tight.

"It's not?"

"Nope. We're here because I love you."

The declaration caught him so off-guard that he couldn't speak. Which, as it turned out, was okay, because Marley wasn't done.

"You're arrogant and bossy and fierce, and you push me when I need to be pushed. You showed me who you are, and you showed me where I belong. I might've had good reasons to guard my heart, but I have even better ones to trust it to you. My heart belongs to you, Greyson. I don't just belong in Millhaven. I belong with *you*. I love you."

"Well, I suppose that's a good thing," he said, when he finally recovered his voice.

Marley's dark brows lifted, the hope on her face along with them. "It is?"

He nodded. "It wouldn't really do for me to love you without you lovin' me back, and anyway, my bed's just not the same without you stealing all the covers."

She laughed, and at the same time, tears filled her eyes. "You forgive me?"

"I can't say I wasn't mad—you stung my pride pretty good. But I know you were scared, Marley, just like I know you're here to stay now. Yes, I forgive you."

"I love you, Greyson," she whispered. "I don't ever want you at arm's length again."

He closed the space between them, pulling her into his arms and knowing she'd always belong there, just as he'd belong right back. "I'm glad for that, darlin'. Because I love you, too, and I don't plan to ever let you go."

EPILOGUE

Marley ran her hand over her dress for the four hundredth time and looked out the window at the lightly falling snow. Fitting for January, she knew, but also fitting for the fact that it was her wedding day.

After all, she *was* marrying a man who was mostly beautiful and just a little stormy.

"Oh, my God, look at you!" Cate—whose own wedding ring was still sparkly and bright from when she and Owen had tied the knot three months ago—poked her head past the door to the tiny room Marley had been instructed not to leave upon penalty of death. Emerson's mother might look polite enough, but Lord above, the woman was a drill sergeant when it came to planning a wedding. Even a small one, like this.

"Are you sure it's not too much?" Marley asked, gesturing to the delicately flowing gown. It wasn't over the top or frilly—God, Marley never would've been able to pull that off with a straight face. But the simple, off-the-shoulder A-line dress had felt just right for her, and the flowers that

Amber Cassidy had volunteered to pin to Marley's hair were a shockingly perfect touch.

"Are you kidding?" came Scarlett's voice from over Cate's shoulder, and both women crowded into the room-slash-closet. "It's perfect. Isn't Aunt Marley gorgeous, J?"

She cooed to the baby on her hip, who gave up a toothless grin that made Marley's heart melt. She'd had no experience whatsoever with babies before Jordan had entered the world only a few weeks after Marley had returned to Millhaven for good, but man. This one had stolen her heart, along with everyone else's, right from go.

"Well, if sweet Jordan says so, then I believe it," Marley laughed, making a silly face at her nephew, who was the spitting image of Eli if ever there was one.

Marley scanned the room, which wasn't tough to do, since it was about the size of a Post-It note. "Where's Emerson?"

"I'm here," the redhead said, slipping in behind Scarlett and looking a little peaked. "Sorry, I was busy trying not to throw up."

"Being knocked up will do that to you," Scarlett said with a knowing laugh, and Cate nodded.

"Let's see if we can find you some ginger ale. We've got to take care of my niece in there so I can spoil her rotten in seven months."

"Or nephew," Emerson said, pausing to kiss Marley on the cheek. "I'm so happy for you, sweetheart. Truly."

All three women echoed the sentiment, hugging her like the sisters they were before slipping out of the room to leave Marley with her thoughts. She'd come a long way since that day in August when she'd returned to Millhaven for good. They all had, really. Although she'd felt a little bittersweet about it, she'd moved out of the main house at Cross Creek and in with Greyson right at the beginning of September, and Louis hadn't grumbled once when they'd gone to adopt Shadow together. Marley had resumed her duties as the manager of the storefront as soon as she'd returned home, and Jade Beckett had proven to be a quick study as her assistant manager and right-hand woman.

Greyson and his father—who had taken some time to come around to the fact that his son was in love with a Cross and that Marley was in love with him right back—had done their best to figure out a way to allow Jeremiah to retire. In the end, it had surprisingly been Cate who had come up with the solution for the Crosses and Whittakers to combine forces in a merger that had provided retirement for both Tobias and Jeremiah, and allowed Greyson, Owen, and Hunter to run equal shares of the land. Both locations were booming better than ever, and this spring was promising to be the best one either farm had ever seen.

For so many reasons.

"Hey, kid." Owen opened the door, flanked on either side by Hunter and Eli, all three of them looking sharp in dark gray suits and huge smiles. "It's time. You ready?"

"Yeah." Marley stood, hugging each of them in turn and letting them lead her into the hallway. "I'm ready."

"Last chance. Are you sure you don't want to run?" Eli asked with a gleam in his eye. "I mean, this *is* Greyson Whittaker we're talking about here."

Marley laughed. "It is Greyson. And that's why I'm one hundred percent sure I *don't* want to run."

"Well, then. I guess we'd best get you inside," Hunter said.

"Sorry, boys, but I believe that job belongs to me," came a voice from behind them, and Marley's heart swelled at the sight of Tobias, standing at the ready. Doc Sanders—Marley had the hardest time calling the woman Ellen—stood right beside him. She squeezed Tobias's arm, just once, then slipped past the double doors down the hall with Owen, Hunter, and Eli in tow.

"You look beautiful," Tobias said, his smile nostalgic and his blue-gray eyes crinkling with happiness. "I've never been more proud."

"It's me who's proud," Marley told him. She'd promised herself she wouldn't get choked up, but apparently she'd been a big, fat liar, because her voice caught as she said, "I'm proud to be a Cross, and I'm so grateful to be your daughter."

Tobias's eyes misted, and he cleared his throat, taking a handkerchief from the pocket of his suit jacket and handing it to her so she could keep her tears in check. "Now, now. No sadness today. I believe you've got a gentleman waitin' for you. If you'll allow me to walk you down the aisle."

He offered his arm, which Marley took with pride. Emerson's mother stood outside the double doors, smiling at the two of them as she opened them to usher Marley and her father inside. Marley was vaguely aware of a few familiar faces—Clementine and her husband, Logan, Amber Cassidy and Billy Masterson, who had finally bitten the bullet and started to date, and Jade and Sierra, who waved like mad as Marley passed by. Lane and Daisy were there, her engagement ring glittering in the soft light, and of course, her brothers, their wives, and Greyson's sisters and parents, too.

But the only person who mattered, the only person in her world, stood right at the front of the room.

"Hey," Marley whispered as they finally finished their walk down the aisle, and Greyson blinked, his long dark lashes framing a wide stare.

"You are perfect," he said, taking her shaking hand in his own.

"I think you're pretty perfect, too."

"Ahem." A sing-song voice Marley knew all too well cut through the room, and Judge Abernathy peered down at them from her perch behind her bench. "If I may interrupt."

"Sorry, Judge," Marley said, grinning as she faced the woman.

"I distinctly remember telling the two of you I didn't ever want to see you in my courtroom again," she said, capping the words with a wry smile. "However, I believe that in this case, I can make an exception. Now let's have a wedding and put this family rivalry to bed once and for all, shall we?"

Greyson laughed, squeezing Marley's hand tight, and she knew he'd never let her go.

"Thought you'd never ask."

SNEAK PEEK AT CROSSING HEARTS

Read on for a look at the book that started the series, CROSSING HEARTS, as well as the links to all of Kimberly's books!

Emerson Montgomery straightened the boxes of elastic bandages on the shelf in front of her for the thousandth time that hour. Turning to survey the one-room physical therapy office tucked in the back of Millhaven's medical center—aka Doc Sanders's family practice—she surveyed her new digs in search of something to keep her occupied. She'd already rearranged the rolls of athletic tape, wiped down the questionably sturdy portable massage table—along with the geriatric treadmill and recumbent bike over by the far wall—and organized the mismatched hand weights and resistance tubing she'd dug out of the storage closet.

She was still an hour shy of lunch on her first day at work, and she'd officially run out of things to do. Beautiful. Now she had nothing but time to dwell on the fact that in the last two weeks, she'd lost a job she'd loved, a boyfriend she hadn't, and the ability to keep the one vow that had saved her life twelve years ago.

She was back in Millhaven.

Emerson blew out an exhale, trying to ignore the stiffness in her knees that made her wonder if her synovial fluid had been replaced with expired Elmer's glue. She knew she should be happy Doc Sanders had been willing to hire her to do supplemental physical therapy, especially when the fifteen job inquiries Emerson had made before her last-ditch call to the doctor had yielded fifteen positions requiring sixty hours a week, with fifty-nine of them on her feet. Under normal circumstances, Emerson would've pounced on any of those employment opportunities before returning to Millhaven. Hell, under normal circumstances, she'd have never left her high-powered, higher-energy job as one of the top physical therapists for the Super Bowl Champion Las Vegas Lightning in the first place. Of course, everything she'd known about normal had been blasted into bits five weeks ago.

And if there was one thing Emerson knew by heart, it was that once you broke something into enough pieces, your chances of putting it back together amounted to jack with a side of shit.

The door connecting the physical therapy room and the hallway leading to Doc Sanders's office space swung open with a squeak, and the woman in question poked her head past the threshold.

"Hi, Emerson." She swept a hand toward the PT room in an unspoken request for entry. Emerson nodded, sending a handful of bright-red hair tumbling out of the loose, low ponytail at her nape.

"Hey, yes, sure. Come on in Doc . . . tor Sanders," she said, awkwardly tacking on the more formal address. But the woman was her boss, an MD who she respected greatly, and at any rate, more than a decade had passed since Emerson had left Millhaven. She was an adult now, a professional. Accomplished. Capable.

Even if her pretense for coming back home was a complete and utter lie.

"Emerson, please," Doc Sanders said, her smile conveying amusement over admonition. "I know with all your experience, you're probably used to different protocol with physicians, but call me Doc. No one in Millhaven has called me Doctor in . . . well, ever. And quite frankly, it makes me feel kind of stodgy."

Emerson dipped her chin, half out of deference and half to hide her smile. While all of the doctors on the Lightning's payroll had been top-of-their-field talented, they'd also sported enough arrogance to sink a submarine, making sure everyone down to the ball boys knew their status as MDs. Even though she'd technically earned the title of "Doctor" along with her PhD five years ago, she never used it, preferring to go by her first name like all the other physical therapists at the Lightning. True, she'd been the only one of the bunch with the varsity letters after her name, but the title meant nothing if she wasn't good enough to back it up hands-on. Plus, she'd always felt something heavy and uncomfortable in her chest on the rare occasion anyone called her Dr. Montgomery. She turned around every time, looking for her father.

Don't go there, girl. Head up. Eyes forward.

Emerson cleared her throat, stamping out the thoughts of both her father and her lost job as she kept the smile tacked to her face. "You got it, Doc. How are things in the office?"

"Not so bad for a Monday, although I could've done without Timmy Abernathy throwing up on my shoes."

"Gah." Emerson grimaced. Broken bones and ruptured tendons she could handle, no sweat. But stomach woes. No, thank you. "Sorry you've had a rough morning."

"Eh." Doc Sanders lifted one white-coated shoulder. "Timmy feels worse than I do, and I had an extra pair of cross-trainers in my gym bag. At any rate, I've got a patient for you, so I thought I'd pop over to see if you have an opening today."

Emerson thought of her schedule, complete with the tumbleweeds blowing through its wide-open spaces, and bit back the urge to laugh with both excitement and irony. "I'm sure I can fit someone in. What's the injury?"

"Rotator cuff. X-rays and MRI are complete, and Dr. Norris, the orthopedist in Camden Valley, ordered PT. But the patient is local, so I figured if you could take him, it'd be a win-win."

"Of course." An odd sensation plucked up Emerson's spine at the long-buried memory of a blue-eyed high school boy with his arm in a sling and a smile that could melt her like butter in a cast-iron skillet. "Um, my schedule is pretty flexible. What time did he want to come in?"

"Actually, he's a little anxious to get started, so he came directly here from the ortho's office . . ."

Doc Sanders turned toward the hallway leading to her waiting room, where a figure had appeared in the doorframe. Emerson blinked, trying to get her brain to reconcile the free-flowing confusion between the boy in her memory and the man standing in front of her. The gray-blue eyes were the same, although a tiny bit more weathered around the edges, and weirdly, the sling was also a match. But the person staring back at her was a man, with rough edges and sex appeal for days, full of hard angles and harder muscles under his jeans and T-shirt...

Hunter Cross.

Emerson stood with her feet anchored to the linoleum, unable to move or speak or even breathe. For the smallest scrap of a second, she tumbled back in time, her heart pounding so hard beneath her crisp white button-down that surely the traitorous thing would jump right out of her chest.

A blanket of stars littering the August sky . . . the warm weight of Hunter's varsity jacket wrapped around her shoulders... the warmer fit of his mouth on hers as the breeze carried his whispers, full of hope . . . "Don't go to New York. Stay with me, Em. Marry me and stay here in Millhaven where we'll always have this, just you and me..."

"Emerson? What... what the hell are you doing here?"

The deeper, definitely more rugged-around-the-edges version of his voice tipped the scales of her realization all the way into the present. She needed to say something, she knew, but her mouth had gone so dry that she'd have better luck rocketing to the moon in a paper airplane right now.

"I work here," Emerson finally managed, the truth of the words—of what they meant—delivering her back to reality with a hard snap. She hadn't returned to Millhaven for a jaunt down memory lane. Hell, she'd only come back when her process of elimination had dead-ended in total despair. She was here for one thing, and one thing only. To bury herself in as much work as her body would allow. Even if her first client probably hated her guts.

Check that. Hunter had probably moved on ages ago and didn't care one whit about her.

OTHER BOOKS BY KIMBERLY KINCAID

Want hot heroes, exclusive freebies, and all the latest updates on new releases? Sign up for Kimberly Kincaid's newsletter, and check out these other sexy titles, available at your favorite retailers!

The Cross Creek series:

- Crossing Hearts
- Crossing the Line
- Crossing Promises

The Station Seventeen series:

- Deep Trouble (prequel)
- Skin Deep
- Deep Check
- Deep Burn
- In Too Deep
- Forever Deep
- Down Deep

The Line series:

Love On the Line
Drawing the Line
Outside the Lines
Pushing the Line

The Pine Mountain Series:
The Sugar Cookie Sweetheart Swap, with Donna Kauffman and Kate Angell
Turn Up the Heat
Gimme Some Sugar
Stirring Up Trouble
Fire Me Up
Just One Taste
All Wrapped Up

The Rescue Squad series:
Reckless
Fearless

Stand-alones:
Something Borrowed
Play Me

And don't forget to come find Kimberly on Facebook, join her street team The Taste Testers, and follow her on Twitter, Pinterest, and Instagram!

Kimberly Kincaid writes contemporary romance that splits the difference between sexy and sweet and hot and edgy romantic suspense. When she's not sitting cross-legged in an ancient desk chair known as "The Pleather Bomber", she can be found practicing obscene amounts of yoga, whipping up anything from enchiladas to éclairs in her kitchen, or curled up with her nose in a book. Kimberly is a *USA Today* best-selling author and a 2016 and 2015 RWA RITA® finalist and 2014 Bookseller's Best nominee who lives (and writes!) by the mantra that food is love. Kimberly resides in Virginia with her wildly patient husband and their three daughters. Visit her any time at www.kimberlykincaid.com

Made in the USA
San Bernardino, CA
18 November 2018